新视野

NEW HORIZON
COLLEGE ENGLISH

大学英语

读写教程
学习必备

主　编　王　波

副主编　王一多

编　者　韩秀荣　何　静

4

外语教学与研究出版社
FOREIGN LANGUAGE TEACHING AND RESEARCH PRESS
北京　BEIJING

图书在版编目(CIP)数据

新视野大学英语读写教程学习必备. 4 / 王波主编；王一多副主编 . — 北京：外语教学与研究出版社，2007.2

ISBN 978 - 7 - 5600 - 6411 - 6

Ⅰ. 新… Ⅱ. ①王… ②王… Ⅲ. ①英语—阅读教学—高等学校—教学参考资料 ②英语—写作—高等学校—教学参考资料 Ⅳ. H31

中国版本图书馆 CIP 数据核字 (2007) 第 021722 号

出 版 人：李朋义
责任编辑：连　静
出版发行：外语教学与研究出版社
社　　址：北京市西三环北路 19 号 (100089)
网　　址：http://www.fltrp.com
印　　刷：北京京师印务有限公司
开　　本：787×1092　1/16
印　　张：19.5
版　　次：2007 年 2 月第 1 版　2007 年 2 月第 1 次印刷
书　　号：ISBN 978 - 7 - 5600 - 6411 - 6
定　　价：29.50 元
* 　　* 　　*

前　言

　　《新视野大学英语》系列教材充分体现了"以学生为中心"的教学思想，强调"主题教学模式"，选材新颖、内容丰富、趣味性强。鲜明的特点使不少高等院校采用了这套教材。为使学生能够充分理解教材精髓，抓住教材要点，解决学习中的疑难问题，我们特编写了此套《**新视野大学英语读写教程学习必备**》丛书。

　　　　本系列丛书共分4册，每册由10个单元组成，包括预习重点、学习难点和重点、文化知识、课文精讲、知识链接和自测题等几大部分。在每个部分中，我们又详细介绍了课文的背景知识、相关的词汇语法知识、难句解析、课后练习的答案和解析以及参考译文等，并针对四、六级考试精心设计了自测练习题。在编写过程中，我们力图保持原教材的编写特色，帮助学生更好地预习和复习课文，激发他们的学习主动性。

　　本套《新视野大学英语读写教程学习必备》丛书具有以下主要特点：

　　1. 严格遵照最新版《大学英语教学大纲》，强化学生的听、说、读、写、译这五方面的能力，帮助学生透彻理解课文内容。

　　2. 坚持细致、全面和实用的原则，从背景知识、词汇、语法、写作以及翻译等多个方面辅导学生的学习。

　　3. 结合CET考试的要求，提供相应的四、六级考试自测题。

　　4. 提供课后练习答案和《听说教程》答案，方便学生自查。

　　本套丛书既可供正在使用《新视野大学英语读写教程》的大学生使用，也可供大学英语教师参考，还可供相应水平的英语自学者使用。

紫金语言工作室

2006年7月

目 录

Unit 1

1 学习重点和难点
词汇和短语、语法项目、写作技巧

2 文化知识
课文大背景、课文知识点

3 课文精讲
词汇与短语详解、难句解析、重点
语法讲解、课文赏析、课后练习答
案及解析、参考译文、写作指导

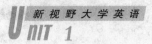 一、预习重点

1. Why Mrs. Baroda was called "a respectable woman"?
2. What were the obligations and responsibilities to marriage?
3. What does love mean to us?

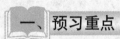 二、学习重点和难点

Ⅰ. 词汇和短语

Section A: temptation, idle, penetrate, nuisance, wit, presence, sheer, fabric, observation, gaze, melt, upright, farewell, hono(u)rablc, propose, overcome, dislike, deserve, tender; for the most part, impose one's company/oneself upon sb., for my part, count upon/on, make a fuss about, run down, object to, a succession of, drink in, yield to

Section B: obligation, offense(offence), relevant, transmission, hollow, investment, guarantee, glue, worship, interpret, faithful, elastic, virtue, procession, sacrifice, pursue, glory, passion, refugee, scatter, acknowledge, gamble, regulate, saddle, sustain, concession; subject... to, take offense, consist of, come apart, at will, throw in, by virtue of, better off, take out one's anger on sb.

Ⅱ. 语法项目
① 虚拟语气
② 倒装句
③ 由疑问句引出的名词从句

Ⅲ. 写作技巧
因果关系结构

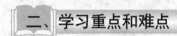 三、文化知识

Ⅰ. 课文大背景

Changes in modern family 现代家庭的变化

Families have undergone a major transformation in the past generation and are poised to change even more in the future. Households will move further away from the family-structure model of a stay-at-home mother, working father, and children, according to a report from the National Opinion Research Center at the University of Chicago. Because of divorce, cohabitation and single parenthood, a majority of families rearing children in the future will probably not include the children's two original parents. Moreover, most households will not include children. Marriage has declined as people marry older and divorce and cohabit more. A growing proportion of children has been born outside of marriage. Even within marriage the changes have been profound as more and more women have entered the labor force and gender roles have become more homogenous between husbands and wives. Those changes are having an impact on how people think about family life, and as a result, the concept of family tends to be more elastic.

II. 课文知识点

1. Kate Chopin 凯特·肖邦

The temptation of a Respectable Woman's original title is *A Respectable Woman*. It is a short story written by Kate Chopin (1851-1904) in *A Night in Acadie*（《阿卡迪亚》）(1897)，her second and final story collections. Kate Chopin was an American novelist and short-story writer. With over 100 short stories, she won recognition for her distinctive and highly imaginative portrayals of early Cajun and Creole life. Her tales are noted for their unique style and structure, their beautiful depiction of the landscape and atmosphere, and their realistic and emotionally powerful treatment of female characters and subject matter.

Kate Chopin

2. Meanings of love 爱的意义

Though love is a variety of feelings and involves a variety of things, the varieties themselves can be meaningfully explained and described, and they can be explained and described simply in terms of everyday experience rather than in scientific jargon or theory. The following show people's understanding of true love: love is a feeling or kind of attraction; love represents a magnetic attraction between two people; love is a feeling of high emotional affiliation which sends a person's ego to dizzying heights. Besides, love has more to do with companionship and compatibility: love is the physical and mental compatibility of two people; love is the end result of a mature union of two compatible personalities; love is helping the other person whenever he needs it being his companion; love is having common goals, dreams, and ambitions; love is doing things together and liking it; love concerns "giving", it is giving time, understanding and trust.

四、课文精讲

Section A

I. 词汇与短语详解

1. temptation

[词义] *n.* ① [U] 诱惑；② [C] 诱惑物

[搭配] resist temptation 抵制诱惑；yield to/give way to temptation 经不起诱惑

[例句] I gave way to the temptation of the delicious chocolate cake.
我经不住美味的巧克力蛋糕的诱惑。

All that money is certainly a big temptation. 那些钱当然是个极大的诱惑。

[派生] tempt *vt.* 引诱，诱惑

2. idle

[词义] *adj.* ① 无目的的；② 闲散的，无所事事的；③空闲的，闲着的

v. (away) 虚度，空费

[例句] He gave me an idle glance. 他漫不经心地瞥了我一眼。

3

There are few idle people in their department. 他们部门几乎没有闲散人员。

We can't leave this expensive machine lying idle.

我们不能让这台昂贵的机器闲置着。

Instead of working, Mike was idling away his time.

麦克不去工作，反而在虚度光阴。

[派生] idleness *n.* 闲散，失业（状态）

[辨析] idle 意为"闲散，悠闲"，强调无事可做；lazy意为"懒惰"，强调不愿意做事。

3. penetrate

[词义] *v.* ① 穿透，渗入，进入；② 弥漫，充满

[搭配] penetrate into 刺入；penetrate through 贯穿，穿透

[例句] The rain penetrated through to his skin. 雨把他淋得湿透了。

A smell of burnt leaves penetrated the woods.

树林里弥漫着树叶烧焦的气味。

[派生] penetrating *adj.* 弥漫的，渗透的，有洞察力的，思维敏锐的；penetrable *adj.* 可被穿透的，可被渗透的；penetration *n.* 刺穿，穿透，渗透，弥漫

4. nuisance

[词义] *n.* [C] 恼人的人或事物

[搭配] make a nuisance of oneself 使自己成为惹人讨厌的人

[例句] These cars are a real nuisance. 这些车真惹人讨厌。

Don't make a nuisance of yourself. 别那么讨厌。

5. wit

[词义] *n.* ① [U] 机敏风趣；② [C] 机敏风趣的人

[搭配] at one's wit's end 束手无策；out of one's wit 头脑不清楚，头脑糊涂

[例句] We conducted a conversation full of wit. 我们进行了一场机智风趣的谈话。

He was a famous wit. 他是个出名的说话风趣的人。

[派生] witty *adj.* 诙谐的，风趣的；witticism *n.* 俏皮话，诙谐语

6. presence

[词义] *n.* [U] 出席，在场

[搭配] in the presence 在……面前，面临着；presence of mind 镇定自若

[例句] The document must be signed in the presence of a witness.

这份文件必须当着证人的面签署。

[派生] present *adj.* 出席的，在场的

[辨析] attendance, presence

attendance [C, U] 指学校、会议等的"出勤、出席"行为时，作不可数名词；指"出席人数"和"出席次数"时，作可数名词；presence [U] 表示会议的"出席"时可与"attendance"互换。但 attendance 强调动作，presence 强调存在、在场的状态。

[联想] absence *n.* 缺席，缺乏；absent *adj.* 缺席的，不在场的

7. sheer

[词义] *adj.* ①（织物）极薄的，轻的；② 完全的，彻底的

[例句] She likes wearing sheer nylon tights. 她喜欢穿透明的尼龙连裤袜。

It is sheer nonsense. 这纯粹是胡言乱语。

8. fabric

[词义] *n.* [C, U] ①布（毛、丝）织物；②组织，结构

[例句] This clothes are made of cotton fabric. 这些衣服由棉织品制成。

The family is the most important unit in the social fabric.
家庭是社会结构最重要的组成部分。

[派生] fabricate *vt.* 制造，捏造；fabrication *n.* 捏造，伪造

[辨析] fabric, textile

fabric 一般用词，指各种经纺织而成的"布、织物、织品"；textile 专业用词，指经工厂制造而成的"纺织品、纺织原料"。

9. observation

[词义] *n.* ① [C] 评论；② [U, C] 观察；③ [pl.] 观察记录

[例句] He made some interesting observations on the current economic situation.
他对当前的经济形势作了一些有趣的评论。

The experiment requires careful observation. 这个实验需要仔细的观察。

You'd better get some firsthand observations.
你最好弄一些第一手的观察资料。

[派生] observe *vt.* 观察，看；observable *adj.* 看得见的，引人注意的；observant *adj.* 善于观察的，机警的；observatory *n.* 天文台，气象台

10. gaze

[词义] *n.* 注视，凝视；*v.* 注视，凝视

[搭配] gaze at 凝视，注视

[例句] She felt uncomfortable under his intense gaze.
在他的密切注视下，她感到不自在。

She gazed at me in disbelief when I told her the news.
当我告诉她这个消息时她难以置信地注视着我。

11. melt

[词义] *v.* ①慢慢走开或消失；②(使) 融化

[搭配] melt away 融化，逐渐消失；melt sth. down 熔毁（金属器物），熔化

[例句] Her anger melted away when she read the letter.
她的愤怒在读信时渐渐平息了。

The spring sun usually melts the snow by mid March.
春天的太阳通常在三月中旬将雪融化。

[派生] melting *adj.* 融化的，柔情的，感伤的；melting-point *n.* 熔点

[辨析] melt, dissolve

melt 指固体因热而溶化，如奶油，雪糕等；dissolve 表示固体遇水而溶化，如盐、糖等。

12. keen

[词义] *adj.* ①强烈的，激烈的，敏锐的；②热衷的，热心的，渴望的

[搭配] be keen on (doing) sth. 对……热心，渴望

[例句] She has a keen desire to study abroad. 她非常想去留学。

She's keen on playing tennis. 她很喜欢打网球。

[派生] keenness *n.* 敏锐

5

13. upright

[词义] *adj.* 正直的，诚实的；*adj. & adv.* 挺直的（地），竖立的（地），垂直的（地）

[例句] She behaved as any upright citizen would have done under the circumstances. 她像所有正直的公民在这种情况下会做的那样做了。

The guards stood upright at the gate. 卫兵笔直地站立在门前。

[辨析] erect, straight, upright, vertical

erect 意为"直立的、笔直的"，尤其强调人的身体是挺直的，不弯曲也不倾斜；straight 意为"笔直的"，即可指水平方向的，也可指垂直方向上的不弯曲，一般修饰客观事物；upright意为"直立的、竖立的、垂直的"，多用来形容直立的位置，也可指人的性格正直的；vertical 意为"垂直的、竖的、纵向的"，指垂直于水平线的，与horizontal意义相对。

14. farewell

[词义] *n.* (formal) 告别，再见

[搭配] bid/say farewell to sb. 向某人告别；a farewell speech 告别演说

[例句] They waved farewell to their friends. 他们挥手向朋友们告别。

[联想] welfare *n.* 福利，安宁

15. hono(u)rable

[词义] *adj.* 可敬的，光荣的

[例句] He is a decent, honorable man. 他是一个体面可敬的男人。

[派生] honor *n.* 光荣，荣誉；honorary *adj.* 名誉的，荣誉的

16. propose

[词义] *v.* ① 打算，计划；② 提议，建议，提出

[搭配] propose (marriage) to sb. 向某人求婚；propose sb. for sth. 推荐某人做某事

[例句] I propose to go to London on Monday. 我打算星期一去伦敦。

They proposed cuts in public spending. 他们建议削减公共开支。

[派生] proposal *n.* 提议，建议

[辨析] propose, intend, mean

propose 指公开明确地提出自己的目的或计划；intend是正式用词，指心里已有做某事的目标或计划，含有"行动坚决"之意；mean可与intend互换，但强调做某事的意图，较口语化。

17. overcome

[词义] *v.* ① 战胜，克服；② 被（烟、气、感情等）压倒，使受不了

[例句] One must overcome many difficulties on the way to success. 在成功的路上必须克服很多困难。

She was overcome with emotion. 她激动得不能自持。

[辨析] conquer, defeat, overcome

conquer 意为"征服"，多指借助武力或斗争击败其他事物，使之置于控制之中；defeat指赢得胜利，尤其是"军事上的胜利"；overcome意为"克服"，强调经过艰苦的斗争，排除障碍而取得胜利，多用于指精神上的克服。

18. dislike

[词义] *n.* 不喜欢，讨厌；*v.* 不喜欢，讨厌

[搭配] have a dislike of/for 不喜欢；take a dislike to sb. 开始讨厌某人

[例句] She has a dislike of/for dark colors. 她讨厌深色。

He dislikes having to get up early. 他讨厌不得不早起。

19. deserve

[词义] *v.* 应得，应受，值得

[搭配] deserve well/ill of 值得……的优/虐待; deserve doing/to be done 值得做某事

[例句] He deserves punishment. 他应受惩罚。

Your suggestion deserves to be considered seriously. 你的建议值得认真考虑。

[派生] deserved *adj.* 应得的; deserving *adj.* 应得的，该受奖赏的

20. tender

[词义] *adj.* ① 温柔的; ② 嫩的; ③ 疼痛的，一触即痛的

[例句] She gave him tender care when he was ill.

当他生病的时候，她对他细心照料。

My steak was juicy and tender. 我的牛排嫩而多汁。

If your stomach feels tender, the best remedy is to have a good rest.
如果你胃痛，最好的疗法就是好好休息。

[辨析] gentle, mild, tender

gentle 主要指人由于克制力量或情绪而显得和蔼、温柔、文雅，带有令人
感到礼貌周全、体贴亲切的意味; mild 意为"温和的、柔和的、温柔的"，
多指人或物固有的温和性情，这种性情往往使人产生宁静而舒适的感觉;
tender 意为"温柔的"，指人的动作、话语等充满温情和善意。

21. for the most part 多半，就大多数而言，通常

[例句] For the most part, he is friendly. 总的来说，他是友好的。

22. impose one's company/oneself upon sb. 硬缠着某人

[例句] A drunken tramp imposed his company on us.
一个醉醺醺的流浪汉缠着我们不走。

[联想] impose on 把……强加于

23. for my part 就我而言，至于我

[例句] For my part, I'm quite tired of this film. 对我来说，我对这部电影很厌倦了。

[联想] for the most part 多半，就大多数而言; as far as I'm concerned 就我而言

24. count upon/on 料想; 依靠; 指望

[例句] We didn't count on so many people being on vocation.
我们没有想到会有那么多人度假。

You can count on me for everything in the future. 你将来的一切可以全靠我。

I'm counting on my teacher to help me. 我正指望我的老师来帮我。

[联想] depend on 依靠，依赖; rely on 依靠，依赖

25. make a fuss about 对……小题大做，对……大惊小怪

[例句] Please don't make a fuss about such a small thing.
请别为这点儿小事大惊小怪的。

26. run down （使）筋疲力尽; （使）衰退

[例句] His health has run down because he's been working too hard.
他劳累过度，把身体搞垮了。

The coal industry is being slocoly run down. 煤炭工业在慢慢衰退。

27. object to 不赞成，反对

[例句] I really object to leaving so early. 我很反对这么早离开。

28. a succession of 一系列，一连串

[例句] A succession of visitors come to the door. 登门造访的人接踵而来。

[联想] in succession 连续地

[例句] He has won the match for three years in succession.
他已经连续三年赢得比赛了。

29. drink in 陶醉于；如饥似渴地倾听

[例句] They drank in the beauty of the landscape. 他们陶醉在美丽的景色中。
I drank in every word of Professor Zhang's lecture.
我全神贯注地倾听了张教授演讲的字字句句。

30. yield to 让步于，屈服于

[例句] In the end, he yielded to his son's request to buy the toy gun.
他终于屈服于儿子买玩具枪的要求。

II. 难句解析

1. Mrs. Baroda was a little annoyed to learn that her husband expected his friend, Gouvernail, up to spend a week or two on the plantation. (Para. 1)

[释义] Mrs. Baroda felt a bit angry when she knew that her husband wanted his friend, Gouvernail, to spend a week or two on the farm.

[分析] "that her husband...on the plantation" 作learn的宾语。
"expect his friend up to spend..." 中，up 是副词，表示 "到较高的地方，北上"。

2. After a few days with him, she could understand him no better than at first. (Para. 2)

[释义] After a few days with him on her plantation, she knew no more about Gouvernail than at the very beginning.

[分析] 这里 "no" 意为 "一点儿也不 (not at all)"，通常在比较级之前作副词。
e.g. The exam is no more difficult than the tests you've been doing in class.
这次考试一点也不比你们一直做的课堂测验难。

3. Then she imposed her company upon him, accompanying him in his idle walks to the mill to press her attempt to penetrate the silence in which he had unconsciously covered himself. (Para. 2)

[释义] Then she forced him to accept her company no matter whether he liked it or not, taking aimless walks with him to the mill and she tried to understand the reserve in which he had enveloped himself unintentionally.

accompany sb. to some place 陪伴某人去某地
e.g. I was six years old and had to be accompanied to the cinema by my two brothers.
我只有6岁，只好由我的两个哥哥陪我去电影院。

[分析] "accompanying him..." 是现在分词短语作状语；"to press her attempt to..." 是目的状语；其中 "in which he had...cover himself" 是介词提前的定语从句，修饰 "the silence"，还原的定语从句是 "he had unconsciously covered himself in which (silence)"。

4. "You are full of surprises," he said to her. "Even I can never count upon how you are going to act under given conditions."(Para. 7)

[释义] He told his wife that she was always saying or doing some unexpected things and he, as her husband, could never know how she would behave in a certain situation.

5. ...he went on, "taking poor Gouvernail seriously and making a fuss about him, the last thing he would desire or expect."(Para. 7)

[释义] ...he continued saying that she was paying too much attention to Gouvernail and showing too much anxiety about him. That was what Gouvernail disliked.

take sth./sb. seriously consider sth./sb. to be important and worth a lot of attention or respect 认真对待，重视

e.g. Some people laughed at her, but after a while they began to take her seriously.
有些人取笑她，可是过了一会儿他们就开始认真看待她了。

the last thing 最不想要发生的事

e.g. The last thing he needed right then was more bad news about his son.
他当时最不想得到的就是关于他儿子的更多的坏消息。

6. I expected him to be interesting, at least. (Para. 10)

[分析] "interesting" 可以指人很有趣，显得滑稽，令人发笑。

e.g. He's a wonderfully interesting man once he starts talking to you.
一旦他开始与你交谈，他可是一个非常有趣的人。

7. He seated himself upon the bench beside her, without a suspicion that she might object to his presence. (Para. 12)

[释义] He sat down on the bench beside her without suspecting that she might dislike his staying there.

seat sb./oneself (formal) 给某人一个座位坐下，坐在某个地方

e.g. He seated himself at one end, and Emily sat beside him.
他自己坐在一头，埃米莉坐在他旁边。

8. ...handing her a length of sheer white fabric with which she sometimes covered her head and shoulders. (Para. 13)

[释义] **length** n. 一段，一节，通常有一定长度或有某种特殊用途

e.g. He attached a small gold ball to a length of chain around her neck.
他把一个小金球系在她的项链上。

9. Gouvernail was in no sense a shy man. (Para. 15)

[释义] **in no sense** 一点也不

e.g. In no sense can the issue be said to be resolved. 这事根本没有解决。

10. His periods of silence were not his basic nature, but the result of moods. (Para. 15)

[释义] **period** n. 周期，时间间歇

e.g. He is suffering from shortness of breath and periods of continuous pain.
他呼吸短促，还有间歇性的持续疼痛。

11. Now, all there was left with him was a desire to be permitted to exist, with

now and then a little breath of genuine life, such as he was breathing now. (Para. 16)

[释义] Now, he only hoped to be allowed to live, enjoying the genuine life as he was doing just then from time to time.

[分析] 这句的主干是 "All was a desire to be permitted to exist."; "there was left with him" 是定语，修饰主语 "all"; "with now and then...life" 是伴随状语，起补充说明作用; "such as he was breathing now" 是举例说明前面的名词 "a little breath of life"。

12. **There was some talk of having him back during the summer that followed. (Para. 21)**

[释义] During the following summer they sometimes talked about inviting him to visit them again.

Ⅲ. 重点语法讲解

虚拟语气 (subjunctive mood) 虚拟语气是一种特殊的动词形式，用来表示说话人所说的话不是一个事实，而只是一种愿望，假设、怀疑、建议、推测、可能或纯粹的空想等。

虚拟结构（不论从句或主句）常可用情态动词的过去式，即could, might, would, should 等加不带to的动词不定式或不带to的动词不定式完成式，来作谓语动词。这些情态动词除表示虚拟结构外，本身还有独立的意思。

If he were here, he *might* agree with you. 假如他在这里，他可能会同意你。

If it had not been for their help, we *could not* have succeeded.

如果没有他们的帮助，我们是不可能成功的。

He *should* have come earlier. 他本应该早点来。

倒装句 英语最基本的词序 "主语部分+谓语部分" 通常十分固定。如果把谓语动词放在主语前面，就叫作倒装。将谓语动词完全移至主语之前，称为完全倒装，如果只是把助动词或情态动词放在主语之前，称为部分倒装。

so 放在句首，用倒装表示强调，结构如下：

1. So + be/have/助动词或情态动词+主语，表示 "也这样"。

—He is a doctor. —So am I. ——他是个医生。——我也是。

—He likes football. —So does she. ——他喜欢足球。——她也是。

2. So + 主语 + be/have/助动词或情态动词，表示 "确实是这样"。

—You said she was very pretty. —So I did. ——你说过她很可爱。——我确实说过。

—I guess they have seen the film. —So they have.

——我猜他们已经看过这部电影了。——他们确实看过了。

Ⅳ. 课文赏析

1. 文体特色

这是一篇以时间顺序为线索的记叙文。在记叙过程中，作者巧妙地运用了多个时间标志词（time marker）来表示时间的推移和故事的发展，把一系列事件按照时间顺序有机地结合为一个整体。在细节描述时，还运用了一系列的因果结构。

此外，文章叙述生动，深入细致，尤其是对女主人公内心的刻画，用词贴切，*丝丝入*

扣，真实地再现了她的情感发展过程，使读者能够感同身受。

2. 结构分析

Part Ⅰ (Para. 1) The general situation and the starting point of the story.

Part Ⅱ (Para. 2-10) Mrs. Baroda's impression of her guest: he is not a man of wit, but a terrible nuisance.

Part Ⅲ (Para. 11-19) At night, meeting each other beneath an oak tree, Gouvernail's talk caused some emotional changes in Mrs. Baroda.

Part Ⅳ (Para. 20) The next morning, Mrs. Baroda took an early train without even saying farewell, and didn't return until Gouvernail was gone.

Part Ⅴ (Para. 21) During the summer that followed, Mr. Baroda greatly desired that his friend should come to visit them again but this was vigorously opposed by Mrs. Baroda.

Part Ⅵ (Para. 22-24) Before the end of the year, Mrs. Baroda proposed to have Gouvernail visit them again as she had overcome everything.

Ⅴ. 课后练习答案及解析

Vocabulary

Ⅲ.

1. idle 译文：当孩子无所事事时她曾对他大呼小叫，但在他夜里醒来害怕的时候又去安慰他。

2. melting 译文：他责备了孩子，但又因为她平安无事感到欣慰。

3. imposes 译文：毫无疑问，日本的传统影响了日本艺术家对待艺术问题一种与众不同的态度。

4. penetrate 译文：巴罗达先生认为妻子总是充满了稀奇古怪的想法，有时他几乎猜不透她的心思。

5. presence 译文：他不愿意加入到他们中去，因为他的出现会让卡斯顿感到尴尬。

6. nuisance 译文：而且，他发现在自己想练习钢琴的时候，她整天待在他的公寓里是一件很麻烦的事。

7. nonsense 译文：她被他们的评论激怒了，就跟他们说她再也不会忍受他们的胡言乱语了。

8. keen 译文：候选人要以以下条件为基础选出：有领导能力、有坚强的性格、思维敏捷、能权衡利弊。

Ⅳ.

1. run down 译文：等他们到山顶时已经筋疲力尽了，但还是为自己能到达山顶感到欣慰。

2. taken seriously 译文：我认为他的思想应该被认真对待，而不是他的表面威望。

3. drinking in 译文：学生们围坐在老师身边，倾听他的谆谆教导。

4. in no sense 译文：当然，你会理解我对这些问题是毫无偏袒或偏见的，因为我对它们的看法既坚定又准确。

5. made excellent observations on 译文：他们设计并实施了一项试验，完整记录了美丽又复杂的自然界，并得出了一定的结论。

6. counted on 译文：一旦某些假设经过验证被认为是正确的并予以采纳，它们就非常可靠了。

7. for my part 译文：如果你愿意，你可以和他们一起去。至于我，我宁愿呆在家里。

8. make a fuss 译文：饭已经不是很热，但我什么都没说，我不喜欢小题大做。

Collocation

V.

1. sanctions 译文：自从去年华盛顿对巴拿马实行经济制裁以来，巴拿马的经济就直线下降了。

2. Restrictions 译文：这个国家南部和东部地区正在遭受本世纪最严重的旱灾，因此这些地区本月已经限制用水了。

3. fine 译文：在经过两年的调查后，委员会因该公司违反规定罚了它五百万美元。

4. limits 译文：按照这项法律，代替家长行使职责的老师要受法律对父母规定的同样的约束。

5. problems 译文：最重要的是，没有窗外马路上那一大群人所带来的麻烦，我们就有时间自娱自乐了。

6. tax 译文：按照常规，只对超出人均仅收入三倍的收入部分征税。

7. duty 译文：此外，策划者宣称，最近国会通过的法案赋予了他们保护奥克尼郡自然环境的责任。

8. responsibility 译文：尽管法律没有规定雇员与雇主合作的义务，但是他们一定不能背叛雇主的信任，如泄漏商业机密等。

Word Building

VI.

1. justify 译文：汤姆声称那天病了，试图为自己没出席会议辩解。

2. glorify 译文：写这首诗并不是为了真实地描述那场战争，而是为了歌颂那些死于战争的人们，让他们的亲友得到一些慰藉。

3. exemplifies 译文：这幅油画是当时盛行的自然主义风格的最佳例证。

4. classified 译文：我们图书馆的书按照主题分类。

5. purified 译文：这里的水必须净化后才能饮用。

6. intensify 译文：随着越来越多的公司投标这一项目，竞争肯定会很激烈。

7. identify 译文：我如此熟悉这些学生，仅凭脚步声就能把他们识别出来。

8. terrified 译文：我被这头牛吓坏了，想跑到场地外面去。

VII.

1. bravery 译文：这些年轻人因其非凡的勇气被授予奖章。

2. jewellery 译文：他们很喜欢珠宝，有的戴耳环，有的戴着纯金的项链。

3. delivery 译文：很显然，部长是在晚宴上发言的合适人选：他的演讲技巧无懈可击。

4. machinery 译文：因为机械再次出故障而停电了。

5. robbery 译文：抢劫是在我们外出度周末的时候发生的。

6. nursery 译文：他们的两个孩子还是婴儿时期就被送到了托儿所。

7. scenery 译文：他们爬上山，在山顶上停下来欣赏风景。

8. discovery 译文：自从发现艾滋病以来，人们越来越关注我们是否能成功克制它。

Structure

VIII.

1. She said it might have been all right, if the weather had been good.

   译文：他说如果当时天气好的话一切可能会很顺利。

2. Mrs. Baroda said she might have liked Gouvernail if he had been like the others.

   译文：巴罗达夫人说如果当时古韦内尔像其他人一样的话，她很可能会喜欢上他的。

3. If I had been there, I could have helped you.

   译文：如果我当时在那里，我会帮你的。

4. He could have got tickets if there had been some cheap ones.

   译文：如果当时有便宜票的话，他本来能买到票。

5. Mrs. Baroda might have yielded to the temptation if she hadn't been a respectable and sensible person.

   译文：假如巴罗达夫人不是一位可敬而明智的女士，那她可能会屈服于诱惑。

IX.

1. "You were different then." "So was she."

   译文："那么你就不同。""她也不同。"

2. "You used to say he was a man of wit." "So he is."

   译文："你过去常说他是个风趣的人。""他确实是的。"

3. "You've made a mistake here." "Oh, so I have. Thank you."

   译文："你这里犯了一个错误。""噢，的确如此。谢谢你。"

4. "Children should behave themselves." "So should adults."

   译文："小孩应该举止得体。""大人也该如此。"

5. "This glass is cracked." "Oh, so it is. I hadn't noticed."

   译文："这杯子裂了。""噢，真的裂了。我没注意到。"

Translation

X.

1. He imposed his company upon her although she repeated the hints of hoping to be left alone.

2. His friends can never count upon how he is going to act under given conditions, as he is always full of surprises.

3. Don't make a fuss about such a small thing because that is the last thing I expected.

4. Besides being an upright and respectable woman Mrs. Baroda was also a very sensible one.

5. She had never known her thoughts so confused, unable to gather anything from them.

6. From Gouvernail's talk, Mrs. Baroda came to know that his periods of silence were not his basic nature, but the result of moods.

7. To Gaston's delight, his wife had finally overcome her dislike for Gouvernail and invited Gouvernail to visit them again wholly from herself.

8. Mrs. Baroda felt confused with Gouvernail's puzzling nature and found it hard to penetrate the silence in which he had unconsciously covered himself.

XI.

1. 在一起待了几天，她仍感到对这个客人很陌生，只得大部分时间让丈夫陪着他。

2. 加斯顿拉了拉妻子的衣袖，双手搂着她的腰，快乐地望着她那充满困惑的眼睛。

3. 他在她身旁的长凳上坐下，丝毫不曾想到她可能会反对他坐在那儿。

4. 她陶醉在他的声音里，他的话变成了一串毫无意义的动词、名词、副词和形容词。

5. 那晚，巴罗达太太很想把自己的一时荒唐告诉丈夫——也是她的朋友，但还是忍住了。

6. 他照例说了些诸如这个季节的夜风对身体不好之类的话。后来，望着茫茫夜色，他开始谈了起来。

7. "噢，"她笑着，在他唇上印了长长的温柔的一吻，"我一切都已经克服了! 你会看到的，这次我会对他很好。"

8. 而现在他只求能生存，只是偶尔才体验到一丝真正的生活的气息，就像此刻这样。

Story Summary

XII.

A D B C A   B C D A B   B C C A D   D B C A D

Text Structure Analysis

XIII.

Cause 1: she could understand him no better than at first

Cause 2: Gouvernil hardly noticed her absence

Cause 3: pressed her attempt to penetrate the silence but without success

VI. 参考译文

一个正派女人受到的诱惑

得知丈夫请了他的朋友古韦内尔来种植园小住一两周，巴罗达太太有点不快。

古韦内尔生性沉默，这令巴罗达太太颇为不解。在一起待了几天，她仍感到对他很陌生。于是她大部分时间只让丈夫陪着客人，但发现自己不在场几乎并未引起古韦内尔的注意。而后她执意要陪他散步到磨坊去，试图打破他这种并非有意的沉默，但仍不奏效。

"你的朋友，他什么时候走?"有一天她问丈夫，"我觉得他太讨厌了。"

"还不到一周呢，亲爱的。我真不明白，他并没给你添麻烦呀。"

"是没有。他要是真能添点麻烦，我倒喜欢他一些了。真希望他能像别人一样，那样我倒可以做点什么使他过得舒心。"

加斯顿拉了拉妻子的衣袖，双手搂着她的腰，快乐地望着她那充满困惑的眼睛。

"你可真让人吃惊，"他说，"我都说不准你什么时候会怎么做。瞧你对古韦内尔顶真的样子，对他那么大惊小怪，这可是他最不希望的。"

"大惊小怪!"她急急回道，"瞎说，你怎么这么说! 大惊小怪，真是! 但你可说过他挺聪明的。"

"他是聪明。但工作太多，这可怜的家伙累垮了，所以我才请他来这儿休息一阵。"

"你常说他是个风趣的人，"太太仍在生气，"我以为他至少该有意思点。明早我进城去试春装。古韦内尔走了你告诉我。他走之前我就住姑妈家。"

那晚她独自一人坐在路边橡树下的长凳上，思绪从未这么乱过，就像头顶飞着的蝙蝠一样，忽东忽西。她理不出丝毫头绪，只感到有一点很明确：她必须第二天一早就离开这里。

巴罗达太太听到从谷仓那边传来了脚步声，她知道那是古韦内尔。她不想让他看见自己，但她的白色长袍泄露了踪迹。他在她身旁的长凳上坐下，丝毫不曾想到她可能会反对他坐在那儿。

"您丈夫要我把这个带给您，巴罗达太太，"说着，他递上一块白色纱巾，这是她有时用来做披肩的。她接了过来，放在腿上。

他照例说了些诸如这个季节的夜风对身体不好之类的话。后来，望着茫茫夜色，他开始谈了起来。

古韦内尔可不是个腼腆的人。他的沉默寡言决非天性，而是情绪使然。坐在巴罗达太太身边，他的沉默暂时消失了。

他以低沉迟缓的嗓音亲切而无拘束地娓娓而谈，谈他在大学里与加斯顿是好朋友，谈那时曾雄心勃勃，志向高远。而现在他只求能生存，只是偶尔才体验到一丝真正的生活的气息，就像此刻。

巴罗达太太只是模模糊糊地感到他在说些什么。他的话语变成了一串毫无意义的动词、名词、副词和形容词；她陶醉在他的声音里。她想在夜色里伸出手去触摸他——要不是个正派女子，她真会这么做。

她越想靠近他，事实上，她却越往后退。为使自己不显得失礼，她借机假装打了个哈欠，起身离开了他。

那晚，巴罗达太太很想把自己的一时荒唐告诉丈夫——也是她的朋友，但还是克制了这种冲动。她是个正派体面的女人，也是个非常明智的女人。

第二天早晨加斯顿起床时，妻子已经走了，也没有跟他道别。脚夫把她的箱子送到火车站，她搭早班车进的城。直到古韦内尔离开后她才回去。

那年夏天，他们有时会谈到再请古韦内尔来种植园一事。也就是说，加斯顿很希望这样，但经不住他那品行高洁的妻子的强烈反对。

然而，快到年底时，妻子主动提出邀请古韦内尔再来。听到妻子的建议，丈夫真是又惊又喜。

"我真高兴，亲爱的，你终于不再讨厌他了。说真的，他不应该使你觉得讨厌。"

"噢，"她笑着，在他唇上印了长长的温柔的一吻，"我一切都已经克服了！你会看到的，这次我会对他很好。"

Ⅶ. 写作指导

随着文章故事情节按照时间顺序的发展，女主角经历了一系列的态度和感情转变，而这些变化是通过一系列的因果关系展开的。

记叙文的组织以按时间顺序描写事物进程最为普通。但在安排文章结构时经常需要对某一事件进行因果分析。一段由因果分析构成的文章可能着重阐述因，也可能重点描述果，也可能因果占有同等重要的位置。在以因果构成段落时要注意：首先，应该客观准确判断因果，不能主观臆断；其次，一个果可能有很多因，一个因也可能有几个果，因此要全面考虑，仔细挑选细节和论证，避免片面或肤浅的论证；最后，在因果论证时，不可忽略中间环节，以免使文章显得残缺而没有说服力。

范文：

Why did Mrs. Baroda vigorously oppose her husband's idea to invite Gouvernail to their plantation again?

When Mr. Baroda mentioned that he would invite his friend, Mr. Gouvernial, to their home again, his wife opposed strongly. Because she thought she had fallen in love with Mr. Gouvernail that night when they came across each other in the garden. His low, hesitating voice amazingly attracted her at that time. But since she was a respectable and sensible woman and she was also clear that it was impossible for them to have a happy ending, Mrs. Baroda managed to resist the temptation. If Mr. Gouvernail appeared again, she was afraid that she could not control herself any more. So Mrs. Baroda spared no efforts to avoid meeting Mr. Gouvernail so as to give herself a period of time to put aside her affection towards him.

Section B
Ⅰ．阅读技巧

读懂言外之意

在第1册第7单元，我们讲过读懂言外之意，那就意味着从已经写出的文字以及字里行间的含义对作者的观点进行推论。在进行推理的时候，我们要超越文章表面的细节，然后"读出言外之意"，并通过逻辑推理，根据提示去找到信息。

文章中读到的实际细节为我们提供了知识基础。但并不是每一点信息都是显而易见或者清晰陈述的。为了完全理解某事，我们可能不得不依靠我们自己的知识和经验。因为信息并不总是以确切的术语来陈述，我们必须从仅仅作者暗示的细节或观点中得到信息。此外，我们对于所理解的东西的正确性也不可能总是确定无疑的。但是如果我们跟随基于证据的直觉，就能相当确信某事，即使这些事只是被暗示的。

例1：他的话语变成了一连串没有意义的动词、名词、副词和形容词……（第1单元第1课第17段）

问题：为什么他的话语变成了一连串没有意义的动词、名词，副词和形容词？

可能的回答：巴罗达夫人心不在焉，在想其它的事情。

例2：她越想靠近他，事实上，她却越往后退。（第1单元第1课第18段）

问题：为什么事实上她被他所吸引，却想离开他呢？

可能的回答：她是一个正派的女性，她在努力抵制诱惑。

Ⅱ．词汇与短语详解

1. obligation

[词义] *n.* 义务，责任

[搭配] fulfill an obligation 履行义务；be/place sb. under the obligation 负有义务

[例句] If you have not signed a contract, you are under no obligation to pay them any money. 如果你没有签合同，你就没有义务付给他们钱。

[派生] obligate *vt.* 强制；obligatory *adj.* 义不容辞的；oblige *vt.* 强迫

[辨析] duty, obligation, responsibility

duty指某人出于道义、信仰、责任感而觉得必须要做的事或必须尽到的"义务"，强调出自内心的自觉要求；obligation多指某个特定时间内，遵照习俗、协议或契约等应尽的"责任、义务"；responsibility指某人对自己的行为和工作负"责任"，包括对产生的后果负法律或道义上的责任。

2. offense (英 offence)

[词义] *n.* ① [U] 冒犯，伤感情；② [C] 犯罪行为，罪行

[搭配] take offense at sth. 因某事而发怒；give/cause offense to sb. 触怒某人；an offense against the law 违法法律

[例句] Do you think he will take offence at what I did?

你认为他会对我做的事生气吗？

Driving without a license is an offence. 无照驾驶是一种违法行为。

[派生] offend *v.* 犯罪，冒犯；offensive *adj.* 令人不快的，讨厌的

[辨析] crime, offense, sin

crime 尤指必须受到法律制裁的"罪、罪行"，也可指道德上的"罪恶、罪过"，此时是一种夸张手法，多见于口语表达；offense 正式用词，应用范围较广，泛指任何违反法律、法规、制度、规矩的行为，既可指轻微的"过错"，也可以指严重的"犯法"。表示"冒犯、得罪"时，有伤害某人感情的意思；sin指违背道德准则或宗教法规而应受到谴责的"罪过、罪孽"。

3. relevant

[词义] *adj.* 有关的，相关的

[搭配] relevant to 与……有关的

[例句] This case is relevant to his reputation. 此案与他的名誉有关。

[派生] irrelevant *adj.* 不相关的；relevancy *n.* 关联，关联事物

4. transmission

[词义] *n.*① [U] 传播，传送；② [C] 广播或电视播送

[例句] The government should take measures to prevent the transmission of disease.

政府应该采取措施阻止疾病的传播。

The football match was a live transmission from German.

这场球赛来自德国的现场直播。

[派生] transmit *vt.* 传输，传达；transmitter *n.* 转送人，传达人

5. hollow

[词义] *adj.* ① 无价值的，空洞的，虚伪的；② 中空的，空心的

[例句] Will their good intentions become realities or hollow promises?

他们的好意会变成现实还是成为空话？

These chocolate eggs are all hollow. 这些巧克力蛋都是空心的。

[派生] hollow-eyed *adj.* 双眼凹陷的；hollow-hearted *adj.* 虚伪的；hollowness *n.* 凹陷，空虚

6. investment

[词义] *n.* ① [U]（大量时间、精力或感情等的）投入；② [U, C] 投资

[例句] It might be a better investment of time to teach these children to learn English.

教这些孩子学英语也许是一种更好的时间投入。

They made an investment in the new company. 他们投资了那家新公司。

[派生] invest *v.* 投资，购买（有用之物）；investor *n.* 投资者

7. guarantee

[词义] *vt.* 保证，担保

n. ① 保证；② 保证，（尤指）商品使用保证书

[搭配] guarantee against/from 保障，保证免受……

[例句] The watch is guaranteed for three years. 这只手表保修三年。

There is no guarantee that it will be nice weather tomorrow.

无法保证明天将会有个好天气。

The new computer had a guarantee with it. 这台新电脑有保修单。

[派生] guarantor *n.* 担保人，保证人；guaranty *n.* 抵押物，保证物

8. glue

[词义] *n.* [U] 胶，胶水；*vt.* 胶合，粘贴

[搭配] glue sth. on to sth. 把……粘到……上；be glued to 盯住不放

[例句] I think we could mend that cup with glue.
我想我们能用胶水来粘合那个杯子。

His eyes were glued to the computer. 他的眼睛老是盯着电脑。

[派生] gluey *adj.* 粘的，似胶的

9. worship

[词义] *n.* [U] 崇敬，敬仰，敬慕
v. ①崇拜，敬重；②(对上帝或神灵) 信奉，敬奉，拜神，敬神

[例句] She became an object of worship after she married the prince.
当她嫁给王子之后，她成了被崇拜的对象。

He worships the money very much. 他非常崇拜金钱。

Their family worship regularly. 他们家人定期做礼拜。

[联想] warship *n.* 军舰

10. interpret

[词义] *v.* ①解释，说明，理解；②翻译，口译

[例句] I interpreted her smile as approval. 我把她的微笑理解为赞同。

Will you interpret what she says for me? 请你把她说的话翻译给我听好吗?

[派生] interpreter *n.* 译员，翻译者；interpretation *n.* 解释，说明

[辨析] explain, interpret, translate
explain 意为"解释、说明"，多指对别人不知道的或不完全了解的事物加以说明，一般不涉及解释者的主观判断和看法；interpret 当意为"解释、诠释"，多指运用特殊的知识、经验、想象力等解释、阐明极难理解的事物，强调解释者的思考过程和对事物的理解；当意为"翻译"时，多指"口译"；translate多指"文字翻译"。

11. faithful

[词义] *adj.* ①忠实的，忠诚的；② 如实的，准确可靠的

[搭配] be faithful to 忠实于……；be faithful in word and deed 言行忠实

[例句] His faithful old dog always accompanied him wherever he went.
无论他去哪里，他那忠诚的老狗都陪伴着他。

His report gave us a faithful account. 他的报告给我们一个如实的陈述。

[派生] faith *n.* 信任，信赖；faithless *adj.* 背信弃义的，不忠的

[辨析] faithful, loyal
faithful 多形容对爱情、友谊、事业、荣誉、工作、职业忠诚的，坚定不移的坚守信义；loyal 可指对爱情、友情、诺言、理想、职责等忠贞不渝的，也可指对君王、国家、政党等忠心的，更强调政治上的效忠。

12. elastic

[词义] *adj.* ①灵活的，可改变的；②有弹性的，可伸缩的

[例句] My timetable for this week is fairly elastic.
我本星期的时间表是相当灵活的。

This swimming costume is made of elastic material.

这件游泳衣是由弹性材料做成的。

[派生] elasticity *n.* 弹性，伸缩性

[辨析] elastic, flexible

elastic 意为"灵活的，可伸缩的"，可指预定的要求、规定或数字，也可用于形容面临危胁或混乱时具有迅速复原的能力；flexible 意为"灵活的，可变通的、能适应环境的"，表示具有为了适应某种变化了的环境而能机敏、熟练地改变习惯的良好素质，还带有为保持平衡而做暂时位置变动之意。

13. virtue

[词义] *n.* ① [U] 高尚的道德，正直的品行；② [U, C] 优点，长处

[搭配] by virtue of 借助，由于

[例句] Patience is a virtue. 耐心是一种美德。

She has the virtue of being a good listener. 她有善于倾听的优点。

[辨析] merit, morality, virtue

merit 意为"长处、优点、价值"，强调品质中值得赞扬的优点或价值，多以复数形式出现，反义词为demerit；morality为中性词，泛指"德性、品行"，用含褒义或贬义的词修饰均可；virtue 为正式用词，褒义词，意为"优点、优越性"，强调人或事物本身的长处、美德，反义词为drawback。

14. procession

[词义] *n.* ① [C] (人或事的) 连续出现；② [C]（人、车等的）行列，队伍

[例句] The family gathering was interrupted by a procession of unwelcome visitors.

家庭聚会被接连而来的不速之客打扰了。

A wedding procession moved slowly down the street.

一列婚礼的队伍沿着街道缓缓行进。

[派生] processional *adj.* 游行的

[联想] process *n.* 过程，进程；precession *n.* 优先

15. sacrifice

[词义] *n.* [U] 牺牲；*vt.* 牺牲，献出

[搭配] sacrifice onself/one's life to sb.'s interest 为了某人的利益牺牲自己/生命；at the sacrifice of 牺牲……；sacrificial lamb 替罪羔羊

[例句] We had to make sacrifices and go without entertainment in order to pay for our children's education.

为了支付孩子们的教育费用，我们放弃娱乐，做出牺牲。

He sacrificed his life trying to save the child from the freezing lake.

为了把这个孩子从冰冷的湖里救出来，他献出了自己的生命。

[派生] sacrificial *adj.* 供奉的，祭祀的，奉献的

16. pursue

[词义] *vt.* ① 追求，从事；② 追赶，追击

[例句] She pursued happiness all her life. 她的一生都在追求幸福。

The police was pursuing a car. 警察正在追赶一辆汽车。

[辨析] chase, pursue

chase 多指"追逐、追捕、追求"在视野之内快速运动的对象，目的在于将其捉住或赶走；pursue 为正式用词，意为"追赶、追踪"，表示为赶超、捕获而坚持不懈地追踪，其追踪距离一般比所经历的远，其目标可隐可现。

[派生] pursuit *n.* 追求，追赶；pursuer *n.* 追随者，追求者

17. glory

[词义] *n.* ① [U] 辉煌，光辉；② [C] 带来荣耀的人或事；③ [U] 荣誉，光荣

[例句] The glory of the Renaissance enlightened the Western world.
文艺复兴的辉煌照亮了西方世界。
The temple is one of the glories of ancient Greece.
这神殿是古希腊的荣耀之一。
He participated the competition and won glory for our motherland.
他参加了竞赛并且为祖国争得荣誉。

[派生] glorious *adj.* 光荣的，壮丽的；glorify *v.* 使更壮丽，赞扬

18. passion

[词义] *n.* ① [U, C] 激情，热情；② [U, C] 热爱，强烈的爱好

[搭配] have a passion for sth./to do sth. 酷爱某事/热切希望做某事；get/fly into a passion 勃然大怒

[例句] Their patriotic passion arose. 他们的爱国热情高涨。
She had a passion for chocolate. 她特别喜欢吃巧克力。

[派生] passionate *adj.* 多情的，充满激情的

19. refugee

[词义] *n.* [C] 难民

[例句] Many homeless refugees filled the streets in the city.
城市的街道上到处都是无家可归的难民

[派生] refuge *n.* 庇护，避难处

[例句] They took refuge in foreign embassies. 他们到外国使馆避难。

20. scatter *vi.* （使）分散，驱散；*vt.* 撒播

[例句] The students scattered in all directions. 学生们朝各个方向散去。
I scattered grass seed all over the lawn. 我把草籽撒在整个草坪上。

[辨析] disperse, scatter
disperse 指把人群或一群东西完全"分散开"；scatter 强调运用某种权力或力量将人或物向不同的方向"驱散"，或强调人、物向四处迅速"散开"，常与 about, around, round 连用，表示四处奔走，到处乱扔。

21. acknowledge

[词义] *vt.* ① 接受，承认，认为；② 告知收到，确认；③ 对……表示感谢，答谢

[例句] She acknowledged that she had been at fault. 她承认自己错了。
You should acknowledge his letter promptly.
你应该及时表明已收到他的来信。
He sent a gift to his friend to acknowledge his favor.
他送了一件礼物给他的朋友以答谢所受的关照。

[派生] acknowledgement *n.* 承认，致谢；acknowledged *adj.* 公认的，得到普遍承认的，被普遍认可的

22. gamble

[词义] v. ① 赌钱，赌博；② 投机，冒险

　　　n. [U, C] 赌博，投机，冒险

[搭配] gamble away 赌掉，输光；gamble on 把赌注押在……上，做……投机生意；take a gamble 冒风险

[例句] He has gambled away all the money. 他赌掉了所有的钱。

　　　He's gambling with his own live driving so fast.

　　　他把车开得那样快，简直是拿自己的生命冒险。

　　　Investing in the stock was a gamble. 投资股票是一种赌博。

23. regulate

[词义] vt. ① 管理，控制；② 调节，调理

[例句] The are strict rules regulating the use of chemicals in food.

　　　有严格的规定限制在食品中使用化学制品。

　　　Please regulate the alarm clock. 请调一下这个闹钟。

[派生] regular adj. 有规律的，整齐的；regulation n. 管理，规定，命令

24. saddle

[词义] v. ① 使负担，强加；② 给（马等）装鞍

　　　n. [C] (马、自行车、摩托车等的) 鞍，坐鞍

[搭配] saddle with 使某人负担（不愿意的责任）；in the saddle 在职，掌权

[例句] I was saddled with the job of leading the worst group.

　　　他们硬是把领导最差组的工作交给我干。

　　　She saddled (up) the horse for her friend. 她替她朋友装好马鞍。

　　　When riding a horse you sit on the saddle. 骑马时要骑在鞍子上。

25. sustain

[词义] vt. 维持，使继续

[例句] The army do not have sufficient food to sustain the battle for long.

　　　部队没有足够的食物把战役长期维持下去。

[辨析] sponsor, support, sustain

　　　sponsor 正式用词，指用语言表明"支持"议案、计划或某人；support 常用词，指支撑重量或作为支柱，以防某人跌倒或某物倒塌。引申为"支持、拥护"，给与积极的帮助或表示赞同；sustain较为正式，可指用具体实物承受压力或重量，引申为给与力量、勇气或信心等意思。

26. concession

[词义] n. [C] 让步

[例句] Both sides involved in the conflict made some concessions in the negotiation.

　　　在谈判中冲突双方都做了让步。

[派生] concessive adj. 让步的；concede v. 容许，勉强承认

27. subject...to（常用被动形式）使遭遇（不愉快之事）

[例句] In recent years, she has been subjected to heart attacks.

　　　近年来，她一再受到心脏病的侵扰。

[辨析] subject...to, be subject to

　　　前者中subject作动词，后者中subject作形容词。意为：① 受……的约束，

应服从……，如：We are subject to the law of the country. 我们受国家法律的制约。②有……倾向的，易患，易受，如：The trains are subject to delays in foggy days. 雾天火车经常会晚点。③以为……条件，须经……，如：The arrangement is subject to your approval. 这一安排须经你批准。

28. take offense 生气，见怪
[例句] He takes offense at the slightest criticism. 他听到一点点批评就生气。

29. consist of 由……组成，由……构成
[例句] The house consists of six rooms. 这房子由六个房间组成。

[联想] be composed of 由……组成

30. come apart 破裂，崩溃，解体
[例句] The old cup came apart suddenly when I touched it.
当我碰到那个旧杯子，它突然裂开了。

[联想] fall apart 崩溃，土崩瓦解

31. at will 任意，随便
[例句] You are free to come and go at will. 你来去自由。

32. throw in 外加，另外奉送
[例句] When they bought the house, the furniture was thrown in at no extra charge.
他们买这房子时，家具是奉送的，不另收费。

[联想] throw away 扔掉，抛弃；throw up 呕吐；产生（想法）；放弃

33. by virtue of 由于
[例句] The player defeated his rivals by virtue of greater experience.
这位选手凭借更丰富的经验战胜了对手。

34. better off 比较幸福，更幸运，更自在
[例句] We'd be better off without the noise outside.
要是没有外面的噪音，我们要舒适得多。

[联想] well off 家境富裕

35. take out one's anger on sb. 向某人发泄自己的愤怒
[例句] He always took out his anger on his wife. 他总是把气发在他妻子身上。

Ⅲ. 难句解析

1. At dinner afterwards I was subjected to a hostile quizzing by a group of women in their thirties who claimed that my whole analysis ignored the most basic change of all. (Para. 1)

[释义] At the following dinner I was questioned in an unfriendly manner by a group of women in their thirties, who stated that my whole analysis failed to consider the most basic aspect of family change.

[分析] "who claimed...of all" 是一个定语从句，修饰先行词women。在这个定语从句中包含了一个宾语从句，即 "that my whole analysis...of all"，作动词claimed的宾语。

2. It's not just a "big stadium" where everyone can enjoy the show. (Para. 3)

[释义] Family is not a place where everyone can come to have their enjoyment and then go, but a place where parents have their duty and responsibility.

3. **The modern nuclear family was rooted in the desire to live happily in a more equal marriage, where the raising of children and the investment of both parents in the children's lives were guaranteed by bonds of friendship between the parents, which were based on rational love. (Para. 4)**

[释义] The modern nuclear family developed from and was strongly influenced by the desire to have a happy life in a more equal marriage, in which the raising of children and the contribution of both parents to the children's lives were ensured by the friendly tie based on the sensible love between the parents.

[分析] 主干为 "The modern nuclear family was rooted in the desire."。"where the raising of...on rational love" 是非限制性定语从句，修饰限定前面的整个句子，where在句中作状语，表示 "在……样的家庭里"。在这个大定语从句中又包含一个小的定语从句，即 "which are based on rational love"，修饰名词friendship。

4. **If marriage exists only as a romantic relationship that can be ended at will, and family exists only by virtue of bonds of affection, both marriage and family come second to the search for love. (Para. 7)**

[释义] If you get married simply to seek a romantic relationship that you can end as you like, and if the existence of family is only through feelings of love, marriage and family become less important than the search of love.

[分析] 整个句子由两个if条件状语从句加一个主句构成，其中第二个从句中if省略，与第一个从句共用if。

5. **But dependent children can't just be left behind when it's time to move on to a new relationship...(Para. 8)**

[释义] **dependent** *adj.* 依靠的，依赖的

　　e.g. The marriage is dependent on your faith towards each other.

　　婚姻取决于你们双方对彼此的忠诚

　　dependant *n.* 需要依靠他人供养的人，食客

　　e.g. This residence document permits you, but no dependant, to live and work in this country. 居住文件允许你，在这个国家生活和工作，但靠你供养的人不享有此权利。

6. **What divorce does is to damage children, making them into refugees as the people in their lives scatter in all directions. (Para. 10)**

[释义] Divorce does great harm to children, who are neglected with no one to care about them, as the people in their lives leave them for different places.

[分析] "What divorce does" 是主语从句，在句中作主语，谓语由不定式 "to damage children" 构成。"making them into refugees" 是现在分词作结果状语，进一步说明离婚对孩子造成的影响，在这个状语从句中包含一个原因状语从句 "as the people in their lives scatter in all directions"。

7. **Nor, I would venture to suggest, is love enough to sustain a marriage relationship. (Para. 12)**

[释义] **venture** *v.* (formal) 冒险，冒昧，斗胆，胆敢（谦语）

e.g. I ventured to suggest that she might have made a mistake.

我冒昧指出她可能犯了一个错误。

[分析] "I venture to suggest" 是一个插入语。因为前面一句是否定句型，此处用了引导的倒装句。

Ⅳ. 重点语法讲解

在句中起名词作用的句子被称为**名词从句**。象任何名词一样，名词从句也可用作动词的主语，但更多作动词的宾语，或作动词be或其他系动词如seem和appear的补语。

if, whether 引导的名词从句

yes-no 型疑问从句

从属连词 if, whether 引导的名词从句是由一般疑问句或选择疑问转化而来的，因此也分别被称为 yes-no 型疑问句从句和选择型疑问从句，其功能和 wh- 从句的功能相同。

Whether he came to the party (or not) didn't matter. (作主语)

The question was whether he came to the party. (在be后作补语)

I wanted to know whether/if he had come to the party. (作动词的宾语，特别是间接宾语)

I was concerned about whether he had come to the party. (作介词的宾语)

如果句子开头是一个从句，则必须用 whether；在 be 和介词之后也必须用 whether。在动词和少数用于否定的形容词之后，如：not sure 和 not certain之后，whether 和 if 两者都可以用。

Ⅴ. 课文赏析

1. 文体特点

本文是一篇结构清晰，通俗易懂的议论文。文章开门见山提出要讨论的问题，主体部分用对比的方法将把婚姻家庭与情爱家庭进行对比，分析离婚会给孩子带来的伤害，从而得出结论：要维系婚姻家庭关系，光有爱是不够的，还需要有责任感和义务感。

2. 结构分析

Part Ⅰ (Para. 1-2) By mentioning one experience, the author introduces a new social change: Love Family.

Part Ⅱ (Para 3-9) Compared with the obligations of marriage, Love Family has its shortcomings.

Part Ⅲ (Para. 10-11) Divorce causes great damages to children.

Part Ⅳ (Para. 12) Love is not enough to sustain a marriage relationship.

Ⅵ. 课后练习答案及解析

Comprehension of the Text

XVI.

B C B B B　C B B

Vocabulary

XVII.

1. obligation 译文：如果你没有签合同，你就没义务付给他们钱。

2. continuity 译文：那个班缺乏连贯性——他们已经连续换了四个老师了。

3. sacrifice 译文：如果你成为一名士兵，就得为国家作出极大的牺牲。

4. acknowledged 译文：他个人收藏的荷兰油画最精美，这是大家公认的。

5. passion 译文：他对她感情如此强烈，以至于连片刻的分开都不能承受。

6. scattered 译文：警察吹响了警笛，示威者四下散开。

7. worship 译文：在崇尚健康的时代，人们对运动和节食都很着迷。

8. elastic 译文：在这个国家，时间是个弹性概念，根本没有时间表这回事。

XVIII.

1. in; in 译文：军队和警察联手搜寻恐怖分子。

2. by/in 译文：他们争辩说，因为塑料袋有干净、柔韧、成本低的优点，可以被用来装许多种食物。

3. to 译文：如果他的感冒还是很严重的话，告诉他试试这种药——这是最好的药。

4. on 译文：她总是回忆那些日子，把它们当作婚后最快乐的日子。

5. at 译文：家里安装好空调后，我们就能随意享受舒适的温度了。

6. behind 译文：男人们都逃跑了，留下了年老的妇女和儿童。

7. to 译文：经历了几次辉煌的战役之后，罗马人控制了整个国家的一半。

8. from 译文：离婚使爸爸离开了家，留下母亲既当妈又当爸。

VII. 参考译文

婚姻的义务与责任

有天晚上，我就家庭的变革发表了一番谈话。在随后的晚宴上，一群三十多岁的女士对我颇不友好地质问攻击了一番。她们声称我的整个分析忽视了家庭变革中最基本的变化。

她们称对我所说的家庭由夫妻和子女组成的观点感到不快。她们这个群体，个个单身，都是好朋友，互相扶持，彼此视作"家人"。如今婚姻与生儿育女都已变得不再重要，她们认为这才是最基本的社会变革。

回想一下，她们也没错，可是问题就出在这日益高涨的变化浪潮本身。可以说，家庭是联系两代人的纽带，是养育孩子和传递文化的中心。它可不是个"大场馆"，人人都可以进来娱乐一场。婚姻和家庭意味着互相关爱的长期义务与责任，而不仅仅是寻求幸福，这一摩登时代的空洞目标。

爱情现在似乎已经失控。现代核心家庭原本基于对更为平等的婚姻关系中幸福生活的渴望。在这样的家庭里，父母间由于理性的爱所带来的友好关系保证了他们能共同抚养孩子和共同在孩子身上投入。

任何建立在自发爱恋基础上的关系都会趋于自然终止，但婚姻建立起家庭纽带，以及父母与子女间的责任义务，这就提供了将夫妇联结在一起的粘合剂。不幸的是，人们称之为"情爱家庭"的新模式以无约束的选择这一理想化的做法取代了夫妻间长相厮守的关系。

现在我们不仅可以选择配偶，也可以任意与其离婚，将我们成人对幸福的崇拜置于孩子的利益之上，也可以阻止另一方与孩子有任何经常性的来往。愿意的话我们甚至可以把"家庭"看作包括一些与我们既无血缘关系、又无婚姻关系的人——些互相扶持的亲密朋友，就像前面所提到的那些女士。如果你愿意的话，可以把那条忠实的狗也算在内。我们想要家庭什么样，它就是什么样。

问题是，对家庭的这种灵活的归类忽视了孩子，也忽视了关怀他人这一更广泛的问题。如果婚姻仅是一种可随意终止的浪漫关系，如果家庭仅由感情来维系，那么婚姻和家庭与追求爱情相比就只能退居其次了。在这样的模式下，个人会去经历一次又一次带来或多或少满足感的浪漫关系，以便追求最大程度的幸福，而将孩子、亲属、相互间的责任和关爱统统置于脑后，全然不顾。

这对能独立生活的成年人没有问题。但在建立新关系的同时不能不考虑尚未独立的孩子。他们需要我们做出自我牺牲和无私奉献，也就是父母对子女在金钱和时间上的长期投入。

婚姻的全部意义就在于它予以夫妻双方清晰的责任义务，而不仅仅是追求个人幸福的权利。而主要的责任就是给孩子感情上和实际上的关爱。激情的光焰可能早已减退，对妻子或丈夫的爱也许不及当初那般令人兴奋、那般美满，但转而寻求新的爱情不会对孩子有好处。"情爱家庭"对孩子来说，要么太随意——新的伴侣对你的孩子没有抚养责任，要么太不稳定，成年人一旦感到他们的关系无法满足自己对完美幸福的追求，就会转而他求。

离婚造成的是对孩子的伤害，使他们随着身边人的离散而成了流亡者。我注意到一些关于离婚对孩子的影响的综合性研究。我承认，如果没有狂暴的父亲，家里的钱没有被浪费在酗酒或赌博上，父母感到不快时不会对家里每个人撒气，一些孩子会生活得更好。

但是离婚摧毁了孩子所需要的稳定感、安全感、整体感，造成了很多妇女儿童的贫困，破坏了父亲与子女间的自然联系，代之以人为安排的定期探视。离婚使父亲离开了家庭，这惟一的父亲与子女间关系赖以存在的合理基础不复存在。离婚使得母亲既当母亲又当父亲而不堪重负，从而造成母子关系的紧张。离婚也常使孩子中断学业、友情、邻里关系，而这正是使孩子能健康地融入社会所必需的信任感和人际关系的开端。离婚甚至削弱了孩子与祖父母、与对方家庭（通常为父亲一方）的联系，而情人间几乎没有人愿为另一人的孩子的幸福真正承担责任。

与双亲家庭和睦相处、相互支持相比，仅有爱是不够的。我想冒昧地说，要维系婚姻关系，仅有爱也是不够的。说到底，"情爱家庭"不用为孩子和亲属做出让步。彻底的自由最终会成为我们的锁链，使我们别无选择，只能生活在孤独中，没有人来关怀我们。

Section C
I . 语言点讲解

1. Consequently, I don't put up obstacles to what you do that enhances you as a person, even though it may result in my discomfort at times. (Para. 3)

[分析] "what you do"是名词性从句，作介词to的宾语。"that enhances you as a person"是定语从句，修饰前面"what you do"。

2. The responsibility does not include my doing for you what you are capable of doing for yourself; nor does it mean that I run your life for you. (Para. 5)

[分析] "what you are capable of doing for yourself"是宾语从句，作动词doing的宾语。"nor does it mean..."是一个倒装句。

3. ...in this sense we see that love involves an acceptance of some responsibility for the impact my way of being has on you. (Para. 5)

[分析] 宾语从句的主干是 "love involves an acceptance of some responsibility for the impact"；"my way of being has on you"是省略了引导词that/which的定语从句，修饰impact；定语从句中的主语是my way of being，谓语动词has，宾语为impact。

Ⅱ. 课文赏析

1. 文体特点

这是一篇说明文。开篇直接点题，主体层层剖析，结尾与开头互相呼应，总结深化主题。文中作者使用了大量的排比句，语言优美流畅，层次清晰地阐释了爱的定义。

2. 结构分析

Part Ⅰ (Para. 1-7) The definition of love.

Part Ⅱ (Para. 8-11) The action of one person for his/her partner for the love between them.

Part Ⅲ (Para. 12) The conclusion that mature love needs to respect the other's uniqueness.

Ⅲ. 课后练习答案及解析

Comprehension of the Text

XX.

TFFFT FTT

Ⅳ. 参考译文

爱的真谛

我们想与大家一起分享我们对爱情的一些积极看法。

爱就意味着了解所爱之人。能够认识到这个人的各个方面——不仅仅是美好的一面，还有他的局限，他的矛盾之处，他的缺点。要看到这个人的情感、思想，感受他的内心。要能够透过他在社交场合的表现和他的社会角色而看到他的内心深处。

爱就意味着关心所爱之人的幸福。真正的爱不是占有，也不是束缚。相反，两人都在爱中得到自由。关心一个人就是关心他的成长，希望他可以尽其所能有所成就。因此，我不会为他的个人发展设置障碍，即使这样有时会给我带来不便。

爱就意味着尊重所爱之人。爱一个人，就是将其视作一个独立的人，有自己的价值观、思想和感情。我不会为了自己而坚持要他放弃个性来变成我所希望的他。我能允许，也鼓励他与众不同，成为他自己。我不会视他为物，或利用他来满足自己的需要。

爱就意味着对所爱之人负责。爱一个人，就要对他作为独立个体的需求做出回应。这种负责并非替他做他可以自己做到的事，也不是操纵他的生活。这种负责是承认我的所作所为会影响到他，他的欢乐痛苦都与我休戚相关。相爱者的确会伤害或忽略所爱的人。从这个意义上说，我们认为，爱就要为自己的行为对对方产生的影响承担某种责任。

爱就意味着对所爱之人做出承诺。这种承诺并非意味着完全把自己交给对方，也并不是说这一关系一定要永远不变。这种承诺意味着不论在恬适欢乐时，还是在艰难困苦、失意绝望时，都愿意厮守相伴。

爱就意味着信赖所爱之人。爱一个人，就要相信他会接受我的关心，接受我的爱，相信他不会故意伤害我；相信自己对他有吸引力，相信他不会抛弃我；相信爱是相互的。如果我们彼此信赖，我们就愿彼此开诚布公，敞开心扉。

爱能够容忍不完美。爱人之间也会有时感到厌烦，有时想放弃，有时感到压力，有时感到羁绊。真正的爱并不意味着永远幸福。但是，在困难时期我能坚守，因为我仍记得我们共同渡过的往昔，我也能想象如果我们愿意直面问题、渡过难关，我们将共同拥有什么样的未来。我们一致认为爱是一种精神，它能改变人生。爱是一种生活方式，它具有创造和改变的力量。但是爱并不只是完美世界所独有，爱本来就是为我们这个不完美、有缺陷的世界而存在的。爱应该是一种能缓解痛苦的精神力量。爱应该给我们这充满荒谬的生活带来意义。换言之，是爱使我们能够在这不完美的世界上生活下去。

爱是包容的。爱一个人，就要鼓励其与他人建立联系。尽管对彼此的爱与承诺不允许我们有某些行为，这种结合也不是全然排他的。两个人密不可分，再无其他发展的余地，这样的爱是不真实、不明智的。

爱又是自私的。只有真正自爱自重、自赏自尊，才能爱别人。如果自己空虚，那么我能给所爱之人的也只有空虚。如果认为自己是完满的、出色的，那么我就能以自己的充实为所爱之人增光。表达爱的最好方法之一就是与所爱之人一起充分体验自己。

爱就要看到所爱之人的内在潜力。爱一个人，爱她/他今日之所作所为，也要视其所能为。视人静止不变，则令其退步，而视其进步发展、待他如同他的潜力已经发挥，则助其进步。

归根结底，成熟的爱就是保持个性条件下的双方结合。两个人由于爱合二为一，又仍是两个独立的个体。

五、知识链接

Can we predict marital success?

Research provides some tentative forewarnings of marital trouble, e.g. ① one or both lovers' parents have an unhappy marriage; ② married at an early age; ③married impulsively; ④have a low income or financial problems; and ⑤one or both lovers have psychological problems.

There are no real surprises here, but also nothing you can really depend on. In fact, some researchers question whether any particular dating or premarital experience helps us make wise choices for a mate. Similar social-economic, religious, ethnic and racial backgrounds of couples are somewhat beneficial, but they don't in general predict marital satisfaction very well, certainly not in individual cases.

Our satisfaction with our marriage is predicted by how well we communicate, even before marriage, and by how we structure our day-to-day lives together after marriage. A good marriage partner will probably have a variety of skills, such as social-communication skills with you and others, emotional maturity and control of his/her emotions, tolerance and affection towards you and others, similar interests and values to yours, ability to be responsible and earn an adequate steady income, and effective problem-solving and conflict resolution ability.

我们能够预测成功的婚姻吗？

研究提供了一些对婚姻问题的预测性的的警告，例如：① 爱人一方或双方的父母婚姻不幸福；② 早婚；③草率结婚；④收入低或有财政问题；以及⑤夫妇一方或双方有心理问题。

这里没有真正的惊喜，但是也没有任何可以真正依靠的东西。事实上，一些研究者质疑是否某种独特的约会或婚前经历能够在选择伴侣时帮助我们做出明智的选择。一对夫妻相似的社会经济、信仰、民族和种族背景在某种程度上是有利的，但是这些基本上不能准确预测婚姻满意度，在单个的案例中肯定不能。

我们对婚姻的满意度是根据我们沟通的好坏程度来预测的，甚至是在婚前，及以根据婚后我们怎样安排在一起的日常生活。一个好的婚姻伴侣可能会有各种技巧，例如与你和与他人的社会交际技巧，情感成熟度以及控制他或她的情感的能力，对你和他人的宽容及友爱，与你相似的兴趣和价值观，担负责任和赚足够且稳定收入的能力，以及有效地处理问题和解决冲突的能力。

六、自测题

1. A lot of ants are always invading my kitchen. They are a thorough _____.
   A. nuisance   B. trouble   C. worry   D. anxiety
2. Parents have a legal _____ to ensure that their children are provided with efficient education suitable to their age.
   A. impulse   B. influence   C. obligation   D. sympathy
3. _____ the high rank and position he holds, Mr. Apple takes social leadership over almost everyone else.
   A. In honor of   B. As regards   C. By virtue of   D. At the cost of
4. Out of _____ revenge, he did his worst to blacken her character and ruin her reputation.
   A. perfect   B. total   C. sheer   D. integral
5. At first, the _____ of color pictures over a long distance seemed impossible, but with painstaking efforts and at great expense, it became a reality.
   A. transaction   B. transmission   C. transformation   D. transition
6. Christmas is a Christian holy day usually celebrated on December 25th _____ the birth of Christ.
   A. in accordance with B. in terms of   C. in favor of   D. in honor of
7. His long service with the company was _____ with a present.
   A. admitted   B. acknowledged   C. attributed   D. accepted
8. The manager spoke highly of such _____ as loyalty, courage and truthfulness shown by hid employers.
   A. virtues   B. features   C. properties   D. characteristics
9. Europe's earlier industrial growth was _____ by the availability of key resources, abundant and cheap labor, coal, iron ore, etc.
   A. constrained   B. remained   C. sustained   D. detained
10. The Car Club couldn't _____ to meet the demands of all its members.
    A. ensure   B. guarantee   C. assume   D. confirm

答案与解析

1. A nuisance 指令人讨厌的人或事物或行为，符合题意。
2. C obligation 责任，义务; impulse 冲动; influence 影响; sympathy 同情
3. C by virtue of 由于; in honor of 为纪念，向……表示尊敬; as regards 关于; at the cost of 以……为代价
4. C sheer 纯粹的，完全的; perfect 完美的; total 总共的; integral 整体的
5. B transmission 传递，传送; transaction 交易，业务; transformation 变迁，变化; transition 转折，过渡
6. D in honor of 向……表示敬意，为庆祝; in accordance with 符合，按照; in terms of 就……而言; in favor of 赞同，支持;
7. B acknowledge 公认; admit 容许，承认; attribute 归结于; accept 接受
8. A virtue 美德; feature 特征; property 特性，性能; characteristic 特点
9. C sustain 维持，持续; remain 保持，逗留; constrain 约束; detain 拘留
10. B guarantee 保证，担保; ensure 确保，后跟从句或用于ensure sb. sth.; assume 假设; confirm 证实

Unit 21

1 **学习重点和难点**
词汇和短语、语法项目、写作技巧

2 **文化知识**
课文大背景、课文知识点

3 **课文精讲**
词汇与短语详解、难句解析、重点语法讲解、课文赏析、课后练习答案及解析、参考译文、写作指导

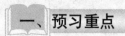

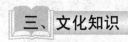

一、预习重点

1. What are the secrets of Chaplin's great comedy?
2. Why did the men vote in a female politician?
3. How is success weighed in the family of first?

二、学习重点和难点

I. 词汇和短语

Section A: comic, tramp, rag, applause, crude, clap, revolt, coarse, behave, nationality, postpone, doubtful, immense, extraordinary, rouse, execute, correspond, betray, collision, relief, spark, clumsy, incident, memorial; cut down, for good, trip up; make up; come down in the word, go along, find one's way into

Section B: revolutionary, opponent, election, sack, loaf, colonial, jealous, assembly, committee, fierce, rally, riot, witness, earnest, refresh; run for, vote in, spy on/upon, shut out of, break up, tear down, in/by contrast, in earnest, lay out, feel like, deliver the goods

II. 语法项目

① 形容词的用法
② 现在分词与过去分词的区别

III. 写作技巧

主题句和细节

三、文化知识

I. 课文大背景

1. Charlie Chaplin 查理·卓别林

Charles Spencer Chaplin (1889-1977) was born in Walworth, London, and lived a Dickensian childhood, shared with his brother, Sydney, that included extreme poverty, workhouses and seeing his mother's mental decline put her into an institution. Both his parents, though separated when he was very young, were music hall artists, his father quite famously so. But it was his mother that Charlie idolised and was inspired by during his visit of the backstage while she performed, to take up such a career for himself.

2. Charles Dickens 查尔斯·狄更斯

Charles Dickens (1812—1870) was an English novelist, considered by many to be the greatest one of all. His many famous books describe life in Victorian England and show how hard it was, especially for the poor and for children. They include *The Pickwick Papers* (《匹克威克外传》), *Oliver Twist* (《奥列佛·退斯特》), *A Christmas Carol* (《圣诞故事集》), *David Copperfield* (《大卫·科波菲尔》), *Great Expectations* (《远大前程》) and *A Tale of Two Cities* (《双城记》).

Ⅱ. 课文知识点

1. Hollywood 好莱坞

Hollywood is an area of Los Angeles which is known as the center of the American film industry. In terms of geography, Hollywood refers to an area consisting of the City of West Hollywood and its vicinity that form part of the Greater Los Angeles metropolitan area. It is generally thought that everyone living in Hollywood is extremely rich, famous and concerned with appearances, but in fact many parts of Hollywood today are poor, dirty and badly cared for.

2. Oona O'Neil Chaplin 沃娜·奥尼尔·卓别林

Oona O'Neil Chaplin (1926-1991) was the only daughter to the famous playwright Eugene O'Neil and his wife, Agnes. Unlike his previous three marriages, Charlie's marriage to Oona was a match made in heaven, despite their age difference. The couple had eight children. Charlie's final marriage realized his ideal girl and love of his life in Oona O'Neil, and it will always be Oona Chaplin who will always be remembered as Mrs. Charles Chaplin.

3. Kenya 肯尼亚

A country in east Africa, on the Equator, which became independent in 1963 and which is known for production of coffee and tea; its capital is Nairobi.

4. Pastrami 胡椒熏牛肉火腿

Pastrami can refer to a technology for preserving meat or meat (very often beef) thus seasoned.

四、课文精讲

Section A

Ⅰ. 词汇与短语详解

1. comic
[词义] *adj.* 喜剧的，滑稽的 *n.* ① [C] 连环漫画（册）；② [C] 喜剧演员
[例句] The speech is rich in comic sensitivity. 这演讲很富有喜剧性。 The child received a comic for Christmas. 孩子圣诞节收到一本连环漫画册。 If you're a famous comic, it means a lot of people are watching your show. 如果你是有名的喜剧演员，这意味着许多人看你的表演。
[派生] comedy *n.* 喜剧; comedian *n.* 喜剧演员，丑角式人物
[联想] tragedy *n.* 悲剧，惨案; tragic *adj.* 悲惨的，悲剧的
2. tramp
[词义] *n.* [C] 流浪者，乞丐; *v.* 踏着沉重的步子行进，长途跋涉
[搭配] on the tramp 到处流浪; take a long tramp to 长途跋涉到……; tramp down 踏坏，踩坏
[例句] He used to be a tramp when he was young. 他年轻时曾当过乞丐。 He has tramped the whole town looking for work. 他走遍全城寻找工作。
[派生] trample *n.* 踩踏，踩躏 *v.* 践踏，轻视

33

3. rag

[词义] *n.* ① (*usu. pl.*) 破旧的衣服；② [C, U] 破布，碎布

[搭配] in rags 穿着破旧的衣服

[例句] The poor beggar was dressed in rags. 那可怜的乞丐衣衫褴褛。

He used a piece of rag to dust the car. 他用一块抹布擦拭车上的灰尘。

4. applause

[词义] *n.* [C] 掌声，欢呼

[搭配] draw applause 引起……鼓掌；give sb. applause for 称赞某人的……

[例句] His speech was followed by loud applause. 他的演讲赢得了热烈的掌声。

[派生] applaud *v.* 拍手喝彩，称赞；applausive *adj.* 拍手欢呼

5. crude

[词义] *adj.* ① 粗鲁的；② 粗制的，粗陋的；③ 天然的，未加工的

[例句] His crude jokes offended her. 他的粗俗笑话冒犯了她。

He was living in a crude hut. 他住在一个简陋的屋子里。

The country exported crude oil. 这个国家出口原油。

[派生] crudely *adv.* 不成熟地，粗杂地；crudity *n.* 生硬，粗野

6. clap

[词义] *vi.* 鼓掌，拍手；*vt.* 拍击，轻拍

[搭配] clap sb. on the back 拍某人的肩；clap hands 拍手

[例句] The audience clapped and cheered after the performance.

在演出之后，观众鼓掌欢呼。

She clapped her son on his back. 她在儿子背上轻拍了一下。

[辨析] applaud, clap

applaud 指拍手喝彩，重点在欢呼喝彩；clap 是拟声词，指的是"拍手"这个单纯的动作，未必表示欢呼喝彩。

7. revolt

[词义] *v.* 反叛，造反；*n.* [C, U] 反叛，造反

[搭配] revolt at 厌恶，憎恨；in revolt 反抗，叛乱

[例句] The people revolted against the military government. 人民反抗军政府。

Troops were called in to put down the revolt. 部队被招来镇压叛乱。

[派生] revolting *adj.* 令人厌恶的；revoltive *adj.* 厌恶的，反感的

[辨析] rebellion, revolt

rebellion 指公开的、有组织的、较大规模的、常以失败告终的"武装反抗"，尤指反叛政府，以图改变国家的政治体系；revolt 与 rebellion 词义相似，但常指很快便失败或成功的"武装体系"。

8. coarse

[词义] *adj.* ① 粗俗的，粗鲁的；② 粗糙的

[例句] His coarse manner made him unpopular with some people.

他粗鲁的举止使他不受一些人的欢迎。

The sand was so coarse that it was quite painful to walk on.

沙子非常粗糙，走在上面很痛。

[派生] coarsen *v.* (使) 变粗糙；coarseness *n.* 粗糙，劣等

[辨析] coarse, crude, rude

coarse 意为"粗糙的、粗劣的",多用来形容某物的质地或组织粗劣、质量欠佳; 比喻意为"粗俗的",指人的举止谈吐由于无知或不注意而显得不文雅;crude原指物品"简陋的、粗糙的、未加工的",比喻义为"粗鲁的、粗俗的",通常可与coarse互换,比coarse语气稍强;rude意为"粗鲁无理的",指言语、行为不礼貌,有时甚至带有侮辱性。

9. behave

[词义] *v.* ① 举动,表现,循规蹈矩;②(机器等)运转,(事物)作出反应

[搭配] behave oneself 行为规矩

[例句] You must behave well at the party! 在晚会上你的表现不错!

How does your new car behave? 你的新车性能怎么样?

[派生] behavior *n.* 举止,行为; well/badly-behaved 行为良好/恶劣的

10. nationality

[词义] *n.* ① [C, U] 国籍;② [C] 种族,民族

[例句] Fill in your name and nationality on the form. 在表上填写你的姓名和国籍。

There are many minority nationalities in China. 中国有很多少数民族。

[派生] nation *n.* 民族,国家; national *adj.* 国家的,国有的,民族的

11. postpone

[词义] *vt.* 延迟,延缓

[例句] They had to postpone their holiday to the next year.

他们不得不将假期推迟到第二年。

[派生] postponement *n.* 推迟,延期

12. doubtful

[词义] *adj.* ① 不大可能的;② 疑惑的,不确定的

[搭配] be doubtful of/about sth. 对……不确定

[例句] It is doubtful whether/if they are still alive. 他们不大可能还活着。

She looked rather doubtful. 她看上去很疑惑。

[派生] doubt *n.* 怀疑,疑惑 *v.* 怀疑,不信; doubtless *adj.* 很可能

[辨析] doubtful, dubious, suspicious

doubtful表示"尚有疑问的",怀疑某人或某事不真实或不正确,但只是一种不确定的推测,尚需进一步的证据来证明;dubious 表示对人或事物"半信半疑、犹豫不决的"时,表示没有把握或缺乏信心,语气没有doubtful强烈;suspicious表示"值得怀疑的"时强调某人的行为动机值得怀疑。

13. immense

[词义] *adj.* 巨大的,无限的

[例句] The air is of immense importance to the plant. 空气对植物非常重要。

[派生] immensely *adv.* 非常,很; immensity *n.* 巨大,巨大之物

[联想] immerse *vt.* 沉浸,使陷入

14. extraordinary

[词义] *adj.* 异常的,非凡的,奇特的

[例句] She has extraordinary beauty. 她异常得美丽。

[派生] extraordinarily *adv.* 格外地，特别地

15. rouse

[词义] *vt.* ① 激起 (某种情感或态度)；② 弄醒，叫醒；③ 唤起，使觉醒

[搭配] rouse sb./oneself to action 激励某人（自己）行动起来

[例句] For what on earth you roused his anger? 到底为什么你引起了他的愤怒？

I was roused by the doorbell ringing. 门铃声把我唤醒了。

The speaker attempted to rouse the crowd to action.

演讲者试图鼓动人们行动起来。

[联想] arise *vi.* 出现，发生；rise *vi.* 升起，上升

[辨析] arouse *vt.* 唤醒，唤起，多用于抽象意味；rouse 多用于具体意味。

The odd sight aroused our curiosity. 奇怪的景象激起我们的好奇。

16. execute

[词义] *vt.* ① 实施，执行，履行；② 将……处以死刑

[搭配] execute one's command 执行某人的命令；execute a plan 实现计划

[例句] We should execute the scheme as previously agreed. 我们应该实行既定方案。

She was executed for murder. 她因谋杀罪被处死。

[派生] execution *n.* 实行，执行；executive *adj.* 执行的，行政的 *n.* 执行者，经理主管人员；executor *n.* 执行者，被指定遗嘱执行者

17. correspond

[词义] *v.* ① 相符，相称，相当；② 通信

[搭配] correspond with sth. 与……调和，符合；correspond to 相当于，相等于；correspond with sb. 与某人通信；correspondence course 函授课程

[例句] His action corresponds less and less with his words.

他的言行越来越不一致。

I frequently correspond with my sister. 我与姐姐经常通信。

[派生] corresponding *adj.* 相应的，相符的；correspondence *n.* 相应，通信，信件；correspondent *n.* 通讯记者，通信者

As the course becomes more demanding, there's usually a corresponding drop in attendance. 随着课程要求逐渐变高，上课的人数也相应少了起来。

18. betray

[词义] *vt.* ① 背叛，出卖；②（非故意地）暴露，表现

[搭配] betray sb. to... 把某人出卖给……；betray oneself 暴露出真实身份

[例句] He was accused of betraying his country during the war.

他被控在战争中背叛祖国。

He smile betrayed his satisfaction with his son.

他脸上的笑容显露出他对儿子很满意。

[派生] betrayal *n.* 被判，出卖；betrayer *n.* 叛徒，背叛者

19. collision

[词义] *n.* ① [C, U] (利益、意见等的) 冲突，抵触；② [C, U] 碰撞，互撞

[搭配] in collision with... 与……相撞 (冲突)；collide with...over sth. 在某事上与……相抵触 (冲突)

[例句] There was a collision of interest in both parties. 双方存在利益冲突。

The cyclist was in collision with a bus.

这位骑自行车的人与一辆公共汽车相撞了。

[派生] collide *vi.* 碰撞，抵触

[辨析] clash, collision, conflict, crash

clash 可指两件或两件以上的事情因同时发生而造成时间上的"相互冲突"，也可指意见等的不一致、观点等的"冲突"；collision 可指两个具体物体的"相撞"，也可指抽象意义上的"冲突"；conflict主要指对立的思想、意识、观点、愿望等导致的"冲突"，常可与clash互换；crash主要指两个坚硬物体之间的"剧烈碰撞"，常用于描述撞车、坠机等。

20. relief

[词义] *n.* ① [U] (*sing.*) (痛苦、忧虑等消除后感到的) 轻松，宽慰；② [U] (痛苦、紧张、忧虑等的) 缓解，减轻

[搭配] on relief 接受救济的；find relief from 从……摆脱出来

[例句] It was such a relief to hear Mary had passed the exam.

听到玛丽通过考试，真是令人十分宽慰。

The drug brings/gives some relief from pain. 这药能减轻一些疼痛。

[派生] relieve *vt.* 减轻，接触，援救，救济

[辨析] relief, release

relief 着重指减轻或暂时解除（痛苦、负担等）；release指释放，从根本上免除，如：I released him from debt. 我免除了他的欠款。

21. spark

[词义] *n.* 火花，火星；*v.* 触发，引起

[搭配] spark sth. off 导致，是……的直接原因

[例句] A single spark can start a prairie fire. 星星之火，可以燎原。

His comment sparked off a quarrel between them.

他的议论引起他们之间的争吵。

[派生] sparkle *vi.* 闪闪发光，闪烁

22. clumsy

[词义] *adj.* 行动笨拙的，不灵活的

[搭配] be clumsy with one's hands 手指不灵活；be clumsy at sth. (干某事) 笨手笨脚

[例句] The first generation of the computer was large and clumsy.

第一代电脑又大又笨拙。

[派生] clumsiness *n.* 笨拙，简陋，丑陋

[辨析] awkward, clumsy

awkward指笨手笨脚，缺乏优雅、闲适、机敏和技巧；clumsy则指行为或构造粗大、笨重而显得笨拙。

23. incident

[词义] *n.* [C] 发生的事，事情，事故

[例句] Strange incidents happened successively. 奇怪的事情接二连三地发生。

[派生] incidental *adj.* 偶然的；incidence *n.* 发生率

[辨析] accident, event, incident

accident 意为"事故"，特指不幸的意外事故；event 普通用语，可指大小事件，如前面加修饰语，常指历史上的重大事件；incident 意为"事件、事变"，可指与某人或某些重要事情有关的、独立的、不太重要的事件，还可指涉及暴力、令人不快的"事变"，在政治上特指引起严重争端甚至战争的事变。

24. memorial

[词义] *n.* [C] 纪念物，纪念碑

[例句] There stood a memorial statue to a great statesman on the square.
一位伟大政治家的纪念雕像矗立在广场上。

[派生] memory *n.* 记忆，回忆；memorable *adj.* 值得纪念的

[辨析] memorial, monument

memorial 主要指"纪念碑、纪念物"，上面刻有纪念性的话语或被纪念人的名字；monument 除可指纪念碑、纪念物之外，多指"纪念馆"，内有被纪念的人或事的资料。

25. cut down (衣服、文章等) 改小，改短

[例句] We had to cut the article down to make it fit the limited space.
我们不得不把文章缩短以符合有限的空间。

[联想] cut down 还可指：

① 削减，缩减 cut down the expenses 削减开支

② 砍倒，杀死 cut down a tree 砍倒一棵树

26. for good 永久地

[例句] The days of happiness had gone for good.
那些快乐的时光已经永远地过去了。

27. trip up 绊，绊倒

[例句] He was tripped up by a stone. 他被一块石头绊倒了。

[联想] trip up 还可以指"使……犯错误"。

The lawyer is always trying to trip the witness up. 这个律师老想让证人出错。

28. make up 虚构，捏造，临时编造

[例句] He made up some excuse for being late. 他编造了一个迟到的借口。

[联想] make up 还可以表示：

① 组成，构成 One year is made up of twelve months. 一年由十二个月组成。

② 为……化妆 She made up her face to look more beautiful. 她在脸上化了妆以便看上去更漂亮些。

29. come down in the world 落魄，潦倒，失势

[例句] He has come down in the world since he started gambling.
他自开始赌博以来变得穷困潦倒。

30. go along 进行下去，前进

[例句] You may have difficulty with this book at first, but you'll find it much easier as you go along.
开始时你或许会觉得这本书难读，但过些时候你便会觉得容易得多。

[联想] go along with sb. 指陪伴某人；同意某人的观点

I'll go along with you as far as I can. 我会尽力一路一直陪伴/支持你。

31. find one's way into 来到（某处），进入

[例句] Recently internet has found their way into most ordinary families.

近来因特网已经进入大部分普通家庭。

Ⅱ. 难句解析

1. Dickens might have created Charlie Chaplin's childhood. (Para.1)

[释义] When he was a child, Charlie Chaplin lived a miserable life, which was much like the one described in Dickens' famous novel named Oliver Twist. Therefore, if he had learnt of Chaplin's childhood, Dickens might have written something about it.

[分析] **might have + v.-ed** 虚拟时态，表示过去可能会发生，但实际上没有发生的事。

e.g. The plan might easily have gone wrong, but in fact it was a great success.

这计划可能会很容易失败的，可是事实上大大成功了。

2. Other countries...have provided more applause (and profit) where Chaplin is concerned than the land of his birth. (Para.2)

[释义] Chaplin was welcomed more enthusiastically and made more money in other countries where he had traveled than in his motherland, Britain.

3. Certainly middle-class audiences did;... (Para.3)

[释义] **certainly** *adv.* 的确地、当然地，经常用来表达肯定的，确实的语气。

e.g. I am certainly not inviting her to my party. I've never liked her.

我肯定不会邀请她来参加聚会，我从来不喜欢她。

[联想] **surely** *adv.* 的确地，经常用来表达惊喜、怀疑或宽慰的语气（尤其在英式英语中）。

e.g. Surely, you aren't going out like this, are you? 你不会就这样就走出去吧？

4. ...Chaplin's comic beggar didn't seem all that English or even working class. (Para.3)

[释义] The amusing character, the beggar created by Chaplin, didn't seem like an Englishman very much, and its appearance wasn't that of working class either.

(not) all that 并不很……，并不特别……，通常用在带有否定意味的陈述中，用来减弱语气。

e.g. He wasn't all that older than we were. 他并不比我们老多少。

5. English tramps didn't sport tiny moustaches, huge pants or tail coats: European leaders and Italian waiters wore things like that. (Para. 3)

[释义] English tramps didn't wear tiny moustaches, very big pants or tail coats: there were something European leaders and Italian waiters wore; therefore, Chaplin's beggar didn't look like an English tramp.

sport *v.* 公开地穿戴或展示某物，带有炫耀的意味

e.g. Back in the 1960s he sported bell-bottom trousers, platform heels and hair down past his shoulders.

回顾20世纪60年代，他那时穿着喇叭裤、木屐式坡形高跟鞋、蓄着过肩长发。

The front of the car sported a German flag. 这辆车前面插着德国国旗。

6. **He was an immensely talented man, determined to a degree unusual even in the ranks of Hollywood stars. (Para.5)**

[释义] He was a man of great talent, who had such a great determindtion that he seemed unusual even among the Hollywood stars.

[分析] determined 是形容词，意为"有决心的，坚定的"，在句中作主语补足语；"unusual even in the ranks of Hollywood stars"是degree的后置定语。

7. **Lifeless objects especially helped Chaplin make "contact" with himself as an artist. (Para.6)**

[释义] For Chaplin, things having no life were especially helpful in his artistic creation, and they can be easily associated with his talent.

8. **In Oona O'Neill Chaplin, he found a partner whose stability and affection spanned the 37 years age difference between them that had seemed so threatening that when the official who was marrying them in 1942, turned to the beautiful girl of 17 who'd given notice of their wedding date and said...(Para.8)**

[释义] **find...in sb.** 发现某人有某种特质

e.g. We have found in her a woman of wit and intelligence.

我们发现她是一位充满幽默感和智慧的女士。

[分析] "that had seemed so threatening that..."是定语从句修饰"the 37 years age difference"，该句中包含了一个"so...that..."的结构，用以强调巨大的年龄差距；在这个"so...that..."结构中，when引导一个时间状语从句，在这个时间状语中又包含了两个由who引导的定语从句，分别修饰"the official"和"the beautiful girl of 17"。

9. **As Oona herself was the child of a large family with its own problems, she was well-prepared for the battle that Chaplin's life became as unfounded rumors of Marxist sympathies surrounded them both...(Para.8)**

[释义] Oona had met with many problems in her own family before marrying, so she was able to deal with the problems in Chaplin's life. For example, at that time, there were unfounded rumors that they sympathized with Marxism; when chaplin caused quarrels in their large family with many talented children, it was Oona who solved such probcems and brought peace back into the family.

unfounded *adj.* 没有事实依据的

e.g. We are pleased to see that our fears about the weather proved unfounded.

我很高兴地发现我们对天气的担心是毫无理由的。

[释义] "that Chaplin's life became"是定语从句，修饰"the battle"；as在句中作连结词，引导原因状语从句；在原因状语从句中"surrounded them both"同时又作sympathies的后置定语。

Ⅲ. 重点语法讲解

形容词（adjective）是用来修饰名词，表示名词属性的词，常放在它所修饰的名词前面。形容词在句中可作：

1. 定语，一般放在被修饰的名词前。

   She is a **beautiful** girl. 她是一个漂亮的女孩。

2. 表语，一般放在be, seem等词后面。

   The movie is **instructive**. 电影有教育意义。

   大部分的形容词既可作定语也可作表语用。

3. 宾语补足语，和die, keep, lie, remain, sit, stand等表示状态的动词一起构成复合宾语。

   You should **keep** your own room **clean** and **tidy**.

   你应当保持你自己的房间的干净和整洁。

   Many famous people have **died young**. 许多名人都英年早逝。

   把形容词放在感觉动词后面，特别是look, taste等这样一些与五官有关的动词后面也可以作补语。用在这些动词后面的词之所以是形容词，是因为它们描述的是动词所属的主语，而不是修饰动词本身，它们起了形容词补足语的作用。试比较：

   You look well. 你看起来很健康。（well=in good health，是一个形容词）

   You did well. 你干地很好。（well是副词，修饰did）

4. 相当于名词，某些形容词前用定冠词，变成名词化形容词，可在句中作主语、宾语。

   The gap between **the poor** and **the rich** is widening. 贫富差距越来越大。

Ⅳ. 课文赏析

1. 文体特点

本文是一篇传记性记叙文，作者通过不同侧面的展示来突出主题思想，其中包括卓别林的生平、艺术成就、感情生活、辞世等几个方面，全面地展现了幽默大师的一生。文章结构清晰，用充满幽默的语言生动地刻画了舞台上塑造喜剧经典的卓别林和生活中饱受折磨的卓别林。

2. 结构分析

Part Ⅰ (Para.1-2) general introduction of Charlie Chaplin

Part Ⅱ (Para.3-6) Chaplin's professional success

Part Ⅲ (Para.7-8) Chaplin's emotional life

Part Ⅳ (Para.9) Chaplin's death

Ⅴ. 课后练习答案及解析

Vocabulary

▶ Ⅲ. ▶

1. coarse 译文：她彬彬有礼，和其他人此类一样，如果有外人说了粗话，她也从来不笑。

2. corresponded 译文：这些国家在政治上的软弱和经济上的虚弱是一致的。

3. doubtful 译文：这些电影制片先驱们是否认识到了这一新发明的潜在影响，这一点令人怀疑。

4. roused/sparked 译文：卓别林的电影激发了我对喜剧的兴趣，于是我去了一家戏剧公司工作。

5. execute 译文：既然我们已经得到了批准，就可以执行先前同意的方案了。

6. relief 译文：巴罗达先生得知太太想让古韦内尔先生再次来拜访他们后，如释重负地舒了口气。

7. applause 译文：所有的演出者要么与观众有联系，要么为观众所熟知，因此每一个节目都被报以同样热烈的掌声。

8. immense 译文：离2008年奥运会还有5年，还有大量工作要做。

IV.

1. for 译文：查理·卓别林出生在伦敦南部的贫民窟，但1913年他就永久地离开了英国。

2. against 译文：欧洲以外的一些国家在反抗殖民统治时，嘴上往往挂着人权、民族自主等口号。

3. up 译文：面试的压力很大，从始至终他们一直想挑我的毛病。

4. with 译文：他昨晚在大剧院的演出被报以热烈的欢呼。

5. up 译文：我想不出什么童话故事可以讲给孩子们听，所以我一面编一面讲给他们听。

6. to 译文：我也认为目前正在讨论的决议有些不妥，因为该决议过分强调了经济危机的问题。

7. down 译文：他们不得不剪去这部影片的某些部分——它太长了。

8. between 译文：昨晚一辆小汽车与一辆出租车迎面相撞，两名司机当场死亡。

Collacation

V.

1. temptation 译文：这些信件对我们尤其有价值，因为普里尼非常清楚地意识到要抵制夸大其词的诱惑，而要客观的描述他的经历。

2. change 译文：当人们认为支持改变就意味着承认他们的决定或想法是错误的时候，他们有时候会为了面子拒绝改变。

3. urge 译文：这是一个如此美丽的地方，人们禁不住停下来，坐在路边的一家小餐馆里，仅仅为了呼吸这里的空气。

4. politics 译文：由于没有充分反思自己的政治纲领，他们无力反对新的政治纲领。

5. pressures 译文：他们也是充满自信的人，对自己的身份有安全感，能够承受朋友及社会带来的各种压力。

6. arrest 译文：警方接到命令，如果恐怖分子拘捕可以开枪。

7. demand 译文：起初他拒绝了进一步调查的要求，理由是证据不足。

8. attempts 译文：研究人员必须努力抵制一些"有倾向的"企图。

Word Building

VI.

1. artist 译文：作为一个艺术家，卓别林在整个演艺生涯中探索并扩展了自己的才能。

2. terrorist 译文：据报道，在恐怖袭击中有一名游客死亡，三名受伤。

3. novelist 译文：伟大的作家狄更斯很可能写出卓别林的童年故事，如果他和卓别林生活在同一个时代的话。

4. activists 译文：镇上的女政治家和活动家说，他们要与根深蒂固的文化传统作斗争。

5. biologist 译文：生物学家就是那些研究有生命的事物的人。

6. idealist 译文：我们都认为莫里斯先生只是一个理想主义者，根本不了解现实世界。

7. capitalist 译文：在那个时期，收入的重新分配使劳动者的出入少了，而地主和资本家的多了。

8. tourist 译文：如布莱克浦和布赖顿海滩等海滨胜地正准备迎接游客的大量涌入。

VII.

1. Terrorism 译文：恐怖主义没有国界——这是国际性问题，需要国际间的合作。

2. industrialism 译文：早期的工业制度开始了一些生产流程（例如制衣、裁缝、罐头制造等）从家庭向市场转移的过程。

3. ageism 译文：他们甚至因为她46岁就不考虑由她来做这项工作——这是典型的歧视老年人。

4. idealism 译文：尽管他的生活充斥了戏剧、令人兴奋的探险旅行、财富和个人的理想主义，他却觉得所有的一切都很空虚。

5. criticism 译文：中产阶级的观众对于卓别林的"流浪者"的评价是，这个人物有点"粗俗"。

6. heroism 译文：我的一个学生因为救了两名溺水儿童这一英勇行为而被授予奖章。

7. racism 译文：很多黑人都深切体会到种族歧视在这个国家根深蒂固，黑人在教育、培训及就业上都面临歧视。

8. Modernism 译文：现代主义要寻求新的表达方式，摈弃传统的或公认的思想。

Structure

VIII.

1. If I had known that your coming, I would have met you at the airport.

   译文：如果我早知道你们要来，我会去机场接你们的。

2. If he had tried to leave the country, he would have been stopped at the frontier.

   译文：如果他试图要离开这个国家，他会在边界被拦截。

3. If we had found him earlier, we could have saved his life.

   译文：要是我们早一点发现了他，我们本可以救活他的。

4. If I had caught that plane, I would have been killed in the air crash.

   译文：要是我当时赶上了那架飞机，我早就在空难中丧生了。

4. If he had been in better health, he could have written more books.

   译文：如果他的健康状态再好一点，他本可以写更多书的。

IX.

1. With so much going on at the office, it is a wonder to find that Mr. Lawrence has much time left for anything else.

   译文：办公室有这么多事，劳伦斯先生还有很多时间做其它的事，这真是个奇迹。

2. It is a surprise to us to find that television enjoys its greatest competitive advantage on information.

   译文：电视机最具竞争性的是信息优势，这一发现真让我们吃惊。

3. It is a possibility for us to expect that the students will get the new facts in the lecture confused with their existing knowledge.

   译文：我们有可能期望学生能从这个与他们的现有知识相混淆的讲座里学到新的知识。

4. It is a fact to know that we have run out of water and food.

   译文：事实就是：我们的水和食物都没有了。

5. It is a relief to learn that the driver controlled the car during the stormy weather.
   译文：得知司机在暴风雨中平安地开车，我们如释重负。

Translation

X.

1. Other writers might have written stories about London. But only he could have created the character David, who gave his creator permanent fame.

2. China has provided more applause, more honour and, of course, more profit where this scientist is concerned than any other countries.

3. He had an urge to execute this skill perfectly.

4. This physical transformation, plus the skill with which he executed it again and again, are surely the secrets of Chaplin's great comedy.

5. But that shock roused his imagination. Chaplin didn't have his jokes written into a script in advance; he was the kind of comic who used his physical senses to invent his art as he went along.

6. He also has a deep need to be loved—and a corresponding fear of being betrayed. The two were hard to combine and sometimes—as in his early marriage—the collision between them resulted in disaster.

7. It's doubtful whether she can find her way into perfect acting, though she never loses her faith in her own ability.

8. It was a relief to know that he finally finished the book before his death, which was regarded as a fitting memorial to his life as a writer.

XI.

1. 但只有查理·卓别林才能塑造出了不起的喜剧角色"流浪者"，这个使其创作者声名永驻的衣衫褴褛的小人物。

2. 尽管如此，卓别林的喜剧乞丐形象并不那么像英国人，甚至也没有劳动阶级的特色。

3. 但假如他在早期那些短小喜剧电影中能操一口受过教育的人的口音，那么他是否会闻名世界就值得怀疑了，而英国人也肯定会觉得这很"古怪"。

4. 随着事业的发展，他感到了一种冲动要去发掘并扩展自己身上所显露的天才。

5. 没有生命的物体特别有助于卓别林发挥自己艺术家的天赋。

6. 然而即使是这种以沉重代价换来的自知之明也在他的喜剧创作中得到了表现。

7. 由于沃娜本人出生在一个被各种麻烦困扰的大家庭，她对卓别林生活中将面临的挑战也做好了充分准备，因为当时有毫无根据的流言说他俩是马克思主义的同情者。后来在他们自己的有那么多天才孩子的大家庭中，卓别林有时会引发争吵，而她则成了安宁的中心。

8. 但是人们不禁会感到，卓别林一定会把这一奇怪的事件看作是对他的十分恰当的纪念——他以这种方式给这个自己曾带来这么多笑声的世界留下最后的笑声。

Story Summary

XII.

DCABB ACADC BADDB ACBCB

Text Structure Analysis

XIII. ►

Different aspects:

the stability and affection that spanned the 37 years age difference between them

the battle against the rumors charging Chaplin as a Marxist sympathizer

the center of rest

VI. 参考译文

查理·卓别林

他出生在伦敦南部的一个贫困地区，他所穿的短裤是从妈妈的红色长裤上剪下来的。他妈妈一度被诊断为精神失常。狄更斯或许会创作出查理·卓别林的童年故事，但只有查理·卓别林才能塑造出了不起的喜剧角色"流浪者"，这个使其创作者声名永驻的衣衫褴褛的小人物。

就卓别林而言，其他国家，如法国、意大利、西班牙，甚至日本和朝鲜，比他的出生地给予了他更多的掌声（和更多的收益）。卓别林在1913年永久地离开了英国，与一些演员一起启程到美国进行舞台喜剧表演。在那里，他被星探招募到好莱坞喜剧片之王麦克·塞纳特的旗下工作。

不幸的是，20世纪二三十年代的很多英国人认为卓别林的"流浪者"多少有点"粗俗"。中产阶级当然这样认为；劳动阶级倒更有可能为这样一个反抗权势的角色拍手喝彩：他以顽皮的小拐杖使绊子，或把皮靴后跟对准权势者宽大的臀部一踢。尽管如此，卓别林的喜剧乞丐形象并不那么像英国人，甚至也不像劳动阶级的人。英国流浪者并不留小胡子，也不穿肥大的裤子或燕尾服：欧洲的领导人和意大利的侍者才那样穿戴。另外，流浪汉瞟着漂亮女孩的眼神也有些粗俗，被英国观众认为不太正派——只有外国人才那样，不是吗？而在卓别林大半的银幕生涯中，银幕上的他是不出声的，也就无法证明他是英国人。

事实上，当卓别林再也无法抵制有声电影，不得不为他的流浪者找"合适的声音"时，那确实令他头痛。他尽可能地推迟那一天的到来：1936的《摩登时代》是第一部他在影片里发声唱歌的电影，他扮演一名侍者，操着编造的胡言乱语，听起来不像任何国家的语言。后来他说，他想象中的流浪汉是一位受过大学教育，但已经家道败落的绅士。但假如他在早期那些短小喜剧电影中能操一口受过教育的人的口音，那么他是否会闻名世界就值得怀疑了，而英国人也肯定会觉得这很"古怪"。虽然没有人知道卓别林这么干是不是有意的，但是这促使他获得了巨大的成功。

他是一个有巨大才能的人，他的决心之大甚至在好莱坞明星中也是十分少见的。他的巨大名声为他带来了自由，更重要的是带来了财富，他因此得以成为自己的主人。随着事业的发展，他感到了一种冲动要去发掘并扩展自己身上所显露的天才。当他第一次在银幕上看到自己扮演的流浪汉时，他说："这不可能是我。那可能吗？瞧这角色多么与众不同啊！"

而这种吃惊唤起了他的想象。卓别林并没有把他的笑料事先写成文字。他是那种边表演边根据身体感觉去创造艺术的喜剧演员。没有生命的物体特别有助于卓别林发挥自己艺术家的天赋。他会将这些物体发挥成其他东西。因此，在《当铺老板》中，一个坏闹钟变成了正在接受手术的"病人"；在《淘金记》中，靴子被煮熟，靴底蘸着盐和胡椒被吃掉，就像上好的鱼片（鞋钉就像鱼骨那样被剔除）。这种对具体事物的发挥转化，以及他一次又一次做出这种转化的技巧，正是卓别林伟大喜剧的奥秘。

他也深切地渴望被爱，同时相应地害怕遭到背叛。这两者很难结合在一起，有时这种冲突导致了灾难，就像他早期的几次婚姻那样。然而即使这种以沉重代价换来的自知之明也在他的喜剧创作中得到了表现。流浪汉始终没有失去对卖花女的信心，相信她正等待着与自己共同走进夕阳之中；而卓别林的另一面使他的《凡尔杜先生》，一个杀了妻子的法国人，成为了仇恨女人的象征。

令人宽慰的是，生活最终把他先前没能获得的稳定的幸福给了卓别林。他找到了沃娜·奥尼尔·卓别林这个伴侣。她的稳定和深情跨越了他们之间37岁的年龄差距。他们的年龄差别太大，以致当1942年他们要结婚时，新娘公布了他们的结婚日期后，为他们办理手续的官员问这位漂亮的17岁姑娘："那年轻人在哪儿？"——当时已经54岁的卓别林一直小心翼翼地在外面等候着。由于沃娜本人出生在一个被各种麻烦困扰的大家庭，她对卓别林生活中将面临的挑战也做好了充分准备，因为当时有毫无根据的流言说他俩是马克思主义的同情者。后来在他们自己的有那么多天才孩子的大家庭中，卓别林有时会引发争吵，而她则成了安宁的中心。

卓别林死于1977年圣诞节。几个月后，几个近乎可笑的盗尸者从他的家庭墓室盗走了他的尸体以借此诈钱。警方追回了他的尸体，其效率比麦克·塞纳特拍摄的启斯东喜剧片中的笨拙警察要高得多。但是人们不禁会感到，卓别林一定会把这一奇怪的事件看作是对他的十分恰当的纪念——他以这种方式给这个自己曾带来这么多笑声的世界留下最后的笑声。

VII. 写作指导

传记式的记叙文分为自传和为他人立传两种情况。自传通常以第一人称，带有作者个人强烈的主观性；为他人立传一般用第三人称，客观地叙述主人公的生平事迹。

在安排记叙文的结构时，首先要考虑选材，无论是事件的发展还是人物的叙述，都离不开细节。当我们把某一段落看作一个整体时，我们会发现在结构上它是一段由中心句和围绕这个中心句的不同方面的句子所构成的。在一篇文章中，作者会使用不同的写作技巧来帮助引出段落的中心思想。从结构上来讲，一个段落就是一个主题句和支撑这个主题句的细节。细节应该充分，但未经严格挑选的细节只会使文章显得杂乱无章。只有那些与事件紧密相连，能有助于突出主题的细节，才能选作文章的材料。

范文：

Charlie Chaplin is a great comic not only for his native land, British, but more for the world. He was born in British, but he wasn't confined to his own country. Instead, he went to America in 1913 and was signed up in Hollywood. On the stage he often wore tiny moustache, huge pants and tailcoats that looked like an Italian waiters. For more than half of the roles Chaplin played were silent movies, even with sound movies he created a nonsense language like no known nationality, people throughout the world had no difficulty in understanding him.

Section B
I. 阅读技巧

事实与观点掺杂

如我们在前三册中所学到的，培养批判的阅读方式牵涉到判断事实和作者的观点或诠释这两者之间的能力。

我们一直以来都意识到把事实和观点分开的重要性，但是作者却经常把事实和观点掺杂在一起，甚至是在一个句子当中就有一些词语代表事实，而另一些则代表观点。

例1：但只有查理·卓别林才能塑造出了不起的喜剧角色"流浪者"，这个使其创作者声名永驻的衣衫褴褛的小人物。（第2课，第1单元，第1段）

尽管"只有"、"了不起的"、"永驻的"这些词陈述了观点，但是整个句子叙述了很多事实——查理·卓别林、创造了、戏剧角色、流浪者、衣衫褴褛的小人物。但是更重要的是，这个句子的重点就在于陈述这个事实——查理·卓别林创造了"流浪者"，这个给他带来声誉的角色。因此，这个句子基本上是事实型的。

例2：这种对具体事物的发挥转化，以及他一次又一次做出这种转化的技巧，正是卓别林伟大喜剧的奥秘。（第2课，第1单元，第6段）

尽管"正是"、"奥秘"、"伟大"这些词是用来陈述观点的，但是这个句子叙述了许多事实——具体事物的发挥转化、他做出的技巧、一次又一次。因为这个句子是关于查理·卓别林的表演技巧，所以它也基本上是事实型的。

II. 词汇与短语精讲

1. revolutionary

[词义] n. [C] 革命者；adj. 革命的，突破性的

[例句] Mike was a revolutionary. 迈克是一个革命者。

Penicillin was a revolutionary drug. 青霉素是一种突破性的药物。

[派生] revolution n. 革命，彻底改变；revolutionize vt. 宣传革命，大事改革

2. vote

[词义] v. 投票，选举，表决

n. ① [C] 投票（结果），选举（结果）；② 选票；③ 选举权

[搭配] vote on sth. 就某事进行表决；vote in sb. 投票选出某人；vote for/against 投票赞成/反对……；vote sth. down/through 投票否决/通过某事

[例句] The representatives voted against/for the bill. 代表们投票反对/支持这个议案。

The vote went in the present mayor's favor. 投票中现任市长领先。

He won the election because he got most votes.

他选举获胜了，因为他得了大多数的选票。

In France, women didn't get the vote until 1945.

在法国妇女直到1945年才获得选举权。

[联想] veto n. 否决，禁止，否决权 vt. 否决

3. opponent

[词义] n. [C] 敌手，对手

[例句] A brave man should face his opponent directly. 勇敢的人应该直面对手。

[辨析] opponent, adversary, antagonist

opponent 表示反对，抵抗或者搏斗的对手；adversary 暗含难以对付的对手，而且可能产生敌意；antagonist 指敌意很强烈的反对者。

4. misunderstand

[词义] vt. 误解，误会

[搭配] misunderstand sb./ sth. to be... 将……误认成……

[例句] You must have misunderstood my meaning. 你一定是误会我的意思了。

[派生] misunderstanding *n.* [C,U] 误解，误会

5. election

[词义] *n.* [C,U] 选举

[例句] Local government elections will take place in May.

地方政府选举将在5月举行。

[派生] elect *v.* 选举，选择; elective *adj.* 有选举权的，可以选择的

6. sack

[词义] *n.* [C] 袋，包; *vt.* 解雇

[搭配] give sb. the sack 解雇某人

[例句] There was a sack of potatoes in the corner of the barn.

在谷仓的角落里有一袋土豆。

He was sacked for thieving. 他因小偷小摸而被解雇了。

7. loaf

[词义] *n.* [C]（一个）面包; *vi.* 游荡，闲逛

[搭配] loaf about 闲着，闲逛; loaf away one' time 浪费时光

[例句] Store the loaf in the refrigerator. 把这条面包储藏在冰箱里。

You thought I just loafed around? 你以为我只是在闲逛?

[派生] loafer *n.* 流浪者

8. colonial

[词义] *adj.* 殖民的，殖民地的

[例句] The people on the Pacific islands have successfully fought against colonial rule.

太平洋岛屿上的人民成功地进行了反对殖民统治的斗争。

[派生] colony *n.* 殖民地

[联想] colonel *n.* 陆军上校

9. jealous

[词义] *adj.* ① 惟恐失去的，小心守护的; ② 妒忌的

[搭配] be jealous of sb./ sth. 嫉妒某人/某事，注意某人/某事

[例句] He was jealous of his property. 他小心守护着自己的财产。

Her colleagues are jealous of her success. 她的同事们妒忌她的成功。

[派生] jealousy *n.* 嫉妒，羡慕; jealousness *n.* 嫉妒，猜忌，吃醋

[辨析] envious, jealous

envious意为"羡慕的，嫉妒的"，不一定带有不满情绪; jealous 意为"嫉妒的"，指一种强烈且令人不快的感情，还指男女间的"吃醋"，比envious更强烈，且带有不满。

10. assembly

[词义] *n.* ① [C] 集会者; ② 议会; ③ [U] 集会，聚会; ④ [U] 装配，安装

[例句] The former president addressed a large assembly.

前总统向众多的与会者讲了话。

The national assembly has/have met to discuss the crisis.

已经召开了国民议会来讨论这次危机。

That anti-government organization was denied the right of assembly.

那个反政府组织被剥夺了集会的权利。

The workers spent a day on the assembly of the machine.

工人们花了一天来装配这台机器。

[派生] assemble *vt.* 集合，聚集，装配 *vi.* 集合；disassembly *n.* 拆卸，分解

[辨析] assembly, convention, conference

assembly 指人多的聚会，并多是按预定日程召开的会议，还专用于立法机关或代表委员会；convention 指全国性的或地区性正式会议，与会代表来自于国内政党、学会或社会团体；conference 可指两个人的聚会，也可指多人的聚会。

11. committee

[词义] *n.* [C] 委员会

[搭配] be/sit on a committee 任委员会委员；go into committee 交委员会详细审查

[例句] She sits/is on the school's economic committee.

她是学校经济委员会的成员。

[派生] committed *adj.* 效忠的，忠于……的

[辨析] committee, commission

commission 指执行某种职能的机构，比committee范围大。国务院下属各种委员会都是commission，如：Economic Commission 经济委员会。

12. fierce

[词义] *adj.* 激烈的，强劲的，凶猛的

[例句] There is a fierce competition for those scholarships.

对这些奖学金的竞争十分激烈。

[派生] fiercely *adv.* 强烈地，厉害地；fierceness *n.* 强烈

13. rally

[词义] *n.* [C] 群众集会，群众大会

[搭配] rally about/around 团结起来，聚集在……周围

[例句] Rallies are being held across the country to celebrate the victory.

全国各地都在集会庆祝胜利。

14. riot

[词义] *n.* [C] 暴乱，骚乱

[搭配] run riot 胡作非为，撒野；riot squad 防暴队

[例句] The football match led to an uncontrolled riot.

这场足球赛导致了一场无法控制的骚乱。

[派生] rioter *n.* 参加暴乱者，聚众闹事者；riotous *adj.* 暴动的，骚乱的

15. witness

[词义] *n.* ① [C] (尤指犯罪或事故等的) 目击者；② [C]（法庭上的）证人
v. 目击，见证

[例句] She was a witness to the road accident. 她目睹了这一交通事故。

He will attend the court as a witness. 他将作为证人出庭。

This city has witnessed quite a few changes over the years.

这座城市多年来已经经历了相当大的变革。

16. earnest

[词义] *adj.* 认真的，坚决的，严肃的

[搭配] in earnest 认真，郑重；earnest money 定金

[例句] There is an earnest conference affecting world peace next month.
下个月将有一个事关世界和平的重要会议。
They are earnest about their studies. 他们学习非常勤奋。

[辨析] earnest, serious
earnest 意为"认真的、诚挚的、热忱的"，多表示人一贯诚挚和认真，强调做事有热心和热情；serious 意为"严肃认真的"，表示说法或做法不是在开玩笑或逗乐。

17. refresh

[词义] *vt.* ① 使振作精神，使恢复活力；② 使清凉

[搭配] refresh sb. with sth. 用某物使某人精神振奋

[例句] Having had a good sleep, he felt thoroughly refreshed.
他睡了个好觉，感到精神已完全恢复。
This glass of iced tea will refresh you. 喝下这杯冰茶你会感到清凉。

[派生] refreshing *adj.* 提神的，凉爽的；refreshed *adj.* 精神振奋的；refreshment *n.* [常pl.] 点心，饮料，精力恢复

18. run for 竞选

[例句] A famous movie star announced he would run for the governor.
一位电影明星宣布要竞选州长。

19. vote in 投票选出

[例句] He was voted in as the president. 投票结果他当选为主管。

20. spy on/upon 监视

[例句] She has spied on her husband for two months.
她已经监视她的丈夫两个月了。

21. shut out of 把……排斥在外

[例句] I wanted to shut John out of my life forever.
我想让约翰永远退出我的生活。

[联想] shut away 把……藏起来，隔离；shut in 把……关在里面，禁闭；shut off 切断（水、电等），关掉，（使）停止运转

22. break up 驱散，解散

[例句] The police broke up the fighting crowd. 警察驱散了打架的人群。

[派生] break away 突然离开，强行逃脱；break even 打成平手，得失相当；break off 中断，突然停止

23. tear down 撕下，拆毁

[例句] They are going to tear down these old buildings. 他们打算拆掉这些旧住房。

[派生] tear away（使）勉强离开；tear apart 扯开，把……弄乱，使心碎

24. in/by contrast 对比之下，相比之下

[例句] She is overweight, by contrast, her sister is slim. 她很胖，相比之下，他的妹妹很苗条。

25. in earnest 认真地

[例句] When I say I'm leaving, I'm in deadly earnest.

当我说要离开，我绝对是认真的。

26. lay out 摆出，张开

[例句] He laid the map out on the table. 他在桌上把地图摊开。

[联想] lay out 还可以指 "安排，布置，设计"，如：well laid-out garden 设计良好的花园。

27. feel like 感觉好像；想要

[搭配] feel like doing sth. 想要做某事

[例句] I was only there two days, but it felt like a week!

我在那儿只有两天，但感觉象过了一个星期。

We all felt like celebrating. 我们都想庆祝一下。

28. deliver the goods 履行诺言，不负众望

[例句] As long as you deliver the goods, she will always trust you.

只要你履行诺言，她会永远信任你的。

III. 难句解析

1. ...because she was voted in by her colleagues on the District Council, all men. (Para.2)

[释义] ...because as a female candidate on the District Council, she was made mayor by her male colleagues through the election.

[分析] all men 是 her colleagues 的补足语。

2. Women politicians and activists say they are fighting deeply held cultural traditions. (Para.7)

[释义] Woman politicans and activists say they are struggling against deeply rooted cultural traditons.

deeply held 根深蒂固的，表示文化传统存在了很长一段时期，很难改变

e.g. It's difficult to change the deeply held patriarchal system in China.

在中国很难改变根深蒂固的家长制。

3. But after independence, leaders jealous to protect their power shut them out of politics, a situation repeated across the continent. (Para.8)

[释义] But after they achieved independence, the male leaders, who were afraid of losing the power they already had, prevented women from entering the political life. That was also always the case in other African countries.

[分析] "jealous to protect their power" 是形容词短语，作主语 leaders 的定语；"a situation repeated across the continent" 是对前面句子的补充说明，repeated 是过去分词，表被动，因为这个动作与主语 a situation 是一种被动关系。

4. Against that background, Agatha Mbogo began her political career. (Para.10)

[释义] **against (particular background)** 在特定的背景下、衬托下；与背景事件相关的

e.g. His red clothes stood out clearly against the snow.

他的红衣服在白雪的映衬下特别突出。

51

The love story unfolds against a background of civil war.

这个爱情故事是在内战的背景下展开的。

5. ...the kinds of abuse that other female politicians have been subjected to, however. (Para. 14)

[释义] **subject...to** 使遭受……（不愉快的事）

e.g. The air bases were subjected to intense air attack. 空军基地遭到了猛烈的空袭。

6. Last June, Kenyan police attempted to break up a women's political meeting northwest of Nairobi, insisting it was illegal and might start a riot. (Para. 14)

[分析] "insisting it was illegal and might start a riot" 是现在分词短语，作主语Kenyan police的伴随状语。

Ⅳ. 重点语法讲解

分词有**现在分词**和**过去分词**两种。现在分词由动词原形后加词尾-ing构成。规则动词的过去分词由动词原形后加词尾-ed构成，不规则动词的过去分词无一定规则。

现在分词和过去分词的主要区别表现在语态和时间关系上。

1. **语态上不同：现在分词表示主动的意思，而过去分词多由及物动词转换而来，表示被动的意思。**

an **exciting** movie 一场令人兴奋的电影

excited audience 激动的观众

He told us many **interesting** things. 他告诉我们很多有趣的事

She is **interested** in art. 她对艺术很感兴趣。

也有一些过去分词是由不及物动词变来的，它们只表示一个动作已完成，没有被动的意味。如：

a **retired** miner 一位退休矿工   **fallen** leaves 落叶

2. **时间关系不同：一般说来，现在分词所表示的动作往往正在进行，而过去分词所表示的动作，往往已经完成。**

the **changing** world 正在变化的世界 the **changed** world 已经起了变化的世界

developing country 发展中国家 **developed** country 发达国家

Ⅴ. 课文赏析

1. 文体特点

本文运用了倒叙和举例说明的方法叙述了女政治家阿加莎·墨丹尼·姆波戈的政治生涯，展示了一位女性在非洲国家从政的社会背景、所遇到的各种障碍、以及女性的当选给当地人民带来的新的变化。文章虽简明易懂，但选题深刻，蕴意深远。

2. 结构分析

Part Ⅰ (Para. 1-2) Ms. Mbogo's victory, a symbol of the increasingly powerful political force women have become in Kenya and across Africa.

Part Ⅱ (Para. 3-12) The social and political background of Ms. Mbogo's political career.

Part Ⅲ (Para. 13-19) Ms. Mbogo brought great changes to the city and hence was welcomed by the people.

VI. 课后练习答案及解析

Reading Skills

XV.

FFOFO

Comprehension of the Text

XVI.

TFFTF TFT

Vocabulary

XVII.

1. fierce 译文: 日本银行曾经是英国银行市场中强劲的竞争对手, 现在几乎销声匿迹了。

2. witnesses 译文: 案件在开庭时是不会告诉受害者的, 除非他们被要求作证。

3. voted 译文: 虽然商会代表们在简短的辩论中一言不发, 但是坚定地跟随领导人投票。

4. scandal 译文: 这位部长在一桩牵涉到他和另一位部长的夫人的丑闻被曝光之后被迫辞职。

5. politics 译文: 姆波戈女士向妇女团体发表演说, 挨家挨户地去做工作, 让妇女了解怎样为自己斗争, 以期望能让更多的女性从政。

6. abuse 译文: 姆波戈女士和她的同事们多年来一直在他们的国家进行反对侵犯人权的活动。

7. jealous 译文: 这些领导人唯恐失去自己的权力, 想方设法将妇女排斥在政界之外。

8. refresh 译文: 只要散散步就能放松大脑, 振作精神——也会让你更健康。

XVIII.

1. Could we take a walk? I feel like a little exercise.
   译文: 我们去走走好吗? 我想稍微锻炼一下。

2. Ms. Mbogo'd made a bold decision: she ran for mayor of Embu, Kenya.
   译文: 姆波戈女士作了一个大胆的决定: 她参加了肯尼亚布恩市市长的竞选。

3. Some leaders in Kenya were afraid of losing their power, so they tried everything to shut Kenyan women out of politics.
   译文: 肯尼亚的一些领导人唯恐失去自己的权力, 就想方设法将妇女排斥在政界之外。

4. She decided long ago that she would study the subject in earnest as soon as she left school.
   译文: 她很久以前就决定一离开学校就认真学习这门课程。

5. He was arrested because he was paid to spy on our air bases.
   译文: 他因为受雇监视我们的空军基地而被捕。

6. After almost four hours of fierce negotiation, the president had the upper hand.
   译文: 在将近四个小时的激烈谈判之后, 总统占了上风。

7. Road accident victims make up almost a quarter of the hospital's patients.
   译文: 交通事故受害者几乎占医院病人的四分之一。

8. Ms. Mbogo's victory was of great significance because all her male colleagues voted her in.
   译文: 姆波戈女士的胜利具有重大意义, 因为她所有的男性同事都投了她的票。

VII. 参考译文

一位女政治家的政治生涯

24岁的阿加莎·墨丹妮·姆波戈, 为人谦虚, 谈吐温柔, 算不上是个革命者的形象, 然而就在6个月前, 她做了一件极富革命性的事情: 她参加了肯尼亚恩布市的市长竞选，并且当选。

更令人感到意外的是，姆波戈女士是由区议会的同事们投票选出的，而那些人全是男性。恩布市是一个位于内罗毕东北部的农业地区，距内罗毕需两个小时的车程。在肯尼亚乃至整个非洲，妇女的政治力量日益壮大。对于生活在此地的数千妇女来说，姆波戈成了这种力量的标志。

1992年，姆波戈女士开始追寻她的从政梦想，她竞选了恩布市议员。像其他打算从政的非洲妇女一样，她面对着很多障碍 她缺钱；她没有政治经验；她要回答许多关于她个人生活的荒唐问题。她说："我的对手一口咬定我要与外市的人结婚，很快就会搬走。"

姆波戈还要面对本市妇女的诸多误解，她们中间有许多人起初并不愿意投票选举她。她成为捍卫妇女政治权利的使者，向妇女团体发表演说。她会挎着手提包，挨家挨户地去做演讲，并给他们讲解政体，一讲就是数小时。

"她胜出我很高兴，因为是男人们选举了她，"恩布市的一位农民政治活动家利迪亚·基曼尼如是说。"这正是对我的祈祷的回应，因为它似乎战胜了这种观念：女人当不了领导者。"

非洲妇女的教育已经成为政治活动家们着重优先考虑的问题。有个机构已经在肯尼亚农村举办了十几个专题讨论会，目的是帮助妇女理解国家宪法以及民主政治制度所体现的程序及理论。一位资深的女政治活动家说，许多妇女连参政的最基本知识都没有。她说，她们在竞选运动中只知道谁"给你半公斤面粉、200克食盐或一条面包"，她们就投票选谁。

妇女政治活动家们说她们正在与根深蒂固的文化传统作斗争。这些传统要非洲妇女做饭、搞清洁、照管孩子、种庄稼、收庄稼以及支持丈夫。她们通常不能继承土地，不能与丈夫离婚，不能理财，也不能从政。

然而，肯尼亚妇女从事政治活动并不是什么新现象。在20世纪50年代争取独立的斗争中，肯尼亚妇女就经常秘密地为部队提供武器、监视殖民军的阵地。但是独立之后，领导者们惟恐失去自己的权力，将妇女排斥在政界之外。这种现象在非洲大陆随处可见。

今天，男性仍占有优势。肯尼亚妇女占选民人数的60%，但在国民大会中的席位仅3%。从来没有一位肯尼亚妇女担任过内阁职务。

在这种背景下，阿加莎·姆波戈开始了她的政治生涯。在赢得市议会席位之后，她拒绝了被同事称为"女人委员会"的教育及社会服务委员会的职位，而加入了城市规划委员会。这是个更显眼的工作。

接着在去年，她决定挑战恩布市市长，一位资深政客。姆波戈女士说，为肯尼亚乡村地区提供大量捐助的团体"不愿意到这里来"，为此她感到很失望。

"我们没看到有人为社区办过什么实事，"她说。"这是一件丑闻，捐资者的钱似乎落入个人腰包了。"

经过一场激烈的竞选，她以7比6当选。她说恩布市的妇女为此兴高采烈，而男人们则很不解，甚至有些心怀敌意。她回忆说，男人们问：那些男人怎么会选一个女人？

但姆波戈女士并没有像其他女政治家那样受到攻击。有人说女政治家们的支持者有时在集会后会受到棍棒袭击。去年6月，肯尼亚警方企图驱散在内罗毕西北部举行的一次妇女政治集会，坚持说它是非法的，可能引发骚乱。目击者报告说，当时有100名妇女，包括一名国民大会委员。她们拒绝离开，于是警官扯下她们的旗帜，并对她们棒打拳击。

与此相反，姆波戈女士通常受到恩布市男士们的热烈欢迎，许多人说现在很高兴议会挑选了她。

如今，捐助团体正式给恩布市的若干项目提供了资金。一个新型市场正在市中心建起。医院新增添了有200个床位的产房。为几十个流浪街头、无家可归的孩子建起了集体宿舍。姆波戈女士为这个市场和医院感到特别自豪，因为"它们对妇女有很大的影响"。

在现在的市场上，数以百计的人在遮阳伞下摆卖果蔬。一个卖柠檬的妇女说她喜欢新市长。

"我感觉如果碰到问题，我可以到她的办公室去找她，"她说。"以前的市长呼来喝去，好像是个皇帝，他并不想听我的问题。"

　　旁边，有个男人说他发觉姆波戈女士带来了一种清新的变化。"我厌倦了男人，"他看着自己那一大堆洋葱说。"他们只会许诺，但没有实际的东西。只要她能不断带来我们所需的东西，她就行。"

Section C

Ⅰ. 语言点讲解

1. The sole standard of being first at something was simply not having heard that somebody else had done it. (Para. 2)

[分析] 主句使用过去进行时，表示通常发生的动作；"that somebody else had done it"是宾语从句，作动词heard的宾语。

2. But I am getting ahead of myself. (Para. 5)

[释义] **get ahead of** 超过，超越，领先

e.g. He's keen on getting ahead of his classmates. 他渴望超越他的同班同学。

3. He married Granny Ethel, who was so beautiful she did not have to be first at anything. (Para. 8)

[分析] "who was so...at anything"是定语从句，修饰Granny Ethel；在这个定语从句中，"she did not have to be first at anything"是一个结果状语从句，在"so...that..."的结构中，省略了that。

4. Why shouldw I mother an invention if all needs are met? (Para. 11)

[释义] **mother** v. 产生，创造

e.g. It is him who mothered the instrument. 正是他发明了这装置。

Ⅱ. 课文赏析

1. 文体特点

本文是一篇以第一人称叙述的记叙文。作者开篇点题，说明了"第一"的含义，是整个家族衡量成功的标准。叙述过程详略得当、主次分明。文章结尾联系个人，继承家族创新精神，深化主题。

2. 结构分析

Part Ⅰ (Para. 1-2) Definition of being first in my family and general idea of my relatives' inventions.

Part Ⅱ (Para. 3-10) Narration of my relatives' inventions.

Part Ⅲ (Para. 11-12) My idea for the inventions and decision to be first.

Ⅲ. 课后练习答案及解析

Reading Skills

▷ **XIX.**

O O F F O

Comprehension of the Text

▷ **XX.**

1. valued　　　　2. doing something which hasn't been heard of before
3. enthusiastic　　4. full　　　　5. fond　　　　6. keep nickels from sliding
7. making use of some used items　　8. takes pride in

Ⅳ. 参考译文

创造"第一"的家族

在我家里，成功与否只由一种标准来衡量，这就是争取第一的能力。只要你在某件事上排第一，就算你行，至于它是什么事情，则无关紧要。

我的前辈们在"机器时代"的高峰期从欧洲来到了美洲。在美国，每天都有"新的"和"第一的"东西产生：第一个抽水马桶，第一部收音机，第一顶装有扇子的帽子。我家里掀起了"第一"热。食物以及其他的好主意都算数，还有款式、发明、用语等方面的"第一"也算数。衡量是否"第一"的惟一标准就是没听说别人做过。那样你就有权讲出这句惊人的话："我是第一个做的！"

我的外曾祖父发明了芥末筒。它是由一块方形小纸片卷上些芥末做成的。早晨上班时带着它，再带一块冷肉，中午吃饭时就可挤一些新鲜芥末在肉上一起吃。

这位发明芥末筒的外曾祖父有三个女儿：露茜，第一个将窗帘制成短上衣的女孩；格尔蒂，第一个将短上衣改成窗帘的女孩；还有波莉，就是我的外祖母，她改进了一把刷子用来清洁水龙头的内部。她喜欢这么说："不能因为你看不到就说它不脏。"

波莉房子里的每一寸地方每年至少都要人工清理两次，她为此深感自豪。她甚至用一种"门顶揩布"来清洁门顶。这东西是用旧长筒袜里面再塞上旧长筒袜做成的。旧长筒袜在我家一直都被视为一种大有可为的东西。我妈妈用她的长筒袜来做洋葱袋，说是她发明的新办法。她还居功说她是第一个将一对长筒袜的两只同时利用起来的人，一只袜筒做洋葱袋，另一只放土豆或大蒜。而我则更是有过之而无不及。

在我的亲属中，最有名的，真正在美国产生影响的，或许就是我的曾祖父莱伯·萨塞尔。据家里人的说法，是他为世人引进了五香烟熏牛肉三明治。1879年，莱伯·萨塞尔离开祖国到纽约的街头寻求功名和财富。在自己国家，他曾在面粉厂干过活，但感觉这种磨面粉的营生真是种折磨人的苦活，就开始背着坛坛罐罐到处兜售。他没有家，往往卖锅罐给谁，就在谁家的地下室或马棚里过夜。有一天早晨，他在祈祷的时候还被马踢了一下。

莱伯·萨塞尔懂得屠宰，所以他决定改行开一家小肉铺。开张第一个星期，有位朋友路过，问能否将他的大皮箱寄存在店铺的后面。"我打算回老家几年，"他说。"如果你让我存放皮箱，我就教你如何制作五香烟熏牛肉。"据说，曾祖父收下了皮箱，学会了制作五香烟熏牛肉，并开始在柜台上出售大块的五香烟熏牛肉。很快他又开始将肉切片出售，然后又将其夹在两片面包中间出售。他偶然碰到了我的外曾祖父，知道了芥末筒这东西。没过多久，到他的店里来买三明治的人比来买肉的人更多了。

我的祖父雅各布·沃尔克则拥有发明"球破碎机"的光荣。他带着"球破碎机"走遍纽约的下曼哈顿区，在他所有卡车的两侧印着"华尔街最强大的破坏力"字样。他娶了格兰妮·爱丝尔。她漂亮得没有必要在任何事情上排第一了，不过她却是新泽西州普林斯顿市的第一位挂历女郎。在20世纪初，她的相片曾被当地的一家银行用在自己的第一本日历上。就是在那里，在银行里，祖父遇上了她。她太美了，她曾收到一封信，信封上写道：

邮递员，邮递员

做做好事

将这封信送给

普林斯顿的美人。

这封信就被投在了她家门前。

我的外祖母则发明了鞋底袋。她相信，若能总是在鞋里留一个五分镍币，就不会有坏事发生。你总可以用它打个电话，总可以用它买点东西，你决不会身无分文。但是镍币会滑来滑去，到处滑动就可能滑出鞋外，因此她制作了一个小口袋固定在鞋内底部。这样，任何一双鞋子都可以有自己的"私房钱"。

至于我，我还没有出名，还在等着找到我的第一。有时候我觉得生活已经太舒服了，所有的需求都满足了，干吗还要去做一项发明？不过，我已经留意到一些东西，开始考虑能否给诸如旧灯泡或鸡蛋壳之类的东西找些新的用途。你出生在一个创造"第一"的家庭，不论喜欢与否，你总是在思考着。

来自一个创造"第一"的家庭，你决不会忘记自己的责任，不会忘记家族历史对你的鼓舞。

五、知识链接

Every few weeks, outside the movie theater in virtually any American town in the late 1910s, stood the life-size cardboard figure of a small tramp—outfitted in tattered, baggy pants, a cutaway coat and vest, impossibly large, worn-out shoes and a battered derby hat. An advertisement for a Charlie Chaplin film was a promise of happiness, of that precious, almost shocking moment when art delivers what life cannot, when experience and delight become synonymous, and our investments yield the fabulous bonanza we never get past expecting. In 1916, Chaplin's third year in films, his salary of $10,000 a week made him the highest-paid actor—possibly the highest paid person—in the world. By 1920, a flood of Chaplin dances, songs, dolls, comic books and cocktails was rampant.

Eighty years later, Chaplin is still here. In a 1995 worldwide survey of film critics, Chaplin was voted the greatest actor in movie history. He was the first, and to date the last, person to control every aspect of the filmmaking process—founding his own studio, producing, casting, directing, writing, and editing the movies he starred in. In the first decades of the 20th century, when weekly moviegoing was a national habit, Chaplin more or less invented global recognizability and helped turn an industry into an art.

1910年代的后几年里，每隔几个礼拜，在几乎任何一个美国小镇的电影院门外都矗立着真人大小的流浪汉形象的厚纸板——穿戴着破烂的、宽松的裤子，圆角礼服和背心，特别大的破旧皮鞋和一顶压扁的圆顶礼帽。查理·卓别林的电影广告就是快乐的承诺，是对那种珍贵的、几乎令人震惊的时刻的承诺，在这个时刻艺术传递生活中所不能传递的，在这个时刻经历和愉悦变成成同义词，在这个时刻我们的投入给我们带来了从未得到，超越我们期待的令人难以置信的财富。在1916年，卓别林从事电影的第三年，他一周10,000美元的薪水使他成为了世界上报酬最高的演员——很可能是报酬最高的人。到1920年，掀起了一股卓别林式的舞蹈、歌曲、玩偶、漫画书和鸡尾酒的狂潮。

80年以后，卓别林依然在这里。在1995年的全世界电影评论者的调查中，卓别林被选为电影历史上最伟大的演员。他是前无古人，迄今为止也是后无来者，控制电影制作过程的每一个方面的人——成立了他自己的工作室，出品、选角、导演、编剧以及剪辑他主演的影片。在二十世纪初始的几十年里，当每周出去看电影还是全国性的习惯时，卓别林或多或少地创造了全球认可性，并且帮助把一个行业变成了一项艺术。

六、自测题

1. The 215-page manuscript, circulated to publishers last October, _____ an outburst of interest.
   A. flared   B. glittered   C. sparked   D. flashed
2. The plane was _____ for two hours because of the heavy fog.
   A. delayed   B. canceled   C. postponed   D. dismissed
3. Lester's face _____ no sign of either thought of relief.

A. granted   B. betrayed   C. pointed   D. projected

4. In order to prevent stress from being set up in the metal, expansion joints are fitted with _____ the stress by allowing the pipe to expand or contrast freely.

A. relieve   B. reconcile   C. reclaim   D. rectify

5. Since it is too late to change my mind now, I am _____ to carry out the plan.

A. obliged   B. committed   C. engaged   D. resolved

6. Boy Scouts hold _____ where they come together for shows and singing.

A. conventions   B. discussions   C. debates   D. rallies

7. The actor was studying his _____.

A. outline   B. sketch   C. script   D. draft

8. It is reported that thirty people were killed in a _____ on the railway yesterday.

A. collision   B. collaboration   C. corrosion   D. confrontation

9. Everybody _____ in the hall where they were welcomed by the secretary.

A. piled   B. assembled   C. joined   D. accumulated

10. The schoolmaster _____ the girls' bravery in his opening speech.

A. applauded   B. enhanced   C. elevated   D. clapped

答案与解析

1. C spark 点燃，激起; flare 闪烁，闪耀; glitter 发光，闪光; flash 闪光，反射

2. A delay常指因遇到阻碍使某事无定期的延迟，常与for加一段时间连用; postpone常指把事情搁在一边，直至另外一件事发生、完成或得到等，常与until/till引出的短语或从句连用

3. B betray 露出……迹象; grant 批准，同意; point 指向; project 投射

4. A relieve 减轻，缓和; reconcile 和解; reclaim 重申; rectify 纠正，校正

5. B committed to 决心做好某事; obliged to 被迫作某事; engaged in 从事，忙于; resolved to 下定决心做某事

6. D rally 集会，聚会; convention 大会; discussion 讨论; debates 辩论

7. C script 剧本; outline 大纲; sketch 草图，素描; draft 草稿，草图

8. A collision 相撞，碰撞; collaboration 合作，协作; corrosion 腐蚀，侵蚀; confrontation 面临，对峙

9. B assemble 集合; pile 堆积; join 参加，加入; accumulate 积累

10. A applaud 鼓掌称赞，表扬; enhance 提高，加强; elevate 举起，提升; clap 轻拍，鼓掌

Unit 3

1 学习重点和难点
词汇和短语、语法项目、写作技巧

2 文化知识
课文大背景、课文知识点

3 课文精讲
词汇与短语详解、难句解析、重点
语法讲解、课文赏析、课后练习答
案及解析、参考译文、写作指导

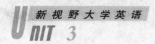

一、预习重点

1. What will a new welfare system should be?
2. How did the blind man help the author see the beautiful world?
3. What can we learn from Alberto Torres?

二、学习重点和难点

Ⅰ.词汇和短语

Section A: raw, pension, rent, opt, entitle, compensation, liberal, paste, receipt, donation, screw, certify, bid, alert, appliance, leak, thrive, convict; drum up, get/be involved in, talk back, break down, look into, fill out, account for, build up, go through; lend oneself/sth. to

Section B: dense, charter, angle, mist, steer, stoop, dye bow, lower, intensity, crown, highlight, curve, pat, skim, veil, realm, magic; bear witness to..., load with, switch on, out of tune, hold up, skim the surface

Ⅱ.语法项目

① there be结构
② 独立主格结构

Ⅲ.写作技巧

举例说明

三、文化知识

Ⅰ.课文大背景

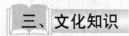
Social Welfare 社会福利

Public assistance programs, commonly called "welfare", provide cash or in-kind benefits for particular categories of the financially needy. The U.S. welfare system operates on both the federal and state levels. The federal welfare program is known as Social Security that provides benefits or assistance for child care, disability, food and medical assistance (also known as medicaid). The state welfare programs, on the other hand, provide assistance to both individuals and local communities with state schooling and social insurance. U.S. welfare programs grew significantly in the decades following World War II, but increases in welfare costs during the 1960s and 1970s brought into question the extent and quality of public assistance. In the early 1980s the Reagan Administration reduced welfare expenditures and suggested turning responsibility for welfare funding over to the states. The cuts in federal funding that took effect during the Reagan Administration did in fact effectively place the responsibility for maintaining funding levels on the states—and, in some cases, on the larger cities. The result has been a widening of the already existing disparities in social services spending between states, and between cities and regions within a state. Social welfare is an integrated part of a country's social policy.

Ⅱ. 课文知识点

1. Thailand 泰国

The kingdom of Thailand, located in Southeast Asia on the Gulf of Thailand and the Andaman Sea（安达曼海）, shares boundaries with Burma（缅甸）on the west and northwest, Laos（老挝）on the east and northeast, Cambodia（柬埔寨）on the southeast, and Malaysia on the south. Known also as Siam（暹罗）, the country was named Thailand, meaning "land of the free", in 1939. Thailand, although rich in rubber and in mineral resources, was never colonized by Europeans and has existed as a unified monarchy since 1350. The capital, Bangkok, was established in 1782.

2. Bangkok 曼谷

Bangkok is the capital and chief port of Thailand and one of the most important cities in Southeast Asia. It is located on the east bank of the Chao Phraya River（湄南河）40 km upstream from the Gulf of Thailand. Bangkok's Thai name is Krung Thep ("City of Angels") . The population of Bangkok Metropolis, which includes that of the industrial city of Thon Buri（吞武里，曼谷外港）on the west bank of the river, is 5, 716, 779. Bangkok was known during the 19th century as the "Venice of the East" because of its many canals, which served as streets and commercial thoroughfares. It is Thailand's economic center as well as the center of transportation system. Tourism is also important.

3. Belgium 比利时

Belgium is a small and densely populated country (10 million inhabitants) at the crossroads of Western Europe. It is one of the founding members of the European Community, and its capital, Brussels（布鲁塞尔）, is also the capital of the European Union. It is a federal state, with 3 relatively autonomous regions: Flanders（弗兰德斯）in the north, where the language is Dutch ("Flemish") , Wallonia（瓦龙）in the south, where the language is French, and the centrally located Brussels, which is officially bilingual.

4. Scandinavian 斯堪的纳维亚人

Scandinavia refers to a group of countries in North Europe including Iceland, Finland, Denmark, Norway and Sweden.

四、课文精讲

Section A

Ⅰ. 词汇与短语详解

1. raw

[词义] *adj.* 未经加工或处理的，生的，未经烹饪的

[搭配] raw material 原材料; in the raw 纯真的，天然的; touch sb. on the raw 触及某人的痛处，伤及某人的感情

[例句] I prefer to eat raw vegetables. 我喜欢吃生蔬菜。

2. pension

[词义] *n.* [C] 养老金，抚恤金

[搭配] pension allowance 养老金; live on a pension 靠养老金生活

[例句] She lived on a small pension. 她靠一点退休金生活。

[派生] pensionable *adj.* 有资格领养老金的; pensionary *n.* 领养老金的人

3. rent

[词义] *n.* [C] 租金，租费; *v.* 租借，租用，出租，出借

[搭配] rent...from sb. 向某人租借……; rent...to sb. 把……租给某人

[例句] The rent for this apartment is $50 a week. 这个房间的租金为每周50美元。

I rented a car from a garage. 我从车行租了辆车。

[派生] rental *n.* 租金收入; rent-free 免租金的; rent-roll *n.* 地租账簿

4. opt

[词义] *vi.* 选择，挑选

[搭配] opt for（从多种方案中）做出选择; opt to do sth. 选择做某事

[例句] Against his father's advice, Daniel opted for music.

丹尼尔违背父亲的意见，选择了音乐。

[派生] optant *n.* 选择者; option *n.* 选择

5. entitle

[词义] *vt.* ① 给……权利; ② 给（书、电影等）定名，题名

[搭配] entitle sb. to sth./to do sth. 给某人权利做某事; be entitled to sth./do sth. 对……享有权利

[例句] The employer is entitled to ask for references. 雇主有权索阅推荐函。

She sang a song entitled "The Moon River".

她唱了一首名为《月亮河》的歌。

[派生] entitled *adj.* 有资格的; entitlement *n.* 权利

6. compensation

[词义] *n.* ① [U] 补偿，弥补; ② [C] 补偿金，补偿物，赔偿金

[搭配] in compensation for... 作为……的补偿，以弥补……; make compensation for 补偿，赔偿

[例句] You should claim compensation. 你应该要求赔偿。

She received $50,000 in compensation for her lost hand.

她得到了5万美金作为失去一只手的补偿费。

[派生] compensate *v.* 赔偿，补偿; compensatory *adj.* 赔偿的，补偿的

7. liberal

[词义] *n.* [C] 思想或行为开明的人

adj. ① 心胸宽广的，开明的; ② 慷慨的，大方的

[搭配] liberal art(s) 文科; liberal economy 自由经济; liberal education 文科教育，普通教育

[例句] He is a man of liberal views. 他是一个思想观点开明的人。

The rich man gave a liberal donation. 这个有钱人慷慨的捐赠。

[派生] liberalism *n.* 自由主义; liberality *n.* 宽大，磊落

[辨析] generous, liberal

> generous 意为"宽厚的、宽宏大量的"，修饰人或其思想、胸怀，偏重其豁达、不偏袒挑剔；作"慷慨大方的"时，表示亲切关照和乐于帮助别人。liberal 意为"心胸宽阔的、开明的、公允的"，含有对有争议的事物或现象能够包涵的意味；意为"慷慨大方的"时，常涉及较大或较重要的服务或施给，或可观的钱财的支出，往往带有大量给与的含义，强调数量可观、充足。

8. paste

[词义] *vt.* 用浆糊粘贴；*n.* [C, U] 浆糊

[搭配] paste in/on 粘住，粘上；paste up a notice 张贴告示

[例句] Her job is pasting a label on a box. 她的工作是把标签贴在盒子上。
> He stuck the sheets of paper together with paste.
> 他用浆糊把这些纸张粘在一起。

9. receipt

[词义] *n.* ① [C] 收据，收条；② [U] 收到

[搭配] on receipt of 一收到就……; make out a receipt 开收据

[例句] Make sure you are given a receipt for everything you buy.
> 一定要确保你买的每样东西都有一张收据。
> Goods will be delivered on receipt of payment. 收到付款即送货。

[派生] receive *vt.* 收到，接到；receiptor *n.* 收受人

[辨析] receipt, reception

> receipt 正式用词，表示"收到、接到"，主要作书信用词，常后接介词of；reception 常用词，可表示一般意义上的"接受、收受"（他人给予的东西），也可表示对某人或某种新事物"接纳、接受力"，还可指无线电、电视等对信号的"接收情况"。

10. donation

[词义] *n.* ① [C, U] 捐赠的钱或物；② 捐赠

[搭配] make/give a donation of...to... 捐赠……给……

[例句] She gave/made a donation of $200 to the Children's Hospital.
> 她捐赠了200美元给儿童医院。

[派生] donate *v.* 捐赠，赠予；donator *n.* 捐赠者

11. screw

[词义] *n.* [C] 螺丝，螺丝钉；*v.* 用螺丝钉固定

[搭配] put the screw(s) on 对……施加压力；screw up 拧紧；把……弄糟

[例句] He needed strong screws for fixing the cupboard to the wall.
> 他需要大螺丝钉把这个碗橱固定在墙上。
> The carpenter screwed the hinges to the door.
> 木匠用螺丝钉将铰链固定到门上。

[派生] screwdriver *n.* 螺丝刀，起子；screwy *adj.* 螺旋形的，扭曲的

12. certify

[词义] *v.* 证明

[搭配] certify to sth. 书面证明；certify to the facts 用事实证明

63

[例句] Here is a document certifying that I was born in China.

这是证明我出生在中国的文件。

[派生] certificate *n.* 证书，证明; certification *n.* 证明; certified *adj.* 被鉴定的;

certifiable *adj.* 可证明的，可确认的; certifier *n.* 证明者

[辨析] certify, prove

certify 正式用词，通常以出具证明书证明某物真实、正确、合格等，如:

This is to certify that... 兹证明……; prove 指拿出证据来证明，为普通用语。

13. bid

[词义] *n.* ① [C] (在拍卖等活动中买主的) 喊价，出价，投标; ② [C] 企图得到

[搭配] bid on sth. 提出价格（承做某事），投标; bid for 期望达到，寻求; bid farewell

to sb. 向某人告别

[构成] Bids for building the bridge were invited from big firms throughout the country.

已向全国各大公司招标建造这座桥梁。

He made a bid for re-election. 他试图再次竞选。

[派生] bidder *n.* 出价人，投标人; bidding *n.* 命令，出价，邀请

14. alert

[词义] *vt.* 使警觉，使警惕，告知; *adj.* 警觉的，灵活的

[搭配] on the alert for sth. 注意/提防/小心……; alert sb. to sth. 提醒某人注意某事;

be alert to sth. 警惕某事

[例句] The sign alerted me to thin ice. 这块告示警告我冰层很薄。

You must be alert to possible dangers. 你必须警惕潜在的危险。

[派生] alertly *adv.* 提高警觉地，留意地; alertness *n.* 警戒，机敏

[辨析] alert, cautious

alert 意为"警惕的、警觉的"，指思想高度集中地注视着可能发生的事

件，尤其是危险的、恐怖的事件，后接介词to; cautious 意为"小心的，谨

慎的"，多表示所有方面都考虑周全后才开始行动，也可表示行为中带有

迟疑、尝试甚至胆怯，后接介词of。

15. appliance

[词义] *n.* [C] 器具，用具，（尤指）家用电器

[例句] Our kitchen is equipped with modern electrical appliance.

我们的厨房里装有现代化的电器设备。

[辨析] appliance, equipment, instrument, tool

appliance 一般多指电器、器械，如: kitchen appliance 厨房用具，medical

appliance 医疗器械; equipment指一台一台的机器或设备等的统称，指为了

生产、工作和研究所需要的"设备、装备、装置"; instrument 特指精细工

作或科学工作上所用的极高精度的仪器，如: optical instrument 光学仪器;

tool 可以广泛地用于一切使工作方便的工具，它还特指小型手工器具。

16. leak

[词义] *v.* ①漏，泄漏; ②（液体、气体等）漏，渗; ③泄漏（秘密）

n. [C] 漏洞，漏隙

[搭配] leak out 泄漏; spring a leak（指船）生裂缝，漏裂

[例句] The car leaked oil all over the drive. 那辆车漏了一路的油。

The rain's leaking in. 雨水漏了进来。

He leaked the names to the press. 他把名单泄漏给了新闻界。

You'd better repair the leak in the roof. 你最好修理一下屋顶的裂缝。

[派生] leakage *n.* 漏，泄漏，渗漏；leaky *adj.* 漏的

17. thrive

[词义] *v.* 兴旺发达，茁壮成长

[搭配] thrive on sth. 靠……旺盛、强壮

[例句] The real estate business is thriving. 房地产业生意兴旺。

[派生] thriving *adj.* 兴旺的

[辨析] flourish, prosper, thrive

flourish 原指树木枝叶茂盛，喻指处于兴旺茂盛期；thrive指由于优越的环境而蓬勃发展和增长；prosper指兴隆，侧重经济上的成功或赚了大钱。

18. convict

[词义] *vt.*（经审讯）证明……有罪，宣判……有罪

[搭配] convict sb. of sth. 宣判某人有罪或有错

[例句] She was convicted of theft. 她被判犯了盗窃罪。

[派生] conviction *n.* 深信，确信，定罪，宣告有罪

19. drum up 大力争取，大力招揽（顾客）

[例句] The department stores are offering discounts to drum up business.

百货商店正提供折扣来招徕生意。

20. get/be involved in 卷入，介入，参与

[例句] More than 100 people are involved in the project. 一百多人参与了这个项目。

21. talk back 顶嘴

[例句] He knew better than to talk back to his father.

他知道最好还是不要和他父亲顶嘴。

23. break down 发生故障，坏掉

[例句] Our car broke down on the freeway. 我们的车在高速公路上抛锚了。

[联想] break down 还可以指（健康等）垮掉。

He broke down due to heavy pressure. 因为压力太大，他的身体垮掉了。

24. look into 调查，仔细检查

[例句] Police are looking into the disappearance of two children.

警察正在调查两名儿童失踪的事情。

25. fill out 填写

[例句] We were asked to fill out a form. 我们被要求填写一张表格。

[联想] fill in 填写，填满；fill up 填补，淤积

26. account for 解释，说明（原因等）

[例句] We have to account for every penny we spend on business trips.

我们得把出差花费的每一分钱都说明清楚。

[联想] account for还可以指（数量等）占。

The raw material accounts for a considerable proportion of exported goods.

原料在出口货物中占相当大的比重。

27. build up 逐步建立，逐步建设

[例句] We've built up good relationships with our clients.

我们与客户建立了良好的关系。

[联想] build up 还可以表示增进，增强。

We must build up both our body and mind. 我们的体质和头脑都要增强。

28. go through 经历，遭受，蒙受

[例句] She's been going through a bad patch recently. 最近她的日子很难过。

29. lend oneself/sth. to 适宜于（某事），有助于（某事），会造成（某结果）

[例句] This hot weather lends itself to sleeping. 这种热天很容易让人昏昏欲睡。

Ⅱ. 难句解析

1. A welfare client is supposed to cheat. (Para.1)

[释义] People believe that a welfare client is cheating.

be supposed to ① 据说；②（依据规则，惯例或安排等等）应该做某事

e.g. I haven't seen the film myself, but it's supposed to be great.

我还没有看过这部影片，但据说它挺不错的。

You're supposed to ask the teacher if you want to leave the room.

如果你要离开教室，得跟老师说。

2. Faced with sharing a dinner of raw pet food with the cat, many people in wheelchairs I know bleed the system for a few extra dollars. (Para.1)

[释义] In the face of sharing uncooked pet food with the cat, many of my wheelchaired acquaintances have to lie about their circumstances, thus getting a little extra from welfare givers.

bleed v. 强迫某人长期付钱，榨取、压榨

e.g. My ex-wife is bleeding me for every penny I have.

我的前妻要榨干我身上的每一分钱。

[分析] "faced with...with the cat"是一个过去分词短语，表示一种状态。

3. I'm not being bitter. (Para. 3)

[释义] I am not feeling angry deliberately/on purpose.

[分析] "be being + adjective/noun" 这种结构被用来谈论某种行为，如：①You're being stupid. = You're doing stupid things. ② I was being very careful. = I was doing something very carefully. 系表结构be+ adjective通常用来表示某种情绪，如：

① I'm happy just now. ② I was depressed.

4. But after a few years...a detective in shorts. (Para. 3)

[释义] **shorts** n. 膝盖以上的短裤（通常儿童穿着或者成年人在天气炎热、休闲运动时穿着）

e.g. She put on a pair of shorts and a T-shirt. 她穿上运动短裤和T恤衫。

5. Suzanne tries to lecture me about repairs... (Para.9)

[释义] **lecture** vt. 训诫某人，向某人说教；n. 训斥，长篇大论的说教

e.g. He's always lecturing me about the way I dress. 他老说我穿着不得体。

I know I should stop smoking—don't give me a lecture about it.

我知道我应该戒烟——别跟我长篇大论。

6. I've heard that you put a lot more miles on that wheelchair than average. (Para.9)

[释义] I've heard that you use your wheelchair more often than the average clients do. No wonder that's why your wheelchair is always breaking down.

7. I'm an active worker, not a vegetable. (Para.10)

[释义] **vegetable** *n.* ① 植物人；② 生活非常无聊的人

e.g. Severe brain damage turned him into a vegetable.

严重的大脑损伤使他变成了植物人。

Since losing my job I've felt like a vegetable.

丢了工作后，我觉得人都变呆了。

8. There needs to be a lawyer who can act as a champion for the rights of welfare clients,...(Para.15)

[分析] 注意 there与某些动词连用表示"有"的意思，如: enter, follow, live, need, remain, seem, tend等；还有与一些动词的被动式，如: say, think, feel, report, understand, presume等。

e.g. There seems to be some problems. 似乎还有问题。

There followed an uncomfortable silence. 随之而来的是令人不适的沉默。

There are thought to be more than 3, 000 different languages in the world.

世界上有3,000多种不同的语言。

9. Would I sit on the governor's committee...(Para.16)

[释义] **sit on** 成为某个代表或控制一个机构的组织的正式成员

e.g. She sat on the company's board for five years.

她在公司的董事会当了5年董事。

10. Someday people like me will thrive under a new system that will encourage them, not seek to convict them of cheating. (Para.17)

[释义] One day in the future, disabled people like me living on welfare will do well and get successful if the old system is transformed into a new one that encourages its clients instead of seeking to prove them to be cheating.

[分析] 本句主干为 "Someday people will thrive under a new system"，其中 "that will...of cheating" 是一个定语从句，在这个定语从句中包含两个并列的谓语动词，即 encourage 和seek to。

Ⅲ．重点语法讲解

there + be 结构在英语中表示"什么地方或时间存在什么事物"，这种句子结构中的there是个引词（由表示地点的副词there变来），本身没有词义，常弱读。be为谓语动词，be后的名词为主语，两者的数必须一致。句子最后为地点（时间）状语。

there +be与have除用法上不同外（have前须有主语，"there + be"则是一种特殊结构），在意义上have表示所属有关系，意为"所有"，there + be则表示"存在"。如: **I have** a bike.

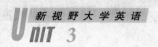

There is a bike in my garden. 前者表示事物的所属关系，后者则表示事物的存在与否。

there + be 的几种特殊结构

1. there + be结构中的谓语动词，有时be可用appear to be, seem to be，happen to be等词组来代替，这种结构主要是用来描写事物。

   There seems to be some misunderstanding between us.

   There happened to be a flood that year.

2. 有时be可被一些不及物动词所代替，表示类似"存在"观念的动词，如：exist, live, come, stand, occur, lie等，这些动词都表示状态，可视为be的异体。

   There stood a tower at the bank of the river.

   There remains nothing to be done.

3. there + be结构也可用作状语和介词宾语，取消句子独立性，这时be变为了being。

   No one had told him something about **there being** a beautiful story about the lake.

   There being nothing to do, they have to go back home.

Ⅳ. 课文赏析

1. 文体特点

本文作者以第一人称的口吻，通过自身的经历说明现存福利制度的弊端，提出对新的福利制度的渴望。在文中作者反复运用了举例说明的写作手法，加上辛辣的语言和夸张手法，使得文章真实可信、风趣幽默，具有强烈的说服力。

2. 结构分析

Part Ⅰ (Para. 1-3) General images of welfare clients and welfare caseworkers under the present system.

Part Ⅱ (Para. 4-14) Problems with the present welfare system.

Part Ⅲ (Para. 15-17) Suggestions to improve the present welfare system.

Ⅴ. 课后练习答案及解析

Vocabulary

Ⅲ.

1. convicted 译文：一旦证实他被指控的罪名成立，他将面临六年监禁。

2. donation 译文：约翰认为给饥民捐食物比给他们钱更有帮助。

3. bleeding 译文：西方国家正通过债务利息榨干贫穷国家的钱。

4. entitled 译文：据估计，大约五分之一有权享用这些利益的领养老金的人根本没有要求这些权利。

5. profile 译文：我决定保持低姿态，毕竟我只是个客人。

6. pension 译文：退休时你可以一次领取一部分应得的养老金，而且在现行法律下，这些钱是免税的。

7. thrive 译文：我的花园太干燥，而且树荫很多——没有多少植物能在这种条件下茁壮成长。

8. receipt 译文：我们准备一旦得到政府批准就开始营业。

Ⅳ.

1. up 译文：他的任务就是想办法从大公司的朋友那里争取捐助。

2. to 译文：人们很容易向签收许多钱的诱惑屈服。

3. back 译文：顶嘴的孩子被认为是脸皮厚，没礼貌。

4. of 译文：当彼得倒茶的时候，他很想知道她是否已告诉詹姆斯她愚弄他的事了，说不定他们还一起嘲笑他了。

5. around 译文：她怀孕的消息不久在邻里间传开了。

6. into 译文：在修改未来的计划之前，你应该观察你的处境，考虑变化，想清楚过去和现在。

7. for 译文：如果像达尔文所深信的那样，人类的高级能力能够用自然选择来解释的话，那些能力也必须有其物质基础。

8. to 译文：电脑有许多复杂的用途。

Collocation

V.

1. pressure 译文：这两个人承受了可以想象的最沉重的压力，却没有背叛他们的朋友。

2. hardships 译文：鉴于许多农民所承受的苦难，他们有时会爆发不满，甚至以暴力的形式就不足为奇了。

3. pain 译文：正如预想的，这是电影的亮点，成功地反映了长跑者所受的痛苦。

4. defeat 译文：将军清楚地知道，在着冰冷的冬季，他的部队不能再经受另一场失败了。

5. delay 译文：乘客们被告知，由于大雾他们得再等两个小时。

6. hunger 译文：到了四月中旬，德国士兵抱怨说他们宁愿挨饿也不愿意为食物进行危险的长途跋涉。

7. conditions 译文：我宁愿作一个舒适的奴隶，也不愿意忍受自由的条件。

8. temper 译文：小汤姆闭上眼睛，握紧拳头，鼓起十一岁的身躯里所有的勇气，不哭不喊，忍受父亲的坏脾气。

Word Building

VI.

1. longish 译文：喝过茶后，他给希尔达写了一封相当长的信。

2. animal-like 译文：当地报纸批评了球迷们的被称为"野兽般的"行为。

3. selfish 译文：我知道，有了孩子后就不能那么自私了。

4. honey-like 译文：成熟的酸橙树开的花会散发出象蜂蜜一样的香味。

5. ball-like 译文：在大楼顶部有一个大的、球形的建筑。

6. boyish 译文：即使他老了，但是他还保有那份年少时的魅力。

7. yellowish 译文：你可以看到，这些树的叶子，有微微泛黄的绿色也有墨绿色颜色变化多样。

8. goodish 译文：这出戏还算好，我曾看过更好的，但也有比它差得远的

VII.

1. politicians 译文：这很奇怪：没有人相信政客，但我们却让他们统治世界。

2. technician 译文：他们正在寻找一个实验室的技术人员，擅长实验室管理细节技术方面。

3. comedian 译文：当这个戏剧演员模仿查理•卓别林时，观众爆发出笑声。

4. musicians 译文：这个盲人告诉他，在西方人听来这音乐有些走调，但是却很动听，

他要求他描述演奏音乐的人。

5. physicians 译文：在这个国家，医生被要求上报对公共卫生有危害的，像艾滋病之类的传染性病例。

6. electricians 译文：我们应经被告知电工周二来重新布线。

7. beautician 译文：在伦敦的时候，她在一家收费不菲的沙龙里当美容师兼皮肤护理专家。

8. magician 译文：所有的孩子都被魔术师表演的神奇戏法逗乐了。

Structure

VIII.

1. The wanted man is believed to be living in New York.
   译文：据说这个被通缉的人正住在纽约。

2. Many people are said to be homeless after the floods.
   译文：据说许多人在洪水之后无家可归。

3. Three men are said to have been arrested after the explosion.
   译文：据说爆炸后有三个人已经被捕。

4. The prisoner is thought to have escaped by climbing over the wall.
   译文：据说囚犯是翻墙逃跑的。

5. Four people are reported to have been seriously injured in the accident.
   译文：据报道事故中有四人受重伤。

IX.

1. He tried sending her flowers, but it didn't have any effect.
   译文：他尝试着给他送花，但没有任何效果。

2. I don't regret telling her what I thought, even if I upset her.
   译文：我不后悔告诉了她我的想法，即使我让她伤心了。

3. She remembered reading a biography about Charlie Chaplin, which described him as a Marxist.
   译文：她记得读过一篇关于查理·卓别林的传记，其中他被描述为一个马克思主义者。

4. We regret to inform you that we are unable to offer you employment.
   译文：我们遗憾地通知你我们不能雇用你。

5. He welcomed the new student and then went on to explain the college regulations.
   译文：他向新同学表示欢迎，然后继续解释学院的规定。

Translation

X.

1. You are legally entitled to take faulty goods back to the store where you purchased them, but you are supposed to account for why you want to do so.

2. You only need to fill out a form to get your membership, which entitles you to a discount on goods.

3. One year ago, the car dealer tried to drum up buyers by offering good services. Now, his business is thriving.

4. The crime was looked into carefully before he was convicted of murder.

5. I called the Freeway Service Patrol for help after my car broke down on the freeway. Twenty minutes later, they came to my rescue and left a $150 receipt.

6. Faced with the threat of losing their jobs, these workers yielded to the management's advice and went back to work.

7. The middle-aged man who took the boy bled the father for $20,000 as a compensation for the loss of his company.

8. The man living on welfare began to set up his own market, one step at a time and his business is thriving.

XI.

1. 人人都觉得福利救济对象是在骗人。
2. 但即使我抗不住这种诱惑，那些大杂志也不愿给自己惹麻烦。
3. 社会工作者心里知道许多救济对象在欺骗他们，因此他们觉得，作为补偿，他们有权让救济对象向他们点头哈腰。
4. 她这是在暗示我得哀求她了。但是我却将她顶了回去。
5. 苏珊娜试图就修理轮椅的问题训斥我。由于福利部门不愿意花钱好好地修理，所以它总是坏。
6. 我当然用得多，我是个工作很积极的人，又不是植物人。
7. 如何逐渐脱离福利照顾，这在法律条款中没有明确规定。
8. 确实需要有一位律师来捍卫福利救济对象的权利，因为这一福利体制不仅容易使救济对象滥用权力，也很容易使福利提供者滥用权力。

Essay Summary

XII.

BCADB ACDBA BCDAD ABADD

Text Structure Analysis

XIII.

Examples:

1. They tell the government that they are getting two hundred dollars less than their real pension so they can get a little extra welfare money.

2. They tell the caseworker that the landlord raised the rent by a hundred dollars.

VI. 参考译文

渴望新的福利救济制度

人人都觉得福利救济对象是在骗人。我认识的许多坐轮椅的人面临与宠物猫分吃生猫食的窘境，都会向福利机构多榨取几美元。为了能领到一点额外的福利款，他们告诉政府说他们实际上少拿了200美元的养老金，或告诉社会工作者，说房东又提高了100美元的房租。

我选择了过一种完全诚实的生活，因此我不会那样做，而是四处找活，揽些画漫画的活。我甚至还告诉福利机构我赚了多少钱！噢，私下里领一笔钱当然对我也挺有吸引力，但即使我抗不住这种诱惑，我投稿的那些大杂志也不会去给自己惹麻烦。他们会保留我的记录，而这些记录会直接进入政府的电脑。真是态度鲜明，毫不含糊。

作为一名福利救济对象，我必须在社会工作者面前卑躬屈膝。社会工作者心里知道许多救济对象在欺骗他们，因此他们觉得，作为补偿，他们有权让救济对象向他们点头哈腰。我并不是故意感到忿忿不平。大多数社会工作者刚开始时都是些大学毕业生，有理想，而且思想开明。可是在这个实际上是要人撒谎的系统里干了几年后，他们就变得与那个叫苏珊娜的人一样了——一个穿运动短裤的侦探。

去年圣诞节，苏珊娜到我家来了解情况，看到墙上贴着新的宣传画，便问："你从哪儿弄到钱来买这些？"

"朋友和家人。"

"那么，你最好要张收据，真的，你接受任何捐献或礼物都要报告。

她这是在暗示我得哀求她了。但是我却将她顶了回去。"那天在马路上有人给我一根烟，我也得报告吗？"

"对不起，卡拉汉先生，可是规定不是我制订的。"

苏珊娜试图就修理轮椅的问题训斥我。由于福利部门不愿意花钱好好地修理，所以它总是坏。"您是知道的，卡拉汉先生，我听说您的那台轮椅比一般人用得多得多。"

我当然用得多，我是个工作很积极的人，又不是植物人。我住在闹市区附近，可以坐着轮椅到处走走。我真想知道如果她突然摔坏臀部，不得不爬着去上班时，是什么感受。

政府削减福利开支已经导致许多人挨饿受苦，我只是其中之一。但这种削减对脊柱伤残的人士更有特别的影响：政府已经不管我们的轮椅了。每次我的轮椅坏了，掉了螺丝，需要换轴承，或刹车不灵等，我都打电话给苏珊娜，但每次都要挨训。她最后总会说：好吧，如果今天我能抽出时间的话，我会找医务人员的。

她该通知医务人员，由他来证明问题确实存在，然后打电话给各家轮椅维修公司，拿到最低的报价。接着医务人员就通知州府的福利总部，他们再花几天时间考虑这件事。而这期间我只能躺在床上，动弹不得。最后，如果我幸运的话，他们会给我回电话，同意维修。

当福利部门获悉我画漫画赚钱时，苏珊娜就开始每两个星期"拜访"我一次，而不是每两个月才一次了。她寻遍每个角落，想找出我未上报的电器，或者是女仆、烤炉里的烤猪、停在房后新买的直升飞机什么的。她从来都是一无所获，但最后我总要填厚厚的一叠表格，说明每一分钱的来历。

如何逐渐脱离福利照顾，这在法律条款中没有明确规定。我是一个独立的生意人，正在慢慢建立起自己的市场。要脱离福利救济，一下子做到每月能挣2,000美元是不可能的。但我很想自己负担部分生活费用，不必在每次需要为轮椅买点配件时都去尴尬地求人。

确实需要有一位律师来捍卫福利救济对象的权利，因为这一福利体制不仅容易使救济对象滥用权力，也很容易使福利提供者滥用权力。前几天，由于药剂师说我使用的医疗用品超出常量，于是福利部门派苏珊娜到我的住所调查。我确实多用了，因为外科手术所造成的排尿孔的大小改变了，于是尿袋的连接处发生渗漏。

她正做着记录，我家的电话铃响了。苏珊娜接听了电话，是一位州议员打来的，这使她慌了一下。数以千计像我这样的福利救济对象，如果允许的话，可以慢慢地负担自己的一部分甚至全部生活费用，对此，我会不会在州政府的委员会里尝试做点儿什么呢？

还用说吗？我当然会！总有一天，像我这样的福利救济对象将在一种新的福利制度下过上好日子，这种制度不是要千方百计证明福利救济对象在欺骗，而是要鼓励他们自立。他们将能自由地、毫无愧疚、毫不担忧地发挥他们的才干，或拥有一份稳定的好工作。

VII. 写作指导

一篇文章，或一个段落，如果只停留在一般性的说理上，文章会显得苍白，缺少说服力；而提供实例，就像律师在法庭上提供证据或证人一样，比起空口争辩要有分量得多。

举例的多少应根据文章的长短和需要而定。有时，充分发挥一个例子就够了，有时则需要多个例子。举例时，要注意所举的例子和所论述的问题密切相关，有助于支持论点；此外，选择的例证应力求不同于一般，这样才能达到吸引读者注意力、产生强烈效果的目的。最后在对提供的例子进行选择的同时，还应该对其先后顺序进行精心安排：按重要性递增的顺序安排例子，使最具说服力的例子出现在段落或结论的最重要的位置，形成一种递进的高潮。

范文：

Welfare clients often face the embarrassing situation of having to lie in bed for weeks before they can get their broken wheelchairs repaired.

Once my caseworker, Suzanne, learned that my wheelchair needed repairing, she would come personally to certify the problem. After giving me a lecture about my overuse of the wheelchair, she would notify the medical worker. Then the medical worker called the wheelchair repair companies to get the cheapest bid and alerted the headquarter office at the state capital. It would normally take them another several days to consider the matter while I was hopelessly lying in bed, unable to move. When they finally got my wheelchair repaired, I would have been confined to bed for more than half a month.

Section B

I. 阅读技巧

> 读懂比喻句

我们在第2册和第3册中学到过怎样读懂比喻句。判断和阐述或解释比喻句的能力可以帮助我们全面理解作者的观点，对于更加深刻地理解我们所阅读的篇章至关重要。为了使语言更加清晰、更加有趣以及更加吸引人，作者经常会使用一些字面上看来不真实的表述，在写作中打比方。比喻句——打比方的句子——为读者描绘出一幅画面。如果光从字面上理解，比喻句很容易使人混淆。看一下第3单元第1课中的几个例子：

例1：Oh, I'm tempted to get paid under the table. (Para. 2)

解释：under the table 在桌子底下 ——私下的，不让其他人知道我在挣钱。

例2：But even if I yielded to that temptation, big magazines are not going to get involved in some sticky situation. (Para. 2)

解释：sticky situation 粘粘的状态 ——不能摆脱的困境

例3：But after a few years in a system that practically requires people to lie, they become like the one I shall call "Suzanne", a detective in shorts. (Para. 3)

解释：a detective in shorts 穿着短裤的侦探 ——社会工作者被比作侦探和运动员，他们追踪福利救济对象，试图发现他们所犯的错误。

II. 词汇与短语详解

1. dense

[词义] *adj.* ① 密集的，稠密的；② 厚的，浓密的

[例句] The road is dense with traffic. 这条路上交通繁忙。

The fog was so dense that we could see nothing.

雾很浓，我们什么都看不见。

[派生] denseness *n.* 稠密，密集，浓厚; densify *v.* 使稠密，使增加密度; density *n.* 密度

[辨析] dense, thick

dense 意为"密集的，稠密的"，强调数量多及布局密，多用于修饰人口的分布，修饰smoke, fog等词时，可与thick互换; thick 意为"浓的，稠的"，通常用来表示气体或液体浓度高或枝叶茂密。

2. charter

[词义] *v.* ① 租，包 (车、船、飞机); ② 特许成立，发放执照

n. [C] 宪章，章程

[搭配] charter flights 包机; chartered accountant 特许会计师

[例句] They chartered a bus for trip. 他们租了一辆巴士去旅行。

This restaurant was chartered in two years ago.

这家饭店是两年前经特许成立的。

Education is one of the basic human rights written into the United Nations charter. 受教育是写入联合国宪章的基本人权之一。

[派生] charterage *n.* 包租，船务代理商之费用; charted *adj.* 受特许的

3. angle

[词义] *n.* ① [C] 角，角度; ② [C] 角度，方面，观点

[搭配] acute angle 锐角; right angle 直角; obtuse angle 钝角; angle of view 视角; at an angle of... 以……角度

[例句] The two lines form an angle of 45. 这两条线构成一个45度的角。

You should consider all angles of this issue.

你应该考虑这个问题的各个方面。

[联想] angel *n.* 天使

4. mist

[词义] *n.* ① [U] 雾气; ② [U] 薄雾

v. (使) 蒙上薄雾，(使) 模糊

[搭配] cast/throw a mist before sb's eyes 蒙蔽人; in a mist (感到) 迷惑

[例句] She looked at me sadly through a mist of tears. 他泪眼模糊，悲伤地看着我。

The early morning mist had lifted, giving us a magnificent view over the lake.

清晨的薄雾散开，我们面前展开了一幅湖上美景。

Her eyes misted with tears. 泪水模糊了她的双眼。

[派生] misty *adj.* 有薄雾的，朦胧不清的; mistiness *n.* 雾，模糊，不清楚

5. steer

[词义] *v.* ① 引导，带领; ② 驾驶

[搭配] steer clear of 绕开，躲开; steer for 向……驶去

[例句] He steered the discussion away from the subject of his personal life.

他把讨论从他的私人生活这个话题引开。

Jenny isn't very good at steering the car. 詹妮的车开得不是很好。

[派生] steerage *n.* 操纵，驾驶，掌舵; steersman *n.* 舵手

[辨析] guide, steer

guide 常指为人带路、指导，暗示避免走弯路或遇到危险，如: guide a ship through a channel 引领轮船通过海峡; steer 常表示引导，暗示引导某人、某物度过难关，如: Soon the country will be steered to peace and prosperity. 这个国家很快便会被带入和平与繁荣之境。

6. stoop

[词义] *n.* [C] (sing.) 弓背; *v.* 俯身，弓腰，弓背

[搭配] stoop to do sth. 降低身份以求……; stoop to (doing) sth. 堕落到……地步

[例句] My brother walks with a slight stoop. 我哥哥走路时有点弓背。

He stooped down and picked up the book. 他俯身把书拣了起来。

He would stoop to do anything for profit. 为了赚钱他什么都干得出来。

7. dye

[词义] *v.* 染; *n.* [U, C] 染料

[搭配] of the blackest/deepest dye 穷凶极恶，彻头彻尾的

[例句] She dyed her hair red. 她把头发染成了红色。

She dipped the material into the dye. 她把布料浸到了染料里。

[派生] dyeing *n.* 染色，染色工艺; dyer *n.* 染布工人

8. bow

[词义] *n.* ① [C] 弦乐器的弓，琴弓; ② [C] 弓，弓形物

vt. 低下（头），压弯; *vi.* 鞠躬

[搭配] bow instrument 弦乐器; bow down 鞠躬，服从; bow sb. in/out 鞠躬恭敬地接/送某人; bow to one's opinion 服从某人的意见

[例句] Violins are played with bows. 小提琴是用琴弓演奏的。

He made his start like an arrow from a bow. 他起跑时就像离弦之箭。

The criminal bowed his head in shame. 那个罪犯羞愧地低下了头。

I can't agree with you but I bow to your greater experience and knowledge. 虽然我不同意你的意见，但我佩服你经验和知识比我丰富。

[派生] bowman *n.* 弓箭手，射手; bowtie *n.* 蝴蝶领结; bow-legged *adj.* 弓形腿的

9. lower

[词义] *v.* ① 降低，调低; ② 放下，降下

adj. 下部的，底层的

[搭配] lower oneself 降低身份，自甘堕落; lower case 小写字母键

[例句] Please lower your voice. 请小点声。

They lowered the flag at sunset. 他们在日落时降了旗。

The lower deck is more convenient. 下层甲板更方便些。

[派生] lowery *adj.* 阴暗的，阴霾的; lowering *adj.* 使低劣的，减少体力的

10. intensity

[词义] *n.* [U] 强烈，强度

[例句] The pain increased in intensity. 疼痛越来越剧烈。

[派生] intense *adj.* 强烈的，剧烈的; intensify *v.* 加强，强化

11. crown

[词义] n. ① [C] 王冠, 皇冠; ② (sing.) 冠军称号

v. 加顶于, 覆盖……的顶部

[搭配] to crown all 尤其是, 锦上添花; be crowned with victory 最后获胜

[例句] The queen wore a crown encrusted with diamonds.

女王带着一顶镶有钻石的王冠。

He won the crown in the Olympic Games. 他在奥运会上获得冠军称号。

The hotel was crowned with golden domes. 这家旅馆有着金色的圆形屋顶。

[派生] crowned adj. 有王冠的, 王室的; crowner n. 最后完成者

12. highlight

[词义] v. 引起注意, 强调; n. [C] 最精彩的部分

[搭配] highlighted text 突出现实的正文

[例句] The report highlights the need for considerable improvements in education.

报告强调了大幅度改良教育的必要性。

The highlight of our trip was the exceptional scenery.

我们这次旅行的最精彩部分是独特的景色。

[派生] highlighted adj. 突出的; highlights n. 拔萃, 集锦

13. curve

[词义] v. 弯曲; 转弯; n. [C] 曲线, 转弯

[搭配] a curve in the road 道路的弯处; curve of beauty 曲线美

[例句] The road curves east. 道路向东转弯。

The model has a figure with beautiful curves. 那位模特的体形具有曲线美。

[派生] curvesome adj. 曲线美的

14. pat

[词义] v. 轻拍, 轻打; n. [C] 轻拍, 拍打

[搭配] pat sb. on the back 赞扬某人, 鼓励某人; pat a ball 拍球

[例句] He patted my head affectionately. 他慈爱地拍拍我的头。

I gave the little dog a pat on the head. 我拍拍小狗的头。

15. skim

[词义] v. ① 掠过, 擦过; ② 浏览, 初步考虑; ③（从液体面上）撇去浮物

[搭配] skim over 掠过, 滑过; skim through 略读, 浏览; skim off 撇去（液体表面的）漂浮物; skim the surface 触及表面

[例句] Birds skimmed (over) the waves looking for food. 鸟儿掠过波浪寻找食物。

I've only skimmed (through/over) his letter. 我只略读了一下他的来信。

She skimmed the cream off the milk. 她撇去了牛奶上的奶油。

[辨析] scan, skim

scan 表示"浏览、粗略地看"篇章文字, 目的在于寻找特定的信息目标;

skim 表示"浏览、略读"篇章文字, 目的在于了解大概内容。

16. veil

[词义] n. ① [C] 面纱, 面罩; ② (sing.) 遮盖物, 掩饰物

v. 遮盖, 掩盖

[搭配] raise/drop/ lower the veil 揭开/拉开/放下面纱; under the veil of 在……掩饰下，假借……之名; draw a veil over 避而不谈，隐瞒

[例句] The bride's face was covered in a white veil. 新娘的脸上蒙着白色的面纱。

A veil of mist covered the woods. 薄雾笼罩着树林。

Dense fog veiled the mountain village. 浓雾笼罩着这个山村。

[派生] veiled *adj.* 以面罩掩盖的，隐藏的; veiling *n.* 面纱布料，帐幔

17. realm

[词义] *n.* [C] 领域，范围，范畴

[搭配] in the realm of 在……的领域里; realm of nature 自然界

[例句] We knew that the music was leading us into new realms of pleasure.
我们知道音乐正引导我们进入新的快乐王国。

18. magic

[词义] *n.* ① [U] 魔法，巫术; ② [U] 魔术，戏法; ③ [U] 魅力，魔力

[例句] The prince was changed into a frog by magic. 王子被魔法变成了一只青蛙。

He'll show you a magic trick. 他会给你表演个魔术。

Although the film was made fifty years ago, it has lost none of its magic.
尽管这部电影摄于50年前，却依然魅力不减。

[派生] magician *n.* 魔术师

[辨析] magic, magical

magic 指会变魔术的，变魔术用的，如: It was a magic stick, and everything it touched turned into gold. 这是一根魔杖，用它一点，任何东西都能变成金的。magical 指用（好像用）魔术变成的，奇妙的，迷人的，如: Her first sight at the Tai Mahal was a magical experience. 她第一次见到泰姬陵的时候好像着了迷似的。

19. bear witness to 对……做出证明，表明

[例句] His neat rooms bear witness to a well-ordered mind.
他那整洁的房间说明了他是一个很有条理的人。

[联想] to 是介词，后面需跟名词、代词或动名词作介词宾语。其他与bear有关的词组还有: bear on/upon sth. 对……有影响; bear down 竭尽全力; bear out 证实; bear with 忍受，容忍。

20. load with 满载着

[例句] The boss loaded her up with extra work. 老板总让她加班，使她超负荷工作。

21. switch on 开（电灯、收音机等），接通（电流）

[例句] Please witch the TV on. 请打开电视机。

[联想] switch off（用开关）关掉

22. out of tune 走调

[例句] The piano is out of tune. 这架钢琴走音了。

[联想] in tune with 与……协调，和谐

23. hold up ①举起，抬起; ②延迟; ③抢劫

[例句] Those who were for the resolution held up their hands.
那些赞成决议的人都把手举了起来。

The ship was held up for two days by the storm. 风暴使船期延迟了两天。

77

It is reported that three men held up a bank last night.

据报道，昨天晚上有名男子抢劫了一家银行。

[联想] hold back ① 阻挡，抑制；② 保守（秘密等），隐瞒

hold down ① 阻止（物价等）上涨；② 保住（工作）

hold on 握住不放，坚持住；hold out 伸出，维持

24. skim the surface 触及表面

[例句] This report has barely skimmed the surface of the problem.

这份报告只是肤浅地涉及了问题。

Ⅲ. 难句解析

1. After a one-hour flight the next morning, we spent the day visiting attractions along with hundreds of other tourists, most of them loaded with cameras and small gifts. (Para.2)

[释义] **attraction** *n.* [C] 旅游胜地

e.g. Buckingham Palace is a major tourist attraction.

白金汉宫是一个主要的旅游胜地。

[分析] "most of them loaded with cameras and small gifts"是一个过去分词的独立主格结构作状语，有其独立的主语 "most of them"。如果变成定语从句，应为 "most of whom were loaded with cameras and small gifts"。

2. Then the truth struck me. (Para.3)

[释义] **strike**（一个主意或想法）突然跃入脑海；对某人留下印象，或产生某种效果

e.g. She was suddenly struck by the thought that she'd left the book on the train.

她突然想起来她把书忘在火车上了

So how does my proposition strike you? 那么你觉得我的建议怎么样?

3. Six young girls appeared, and I described their violet-colored silk skirts, white blouses, and gold-colored hats like small crowns, with flexible points that moved in rhythm with the dance. (Para.14)

[释义] **in rhythm (with)** 与……合拍

e.g. The boat rocked up and down in rhythm with the sea.

船随着海浪上下颠簸。

[分析] "with flexible...the dance"是介词短语，作中心语hats的定语，在这个定语从句中，又包含一个定语从句 "that moved in rhythm with the dance"修饰points，关系代词that作主语。

4. ...and I excused myself...(Para.16)

[释义] **excuse oneself/sb.** 礼貌地请他人允许某人离开

e.g. I excused myself from the dinner table to make a phone call.

我请求离开餐桌去打电话。

5. She shyly extended both hands towards him, the brass fingernails shining in the overhead light. (Para.17)

[分析] "the brass fingernails shining in the overhead light"是现在分词的独立主格结构，独立的逻辑主语 "the brass fingernails"，在句中作状语。

6. A lump formed in my throat. (Para.17)

[释义] I felt the scene very touching.

> **a lump in one's/the throat**（由于感动、悲伤等强烈的感情）而哽咽
>
> e.g. I seized her bony hand with a lump in my throat.
>
> 我握住她骨瘦如柴的手，伤心得哽咽欲泣。

Ⅳ. 重点语法讲解

当短语有自己的逻辑主语，且逻辑主语与主句主语不一致，这种结构叫**独立主格或无依附结构**。短语的主语由作主语的名词或代词来表示，放在短语前面，与短语结构构成逻辑上的主谓关系。

独立主格结构在句中常常作状语，可以表示时间、条件、原因和伴随状况等。这种结构可以是现在分词形式，过去分词形式（名词+形容词）或者名词+介词等形式。如：

Many strange new means of transport have been developed in our country, the strangest of them **being** perhaps the hovercraft.

All flights **having been** cancelled because of the storm, they decided to take the train instead.

Late that year, his novels **published**, he went abroad for vacation.

Everything **taken** into consideration, you'd better put off the plan.

But he stepped forward with no fear sign of hesitation or stoop, **his shoulders squared, his head high**, as though he were guiding me.

Just below her a yellow-haired Scandinavian boy of about five is leaning forward, **his face just below hers**.

Ⅴ. 课文赏析

1. 文体特点

这是一篇记叙文，叙述了作者的亲身经历：在一位盲人的带领下，领略到了生活中他从未感受过的美妙，改变了他的生活态度。文章采用了大量的拟人、比喻等修辞手法，生动有趣，真实感人。结尾和开头形成鲜明的对比，互相呼应，更加深化了文章的主题。

2. 结构分析

Part Ⅰ (Para. 1-2) Going to Thailand accompanying a Chinese business man.

Part Ⅱ (Para. 3-17) Meeting a blind Belgian and describing scenes for him.

Part Ⅲ (Para. 18-21) Going back and recognizing that the blind man helped me see the beautiful world.

Ⅵ. 课后练习答案及解析

Reading Skills

XV.

1. The stack of papers is being personified as sb. who can bear witness to sth.

2. The fact that his eyes were covered with a layer of white coating is described as if the eyes contained a white mist.

3. To steer him is a figurative way of saying "to lead him or to guide him".

4. Western ears symbolize people from western countries.

5. A gallery of human faces symbolizes a gathering of people from many nationalities.

6. As we know a portrait does not have life: it is impossible to say a "living portrait". It is a figurative way of saying "a vivid portrait".

7. The word "like" clearly tells us that these are hats only but are being compared to small crowns.

8. Two tiny birds are clearly a metaphor of the girl's two small hands to show that it was with loving care that the blind man held the girl's hands.

Comprehension of the Text

XVI.

1. even though	2. annoyed	3. struck me	4. out of tune
5. motionless	6. just as	7. hardly	8. satisfaction

Vocabulary

XVII.

1. skimmed 译文：尽管老师只是浏览了一下我的论文，他却说我写得很好。

2. steer 译文：然而克雷森夫人会运用它所有的技巧使她的提案得以在国会通过。

3. chartered 译文：国际援助机构已经租船把物资运到受灾地区去。

4. angle 译文：当然，从那一特定的角度来看整件事是有点可疑。

5. overhead 译文：她所知道的就是她来到花园中的长凳上躺下，那时天已经黑了，头顶上的星星闪闪发光。

6. magic 译文：直到做出科学解释之前，很多人认为照片是魔术变出来的。

7. realm 译文：我们所有人对弗兰克林博士的工作都评价很高。在外科领域，他是无与伦比的。

8. stack 译文：那天，经理忙于处理接连不断的电话和一大堆上面别着紧急处理标签的文件。

XVIII.

1. Only a few crumbling wall bear witness to the past greatness of the city of Aksum.
   译文：只有一些残垣断壁还显示出古城阿克苏姆过去的辉煌。

2. At first he was way ahead of me, but I'm slowly but surely catching him up.
   译文：一开始他远在我前面，但我正在慢慢赶上他。

3. I was loaded with many parcels, unable to walk any faster.
   译文：我带着许多包裹，不能再走快了。

4. The place was deserted and there was no sign of human beings living there.
   译文：这个地方很荒凉，没有人类居住的迹象。

5. These instruments should be switched on and checked before we start our work.
   译文：在我们开始工作之前，应该先开动这些仪器进行检查。

6. My friend was dressed in a black coat whereas I had gone there in jeans.
   译文：我的朋友穿着黑色的外套，而我穿着牛仔裤去那里。

7. All those connected with the mission were in prayer for her, but her life was not spared.
   译文：所有和这一使命有关的人都在为她祈祷，但她还是没能活下来。

8. May I excuse myself/be excused for a while, Mr. Davis?
   译文：戴维斯先生，请原谅，我失陪一会儿。

VII. 参考译文

盲人帮我看到了美妙的世界

已经是下午很晚了，我们驻曼谷公司的主席分配给我一个任务：我必须在第二天出发陪一位重要的中国商人到泰国北部的旅游点。我眼睛瞪着桌子，心里直冒火。桌上成堆的文件足以证明，尽管我一周七天都在工作，可还有大量的工作等着我去做。我真不知道如何才能把这些活儿赶出来。

第二天早晨，坐了一个小时飞机后，我们当天就与其他数以百计的游客一起，参观了一些景点。他们大多数都带着相机，满载着小礼物。我仍记得那天挤在密集的人群中，心里很恼火。

当天晚上我和这位中国伙伴一起坐上了旅游包车去吃晚饭、看表演。那场表演我以前看过许多次了。他跟其他游客聊着天，我则在黑暗中礼貌地跟一位坐在我前面的男士谈话。他是位比利时人，讲一口流利的英语。当时我感到奇怪，为什么他的头一动不动地保持着一个古怪的角度，好像在祷告一样。后来我恍然大悟，他是个盲人。

我身后有人打开了灯，我看到了他浓密的银发，还有方正有力的下巴。他的双眼里似乎有一层白膜。"我吃饭时能坐在您的旁边吗？"他问道。"我很想您能把看到的向我略作介绍。"

"我很乐意，"我回答说。

我的客人与几位新交的朋友径直走进了餐馆，我和这位盲人跟了进去。我用手搀着他的肘部给他领路，但他昂首挺胸地前行，没有丝毫的犹豫或屈从，好像是他在给我带路。

我们找了一张靠近舞台的桌子，他要了半升啤酒，我则要了一杯葡萄汽水。我们正等着饮料时，盲人说："我们西方人听起来这首乐曲似乎变调了，但还是挺有魅力的，您能描述一下奏乐的人吗？"

我并没注意到舞台那头的五个人，他们在奏着演出的开场乐曲。"他们盘着腿坐在小地毯上，身着宽松的白色棉布衬衫和肥大的黑裤，腰系染成鲜红色的布带。他们中三个是年轻小伙子，还有一位中年乐手和一位老年乐手。他们中一个击鼓，另一个奏着木制的弦乐器，另外三个用琴弓拉着一种类似小提琴的小小的乐器。"光线又暗下来，盲人问："您的那些游客们都长什么模样？"

"他们各种国籍、各种肤色都有，体形、个子大小也都不同，简直就是一个人种大聚会，"我低声说。

我把声音压得更低，凑近他的耳朵说话，他也热切地把头靠过来。从来没有人如此强烈地想听我讲话。

"离我们很近的是一位日本老妇人，"我说。"就在她旁边，有一位黄头发的斯堪的纳维亚男孩，大约五岁，身体往前倾，他的脸刚好在妇人的脸下面。他们一动不动，等着演出开始。这真是一幅生动完美的画像，有儿童也有老人，有亚洲也有欧洲。"

"是的，是的，我见到他们了，"盲人微笑着轻声地说。

舞台后部的帷幕打开了，走出六位年轻女孩子。我向他描述她们身着紫罗兰色丝裙，白色外套，头戴形似小皇冠的金色帽子，帽上的饰物随着舞蹈节奏有弹性地跳动着。"她们的手指上有金黄色的指甲，有八厘米长吧，"我告诉盲人。"长指甲使手部的每一个动作都更显得十分优美，效果真好看。"

他微笑着点点头："太美妙了，我真想摸一下那些金黄色的指甲。"

第一个节目结束时，我们刚好吃完甜食，我找了个借口过去与戏院经理搭话。我一回来就告诉我的伙伴："有人请你到后台去。"

几分钟后他站到了其中一位舞蹈演员的身旁，她带着小皇冠的头还不及他胸部那么高。她害羞地将两只手伸向他，黄铜指甲在头顶射下的灯光下闪闪发光。他慢慢地伸出双手，那双手足有女孩的手四倍大，握住了那双小手，就好像捧着两只小鸟一样。他抚摸着那些光滑、呈弧形弯曲的金属尖指甲时，女孩静静地站着，惊奇地注视着他的脸。我不禁哽咽了。

乘出租车回酒店后，我的中国客人仍然与别人在一起。盲人拍拍我的肩膀，把我拉向他，紧紧地拥抱着我。"你帮我看到的一切太美了，"他低声说，"真不知道怎么感谢你。"

后来我想，是我该谢谢他。其实盲的人是我，我看事物只是在表面一掠而过。在这忙碌的世界里，一层快速形成的面纱遮住了我们的双眼，是他帮我揭开了这层面纱，见到了一个以前从未好好欣赏的崭新世界。

此行之后的一周，主席告诉我，那位中国经理来电话说他对旅程非常满意。"干得好，"主席笑着说，"我就知道你会有神奇的表现。"

我无法告诉他，是别人的神奇改变了我。

Section C
Ⅰ．语言点讲解

1. **Total darkness came as a result of a swelling of the nerve leading to his eye — a condition that was unrelated to the eye disease that had limited his vision since birth. (Para. 2)**

   [分析] "a condition that...since birth"是对a swelling of the nerve进一步的解释说明；that引导的是定语从句，修饰condition；"leading to his eyes"是现在分词短语，作the nerve的定语。

2. **Earlier this month, Alberto Torres's wife, who had just been laid off from her job, had to have a breast removed due to cancer...(Para. 4)**

   [释义] **lay off**（因为不景气等）解雇（人员），下岗

   e.g. The manager of this factory was also laid off. 这家工厂的经理也被解雇了。

3. **Before he got the job, Mr. Torres was determined to escape from the workshop run by the Lighthouse, an organization dedicated to help people who can't see, and to try to make it on his own. (Para. 11)**

   [释义] **dedicate** *vt.* (to) 献身，致力于

   e.g. He dedicated his life to the service of his country. 他献身于为国服务。

   [分析] 这句的主干是："Mr. Torres was determined to escape from the workshop and to try to make it on his own."；"run by the Lighthouse"是过去分词短语作定语，表示被动的含义，意思是"由……经营的"；"an organization...can't see"是the Lighthouse的同位语。

4. **The lighthouse people would have much preferred for him to find a job closer to his home. (Para. 12)**

   [释义] **prefer to** 宁愿，更喜欢

e.g. He preferred to die rather than surrender. 他宁死不屈。

He preferred coffee to tea. 和茶比起来，他更喜欢咖啡。

Ⅱ. 课文赏析

1. 文体特点

本文描述了盲人阿尔伯图·多里斯不接受救济，自力更生的事迹。通过对主人公思想活动和话语行为等多处细节描述，真实生动地再现了他身残志坚、乐观向上的意志，具有强烈的震撼力，发人深省。

2. 结构分析

Part I (Para. 1-5) Alberto Torres's bad luck and his optimistic spirit.

Part II (Para. 6-14) A hard job to come by for Alberto Torres and his treasure for the job.

Part III (Para. 15-18) Achievements from a hard job and his active emotion.

Ⅲ. 课后练习答案及解析

XIX. ▶

Reading Skills

1. It is not the world went blank but his eyes that went blank. The world is a substitution of the blind man's eyes.

2. Bad luck is personified here as a stranger. The sentence means that the man is familiar with bad luck.

3. "Good luck" and "dark side" are self-contradictory as being contrary to established fact or practice. But it is used here to the effect that Mr. Torres suffered from one blow after another in his life.

4. Here "get the money" is being compared to "pocket the money" to show that the blind man was entitled to obtain financial help from a pension.

5. Of course here "go into a hole" does not mean physically falling into a hole. It is a comparison of "falling into a difficult situation".

Comprehension of the Text

XX. ▶

C C B A   A B C B

Ⅳ. 参考译文

> **一份来之不易的工作**

您也许会为盲人阿尔伯图·多里斯感到难过，他记得他看到的最后一件事就是13年前他女儿出生的情景，然后世界就变得一片空白。他惟一的孩子——一个10多岁的优等生——现在长什么模样，他只能想像了。

双目失明是由视神经发炎膨胀造成的——这病与他的眼疾无关。自出生起他就有眼疾，视力有限。"我入睡后一觉醒来，什么都看不见了，"他说。

厄运已经不是一次捉弄这位37岁、热心而又体贴的人了。他4岁时，母亲死于癌症；多里斯的父亲时常患病，不得不在他11岁时将他送给政府照顾。后来他到一个工场干了19年活，装配扫帚和其他家庭用品。那真是使人厌烦得要死的工作。这个月初，阿尔伯图·多里斯刚刚失业的妻子，由于患癌症而不得不将一侧乳房切除，而今又面临一年的放射性治疗。事情似乎总是从糟糕透顶变得更加恶化，甚至多里斯先生的好运也总伴随着不幸。五年前，他钟爱的导盲犬把他从卡车前拉了出来，多里斯先生没有受伤，但狗却被撞死了。

但是你要知道，要清楚地知道，多里斯先生并不为自己感到伤心。他说："这些只是生活中必须经历的小小磨难。"

最近，有一天早晨5点钟，我们看到多里斯先生来到了纽约布鲁克林的一个地铁站；此处靠近他的住所：没有电梯的三层楼上的一套公寓。他早晨3点就起来了，喂好他新养的狗，煮好咖啡，准备好一切。他说："人一看不见，做什么事都会费点时间。"

多里斯先生正准备上班，这一路得花两个小时，十分麻烦。他在布朗克斯市立中心医院的急诊放射科干冲洗胶片的工作。他得坐G线列车到皇后广场站，在该站他要先上楼梯，再下楼梯去换乘开往曼哈顿的R线列车。然后他得乘R线在59街下车，再往上走一层楼转搭6号列车。

在上班途中，有时他会与陌生人聊天，有时又有人会拍拍他的狗，直呼其名与他打招呼。人们给他帮助，甚至给他让座。

到了第125街，多里斯先生就要穿过月台去转4号列车。到了第149街后，他就得往下走搭乘2号车，在东180街下车；在这里，他几乎总要花很长时间等他的最后一趟车到帕尔汉大道。从那儿他和他的狗得走20分钟才到医院。

"他们没必要特别为我做什么规定，"多里斯先生说，"这是工作，我应该准时到达。"

这份工作来之不易。得到这份工作之前，他就决心离开"灯塔"所经营的一个工场——"灯塔"是一个专门为盲人提供帮助的机构。他想靠自己的能力去工作。他想干一份冲洗X光胶片的工作，这工作任何人都只能在黑暗中完成。"灯塔"给许多医院打了电话，甚至提出由他们发头三个月的工资，并且提供培训，但都没有结果。

"灯塔"的人本来很想为他找一份离家近一些的工作，但他们相信他有能力做好这份工作，也有能力克服这遥远的路途。"我们的观点是，除了开车以外，盲人完全有能力胜任任何工作。"一位一直在努力帮盲人找工作的"灯塔"员工如是说。

事实上，这也是布朗克斯医院对残疾人的看法。正如医院的副院长所说："我们要看一个人能做什么，而不是看他不能做什么。"

"关键是这种做法行之有效，"医院院长说。

不久前的一天是多里斯先生受聘一周年的日子。他以平日的工作量，冲洗大约150张X光胶片来庆祝这个日子。这些带有名字和数据的胶片，都在右上角折了一下，这样他能正面朝上冲洗它们。这是对他作为盲人的惟一照顾。

多里斯先生单独在一间充满化学药品味、又小又暗的房间里工作。他不能戴手套，因为他必须靠触觉。这是很严格的工作，而且又是在急诊室，生命攸关。他的顶头上司说他百分之百信任他。

多里斯先生每年可挣20,000美元。他本来可以领取12,000多元的抚恤金，但他并不只是为了钱。"如果我开始觉得自己是个受害者，我会很痛苦的。为什么要痛苦呢？"他说。"那样会使你陷入困境，并永远陷在那儿。"

"我并没有做什么非凡的事，"多里斯先生坚决地说，一边利索地干完了手头上的活儿。

五、知识链接

According to the World Health Organization, 37 million people are blind worldwide, and another 124 million have low vision and are at risk of becoming blind. A child goes blind every minute, an adult every 5 seconds.

An estimated 75% of global blindness is treatable and/or preventable, but 90% of the blind live in the poorest areas of the developing world without access to quality eye care at an affordable price.

Of the three million children who suffer from clinical vitamin A deficiency (VAD) , an estimated 250,000-500,000 annually go blind. Most (70%) die within 12 months of losing their sight.

As many as a third of the world's people are affected by micronutrient deficiencies. Six million children under the age of five die needlessly each year as a result of malnutrition. That's one child every 6 seconds.

Despite the gravity of global blindness and malnutrition, solutions have been available for decades. Nearly 75% of all blindness is either preventable or treatable using techniques easily accessible in developed countries. VAD and other micronutrient deficiencies can be tackled through supplementation, food fortification and other food-based programs. In fact, vitamin A supplementation has long been regarded as the most cost-effective public health intervention in the world. Interventions to provide other micronutrients are constantly being innovated to achieve similar cost and operational effectiveness.

根据世界卫生组织的报告，全世界有三千七百万盲人，以及一亿两千四百万弱视者，正面临着失明的危险。每一分钟就有一名儿童失明，每五分钟就有一名成年人失明。

据估计，全球百分之七十五的失明是可治疗的，以及/或者能够预防的。但是百分之九十的盲人居住在发展中国家最贫困的地区，不能得到便宜又优良的眼部治疗。

在三百万患有临床维生素A缺乏症（VAD）的儿童中，估计每年有250,000 到500,000名儿童失明。其中大部分（70%）由于失去视力在十二个月之内死去。

全世界有多达三分之一的人被微量营养素缺乏所影响。由于缺乏微量营养素，每年有六百万五岁以下的儿童不必要地死去。那就是说每六秒钟就有一名儿童死去。

尽管全球失明和营养不良形势严峻，但是几十年来一直都有解决办法可以使用。利用在发达国家容易享用的技术，将近百分之七十五的失明是可预防的或可治疗的。VAD和其他微量营养素缺乏可以通过补充、加强食物以及其他食疗方法来治疗。事实上，维生素A补充一直被认为世界上花费最小、效果最明显的公共健康干预。提供其他微量营养素的干预正在不断被创新以取得同样的花费和操作效果。

六、自测题

1. The mountain's jagged _____ stood out against the darkening sky.
   A. framework   B. skeleton   C. sketch   D. profile
2. The Timber rattlesnake is now on the endangered species list, and is extinct in two eastern states in which it once _____.
   A. thrived   B. swelled   C. prospered   D. flourished

3. The insurance company paid him $10,000 in _____ after his accident.

    A. compensation   B. installment   C. substitution   D. commission

4. The remaining two-thirds of the book _____ the disastrous consequences of unmarried love.

    A. commented   B. dealt   C. accounted   D. highlighted

5. _____ are often paid because of long service, special merit, or injuries received.

    A. Subsidies   B. Allowance   C. Bonuses   D. Pensions

6. There is supposed to be a safety _____ which makes it impossible for trains to collide.

    A. appliance   B. accessory   C. machine   D. mechanism

7. The sign set up by the road _____ drivers to a sharp turn.

    A. alerts   B. refreshes   C. pleads   D. diverts

8. High grades are supposed to _____ academic ability, but John's actual performance did not confirm this.

    A. certify   B. clarify   C. classify   D. notify

9. The mayor was asked to _____ his speech in order to allow his audience to raise question.

    A. constrain   B. conduct   C. condense   D. converge

10. People who live in small towns often seem more friendly than those living in _____ populated areas.

    A. intensely   B. densely   C. abundantly   D. highly

答案与解析

1. **D** profile 轮廓; framework 框架, 结构; skeleton 骨架; sketch 草图

2. **A** thrive (动、植物) 苗壮生长; swell 膨胀; prosper 成功, 繁荣; flourish 兴旺, 成功

3. **A** compensation 赔偿; installment 分期付款中每一次所付的款项; substitution 代替; commission 佣金

4. **D** highlight 突出; comment 评论, 常与on连用; deal 处理, 常与with连用; account 说明

5. **D** pension 养老金, 抚恤金; allowance 津贴; subsidy 补助金; bonus 奖金, 红利

6. **A** appliance 装备, 装置; accessory 配件, 零件; machine 机器; mechanism 机械, 机制

7. **A** alert sb. to sth. 使某人警觉某事; refresh 使 (人) 精神振奋; plead 恳请, 请求; divert 使……转向, 使……转移

8. **A** certify 证明, 证实; clarify 澄清, 阐明; classify 分类; notify 通告

9. **C** condense 压缩, 缩短; constrain 压抑, 抑制; conduct 引导, 指导 converge 会合, 趋同

10. **B** densely 密集地, 稠密地; intensely 强烈地, 极度地; abundantly 丰富地, 充裕地; highly 高度地, 非常

Unit 4

1 学习重点和难点

词汇和短语、语法项目、写作技巧

2 文化知识

课文大背景、课文知识点

3 课文精讲

词汇与短语详解、难句解析、重点语法讲解、课文赏析、课后练习答案及解析、参考译文、写作指导

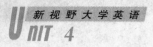

一、预习重点

1. How important is the telecommunications revolution?
2. What are the advantages and disadvantages of the information superhighway?
3. What should we do to protect privacy in the information Age?

Ⅰ. 词汇和短语

Section A: telecommunications, dumb, utility, optical, parade, condense, intensive, desperate, lick, strategic, recession, log, stake, lease, reliable, disposal, revenues, persist; (be) stuck with, a matter of sth./doing sth., date from, be stuck in, scratch the surface, log on to, keep pace with, lag behind

Section B: edition, tutor, feedback, transmit, carrier, hence, dose, correspondent, vacuum, synthetic, crucial, diagram, portion, insure, terminal; sign up, refer to, be compared to, come up with, in the hands of, have access to, rely on, fall behind, devote to

Ⅱ. 语法项目

① 倍数增减的表达方式
② 现在分词的用法

Ⅲ. 写作技巧

比较对照法

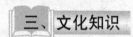

Ⅰ. 课文大背景

> **Telecommunications 电讯**

Telecommunications, from Greek, means "communications at a distance". Telecommunications through voice, data, and image communication is changing the world. The ease of accessing information and people anywhere at anytime is having major impacts on society, business, and finance. Two major trends have occurred in the technology that is applicable to telecommunications. The first trend has been the incredible increase in the processing power of digital computers, namely, dramatic decreases in physical size along with equally dramatic increases in complexity, speed, and capacity. The second trend has been the explosive growth in transmission capacity through the widespread use of optical fiber across continents and under oceans. These two trends have had impressive long-term consequences for telecommunications around the world. The Internet and the World Wide Web have already created a global system for the access of information. It has become popular that people check flight, weather, and hotels before traveling to a foreign country. E-mail makes it easy to keep in contact instantly with colleagues and friends around the globe. But many of the peoples of the world do not even have a telephone, much less access to the Internet and the information. The challenge to the telecommunications industry is to bridge the digital gap and extend the availability of telecommunications to all parts of the planet.

Ⅱ. 课文知识点

1. information age 信息时代

When we say that we live in the information age, we mean that we live in a time when information is very important and easy to get. The information age is an era of fundamental and global change in intellectual, philosophical, cultural and social terms. Today's information age began with the telegraph. It was the first instrument to transform information into electrical form and transmit it reliably over long distances. New techniques of encoding and distributing digital information are pacing the spread of the information age throughout society.

2. optical fiber 光纤

Optical fiber (or "fiber optic") often refers to the medium and the technology associated with the transmission of information as light pulses along a glass or plastic wire or fiber. Optical fiber carries much more information than conventional copper wire and is in general not subject to electromagnetic interference and the need to retransmit signals. Most telephone company long-distance lines are now of optical fiber. Transmission on optical fiber wire requires repeater at distance intervals. The glass fiber requires more protection within an outer cable than copper. For these reasons and because the installation of any new wiring is labor-intensive, few communities yet have optical fiber wires or cables from the phone company's branch office to local customers (known as local loop). Single mode fiber is used for longer distances; multimode fiber is used for shorter distances.

3. information superhighway 信息高速公路

A name first used by (former) U.S. Vice President Al Gore for the vision of a global, high-speed communications network that will carry voice, data, video, and other forms of information all over the world, and that will make it possible for people to send email, get up-to-the-minute news, and access business, government and educational information. The Internet is already providing many of these features, via telephone networks, cable TV services, online service providers, and satellites. In the U.S., the information superhighway is also known as National Information Infrastructure. The information superhighway can be understood to be a highway which has computer technology and modern communication technology serving as the base of the road and fiber-optic cables serving as the surface of the road. The "vehicles" are the multimedia machines equipped with computer, television and telephone, and high speed transmission and exchange of various multimedia information forms the web covering the whole nation. If the national superhighways all over the world are linked together, the global information superhighway will be created.

4. BellSouth Corporation 南方贝尔电话公司

BellSouth is a telecommunications company in the U.S. that mainly serves the southern states. Its business ranges from voice (such as local and long-distance telephone and wireless) to data

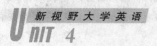

(computer networks) services.

5. Beauty and the Beast《美女与野兽》

Beauty and the Beast was written at the beginning of the 19th century by a Russian writer— Petjerski. It immediately became one of the most popular and exciting fairy tales ever since. Many creators in different facets of the arts have used it, whether in theatre, cinema, opera, musical as well as animation. This classic love story with a definite moral and message has enchanted audiences throughout the ages. The author of the fairy tale wanted to say that every human being has a beast in him. We sometimes behave like beasts to others because of hate, anger, etc. But it takes love and kindness to change even a beast into a beautiful being.

6. Social Security Number 社会保障号码

Social Security Number in the U.S. is similar to Personal Identification Number in China. When Social Security Numbers were first issued in 1936, the U.S. federal government assured the public that use of the numbers would be limited to Social Security programs. Today, however, the Social Security Number (SSN) is the most frequently used record-keeping number in the United States. SSNs are used for employee files, medical records, health insurance accounts, credit and banking accounts, university ID cards, and many other purposes.

四、课文精讲

Section A

Ⅰ. 词汇与短语详解

1. telecommunications

[词义] *n.* [U] 电信，远距离通信

[例句] The telecommunications industry is developing fast in recent years.
近年来电信业发展迅速。

2. dumb

[词义] *adj.* 哑的，不会说话的

[例句] He was struck dumb with fear. 他吓得说不出话来。

[派生] dumbbell *n.* 哑铃; dumbness *n.* 无言，沉默

3. utility

[词义] *n.* ① [C] 公用事业，公用事业设施；② [U] 功用，效用，利用

[搭配] of no utility 没用的，无益的; from the point of view of practical utility 从实用观点出发

[例句] Railroads, bus lines, gas and electric companies are public utilities.
铁路、公共汽车、煤气和电力公司都是公用事业。
Some kitchen tools have very little utility. 有些厨房用具几乎没有什么用处。

[派生] utilize *v.* 利用; utilizable *adj.* 可利用的

4. optical

[词义] *adj.* ① 光学的，光的；② 视力的，视觉的，眼睛的

[例句] Telescopes and microscopes are optical instruments.
望远镜和显微镜都是光学仪器。

She was born with an optical defect. 她天生有视觉障碍。

[派生] optic *adj.* 眼睛的，视觉的；optician *n.* 光学仪器商，眼镜商

5. parade

[词义] *n.* ① [C] 一连串，一批；② [C]（庆祝）游行，检阅

[搭配] be on parade 在游行；a dress parade 阅兵典礼；parade the troops 检阅军队

[例句] There are an endless parade of advertisements on the TV.
电视里有一连串没完没了的广告。
The small boy loves watching the soldiers on parade.
这个小男孩喜欢看士兵的检阅队伍。

[辨析] demonstrate, march, parade
demonstrate, march均指抗议、示威游行，前者更常用、更正式一些，且侧重其集会的有组织性，而后者侧重行动本身；parade 可指"游行、检阅、阅兵"，主要以庆祝、展示为目的。

6. condense

[词义] *v.* ① 缩短，压缩；②（使）冷凝

[搭配] condense sth. into... 压缩/浓缩成……；condensed milk 炼乳

[例句] I tried to condense the essay into ten pages. 我试图把论文缩短成十页。
Steam condenses into water when it touches a cold surface.
蒸气接触冷的表面就凝成水珠。

[辨析] compress, condense
compress意为"压缩、压紧"，表示通过外力的作用，对形状不确定的东西进行挤压而使之形成固定的形状或使范围变小；condense 意为"浓缩、压缩、简缩"，指增加某物的密度或浓度，含有精简，提炼的意思，但保持其原有本质；当condense表示"缩短、压缩"时，可与compress互换。

7. intensive

[词义] *adj.* 密集的，集中的，加强的

[搭配] intensive training 强化训练；intensive reading 精读；intensive care 特别护理

[例句] A lot of farming techniques have been abandoned because they were too labor-intensive. 许多农业技术因过于劳动密集而被放弃了。

[派生] intensify *v.*（使）增强，（使）加剧；intensity *n.* 强烈、剧烈，强度

[联想] intense *adj.* 强烈的，剧烈的，紧张的

8. desperate

[词义] *adj.* ① 极度需要的，非常想要的；② 拼死的，铤而走险的，绝望的

[搭配] a desperate remedy 最后/非常手段；a desperate enemy 作困兽之斗的敌人；a desperate situation 严重的形势

[例句] They are desperate for help. 他们极需要帮助。
The doctors made one last desperate attempt to save the boy's life.
为挽救男孩的生命，大夫们做了最后一次努力。

[派生] despair *n.* 绝望 *vi.* 失去希望；desperation *n.* 绝望，自暴自弃；desperado *n.* 亡命之徒，暴徒

[辨析] desperate, hopeless
desperate 正式用词，意为"绝望的"，表示因身处绝境、毫无希望而不顾

一切，铤而走险；hopeless 常用词，意为"没有希望的"，即可表示本身没有前途、令人失去希望的，也可表示对他人不抱希望，而甘愿忍耐可能发生的一切。

9. lick

[词义] *vt.* ① 击败，克服；② 舔

[搭配] lick off/away 舔掉；lick up 舔尽

[例句] The computer people seem to have licked the problem.
电脑人员看起来已经克服了这个问题。
The dog licked her hand. 那条狗舔了舔她的手。

[派生] lickerish *adj.* 讲究吃的，贪婪的

10. strategic

[词义] *adj.* 战略的

[例句] The company discussed the strategic marketing factors for the coming year.
公司讨论了来年的战略性市场因素。

[派生] strategy *n.* 策略，战略；strategize *vi.* 制定战略、策略

[联想] tactic *n.* 战术；tactical *adj.* 战术的

11. recession

[词义] *n.* [C] 经济衰退

[例句] Many businesses are failing because of the continuing recession.
由于经济持续衰退，许多公司都倒闭了。

[派生] recess *n.* 休息，放假；recessive *adj.* 后退的，逆行的

12. scratch

[词义] *vt.* 抓，搔，划

[搭配] scratch a match 擦火柴；without a scratch 安然无恙，完好无损

[例句] His scratohed the insect bit on his leg with his nails.
他用指甲在腿上搔虫咬的地方。
Be careful not to scratch yourself on the roses. 当心不要被玫瑰刺扎伤。

13. log

[词义] *v.* ① 记载；② 砍伐
n. ① [C] 原木，木料；② [C] 航海（或飞行）日志

[搭配] log in/out 进入/退出计算机系统

[例句] They have logged more than 90 complaints. 他们已经记录了90余例投诉。
The forest has been so heavily logged that it is in danger of disappearing.
森林被严重砍伐，面临毁灭的危险。
The cabin was built of logs. 这个小屋是用原木造的。
The captain described the accident in the ship's log.
船长在航海日志中描述了这次事故。

[辨析] log, timber, wood
log 指从树上砍伐下来但未经过深加工的"原木、圆形木材"；timber 作不可数名词时，指可作建材用的生长中的"树木、林木"，作可数名词时，指经过加工的用于建造房屋、桥梁等的"大木料、栋木"，或指木板、木条等的"木料"；wood 常用词，可指用于各种目的的"木头、木材、木柴"，强调材料的木质。

14. stake

[词义] *n.* ① (sing.) 股份，利益关系；② [C] 桩，标桩

[搭配] at stake 濒临危险；have a stake in sth. 与某事有利害关系

[例句] He holds a 40% stake in the company. 他在这家公司拥有40%的股份。

Joan of Arc was burned at the stake. 圣女贞德被烧死在火刑柱上。

[辨析] share, stake, stock

share指的是被平均分成若干股的股权中的"一股"，在英国英语中可指"股票"；stake意为"股本、股份"，指投机生意等的巨大利益分成；stock指一般说的"股票"，在英国英语中，the stock指国债总额。

15. lease

[词义] *v.* 租借，出租；*n.* [C] 租约

[搭配] by/on lease 以租借的方式；lease sth. from sb. 从某人那里租借某物；lease sth. to sb. 把某物租给某人

[例句] We have leased an apartment for one year. 我们已租到一套公寓，租期为一年。

He has the flat on a long lease. 他长期租用该公寓。

16. reliable

[词义] *adj.* 可靠的，可依赖的，值得信赖的

[例句] It's not reliable to judge one person only by his appearances.

单凭外貌来判断一个人是不可靠的。

[派生] rely *vi.* 依靠，依赖；reliance *n.* 依靠，依赖；reliability *n.* 可靠性

17. usage

[词义] *n.* ① [U] 使用，对待方式；② [U] 用法

[例句] The radio is designed for rough usage. 这个收音机是为耐用而设计的。

The earliest recorded usage of the word is in the twelfth century.

最早有关该词用法的记录见于12世纪。

[辨析] usage, use

usage 指的是使用处理或处理的方法；当作用法时，特指习惯性的或约定俗成的做法，是指词语的惯用法。如：It's not a word of common usage. 这个词不是普通常用词。use 是常用词，意为"使用，运用"。如：I use my bike to go shopping. 我买东西时骑自行车去。

18. disposal

[词义] *n.* ① [U] 支配权，处置权；② [U] 处理，消除

[搭配] at one's disposal 任某人处理，供某人使用；a waste-disposal unit 废品处置部门；the disposal of business affairs 处理商业事务

[例句] During your visit, I will put my room at your disposal.

在你来访期间我会把我的房间给你用。

Please see to the disposal of that rubbish. 请负责处理掉那堆废物。

[派生] dispose *vt.* 排列，布置 *vi.* 去除，除掉，处理，解决；disposition *n.* 性情，性格，排列，部署；disposable *adj.* 可任意处置的

[辨析] disposal, disposition

disposal 侧重于表示把某物"处理掉"，其方式可以是"卖"、"白送"或者是"毁掉"等。如：the disposal to the jewels 珠宝的处理；disposition 侧重

93

于把物品整齐排列起来，如：disposition of the furniture 布置家具。

19. revenue

[词义] *n.* [U]（政府的）岁入，税收，（公司的）收入

[搭配] revenue tax 财政税；a revenue stamp 印花税票；a revenue officer 税务员；
revenue charge/expenditure 营业支出/收益支出

[例句] The government got much revenue from taxes last year.
政府去年从税收中获得大量收入。

[派生] revenuer *n.* 税务官员；revenual *adj.* 税收上的

20. persist

[词义] *v.* 坚持不懈，执意

[搭配] persist in sth./doing sth. 坚持做某事；persist with 坚持不懈

[例句] You could never expect to master the heart persisting in leaving.
你永远征服不了执意要离开的心。

[派生] persistence *n.* 坚持，持续；persistent *adj.* 坚持不懈的，持续的

21. (be) stuck with 无法摆脱，解脱不了

[例句] I'm always stuck with that nightmare. 我总是摆脱不了那个梦魇。

[联想] stick with 意为"缠住，萦绕，继续忠于（支持）"，如：stick with crowds 混
在人群中；stick with one's old friends 仍然忠于老朋友。

22. a matter of sth./doing sth. 需要……的问题，需要……的事情

[例句] It's a matter of life and death, so we should handle it with care.
这是件生死攸关的事，我们应该慎重处理。

23. date from 始于

[例句] Our friendship dates from middle school days. 我们的友谊始于中学时代。

[联想] date back 回溯至；out of date 过时的

24. be stuck in 陷入

[例句] We were stuck in traffic for over an hour. 我们被交通堵塞困了一个多小时。

25. scratch the surface 触及表面

[例句] We left feeling that we had just scratched the surface of this fascinating country.
我们离开这个神奇的国家时，觉得只了解了她表面的一些东西。

26. log on to 进入（计算机）系统，登录

[例句] You need a password to log on to the system. 你要有密码才能登录该系统。

27. keep pace with 与……齐步前进

[例句] It's important for us to keep pace with the development of the society.
与社会发展齐步并进对于我们来说很重要。

28. lag behind 落后，落在……后面

[例句] We still lag far behind many countries in using modern technology.
在应用先进技术方面，我们仍落后于许多国家。

Ⅱ. 难句解析

**1. A transformation is occurring that should greatly boost living standards in
the developing world. (Para. 1)**

[释义] A change is taking place that should greatly improve and promote standards of living
of the developing countries.

boost *v.* ① 增强，提高；② 大力推广

e.g. Getting that job did a lot to boost his confidence.

得到那份工作大大增强了他的自信。

Her books have been boosted in The Observer recently.

她的书近来得到了《观察者》杂志的推介。

2. All these developing regions see advanced communications as a way to leap over whole stages of economic development. (Para. 2)

[释义] All these developing regions regard directly acquiring and making use of up-to-date communications as a way to catch up with the advanced countries economically.

leap over 跳跃过……

e.g. The dog leapt over the hedge into the field. 那条狗跃过篱笆奔向田野。

3. Widespread access to information technologies, for example, promises to condense the time required to change from labor-intensive assembly work to industries that involve engineering, marketing, and design. (Para. 2)

[释义] A great number of opportunities of using information technologies, for example, will make it possible to lesson or shorten the time needed to change from labor-intensive assembly work to industries that involve engineering marketing, and design.

[分析] 句子的主干是：Widespread access to information technologies promises to condense the time。"required to change...and design" 是过去分词短语作定语从句，修饰 the time，在这个定语从句中，又包含一个定语从句 "that involve engineering, marketing, and designing"，修饰 industries。

4. Many experts think Vietnam is going too far by requiring that all mobile phone be expensive digital models, when it is desperate for any phones, period. (Para. 3)

[释义] **go too far** 做得过火，走极端

e.g. Sometimes you go too far and say hurtful things.

有时候你做得太过分了，而且说一些伤人的话。

period *n.* 原意为句号，经常用于一种观点的后面，表示就此话题的观点已阐述完了，不愿就此话题再发表意见。

e.g. We are all against the proposal, period. 我们都反对这个建议，我说完了。

[分析] "that all mobile phone be expensive digital models" 是一个省略了 that 的虚拟语气，因为前面的动词是 require，类似用法的词还有 demand, request, suggest 等。

5. To lick the problem, Russia is starting to install optical fiber and has a strategic plan to pump $40 billion into various communications projects. (Para.4)

[释义] To overcome this problem, Russia is beginning to install optical fiber and has a strategic plan to put $40 billion into various communications projects in order to make these projects successful.

pump (money) into (sth.) 投资

e.g. They had been pumping money into the business for some years without seeing any results. 几年来他们在这项生意中投入了大量资金，却看不到任何成果。

6. To offer peak performance in providing the electronic data and paperless trading global investors expect, Shanghai plans telecommunications networks as those in Manhattan. (Para.6)

[分析] "To offer...investors expect" 引导的是目的状语从句，在这个状语从句中，"global investors expect" 是省略了关系代词that的定语从句，修饰the electronic date and paperless trading。

7. ...Hungary has leased rights to a Dutch-Scandinavian group of companies to build and operate what it says will be one of the most advanced digital mobile phone systems in the world. (Para.7)

[分析] "what it says" 是 "to build and operate" 的宾语，"it says" 是插入成分，意为"据说"，it 指代前面提到的Dutch-Scandinavian group of company。

8. Wireless demand and usage have also exploded across the entire width and breadth of Latin America. (Para. 8)

[释义] There is a sudden popularity of mobile phones all over the countries in Latin America.

Ⅲ. 重点语法讲解

倍数增减的表达方式

1. 倍数+形容词/副词比较级+than

He is **twice heavier than** his brother. 他是他弟弟的两倍重。

Computers can work **500,000 times faster than** any person can.

计算机的速度是人类的五十万倍。

2. 倍数+as+形容词/副词+as

John's house is **three times as big as** ours. 约翰的房子是我们的三倍大。

The output of the factory increased **fours times as great as** that of last year.

这家工厂的产量比去年增加了三倍。/……是去年的四倍。

3. 倍数+名词

The earth is **49 times the size of** the moon. 地球是月亮的49倍大。

The pine tree is **twice the height of** the building. 这个松树是这个楼房的两倍高。

4. 动词+百分比或倍数

The personal income this year **rose 10%**. 今年的个人收入增加了百分之十。

The loss of metal has been **reduced to 5 times**. 金属损耗减少到原先的五分之一。

5. 动词+by+数词/百分比/倍数

Investment in this project will be **reduced by US $3 million**.

对这个项目的投资将会减少三百万美元。

The total volume of municipal expenses in the first half year **rose by 3.5 percent**, compared with the same period of last year. 和去年同期相比，市政府上半年的花销增长了百分之3点5。

Ⅳ. 课文赏析

1. 文体特点

这是一篇议论文（argumentation），作者在文章的结构安排上使用了议论文常用的总—分—总的结构。围绕电信革命这一中心从不同方面进行论述，包括电信技术的优点、发展中国家遇到的问题和应对方法，最后得出结论。文章层次分明，语言简洁客观。在论证过程中，主要运用例证法和比较对照法，举例说明电信革命过程中的问题，通过互相对比各国的不同情况，增强了文章的逻辑性和针对性。

2. 结构分析

Part I (Para. 1-2) The overwhelming advantages of telecommunications revolution for developing countries.

Part II (Para. 3) How fast to develop telecommunications technologies in developing countries.

Part III (Para. 4-10) Different countries solve different problems and have different solutions.

Part IV (Para. 11) Conclusion: One day the developing countries can catch up with Americans and western Europeans in telecommunications technologies if they persist in their efforts.

V. 课后练习答案及解析

Vocabulary

Ⅲ.

1. recession 译文：经济衰退使得托马斯公司的无线电话客户大大减少，变卖多余财产所得的利润也几乎没有了。

2. disposal 译文：在未来几天里，美国人将丢掉大约3,500万棵圣诞树，这将造成城市垃圾处理的一个大难题。

3. condensed 译文：作者将大量资料压缩到仅仅400多页，并以合理的、可读的风格表述出来。

4. strategic 译文：缺乏战略性眼光以及客户针对性不强是这家移动通讯公司面临的另外两大主要问题。

5. revenue 译文：你年收入的百分之几用来交纳政府税收？

6. persist 译文：如果你总是打扰我的话，我就绝对不可能有足够的时间完成你说你急于得到的画。

7. utilities 译文：因建公共设施我们每天都要挖掘路面，今天我要宣布我们将结束这些未经协调的、效率低下的施工工作。

8. desperate 译文：发展现代通讯对越南来说是绝对必要的，因为相对于那些使用旧技术的国家来说，这将成为越南的巨大优势。

Ⅳ.

1. lags far behind 译文：在现代技术的应用方面，我们公司仍然落后于其他竞争对手。

2. are stuck with 译文：他们暂时不得不使用旧技术，但不久他们就会采用新技术。

3. going for 译文：通过寻求最先进的技术，上海意在使自己成为世界一流的金融中心。

4. remain in contact 译文：他们这些年虽然没见过面，但一直有书信来往。

5. keep pace with 译文：我们必须确保跟上计算机技术的新发展，否则不久我们就会落伍。

6. at your disposal 译文：教授答应将她的办公室和电脑供你使用一整年。

7. dates from 译文：他们发现这座大楼最古老的部分可以追溯到十六世纪早期。

8. only scratch the surface of 译文：还有很多事情要做——他们所有的钱只能解决一小部分问题。

Collocation

Ⅴ.

1. sales 译文：许多产品广告都使用名人如电视明星、体育明星来促销。

2. health 译文：他们把增进健康和帮助预防疾病放在首位。

3. will 译文：我们将利用海外援助来促进政府良好意愿的实现、合理经济政策的实施以及对人权尊重的深入。

4. trade 译文：我们将更广泛、更公平地同贫穷国家做贸易以发展其经济并使其经济多元化。

5. education 译文：教育部长的职责是提高人民教育水平，逐步发展以此为目的的教育机构并确保全国每个地区都可以提供综合教育服务。

6. growth 译文：良好的饮食应该保持健康，提供能量，促进生长。

7. understanding 译文：学生应该被鼓励以他们乐于接受的方式回应各种文学形式，这将提高他们的理解力。

8. idea 译文：他们的一个重要职责就是在社区里为学校开展的工作与活动的每一方面宣传平等的概念。

Word Building

▶ **VI.** ▶

1. superpower 译文：美国被认为是当今的军事、经济强国。

2. superabundant 译文：我们今年苹果大丰收，我真不知道如何处理它们。

3. supermarket 译文：一个新超市刚刚开张，你几乎能在那里买到你需要的任何东西。

4. super-speed 译文：据报道，上海将在地铁二号线的龙阳路站和浦东机场之间兴建超高速磁悬浮列车，乘客在6至7分钟内可达到目的地。

5. super-computers 译文：最近超级电脑的功能已被运用于发展医学。

6. superman 译文：只有超人才能使公司摆脱目前的医学领域。

7. superstar 译文：尽管她是好莱坞的超级明星，但她平易近人，生活俭朴。

8. super-efficient 译文：科学家在实验室里已成功地使足球状的碳分子在相对温暖的环境下像超导体一样运动，这增加了制造更快、更有效的计算机的希望。

▶ **VII.** ▶

1. auto-timer 译文：刚才停电了，你得重新设置炊具上的自动计时器。

2. auto-racing 译文：看过赛车比赛的人都知道多数的刺激来自于显而易见的危险。

3. auto-focus 译文：这台照相机很容易使用，因为它有自动对焦功能。

4. autograph 译文：他把我错当成麦当娜，向我索要签名。

5. auto-reverse 译文：去年格伦蒂承诺推出一款自动回转机，可以24小时连续录制电台节目，但这种机器一直没出现。

6. autopilot 译文：调查显示飞机坠毁时处于自动驾驶状态。

7. autobiography 译文：这部电视连续剧是根据新西兰作家珍妮特•弗雷姆的自传拍摄的。

8. auto-industry 译文：根据汽车工业的预测，这家公司明年必须更加努力地工作才能挺过去。

Structure

▶ **VIII.** ▶

1. Concentrated on indoor delights rather than outdoor fights and you will be much better appreciated.

   译文：注重室内娱乐而不是户外打斗，你会得到更好的赏识。

2. As a result of the development of the information superhighway many people may

eventually be able to work at home rather than go to an office.

译文：由于信息高速公路的发展，很多人最终能够在家工作而不用去办公室。

3. some people say that this term pupils' achievements will be measured by a formal test rather than by their teacher's assessment.

译文：有些人说，这学期学生的成绩将由一次正式的考试而不是由老师的评价来测评。

4. They argued that their products should be developed on the basis of need rather than profit.

译文：他们主张产品开发应以需要为基础而不是利润。

5. During weekends the businessmen may spend some time establishing friendship and mutual trust rather than discussing any particular item of business.

译文：在周末，生意人通常会花一些时间来建立友谊和相互之间的信任，而不是讨论任何特定的生意项目。

IX.

1. Petrol now is twice as expensive as it was a few years ago.

译文：汽油价格长得太快了。现在汽油的价格是几年前的两倍。

2. Theirs is about three times as big as ours.

译文：你去过他们家吗? 他们的屋子是我们的两倍大。

3. Latin American customers talk two to four times as long on the phone as people in North America.

译文：公司预计，同美国国内客户年平均收入860美元相比，拉丁美洲的年收入大约是每个客户2,000美元，其中部分原因是：拉丁美洲电话客户的通话时间是北美洲人的两倍。

4. the fee for cell phones is typically as much as for calls made over fixed lines.

译文：尽管移动电话的资费通常是固定电话费的两倍，他们仍然十分受欢迎，特别是在年轻人当中。

5. can transmit 250,000 times as much data as a standard telephone wire.

译文：光纤电缆是容量巨大的高效信息载体，可以通过玻璃光纤传送高达标准电话线25万倍的数据。

Translation

X.

1. By installing the latest wireless transmission systems, a parade of urban centers and industrial zones from Beijing to Budapest are stepping directly into the Information Age.

2. Widespread access to information technology promises to condense the time required to change from labor-intensive assembly work to industries that involve engineering, marketing and design.

3. Modern communications will give countries like China and Vietnam a huge advantage over countries stuck with old technologies.

4. There is little dispute that communications will be a key factor separating the winners from the losers.

5. The economy of the country is stuck in recession and it barely has the money to scratch the surface of the problem.

6. Businesses eager for reliable service are willing to pay a significantly high price tag for a

wireless call.

7. Having an operation there is like having an endless pile of money at your disposal.

8. For countries that have lagged behind for so long, the temptation to move ahead in one jump is hard to resist.

XI.

1. 一个将会大大提高发展中国家生活水准的转变正方兴未艾。

2. 所有这些发展中地区都把先进的通信技术看作一种能跨越经济发展诸阶段的方法。

3. 问题是，它的国内电话系统是一堆生了锈的20世纪30年代的老古董。

4. 通信工程也是上海实现其成为一流金融中心这一梦想的关键。

5. 整个拉丁美洲对无线通信的需求和使用已急速增加。

6. 泰国也在求助于无线通信方式，以便让泰国人在发生交通堵塞时更好地利用时间。

7. 移动电话在商界成为时尚，使人们在交通堵塞时也能与外界保持联系。

8. 总有一天，他们将能在信息高速公路上与美国和西欧并驾齐驱。

Essay Summary

XII.

DABCA BDADB DADAC BADCA

Text Structure Analysis

XIII.

1. A strong educational system in mathematics and science.

2. advantage of its backwardness because new technologies are even cheaper than copper wire systems.

3. to pump $40 billion into various communications projects

4. it barely has the money to even scratch the surface of the problem

5. China's major cities are getting the basic infrastructure to become major parts of the information superhighway

to realize its dream of becoming a top financial center

VI. 参考译文

电信革命

　　一个将会大大提高发展中国家生活水准的转变正方兴未艾。一些不久前还是信息闭塞的地方正在快速获得最新的通信技术，这将促进当地对国内外投资的吸纳。亚洲、拉丁美洲和东欧的许多国家也许需要10年的时间来改善其交通、电力供应和其他公用设施。但是单单一根直径小于半毫米的光纤电缆就可以比由铜丝制成的粗电缆负载更多的信息。由于安装了光纤电缆、数字转换器和最新的无线传输系统，从北京到布达佩斯的一系列城区和工业区正在直接跨入信息时代。一个蛛网般的数字和无线通信网络已经伸展到亚洲的大部分地区和东欧的部分地区。

　　所有这些发展中地区都把先进的通信技术看作一种能跨越经济发展诸阶段的方法。例如，信息技术的广泛应用有望缩短从劳动密集型的组装工业转向涉及工程、营销、设计等产业所需的时间。现代通信技术将使像中国、越南那样的国家与那些困于旧技术的国家相比拥有巨大的优势。

　　这些国家应以多快的速度向前发展是人们争论的一个问题。许多专家认为，越南在目前急需电话的情况下，却要求所有的移动电话都必须是昂贵的数字型电话的做法就是太超前了。一位专家说，"这些国家缺乏估算成本和选择技术的经验。"

然而毋庸争辩，通信技术将是区分赢家和输家的关键因素。看一看俄罗斯的情况吧。由于其坚实的数学和科学教育基础，它应该在信息时代有繁荣的发展。问题是，它的国内电话系统是一堆生了锈的20世纪30年代的老古董。为了解决这一问题，俄国已经开始铺设光纤电缆，并制定了投入400亿美元建设多种通信工程的战略计划。但是由于其经济陷于低迷，几乎没有资金来着手解决最基本的问题。

与俄国相比，在未来10年中，中国大陆计划对通信设备投入1,000亿美元。从某种意义上说，中国的落后成了一种有利因素，因为这一发展正好发生在新技术比铜线电缆系统更便宜的时候。到1995年底，中国除了西藏以外的省会都将有数字转换器和高容量的光纤网。这意味着其主要城市正获得必需的基础设施，成为信息高速公路的主要部分，使人们能够进入系统，获得最先进的服务。

通信工程也是上海实现其成为一流金融中心这一梦想的关键。为了能给国际投资者提供其所期望的电子数据和无纸化交易的出色服务，上海计划建设与曼哈顿的网络同样强大的远程通信网络。

与此同时，匈牙利也希望跃入互联网世界。目前有70万匈牙利人等着装电话。为了部分地解决资金问题，加速输入西方技术，匈牙利将国有电话公司30%的股权出售给了两家西方公司。为进一步减少电话待装户，匈牙利已将权利出租给一家荷兰-斯堪的纳维亚企业集团，来建造并经营一个据说是世界上最先进的数字移动电话系统。事实上，无线方式是在发展中国家快速建起电话系统的最受欢迎的方式之一。建造无线电发射塔要比翻山越岭架设线路更便宜。而且，急切想得到可靠服务的企业乐于花费可观的高价来换取无线电话——通常是固定线路电话资费的二至四倍。

整个拉丁美洲对无线通信的需求和使用已急速增加。对于无线电话服务商来说，没有任何地方的业务比拉丁美洲更好了——在那里有一个营运点就好像有一堆无穷无尽供你使用的钞票。在四个无线电话市场有营运点的贝尔南方电话公司估计它的年收入约为平均每个客户2,000美元，与之相比，在美国国内的收入是860美元。产生这种情况的部分原因是拉丁美洲客户的通话时间是北美洲人的二至四倍。

泰国也在求助于无线通信方式，以便让泰国人在发生交通堵塞的时候更好地利用时间。而且在泰国，从办公室往外打电话或发传真并不那么容易：待装电话的名单上有一、二百万个名字。因此移动电话在商界成为时尚，使人们在交通堵塞时也能与外界保持联系。

越南正在做出一个最大胆的跳跃。尽管越南人均年收入只有220美元，它计划每年增加的30万条线路将全部为有数字转换的光纤电缆，而不是那些以铜线传送电子信号的廉价系统。由于现在就选用了下一代的技术，越南负责通信的官员说他们能够在数十年中与亚洲的任何一个国家保持同步。

对于那些长期落后的国家来说，一跃而名列前茅的诱惑难以抵御。而且，尽管他们会犯错误，他们仍会坚持不懈——总有一天，他们将能在信息高速公路上与美国和西欧并驾齐驱。

VII. 写作指导

当我们要了解两项或多项事物的异同之处时，比较对照是一种常用且非常有效的方法。以一种人们熟悉的事物来描述和说明另一种人们尚不很熟悉的事物，通常是比较对照法的核心。比较（comparison）是把两个事物的共同找出来，而对照（contrast）则是着重于两个事物的、观念之间的差异。但这两种方法通常有机地结合在一起。

在进行比较对照时，通常有两种模式可选。如果较为宏观地观察两个事物，可采用纵向的个别事物观察法：即先观察A事物的各点，在观察B事物的各点；如果需要微观地对照两个事物，也就是说这两个事物较复杂，细节很多，则宜采用横向的共同观察法，即先观察A事物的第一点，对照比较B事物的第一点；然后再观察A事物的第二点，对照比较B事物的第二点，以此类推。

范例：

Telecommunications have made a world of difference in the life today. Many countries including countries in Asia, Latin American and Eastern Europe are rapidly acquiring up-to-date telecommunications technologies.

At first, compared with the former cable made of copper wires, a single optical fiber with a diameter of less than half a millimeter can carry much more information. So telecommunications technologies are highly efficient ways to relate each other closely. Secondly, telecommunications technologies provide a chance to leap over whole stages of economic development by condensing the time required to change from labor-intensive model to high-tech intensive one. Last but not least, those countries with telecommunications have a huge advantage over countries stuck with old technology. One day they can cruise alongside Americans and Europeans in the Information Age. It is the telecommunications that separate the winners from the losers.

Section B
I. 阅读技巧

认识段落模式（I）

段落是在我们所阅读的文章和故事里重要的思想单元。推测出一个段落的含义是我们作为读者所面对的基础挑战。有助于找出含义的线索则存在于作者在段落中安排信息的方式。

段落的信息通常出现在能够被认出或分析的模式中。如果你了解一些典型的信息出现模式，你就可以更加轻易地理解文章。当然，没有作者会严格地按照任何一种单一的模式写作。通常在一篇文章或故事里，许多不同的段落模式都会出现。事实上，在一个单独的段落里，各种模式经常会被重叠或混合使用。当读者熟悉了段落模式之后，就能更好的处理信息，把握作者的思路。进一步讲，恰当的结构有助于读者预测下文内容，梳理出主体及要点，分清论据之间的关系。

作者的写作目的即文章的主题有助于确定采用哪种(些)结构。另外还应当熟悉一些特定的词语，它们标志着作者所用的段落模式。

一、分类式（Classification）

信息可以根据其相似性或差异性做归类，划分为不同的数据组。教科书尤其是科技类教科书广泛使用"分类式"。其目的在于将涉及面广泛的主体加以细分，从而得以分析由庞杂信息分割出来的各部分；或通过讨论个别元素进而解释整个系列事件。

采用分类法的文章通常以概述的形式出现，常用数字来表示内容的划分。

二、排序式（Sequence or Process）

排序式可按事件发生的顺序，即时间顺序来展现事实；而空间顺序着重强调事物的大小、规模及位置；运用主次顺序时，可由主到次，也可由次到主排列；过程分析结构可以按照事物发展过程逐一列出阶段和步骤。

排序中的顺序至关重要，不能随意调换，这是分类式和排序式的区别。与分类式一样，排序式也可能用数字做标记，只不过其目的是显示时间顺序或某过程的步骤，而不是按随意的顺序排列。

Ⅱ. 词汇与短语详解

1. edition

[词义] *n.* [C] 版本

[例句] I've ordered the paperback/hardback edition of their dictionaries.
我已订购了他们词典的平装/精装本。

[派生] editor *n.* 编辑; editorial *adj.* 编辑的，主笔的

[辨析] edition, copy, number, issue, version
edition 表示版数; copy 表示册数; number，issue 表示期数，即期刊的某一期; version 是同一作品的不同"译本、文本"。

2. tutor

[词义] *n.* [C] 家庭教师，私人教师，辅导教师，导师; *v.* 教授，指导

[搭配] home tutor 家庭教师; course tutor 选课指导老师

[例句] His tutor encouraged him to read widely. 他的导师鼓励他广泛阅读。
He tutored the child in mathematics. 他辅导这孩子的数学。

[辨析] tutor, teacher
tutor 多指教授单个学生或少数学生的教师; teacher 为常用词，泛指从小学到大学的教师。

3. feedback

[词义] *n.* [U] 反映，反馈信息

[搭配] feedback circuits 反馈电路; feedback adjustment 反馈调整

[例句] The company welcomes the feedback from the customers.
那家公司欢迎来自客户的反馈信息。

4. transmit

[词义] *v.* 传播，传送

[例句] Fiber-optic cables will transmit electronic signals. 光纤电缆能传送电子信号。

[派生] transmitter *n.* 发射机，发射台; transmittable *adj.* 可播送的，可发射的

5. carrier

[词义] *n.* ① [C] 运送工具，运载工具; ② [C] 搬运东西的人

[搭配] aircraft carrier 航空母舰; air carrier 航空公司; active carrier 活动性（病菌）携带者

[例句] Mosquitoes are carriers of malaria. 蚊子是疟疾的传播媒介。
He got a job as a carrier on a building site.
他在建筑工地找到了一份搬运工的工作。

6. hence

[词义] *adv.* 因此，所以

[例句] Nobody listened to the speaker, hence he got angry.
没有人在听演讲者讲话，因此他生气了。

[辨析] hence, therefore

hence和therefore两词均为连接副词，表示因果关系；两词后均可接从句，但hence后可直接跟名词，而therefore通常不能。如：This town was built on the side of a hill, hence the name Hillside. 这座小镇建立在小山边上，因此名为山边镇。

7. dose

[词义] *n.* [C]（药的一次）用量，剂量

[例句] He was not able to sleep without heavy doses of sleeping pills.
他不服大剂量的安眠药就无法入睡。

[派生] dosage *n.* 剂量，配药，用量

8. correspondent

[词义] *n.* [C] 记者，通讯员

[例句] He used to be a war correspondent. 他以前曾是战地记者。

[派生] correspond *v.* ① (with) 相符合，与……一致；② (to) 通信

correspondence *n.* [U] ① 信件，函件；② 通信，通信联系

corresponding *adj.* ① 相应的，相当的；② 符合的，一致的

9. vacuum

[词义] *n.* [C] ① 真空般的状态，空白；② 真空

v. 用真空吸尘器清扫

[例句] Her death left a vacuum in his life. 她的去世使他的生活变得空虚。

Nothing can live in a vacuum. 任何生命都不能在真空中生存。

She vacuumed the carpet. 她用吸尘器清扫地毯。

10. synthetic

[词义] *adj.* ① 人造的，合成的；② 虚假的

[搭配] synthetic leather 人造皮革; synthetic method 综合法

[例句] This synthetic dress material are welcomed by young people.
这种合成纤维衣料很受年轻人欢迎。

I hate her synthetic skin-deep smiles. 我讨厌她那副皮笑肉不笑的样子。

[派生] synthesis *n.* 综合，合成; synthesize *v.* 综合，合成

[辨析] artificial, synthetic

artificial 意为"人造的，人为的"，强调某物为"非天然的"，指人使用技术和通过人工方式模仿自然物质而制造出来的事物; synthetic 指用自然物质经化学处理而成的合成物，常用作自然品的代用品。

11. crucial

[词义] *adj.* 至关重要的，关键的

[搭配] be crucial to 对……至关重要的; at a crucial moment 关键时刻

[例句] Consumers' confidence is crucial to the recovery of our company.
顾客的信心对我们公司的复苏至关重要。

12. diagram

[词义] *n.* [C] 图解，示意图

[例句] The teacher drew a diagram showing the parts of a car engine.
老师画了张示意图，说明汽车发动机的部件。

[辨析] chart, diagram, graph

chart 指以图形、表格或符号表现数据变化的图表; diagram 常指标明事物主要构成部分、用来说明物体的结构、功能、原理、性质等的"图解、简图"; graph多指由点或线组成的表现两种或多种事物相互关系的曲线图。

13. portion

[词义] *n.* [C] 一部分，一份

[例句] The profits was divided into seven portions. 利润被分成了七份。

[辨析] portion, part, section, share

portion 指在某物中所占的份额、比例，也可指物体或交通工具的某一独立的"部分"; part 纯粹表示部分，并无比例的内涵; section 指通过或似乎通过切割或分离而成的部分，如指书、文章或城市的某一部分; share之多分享、分担的一部分，侧重的是共性。

[联想] proportion *n.* 比例

14. insure

[词义] *v.* (AmE ensure) ① 保证，担保给……; ② 保险，投保

[搭配] insure against 投保……险，使免受……

[例句] The airline is taking further steps to insure public safety on its aircraft.
航空公司正采取进一步的措施以保证其飞机上乘客的安全。
His house is insured against accidental damage. 他的房子投了意外损失险。

[派生] insurance *n.* 保险，保险费

[辨析] assure, ensure, insure

assure 意为用十分肯定的语气向某人保证（某事一定会发生），常用句型为: assure sb. of sth或接that从句; ensure意为确保某种行动或动因的结果一定会发生，常用句型为: ensure that...或ensure sb. sth; insure 意为保险、确保时相当于ensure，但不及后者正式，两者常可通用。insure更多是表达纯粹法律上的给……保险的专门术语，常用句型为: insure against...。

15. terminal

[词义] *n.* ① [C] 计算机终端; ② [C] 候机楼，码头，出入口

[搭配] terminal exam 期末考试; terminal point 终点; terminal stages of cancer 晚期癌症

[例句] The data will be fed into a computer terminal. 这些资料将被输入计算机终端。
We got off at the terminal station. 我们在终站下车。

[辨析] terminal, ultimate

terminal 意为"终点的、末端的"，指处于事物或时期的末尾，标明范围极限、发展极限，或标明一个系列、一个周期的结束; ultimate 正式用词，意为"最终的、最后的"，多修饰需花费很大努力才能达到的最终目的，带有感情色彩。

16. sign up（经报名或签约）获得，从事

[例句] Many students have signed up for the course. 许多学生报名修这门课程?

[联想] sign on (for sth.) = sign up。sign away/over 签字放弃，签收; sign in（使）签到，（使）登记; sign out 签名登记离开; sign off 停止播送

17. refer to 指的是，涉及

[例句] What I want to say refers to all of you. 我要说的话涉及到你们所有人。

[联想] refer to 还可以指：① 参考、查询；② (as) 把……称为……，把……当作。

e.g. He often refers to that dictionary. 他经常查阅那本字典。

The American Indians referred to salt as "magic white sand".

美洲印第安人把盐称为"魔力白沙"。

18. be compared to 比作

[例句] Man's life is often compared to a candle. 人生常被喻为蜡烛。

[联想] 表示"与……比较"时，既可以用compare with也可以用compare to，但表示"把……比作……"时只能用compare to。

19. come up with 拿出，提供；提出，想出

[例句] She came up with some pictures taken by her father.

她拿出一些她父亲拍的照片

She came up with a new idea for increasing sales.

她想出一个增加销售的新办法。

[联想] 此短语还有"赶上"之意，如：We came up with a group of tourists. 我们赶上了一群游客。

20. in the hands of 在……手上，在……掌握之中

[例句] At that time, the castle was in the hands of their enemy.

那时城堡还在他们的敌人手里。

[联想] in good hands 意为"在可靠的人手上"，如：The child is in good hands.

这孩子有人妥善照看。

21. have access to 享有接近（或进入）……的机会，享有使用……的权利

[例句] Many divorced fathers only have access to their children at weekends.

许多离了婚的父亲只在周末获许见他们的孩子。

[联想] gain/give access to 接近/接见某人；a man of easy/difficult access 容易/难以接近的人

22. rely on 依靠

[例句] She relies on her parents for tuition. 她靠父母替她交学费。

23. fall behind 落后，落在……后面

[例句] He is falling behind all the other classmates. 他落后所有同班同学。

[联想] fall behind in (with) 在某方面落后；fall back 后退，退却；fall back oon 借助于，依靠；fall in with 同意，赞成，符合；fall on 开始，着手

24. devote to 专心于，把……专用（于）

[例句] He devoted all his time to his job. 他把他的全部时间都用在工作上了。

Ⅲ. 难句解析

1. Just sign up for the language course offered by a school in another district or city, have the latest edition of the course teaching materials sent to your computer, and attend by video. (Para. 2)

[释义] Just sign a document or contract to show that you want to take the language course that is offered by a school in another district or city, ask them to send the most recently published edition of the teaching materials for the course via computer and attend the course by video.

have sth. done 让某人做某事。因为"某人"不是意思的重点，所以不在句中体

现。相反，"某事"才是语义的重点，因为事情是被人做的，所以动词用过去分词形式，如：I have my hair cut. 我把头发剪了。相同的意思也可以用 have sb. do sth. 的句型来表示，但此时语义重点不同了。

[分析] 本句由三个并列的祈使句构成。

2. **While nearly everyone has heard of the information superhighway, even experts differ on exactly what the term means and what the future it promises will look like. (Para. 4)**

[释义] While almost everyone knows something about the information superhighway, even experts have different ideas about what the term really means and what it will bring about in the future.

differ on/about 对……有不同的意见

e.g. The committee differ on the question of appointing the next chairman.

委员会的成员对下一任主席的任命有不同意见。

[分析] "what the terms means" 和 "what the future it promises will look like" 是两个名词性从句作并列宾语；在第二个宾语中，"it promises will look like" 时省略了关系代词that 的定语从句，修饰the future，it指代前面的term，即information superhighway。

3. **The greatly increased volume and speed of data transmission that these technologies permit can be compared to the way in which a highway with many lanes allows more cars to move at faster speeds than a two-lane highway—hence, the information superhighway. (Para. 6)**

[释义] The greatly increased volume and speed of data transmission made possible by these technologies are similar to the situation in which a highway with many lanes allows more cars to move at faster speeds than a two-lane highway, and for this reason, people use the term "information superhighway".

[分析] "that these technologies permit" 是定语从句，修饰限定先行词 volume and speed，关系代词在从句中作宾语；"in which a highway...a two-lane highway" 是一个定语从句，介词 in 提到了关系代词的前边，所以应用 which，而不是 that。

4. **But while the Internet primarily moves words, the information superhighway will soon make routine the electronic transmission of data in other formats, such as audio files and images. (Para. 8)**

[释义] But while the Internet mainly transmits words, the information superhighway will soon make it normal to allow the electronic transmission of data in other for mates, for example, audio files and images.

[分析] "the electronic transmission...files and images" 是动词make的宾语，routine 作宾语补足语，因为宾语较长，所以后置。

5. **...predicts one correspondent who specializes in technology. (Para. 9)**

[释义] **specialize in** 擅长于……，专攻……

e.g. He has hired a lawyer who specializes in divorce cases.

他雇了一位专门受理离婚案的律师。

6. "**If left in the hands of private enterprise, the data highway could become little more than a synthetic universe for the rich.**"(Para. 11)

[释义] "If it were to be controlled by private enterprise, the data highway could be come almost nothing but a man-made world for wealthy people."

little more than 只是……而已

e.g. He is little more than a puppet. 他只是一个傀儡而已。

[分析] "if left..."结构在句中作状语，由"关系代词+分词/介词短语"构成，类似的用法还有：If asked, she can tell him about it in detail. 如果被问起来，她可以详细地告诉他这件事。Once in trouble, you can turn to the police. 一旦有麻烦，你可以向警方求助。

7. **In order for it to be of value to the most people, individuals need to become informed about what is possible and how being connected will be of benefit. (Para. 16)**

[释义] In order for the superhighway to be valuable to most people, individuals need to know about what is possible and how being connected to it will be beneficial to them.

be of+名词=形容词，如：be of value=valuable；be of benefit=beneficial。

[分析] "what is possible"和"how being connected will be of benefit"是两个并列的宾语从句，作介词 about 的宾语。"being connected"是一个插入的现在分词短语，作状语，表示"连通后"。

IV. 重点语法讲解

现在分词的用法 现在分词是动词的一种非谓语形式，由动词原形+ing构成，具有完成时态和被动语态，就其语法功能而言，它可以作主语、表语、宾语、宾语补足语、状语和定语。

1. 作主语

Swimming is a good means to keep fit.

2. 作表语

The only thing that he is interested is **playing basketball**.

3. 作主语补足语

常见作主语补语的现在分词有amusing, boring, confusing, disappointing, tiring等，有时这些词被视为形容词。如：

The game sounds **interesting**.

4. 作动词宾语

有些动词或短语后面跟作宾语的非限定性动词只能是现在分词，如：admit, advise, delay, include, risk, threaten, keep on, give up等。

They don't allow **smoking** in the library.

5. 作介词宾语

几乎所有介词，不管是单个介词还是介词词组，不管他们是否谓语动词的组成部分，都能用-ing分词的动名词作宾语。如：

What about **having** a party?

6. 宾语补足语

表示感觉和心理状态的动词，如：hear, feel, give, listen to, observe, smell, watch等词的宾语可以用-ing分词作补足语。

Suddenly she heard someone **knocking** at the door.

7. 状语

现在结构作状语表示助于在进行一动作的同事所进行的另一种动作，他对谓语起修饰或陪衬作用。这时要注意现在分词与其逻辑主语在时态、意义上的统一。可表示时间和伴随、方式、原因、条件、结果、目的、让步等。

Facing so many people, the young girl became nervous.

8. 定语

现在分词可单独作定语，也可构成合成词作定语，在意义上相当于一个定语从句（包括限定性从句和非限定性从句）。

This is a new computer system which has made old method of **data processing** obsolete.

V. 课文赏析

1. 文体特点

本文是一篇说明文，语言通俗易懂，客观可信。文章开头通过事例提出了信息高速公路这一概念，吸引读者的注意。正文部分作者运用列数字、举例子的方法，说明了信息高速公路对人类的益处和所面临的挑战。最后，作者对主题进行全面的评价，并提出相应的具体措施，增加了文章的完整性。

2. 结构分析

Part I (Para. 1-2) Examples about what is information superhighway are given.

Part II (Para. 3-9) What is Information highway and the advantage of information Superhighway.

Part III (Para. 10-15) Potential challenges which exist for information superhighway.

Part IV (Para. 16) Summary about information superhighway and some measures which should be taken.

VI. 课后练习答案及解析

Reading Skills

XV.

1. A. Your school has no professors of Japanese and you want to learn the language.

   B. Just sign up for a language course offered by a school in other places and the materials and instructions can be sent to you via your computer.

   C. A problem-solution pattern.

2. A. Poor people must also have access to high technology.

   B. The author offers reasons such as the access to high technology is crucial to obtaining a high-quality education, getting a good job, and also important to banking, shopping, communication, and information.

   C. The paragraph starts with a general statement, which is supported by reasons.

Comprehension of the Text

XVI.

FFTTF　TTT

Vocabulary

XVII.

1. transmit 译文：现在人们可以互相发电报、打电话，信息的传递要比以前任何时候都快得多。
2. insuring 译文：在这个国家，生很多孩子是为了到老时不感到孤独。
3. format 译文：他们所需要的所有图像和数据都以数字形式储存在数据库中。
4. feedback 译文：岗位设计、考评、目标设定、信息反馈和总结都是与管理有关的活动。
5. correspondence 译文：他要求得到公司与杨伯爵在1988年7月间的所有往来信件。
6. vacuum 译文：他的辞职已经造成一个很不易填补的职位空缺。
7. Synthetic 译文：合成橡胶作为天然橡胶的替代品被广泛应用。
8. diagrams 译文：这本书包含了很多图表，它们显示了信息高速公路的组成部分。

XVIII.

1. differ on 译文：医学专家对这种病的治疗有不同意见。
2. refer to 译文：在这篇文章中，作者使用了"聋哑"地区来描述那些没有通讯设施或被困于旧技术的地区。
3. be compared to 译文：作者认为乡村的社会生活与大城市社会生活毫无可比之处。
4. specialize in 译文：他行医多年以后决定专攻儿科。
5. make routine 译文：先进技术很快可以使得许多网上交易和交流变成常规。
6. come up with 译文：老师鼓励学生在课堂上对一些社会问题提出解决方案。
7. has access to 译文：在加州伯克利，社区储存器项目已经启动，以确保每个人都可以使用高科技。
8. Some concrete steps should be taken 译文：为了使信息高速公路变为现实还需要做很多具体的事情。

VII. 参考译文

信息高速公路

你是否太累了，不想去录像店却又想在家看《美女与野兽》? 是不是想听听你最喜欢的吉他手最新的爵士乐磁带? 或需要一些新的阅读材料，比如杂志或书? 没问题。只要坐在家中的电脑或电视机前，在一个含有上千个条目的电子目录中输入你想要的东西和需要的时间就行了。

在暑假去日本之前你想学日语，可学校又没有日语老师。不用担心，你可以向另一地区或城市的学校报名，上他们提供的日语课，让他们将这门课程最新的教材传送到你的电脑上，然后通过视听方法上课。如果你在翻译作业或发音上还需额外帮助，辅导教师可通过电脑给你反馈。

欢迎来到信息高速公路。

尽管几乎人人都听说过信息高速公路，可即使专家们对这一名称的确切含义，以及它预示着什么样的未来也有分歧。但广义地说，信息高速公路是指由今天的广播、电视、录像、电话、电脑、半导体等产业组合而成的一个互相关联的大产业。

是技术进步在引导着这一大联合。这些技术进步已使储存信息以及向家庭和办公室快速传输信息更为容易。例如，光纤电缆——由细如发丝的玻璃纤维制成——是一种极为高效的信息载体。射过玻璃纤维的激光可以传送高达标准电话线25万倍的数据，或者说，每秒可传送几万段像这样的文字。

这些技术使得数据传送的容量和速度大大提高。这种情况可与一条高速公路相比，多车道比双车道能使更多的车以更高的速度行驶——信息高速公路由此得名。

今天，与信息高速公路最接近的就是互联网，这是一个由电脑连接而成的网络系统，它使得135个国家多达2,500万的人能进行信息交换。

但是，互联网主要是传送文字，而信息高速公路不久将使其他形式的电子数据传送（如声音资料和图像的传送）成为常规。那就是说，举个例子，欧洲的一位医道高明的医生通过电脑看了病历就能给美洲的病人治病，决定病人用药的剂量，甚至还可以遥控一个操手术刀的机器人施行手术。

一位专门从事技术方面报道的记者预言道："把录像邮件的片段传送到大楼的其他地方或国内的其他地方要比在键盘上打出文字来更为容易。"

美国前副总统阿尔·戈尔说，我们这个世界正处于"新时代的前夜"，他是克林顿政府中推行高科技的主要人物。戈尔希望联邦政府在决定信息高速公路的发展方面发挥领导作用。然而，在一个预算拨款相对较少的时期，美国政府不可能拿得出今后20年里建造信息高速公路所需的钱款。

这就使得私人企业——电脑公司、电话公司、有线电视公司——得以填补由于政府无法顾及所留下的空缺。尽管这些企业在最令人振奋的新技术上领先，一些批评者仍担心追逐利润的企业会只开发面向富人的服务项目。首都华盛顿大众媒介教育中心主任杰弗里·切斯特担心地说："如果数据高速公路控制在私人企业手中，它可能只会成为富人的虚拟世界。"

另一位专家说，穷人也必须有权获得高科技。他说："这种权利对于获得高质量的教育、找到好工作都将至关重要。那么多的交易、交换都将通过这一媒体进行——银行业务、购物、通信、信息——因此那些只能靠邮递员发送信件的人实在是有落伍的危险了。"

今年年初，当图表显示正在建造信息高速公路设施的四家地区性电话公司只接通了富人社区时，一些专家对此不无担忧。

这几家公司否认自己避开穷人，但也承认有钱人会成为首批受益者。其中一家公司的发言人说："我们总要先从某些地区开始，而(那)就应该是我们认为会有顾客购买这些服务的地区。做生意就是这样。"

维护穷人权益的人士希望这些正在建设数据高速公路的公司能够将其利润的一部分用于此项技术的普及。提倡普及的人已启动了他们自己的几个项目。在加利福尼亚的伯克利，"社区存储器项目"已在公共建筑物和地铁站里安装了电脑终端，花25美分就可发送信息。在加州的圣莫尼卡，所有公共图书馆里的打字机都已换成了电脑；任何人，不仅仅是图书馆管理员，都可通过电脑发信件。

随着我们日益接近信息高速公路的现实，我们也面临着许多挑战。为了使其对大多数人有价值，人们应该了解哪些是可能做到的，以及连通后如何能从中受益。信息高速公路带来的可能性不胜枚举，但要使其成为现实，还必须采取具体的措施来开展这一工作。

Section C

Ⅰ. 语言点讲解

1. Operation Match went after government employees who had not paid back student loans the government had given them for colleges, and welfare clients with large unreported incomes. (Para. 3)

[分析] "who had not...for college" 是定语从句，修饰先行词employees；在这个定语从句中又包含一个小的定语从句，即 "the government had given them for college"，修饰先行词loans，因为关系代词that在从句中作宾语，所以省略。

2. The government has been pressing for computer makers to include a special chip in their machines to allow police agencies to listen to electronic communications. (Para. 4)

[释义] **press for** 督促，催促

　　e.g. The workers press for higher wages. 工人极力要求提高工资。

3. That may still seem like something form a spy movie; more troubling is the growing case with which everyday information can be accessed. (para. 5)

[分析] "more troubling is..." 是一个倒装句，里面包含了一个介词提前的定语从句，即 "with which everyday information can be accessed"，修饰cases。

Ⅱ. 课文赏析

1. 文体特点

本文的结构按照"提出问题—分析问题—解决问题"的模式展开。文章开篇开门见山，提出设想，引起读者的好奇。正文则通过列数字和举例子等方法向读者说明了信息时代的缺点。最后，文章结尾提出了保护隐私的方法。文章语言朴实生动，事例真实可信，具有很强的说服力。

2. 结构分析

Part Ⅰ (Para. 1-3) Such a phenomenon is expressed that it is more difficult to keep personal privacy in Information Age.

Part Ⅱ (Para. 4-8) Examples are given about how to get personal privacy.

Part Ⅲ (Para. 9-10) Methods are told about how to keep personal privacy.

Ⅲ. 课后练习答案及解析

Reading Skills

XIX.

1. A. A small plastic card can hold all manner of information about you.

   B. The personal information includes your date of birth, Social Security number, credit and medical histories and you can use it to drive a car, get medicine, get cash from machines, pay parking tickets, and collect government benefits.

   C. A general statement supported by detail.

2. A. Medical records are used to make a whole host of decisions about you that aren't related to your health.

B. The medical records are used by employers or companies to make decisions whether or not to hire or promote an employee.

C. A general statement supported by details.

Comprehension of the Text

XX. ▶

1. negative   2. harder   3. different   4. Ronald Reagan's

5. effective   6. could monitor electronic communications

7. easier   8. uninformed

IV. 参考译文

信息时代的个人隐私

设想一下一张小小的塑料卡，在微小的记忆芯片上存有关于你的所有信息：出生日期、社会保障号、信用记录和病史。想一想，这同一张卡能使你驾车、就医、从取款机中提款、付停车费、领政府补助。

这种所谓的智能卡已有一款正在使用。有些保险公司发行了客户的医疗记录卡，客户凭这些卡才能就医。《私密时代》报纸编辑伊万·亨德里克斯说，为方便起见产生了这门技术，但是，"其不便之处就是房东、雇主或保险公司等会说，我们不会与你谈正事的，除非你出示该卡。"

随着更多的公司与政府机构建立了电脑管理的、可随时联网的数据库，个人信息更难保护了。"你可以从一个数据库进入另一个数据库，就像人们从一间酒吧到另一间酒吧一样，"亨德里克斯说。"信息高速公路很可能由大企业开发，但政府总喜欢参与这些事情。企业开发数据库以更好地定位客户，然后政府就用这些数据库来调查犯罪。"

据作者辛姆森·L·加芬克尔说，这种利用数据库掌握情况的趋势始自罗纳德·里根关于领救济金的人对政府有欺骗行为的说法。一位隐私权方面的专家说："这被称作'匹配行动'，它将那些欠有政府款项的人的数据库与那些从政府获得款项的人的数据库——对应。'匹配行'跟踪记录那些未归还政府助学贷款的政府雇员，以及隐瞒大笔收入的福利救济对象。"

保护公众不受欺骗和侵害一直是降低个人隐私程度的有效借口。政府一直在敦促电脑制造商在机中加装一块特殊的芯片以使警方能接听电子通信。政府称不这样做就等于让恐怖分子和犯罪分子通过信息高速公路来共同策划阴谋。

这仍感觉像是间谍片中的场景；更使人不安的是日常信息可以越来越容易地被获取。以医疗档案的电脑化管理为例。正如一位作者所指出的那样，"你租借录像带的习惯都能比你的医疗记录得到更好的法律保护。"那是因为医疗档案涉及到更多的钱。一位隐私权专家说，保险公司列出"有某些健康问题的人员名单，又转而将这些名单卖给制药公司和其他的企业"。

医疗档案被用来做出很多与你相关的决定，而这些决定却与你的健康无关。据一份1991年的政府报告称："50%的雇主经常用医疗档案里的信息来决定是否雇用或提拔某人。那些利用这种信息的人中，约20%的人……不会告诉雇员他们的医疗档案曾被用于此种目的。"某公司不雇用吸烟者，另一家则在发现雇员在晚会上酗酒后将其解雇。

雇主、房东们常向开发数据档案的公司购买这类信息。除了犯罪记录、劳工保险索赔、民事法庭记录外，这些公司的核心产品之一是信用信息，而这种信用信息却并非总是准确的。几年前，19个州指控国内一家大型信用机构的报告错误百出，这家公司因此付了一大笔钱。

不过据加芬克尔说，最大的信息收集机构还是各州的汽车管理部门，简称DMV。他写道："对想要影响我们、管得过宽的政府机构来说，DMV正是它们获得所需信息的一站式供应处。"现有的系统将美国所有51个汽车管理部门连接起来，在这一点上，"任何其他的政府机构都不可能比它更准确地跟踪人们的行为。"

DMV的数据也并非仅用于与开车有关的事情。加芬克尔写道："俄勒冈州有109种不同的违规行为可导致暂时吊销驾驶执照，而其中50种与开车毫无关系。"他提到，威斯康星州的居民可能会因未付图书馆罚款，未将门前步道上的积雪清除，未将伸到邻家宅院上的树枝修剪掉而失去驾驶执照。在肯塔基州，退学的学生，无故旷课达9次以上的学生，或分数达不到某一标准的学生，都会失去驾驶执照，"除非他们能证明其家庭有困难"。

很难使自己的信息不出现在DMV的电脑屏幕上。但还是有办法在其他方面使自己的情况少为人知。一位卫生官员建议，当填写医疗表格时，你可改变一下，清楚地表明"你不同意在没有你的直接书面同意的情况下将你的信息泄露或出卖给第二方"。

《全球评论》（1993年秋季号）列出了一些提供了很多其他建议的出版物。这一书单上两本最令人感兴趣的书是杰弗里·罗斯费德所著的《出卖隐私》和通信刊物《私密时代》的伊万·亨德里克斯所写的《你的隐私权》。另一本著名而实用的期刊是月刊《隐私月报》。

五、知识链接

Employment in the telecommunications industry is expected to decline 7 percent over the 2004-2014 period, compared with 14 percent growth for all industries combined. Industry consolidation and strong price competition among telecommunications firms will decrease employment as companies try to reduce their costs.

The industry will continue to grow despite the lower employment as people and businesses will demand ever wider ranges of telecommunications services. The growth of high-speed Internet and video services will lead to continued upgrades of telecommunications networks. Residential customers will use an increasing range of services as technology and competition lower the price of high-speed Internet access, video-on-demand, and wireless and Internet-based telephone services. Cable companies and telephone companies will both offer cable television, high-speed Internet, and phone services. Wireless carriers will compete directly with the residential wired services, providing increasingly reliable cellular communications and increasingly faster Internet service.

Business demand will rise as companies increasingly rely on their telecommunications systems to conduct electronic commerce, ordering, record keeping, and video conferencing. In order to remain competitive, businesses will require higher speed access to the Internet.

Technology is continuing to transform the industry and will continue to bring on line a wider array of services to homes and businesses.

预计在2004-2024年期间，与所有工业雇员总共增长百分之十四相比，电信业的雇员将下降百分之七。由于电信公司试图降低成本，工业合并以及电信公司之间激烈的价格竞争将会导致雇员减少。

随着人们和商业需要更加广泛的电信服务，尽管雇员人数降低，但电信业却会持续增长。高速网络和视频服务的增长将会引领电信网络的不断升级。随着技术和竞争降低使用网络、即时视频和无线及网络电话服务的价格，居民用户将会使用更加多样的服务。有线电视公司和电话公司会同时提供有线电视、高速网络和电话服务。无线传输和将会直接与居民有线服务竞争，提供日益可靠的无线通讯和日益高速的网络服务。

商业对于电信的需求将增长，因为公司越来越依赖于它们的电信系统来进行电子交易、定购、保存记录和视频会议。为了保持竞争力，商业会要求更高速的网络使用。技术正在持续改造电信业，并且将继续给家庭和商业带来更多种类的服务。

六、自测题

1. The town planning commission said that their financial outlook for the next year was optimistic. They expect increased tax _____.
   A. efficiency　　　　B. revenues　　　C. privileges　　　D. validity

2. He _____ in carrying on his work in spite of his poor health.
   A. insisted　　　　B. persisted　　　C. maintained　　　D. resisted

3. The captured criminal were _____ in chains through the streets.
   A. exhibited　　　　B. displayed　　　C. paraded　　　D. revealed

4. We must bring our ideas into _____ with the laws of the objective external world.
   A. correspondence　　B. conflict　　　C. contact　　　D. relations

5. The _____ on this apartment expires in a year's time.
   A. treaty　　　　　　B. lease　　　　C. engagement　　D. subsidy

6. We should concentrate on sharply reducing interest rates to pull the economy out of _____.
   A. rejection　　　　B. restriction　　C. retreat　　　D. recession

7. Help will come from UN, but the aid will be _____ near what's needed.
   A. everywhere　　　B. somewhere　　C. nowhere　　　D. anywhere

8. The farmers were more anxious for rain than the people in the city because they had more at _____.
   A. danger　　　　　B. stake　　　　C. loss　　　　D. threat

9. Today, household chores have been made much easier by electrical _____.
   A. equipment　　　B. appliance　　　C. facilities　　　D. utilities

10. If you decrease the _____ of alcohol in this solution, it would be less dangerous.
    A. part　　　　　　B. portion　　　C. section　　　D. share

115

答案与解析

1. B   revenue 税收收入; efficiency 效率; privilege 特权; validity 效力

2. B   persist in 坚持，持续; insist on 坚持; maintain 维持，维修; resist 抵制，反抗

3. C   parade 游行，多作贬义词; exhibit 展览，展示; display 陈列，展出; reveal 显示，泄露

4. A   bring...into correspondence 使……与……相符合; conflict 冲突; contact 接触，联系; relation 关系

5. B   lease 租约，租契; treaty 协议，条约; engagement 正式的承诺或保证; subsidy 津贴，补助金

6. D   recession 经济衰退; rejection 拒绝; restriction 限制; retreat 撤退

7. C   nowhere near 固定搭配，意为"远非，远不及"

8. B   be at stake 利益攸关，在危险中; in danger 有危险; loss 损失，遗失; threat 威胁

9. B   appliance 常指家用器具; equipment 设备，范围较广; facility 指使人便利的"设施"; utility 公用设施

10. B   portion 份额，比例; part 部分; section 通过分割而形成的某一部分; share 所分享的一部分，侧重共性

Unit 5

① **学习重点和难点**

词汇和短语、语法项目、写作技巧

② **文化知识**

课文大背景、课文知识点

③ **课文精讲**

词汇与短语详解、难句解析、重点
语法讲解、课文赏析、课后练习答
案及解析、参考译文、写作指导

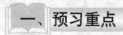

一、预习重点

1. Why loneliness has become a sort of national disease?
2. How to solve the roommate conflicts according to the author?
3. Is an Indian arranged marriage good or not?

二、学习重点和难点

Ⅰ. 词汇和短语

Section A: solitary, tame, inspiration, benign, dictate, saucer, humble, soak, waterproof, slippery, choke, supreme, justice, niece, seal; on purpose, speak highly of, seek out, set forth, stretch out, back up, stay up late, at length, in line, settle down, after all

Section B: oral, minus, vibrate, organic, holy, stale, depression, tolerate, abstract, resort, disorder, selection, exclaim, paw, chip, slap; strike out, range from...to, give up on, turn up, end up, spring from, tear apart, resort to, in case, head off, fill in, sum up, against all (the) odds

Ⅱ. 语法项目

① 动词不定式的用法
② 省略句

Ⅲ. 写作技巧

分类法

三、文化知识

Ⅰ. 课文大背景

1. Henry David Thoreau 亨利·大卫·梭罗

Henry David Thoreall was a U.S. thinker, essayist, and naturalist (1817-1862). Born in Concord, Mass（康科德，马斯）, Thoreau graduated from Harvard University and taught school for several years before deciding to become a poet of nature. Back in Concord, he came under the influence of R. W. Emerson（爱默生）and began to publish pieces in the transcendentalist（先验论者的）magazine *The Dial.* In the years 1845-1847, to demonstrate how satisfying a simple life could be, he lived in a hut beside Concord's Walden Pond; essays recording his daily life were assembled for his masterwork, *Walden*（《瓦尔登湖》）(1854)
. His *A Week on the Concord and Merrimack Rivers*（《康科德河和梅里麦克河上的一星期》）(1849) was the only other book he published in his lifetime. He reflected on a night he spent in jail protesting the Mexican-American War in the essay *On Civil Disobedience*（《消极反抗》）(1849), which would later influence such figures as M. Gandhi（甘地）and M. L. King（马丁·路德·金）.

2. John Milton 约翰·弥尔顿

Milton (1608-1674) was an English poet. Milton attended Cambridge University (1625-1632), where he wrote poems in Latin, Italian, and English. During 1632-1638 he engaged in private

study——writing the masque *Comus*（《酒神的假面舞会》）(1637) and the extraordinary elegy *Lycidas*（挽歌《利西达斯》）(1638)——and toured Italy. Concerned with the Puritan（清教徒）cause in England, he spent much of 1641-1660 pamphleteering（编写小册子）for civil and religious liberty and serving in Oliver Cromwell's（奥利弗·克伦威尔）government. He lost his sight in the year of 1651, and thereafter dictated his works. After the Restoration（王政复辟）he was arrested as a noted defender of the Commonwealth（英联邦）, but was soon released. In *Paradise Lost*（《失乐园》）(1667), his epic masterpiece on the Fall of Man（人类的沉沦）written in blank verse（无韵诗）, he uses his sublime "grand style" with superb power; his characterization of Satan（撒旦）is a supreme achievement. He further expressed his purified faith in God and the regenerative strength of the individual soul in *Paradise Regained*（《复乐园》）(1671), and *Samson Agonistes*（《力士参孙》）(1671). Considered second only to W. Shakespeare in the history of English-language poetry, Milton had an immense influence on later literature.

3. William Wordsworth 威廉·华兹华斯

Wordsworth was an English poet (1770-1850). Orphaned at 13, Wordsworth attended Cambridge University. He became friends with S. T. Coleridge（科尔律治）, with whom he wrote *Lyrical Ballads*（《抒情歌谣集》）(1798), the collection often considered to have launched the English Romantic Movement（英国浪漫主义运动）. Wordsworth's contributions include *Tintern Abbey*（《丁登诗》）and many lyrics controversial for their common, everyday language. Around 1798 he began writing the epic autobiographical poem that would absorb him intermittently for the next 40 years, *The Prelude*（《序曲》）(1850). His second verse collection, *Poems* (1807), includes many of the rest of his finest works. His poetry is perhaps most original in its vision of the almost divine power of the creative imagination reforging the links between man and man, between humankind and the natural world. In 1843 he became England's poet laureate. He is regarded as the central figure in the initiation of English Romanticism.

II. 课文知识点

1. Gettysburg College 葛底斯堡学院

The college was founded in 1832. With a student body of approximately 2,400, Gettysburg College is a highly selective four-year residential college of liberal arts and sciences located on a 200-acre campus adjacent to the Gettysburg National Military Park. Gettysburg College education blends a rigorous foundation in the sciences, the social sciences, and the humanities with a highly personal atmosphere of challenge and support.

2. Harvard University 哈佛大学

Harvard University is the oldest institution of higher learning in the United States. Founded in 1636, 16 years after the arrival of the Pilgrims（清教徒）at Plymouth（普利茅斯）, the University has grown from nine students with a single master to an enrollment of more than 18,000 degree candidates, including undergraduates and students in 10 graduate and professional schools. Seven presidents of the United States were graduates of Harvard. Its faculty has produced nearly 40 Nobel laureates.

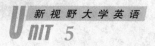

3. India 印度

The country is located in Southern Asia, bordering the Arabian Sea and the Bay of Bengal （孟加拉湾）, between Burma（缅甸）and Pakistan（巴基斯坦）. It has a population of over one billion. The Indus Valley（印度河河谷）civilization, one of the oldest in the world, goes back at least 5,000 years. Aryan（雅利安人）tribes from the northwest invaded about 1500 B.C.; their merger with the earlier inhabitants created classical Indian culture. By the 19th century, Britain had assumed political control of virtually all Indian lands. Non-violent resistance to British colonialism under Mohandas Gandhi（莫罕达斯·甘地）and Jawaharlal Nehru（贾瓦哈拉尔·尼赫鲁）led to independence in 1947. The subcontinent was divided into the secular state of India and the smaller Muslim state of Pakistan. A third war between the two countries in 1971 resulted in East Pakistan becoming the separate nation of Bangladesh（孟加拉国）.

4. Hasidic Jews 哈西德派犹太教徒

Hasidic Jews are those who follow Hasidism. Hasidism is a (Jewish) religious movement which gave rise to a pattern of communal life and leadership as well as a particular social outlook. This movement emerged in the second half of the 18th century.

5. Wall Street 华尔街

Wall Street is the name of a street in lower Manhattan, New York City. It was the first permanent home of the New York Stock Exchange, and is the approximate center of New York's financial district. The phrase is also used to refer to the financial industry. In 1792, in order to fund the country's first public-federal debt, two dozen brokers and speculators gathered under a buttonwood tree on Wall Street to formalize a system of standard minimum fees for the buying and selling of securities. This was the beginning of the New York Stock Exchange.

四、课文精讲

Section A

Ⅰ. 词汇与短语详解

1. solitary
[词义] *adj.* 独自的，孤独的
[搭配] a solitary valley 人迹罕至的山谷
[例句] She lives a solitary life. 她过着孤独的生活。
[派生] solitude *n.* 单独，独居; solitariness *n.* 单独，孤独
[辨析] alone, lonely, solitary 　　　alone 意为"独自一个人"，并不一定感到寂寞; lonely 意为"孤单，寂寞"，侧重因孤独而感到心情沮丧的; solitary 主要指"喜欢独处的，惯于独居的"。
2. tame
[词义] *v.* ① 制服，控制并利用; ② 驯化，驯服 　　　*adj.* ①（尤指动物）温顺的，驯化的; ② 沉闷的，乏味的
[例句] Man has tamed the river to work for him. 人类利用河流为自己服务。

He is an expert in taming animals. 他是驯兽专家。

He keeps a tame lion as a pet. 他养着一头驯服的狮子作为宠物。

The book was so tame that I fell asleep while reading it.

这本书如此乏味，以至于我读着就睡着了。

[派生] tameless *adj.* 难驯养的，性野的; tameness *n.* 驯服，制服

3. inspiration

[词义] *n.* ① [U] 灵感; ② [C] 鼓舞人心的人或事物

[搭配] get/draw inspiration from 从……得到启示; give the inspiration to 启发，鼓舞; have a sudden inspiration 灵机一动

[例句] Wordsworth found his inspiration in the lake district.

华兹华斯从湖泊地区获得灵感。

Her mother was a constant inspiration to him. 她母亲是不断鼓舞她的人。

[派生] inspire *vt.* 鼓舞，使生灵感; inspirational *adj.* 有灵感的，给予灵感的; inspirationism *n.* 灵感论

4. benign

[词义] *adj.* ① (fml.) 善良的，慈祥的; ② 无危险的

[例句] She is a benign girl. 她是一个善良的女孩。

A benign tumor can usually be cured. 良性肿瘤通常能够治愈。

[联想] malignant *adj.* 恶性的 (肿瘤)

5. dictate

[词义] *v.* 听写，口授

[搭配] dictate to sb. 口述，使听写

[例句] The teacher dictated a whole passage to the whole class.

老师让全班同学听写一段文章。

The manager dictated a letter to his secretary. 经理向他的秘书口授了一份信稿。

[派生] dictation *n.* 口授，听写; dictator *n.* 独裁者，口授者

6. saucer

[词义] *n.* [C] 茶托

[搭配] a cup and saucer 一套杯碟

[例句] Madame White offered us tea in her best cup and sauce.

怀特夫人用它最好的一套杯碟请我们喝茶。

[辨析] dish, plate, saucer, tray

dish 多指椭圆或圆形的"大平盘"，用于将食物端上餐桌; plate 指圆形的、周边稍微翘起的"盘子"，可用于进餐者个人放食物或直接进食; saucer 指"茶托、碟子"，一本用来放调味品或单个茶杯等; tray 多指较大的"平底托盘"，用于盛放数个较小的盘、碟、盏。

[联想] sauce *n.* 佐料，酱汁

7. humble

[词义] *adj.* ① 谦逊的，谦虚的; ② 地位 (或身份) 低下的，不显要的

[例句] He strikes me as a very humble person. 他的谦虚给我留下了深刻的印象。

The princess is a woman of humble origin. 王妃出生低微。

[派生] humbly *adv.* 谦逊地，卑贱地; humbleness *n.* 谦逊，卑贱

121

[辨析] humble, modest

humble 表示因为意识到自己的弱点或微不足道而举止、态度谦卑，并且尊重他人；modest 常用词，表示不夸耀自己、不自负，态度平和谦虚，但不含有谦卑恭顺的意思。

8. soak

[词义] *v.* 浸泡，（使）湿透

[搭配] be soaked in 沉浸在……; be soaked to the skin 浑身湿透

[例句] He soaked bread in milk. 他把面包浸在牛奶中。

[辨析] dip, saturate, soak

dip 意为"蘸、浸一浸"，动作短暂；saturate 意为"使湿透、浸透、浇透"，强调程度透彻；soak 意为"（使）浸泡、浸透"，强调在液体中较长时间的浸泡过程。

9. waterproof

[词义] *adj.* 防水的，不透水的

[例句] The coat was made from waterproof material.
这件外套是由防水材料做成的。

[联想] rustproof *adj.* 防锈的; bulletproof *adj.* 防弹的; fireproof *adj.* 耐火的

10. slippery

[词义] *adj.* ① 滑的; ② (infml.) 不可靠的, 狡猾的

[搭配] a slippery customer 滑头; a slippery situation 变化不定的形势; a slippery term 难以捉摸的字眼

[例句] The roads are slippery after rain. 雨后道路很滑。
He's as slippery as an eel—you can never get a straight answer out of him.
他像鳝鱼般难以捉摸——你永远不可能从他口里得到直接的回答。

[派生] slip *vi.* 滑倒，滑落 *vt.* 悄悄放进 *n.* 疏漏，差错

[辨析] slippery, smooth

slippery 意为"滑的、滑溜的"，强调摩擦力很小，常用于形容街道、冰面等容易让人摔倒的地方；smooth 意为"平滑的、光滑的"，强调没有粗糙感。

[联想] slipper *n.* 拖鞋

11. choke

[词义] *v.* ① 说不出话来; ② 窒息

[搭配] choke up (因激动等)说不出话来; choke back 抑制，忍住

[例句] The surprise farewell party left them all choked up.
这一意外的告别聚会令他们激动得说不出话来。
The heavy smoke from the stove almost choked me.
炉子里冒出的浓烟呛得我几乎透不过气来。

12. supreme

[词义] *adj.* ①（地位、权力等）最高的，至上的; ②（程度上）最大的，极度的

[例句] The king was a supreme ruler of a country. 国王是一个国家的最高统治者。
Soldiers who die for their country are said to have made the supreme sacrifice.
为国捐躯的将士被认为是做出了最大的牺牲。

[派生] supremacy *n.* 地位最高的人，霸权

13. justice

[词义] *n.* ① [C] 法官；② [U] 公正，正义；③ [U] 司法，审判

[搭配] bring...to justice 把……交付审判; do justice to 公正地评判

[例句] The justice found him guilty and sentenced him to five years in prison.
法官判他有罪，入狱5年。
All men should be treated with justice. 所有的人都应受到公正对待。
The criminal was finally brought to justice. 罪犯最终被审判。

[派生] just *adj.* 公正的，公平的; justify *vt.* 证明……正当或有理

14. niece

[词义] *n.* [C] 侄女，甥女

[例句] My brother's two daughters are my nieces. 我兄弟的两个女儿是我的侄女。

[联想] nephew *n.* 侄子，外甥

15. seal

[词义] *n.* ① 封条，封铅；② 印，图章；③ 海豹
v. ① 密闭，闭紧，钉住；② 封，密封

[搭配] seal off 封闭，封锁; seal up 密封

[例句] An unused wing of the hospital was sealed off.
一个未启用的医院侧厅被封锁了。
Make sure the parcel of examination scripts is properly sealed up.
确保装考卷的袋子密封好了。
He affixed his seal to the document. 他在文件上盖了印。
The seal on the jar was broken. 坛子的封口被打开了。

16. on purpose 故意，特意

[例句] She did it on purpose. 她是故意那样做的。

[联想] for the purpose of 为的是，为了……起见; with the purpose of 以……为目的; for (all) practical purposes 事实上，实际上

17. cast out 赶出，驱逐

[例句] After the scandal, he was cast out of the committee.
在出了丑闻之后，他被委员会所摈弃。

[联想] cast aside 把……丢在一边; cast off 抛弃; cast around 到处寻找

18. speak highly of 对……给予高度评价，赞扬

[例句] They spoke highly of his behavior. 他们对他的行为赞颂备至。

[联想] speak ill of 说某人的坏话

19. seek out 找出，搜寻出

[例句] The magazine is seeking out readers' opinions.
这本杂志正在征求读者的意见。

[联想] seek after/for 寻求，追求

20. set forth 启程，动身；阐述

[例句] He will set forth on a trip next month. 他下个月将要动身去旅行。
The author set forth the reasons for writing the book in the preface.
作者在前言里阐述了写这本书的原因。

21. stretch out 拉长，伸长，伸出

[例句] The process often stretches out to years, even decades.

这一过程常要延续好几年，甚至几十年。

[联想] at a stretch 不停的，连续的

22. back up（使）积压，（使）拥塞；支持

[例句] Many vehicles were backed up at the crossroads because of the accident.

由于事故，很多车辆被堵在十字路口。

My husband will back me up wholeheartedly as he used to.

我丈夫会像过去一样全心全意地支持我。

23. stay up late 熬夜，不睡觉；处于原位不动，不沉，不被移走

[例句] She stayed up to complete the task. 她熬夜完成任务。

Your notice can stay up for a week. 你的通知可保留一个星期。

24. at length 长久地，详尽地

[例句] We have already discussed this matter at length. 我们已详细讨论过这件事了。

25. in line（排）成一行，（排）成一队；与……一致，与……符合

[例句] The children stood in line. 孩子们排成一队。

This plan is in line with my ideas. 这个计划符合我的想法。

[联想] out of line 不成一线，不一致

26. settle down 安静下来，安下心来；适应（或习惯于）新环境；定居，过安定的生活

[例句] He settled down to do his homework. 他安下心来做家庭作业。

I hope the child will soon settle down in his new school.

我希望这孩子很快就会对新学校习惯起来。

They settled down in Europe at last. 他们最终在欧洲定居。

27. after all 毕竟，终究

[例句] The day turned out fine after all. 终究天还是转晴了。

Ⅱ. 难句解析

1. On the other hand, to be alone on purpose, having rejected company rather than been cast out by it, is one characteristic of an American hero. (Para. 2)

[释义] On the other hand, the deliberate choice of solitude by refusing companions instead of being excluded by others in one special quality of an American hero.

[分析] 不定式"to be alone on purpose"作句子的主语；"having rejected...by it"是现在分词作状语，it指代的是company。

2. The solitary hunter or explorer needs no one as they venture out among the deer and wolves to tame the great wild areas. (Para. 2)

[释义] **venture out** 冒险出去

e.g. I'd rather not venture out in pouring rain if I don't have to!

如果不是非出去不可，我可不愿冒着倾盆大雨出去。

3. Inspiration in solitude is a major commodity for poets and philosophers. They're all for it. (Para. 3)

[释义] Inspiration in solitude is the most useful thing for poets and philosophers. They are all in favor of it.

4. No doubt about it, solitude is improved by being voluntary. (Para. 5)

[释义] Undoubtedly, one can even find pleasure in living alone if he or she chooses to stay alone of his or her own free will.

5. Look at Milton's daughters arranging his cushions and blankets...(Para. 6)

[释义] **creep away** 轻手轻脚地离开

    e.g. They crept away in order not to wake the baby.

        为了不弄醒婴儿，他们蹑手蹑脚地走开了。

6. While the others are absent,..., eating ice cream at one sitting,...(Para. 11)

[释义] **at one sitting** 持续进行某一活动的时间

    e.g. I read the book at one sitting. 我坐着一口气把书读完了。

7. It's good for us, and a lot less embarrassing than the woman in front of us in line at the market who's telling the cashier that her niece Melissa may be coming to visit on Saturday, and Melissa is very fond of hot chocolate, which is why she bought the powered hot chocolate mix, though she never drinks it herself. (Para. 13)

[分析] "the woman in front of us in line at the market"是介词than的宾语，"who's telling...drinks it herself"是修饰the woman的定语从句，在这个定语从句中又包含了两个并列的宾语从句"that her niece Melissa...on Saturday"和"and Melissa...hot chocolate"；"which is why...drinks it herself"是非限制性定语从句，先行词which指代前面两个宾语从句的内容。

Ⅲ．重点语法讲解

  动词不定式 (infinitive) 是一种非限定动词，由不定式符号to加动词原形所构成。动词不定式有动词的特征，同时也有名词、形容词和副词的特征。

  动词不定式在句中可作主语、表语、宾语、定语和状语等。

1. 主语 动词不定式可前置作主语，但往往放在谓语动词的后面，而在句首用代词it作形式主语。

To talk with her is a pleasant thing.

It is a real pleasure **to talk with him**.

2. 表语 不定式表语对主语做补充说明。

Her dream is **to be a pilot**.

Our project is **to help those disabled people**.

3. 宾语 动词不定式常用作某些及物动词或形容词的宾语。

He was pledged **to take part in** the party.

We are ready **to set out**.

4. 定语 动词不定式作定语时，须放在被修饰的名词或代词之后。

He is always **the first to come**.（主谓关系）

I have three letters **to write**.（动宾关系）

They are discussing ways **to guarantee high output**.（同位语关系）

5. 状语 动词不定式作状语时，一般放在它所修饰的动词之后。

He applied to a British university **to study abroad**.（表示目的）

He went upstairs **to find** that the door of the bedroom was closed.（表示结果）

We are proud **to be members of this class**.（表示原因）

Ⅳ. 课文赏析

1. 文体特点

本文是一篇议论文，就一种普遍的社会现象——有意选择独处展开讨论。作者运用了摆事实、举例子和对照比较等论证方法，最后得出文章的结论。文章结构层层推进，论证有理有据。虽然在讨论一个哲学问题，但是作者笔调轻松随意，语言幽默机智。

2. 结构分析

Part Ⅰ (Para. 1) Living alone has become a common social phenomenon.

Part Ⅱ (Para. 2) People have different opinions on living alone.

Part Ⅲ (Para. 3-10) Inspirations in solitude brings inspiration to poets and philosophers.

Part Ⅳ (Para. 11-16) Comments on the phenomenon of living alone.

Ⅴ. 课后练习答案及解析

Vocabulary

Ⅲ.

1. dictate 译文：尽管他没有口述内容，但是他的速度很慢，以便让听众有足够的时间记下他说的话。

2. choked 译文：她等不及天亮，半夜就打电话给她的朋友，告诉他那段令她窒息的不愉快的经历。

3. humble 译文：职位低的职员不得不仔细掂量老板的话语，密切关注老板的神情。

4. justice 译文：公众对于警察和法院等司法机关的信任度已处于半崩溃的状态，必须重建。

5. waterproof 译文：我认为在又冷又湿的天气中外出旅行并不是不好，但是你得准备好地图、指南针和防水的防寒服。

6. slippery 译文：据预计，找到并重新铺筑打滑的地面一年能够减少1,800起事故。

7. poetry 译文：当威廉·华兹华斯在户外创作诗歌时，她的妹妹多罗茜在家里收拾家务。

8. supreme 译文：尽管他有最高权力，但是他宁愿被当作一个伙伴，而不是独裁者，和导演、演员以及俱乐部的其他人为了同一个目标共同努力。

Ⅳ.

1. cast out 译文：在丑闻之后，人们不愿与他谈话，并且他被上流社会抛弃。

2. all by himself 译文：梭罗不需要任何陪伴，相反，他更愿意独自一个呆在小屋里。

3. stay up late 译文：在周末我们通常被允许晚点睡觉以看会儿电视。

4. was fond of 译文：甚至在小学里时，他就十分喜爱足球。

5. at one sitting 译文：故事情节如此吸引人，以至于她一口气就看完了。

6. filled up with 译文：在暴雨之后，水沟里满是泥浆和垃圾。

7. speaks highly of 译文：作者高度评价了梭罗在瓦尔登湖畔的独居生活。

8. have sought out 译文：有些诗人和哲学家认为他们在独处时找到了灵感。

Collocation

Ⅴ.

1. idea 译文：因此，在这个时期主要的哲学流派倾向于摒弃进步的观点而认为时间的本质是循环往复的，这一点也不奇怪。

2. offer 译文：但是巴勒斯坦拒绝了这个提议，而且说到他们的所有要求得到满足之前不会重新恢复和谈。

3. proposal 译文：今天，将近有1000名公共汽车司机、工程师和办公室职员准备投票决定是否接受或否决这项提议，其中也包括节假日减少薪水。

4. belief 译文：他并没有因为马克思主义还没有被历史证明而否定它，而是通过分析前苏联的具体历史来说明马克思主义。

5. request 译文：银行可能会拒绝你的贷款要求，因为他们认为你不能按时还款。

6. control 译文：他争辩道拒绝教堂的控制并不等于表示人们不相信上帝的存在。

7. promotion 译文：他拒绝了公司的提升，说他更愿意自由地选择自己的将来，而不愿意由于新的提升而被合同所限制。

8. products 译文：在抗日战争中，许多中国人把抵制日货作为爱国主义运动的一部分。

Word Building

VI. ▶

1. underestimated 译文：修理费比我想得多了一倍，我确实低估了受损的程度。

2. underpaid 译文：许多人抱怨他们超额工作却没有足够的报酬。

3. overslept 译文：今天早上我没有赶上火车，因为我又睡过头了。

4. Underdeveloped 译文：发展中国家应该得到帮助，允许他们使用信息技术，以便有一天能够在信息高速公路上与发达国家并驾齐驱。

5. overestimated 译文：销售经理过高估计了需求量，结果公司剩余20,000件商品未出售。

6. overcharged 译文：他说出租车司机多收了他十美元，并决定就此投诉。

7. underweight 译文：在这个国家有将近三分之一的孩子体重不达标。

8. overloaded 译文：飞行员警告他飞机超载，因此不能起飞。

VII. ▶

1. simplified 译文：老师简化了指令以便使孩子们理解。

2. electrician 译文：哦，天哪，灯又灭了。这次我们最好还是找电工。

3. recovery 译文：在9-11事件以后，这个国家的许多人对于在几年内经济复苏的前景一直持悲观态度。

4. underwent 译文：亚伯丁皇家医院发言人称，女王在星期四晚上进行了一个小时的喉部手术，最新的检查结果表明一切状况良好。

5. autobiography 译文：他一生的经历记录在他的两卷精彩的自传中。

6. underline 译文：用红笔划出所有你认为对你的健康不利并且应该控制的食物。

7. terrorist 译文：1933年2月，在恐怖分子在地下室引爆了炸弹之后，警方的直升机撤离了北塔屋顶上的人。

8. over-react 译文：如果你的孩子在学校里惹上了麻烦，请不要反应过激。

Structure

VIII. ▶

1. The more openly you and your doctor talk together, the better the service your doctor will

be able to give you.

译文：你与你的医生谈得越开诚布公，他能够给你的服务就越好。

2. The more Renee Henry learnt about the therapy, the more she became convinced that it was right for her.

译文：瑞尼·亨利对这个疗法了解得越多，她就越坚信这适合她。

3. The more a nation's companies locate factories abroad, the smaller will be the country's recorded exports.

译文：一个国家的公司在海外的工厂越多，这个国家的出口量就越少。

4. The less exercise you do, the more unfit you will become, and the harder everyday tasks will seem.

译文：你越不锻炼，身体越不健康，每天的任务就显得越难。

5. Remember that the less processed a food, the higher its mineral and vitamin content.

译文：记住，食物的加工过程越少，其中的矿物质和维生素含量就越高。

IX.

1. You might as well go there to see whether there is the information you need.

译文：我爸爸总是在当地图书馆查阅资料，你不妨去那里看看有没有你需要的资料。

2. You might as well call it freedom.

译文：当你独处时你可以做你想做的事，我们不妨称之为自由吧。

3. You may as well ring and tell them you're going to visit them.

译文：他们经常想念你，你不妨打电话告诉他们你要去看望他们。

4. We might/may as well walk home.

译文：等车没用的，我们不妨走回家吧。

5. We might/may as well find an easier one to read.

译文：这篇文章对我们来说太难了，我们不妨找一篇容易一些的来读。

Translation

X.

1. Poets and philosophers all speak highly of/have a high opinion of themselves for seeking out solitude, from which they can draw inspiration.

2. A humble person tends to/is likely to suffer from solitude, feeling himself inadequate company, longing to be around.

3. The widowed old lady was so lonely that she would talk at length to the strangers in the supermarket about her pets.

4. The condition of loneliness rises and falls, but our need to talk goes on forever——the need of telling someone the daily succession of small observations and opinions.

5. To a person living alone, it's important to stay rational and settle down and make himself comfortable, and find some grace and pleasure in his condition.

6. If you live with other people, their temporary absence can be refreshing.

7. Scientific surveys suggest that those who live alone talk at length to themselves and their pets and the television.

8. It's important to stop waiting and settle down and make ourselves comfortable, at least temporarily.

XI. ▶

1. 孤独或许是这里的一种民族弊病，它比起其他任何过错更加令人难以启齿。而另一方面，故意选择独处，拒绝别人的陪伴而非为同伴所抛弃，这正美国式英雄的一个特点。

2. 孤独的猎人，孤独的探险者，在鹿群和狼群中间冒险，去征服广袤的荒野，这时他们并不需要有人陪伴。梭罗独居在湖畔的小屋，有意抛弃了城市生活。现在，这成了你的个性。

3. 独处时产生的灵感是诗人和哲学家最有用的东西。他们都赞成独处。

4. 也许你已经注意到，这些艺术家类型的人，大多是到户外独处，而家里则自有亲人们备好了热茶，等着他们回家。

5. 美国的独处高士是梭罗。我们钦佩他，并非因为他倡导自力更生精神，而是因为他孤身一人在瓦尔登湖畔生活，这是他自己想要这么做的。他独居在湖畔的树林中。

6. 其他人不在的时候，你可以放飞你的灵魂，让它充满整个房间。你可以充分享受自由。你可以随意来去而无需道歉。

7. 在我们自身的条件下发现一些优雅和乐趣很重要，不要做一个以自我为中心的英国诗人，而要像一个被关在塔楼里的公主，耐心地等待着我们的童话故事进入快乐的结局。

8. 毕竟，事已至此，这或许不是我们所期望的局面，但眼下我们不妨称之为家吧。

Essay Summary

XII. ▶

DBACB　DACBC　DADBC　ADCAC

Text Structure Analysis

XIII. ▶

1. their temporary absence can be refreshing.

2. the temporary absence of your friends and acquaintances leaves a vacuum.

3. We can tell our friends important things or complain about losing job, falling on a slippery floor, breaking our arm...

4. talking at length to ourselves and our pets and the television, asking the cat and the parrot what to do, arguing with ourselves...

VI. 参考译文

有意选择独处

　　事实如此，我们孤独无伴地生活着。据最近的统计，共有2,200万人独自生活在自己的屋里。其中有些人喜欢这种生活，有些却不是。有些离了婚，有些鳏寡无伴，也有些从未结过婚。

　　孤独或许是这里的一种民族弊病，它比起其他任何过错更加令人难以启齿。而另一方面，故意选择独处，拒绝别人的陪伴而非为同伴所抛弃，这正美国式英雄的一个特点。孤独的猎人，孤独的探险者，在鹿群和狼群中间冒险，去征服广袤的荒野，这时他们并不需要有人陪伴。梭罗独居在湖畔的小屋，有意抛弃了城市生活。现在，这成了你的个性。

　　独处时产生的灵感是诗人和哲学家最有用的东西。他们都赞成独处，都因能够独处而自视甚高,至少在他们匆匆忙忙赶回家喝茶之前的一两个小时之内是如此。

就拿多萝西·华兹华斯来说吧,她帮她兄弟威廉穿上外衣,为他找到笔记本和铅笔,向他挥手告别,目送着他走进早春的阳光去独自对花沉思。他写道:"独处多么悠闲,美妙。"

毫无疑问,如果自愿独处,则感觉要好得多。

瞧瞧弥尔顿的女儿们:她们为他准备好垫子和毯子,然后蹑手蹑脚地走开,以便他能创作诗歌。然而他并不自己费神将诗歌写下来,而是唤回女儿们,向她们口述,由她们写下来。

也许你已经注意到,这些艺术家类型的人,大多是到户外独处,而家里则自有亲人们备好了热茶,等着他们回家。

美国的独处高士是梭罗。我们钦佩他,并非因为他倡导自力更生精神,而是因为他孤身一人在瓦尔登湖畔生活,这是他自己想要这么做的。他独居在湖畔的树林中。

实际上,他最近的邻居离他只有一英里,走路也就20分钟;铁路离他半英里;交通繁忙的大路距他300码。整天都有人进出他的小屋,请教他何以能够如此高洁。显然,他的高洁之处主要在于:他既没有妻子也没有仆人,自己动手用斧头砍柴,自己洗杯碟。我不知道谁为他洗衣服,他没说,但是他也肯定没提到是他自己洗的。听听他是这么说的:"我发现没有任何同伴比独处更好。"

梭罗以自尊自重为伴。也许这里的启示是:自我意识越强,就越不需要其他的人在周围。我们越是感觉谦卑,就越受孤独的折磨,感到仅与自己相处远远不够。

若与别人同住,你会在与他们小别时感觉耳目一新。孤独将会于星期四结束。如果今天我提到自己时使用的是单数人称代词,那么下星期我就会使用复数形式。其他人不在的时候,你可以放飞你的灵魂,让它充满整个房间。你可以充分享受自由。你可以随意来去而无需道歉。你可以熬夜读书、大泡浴缸、坐下一口气吃掉整整一品脱的雪糕。你可以按自己的节奏行动。暂别的人会回来。他们的冬季防水大衣还放在衣橱里,狗也在窗边密切留意他们归来的身影。但如果你单独居住,那么朋友或熟人的暂时离别会使你感到空虚,也许他们永远也不会回来了。

孤独的感觉时起时落,但我们却永远需要与人交谈。这比需要倾听更重要。噢,我们都有朋友,可以把大事要事向他们倾诉。我们可以打电话对他们说我们丢了工作,或者说我们在湿滑的地板上摔倒了,跌断了胳膊。但是每日不断发生的琐碎抱怨,看到的和想到的琐事,却积在那儿,塞满了我们的心。我们不会真打电话给一位朋友,告诉他我们收到了姐姐的一个包裹,或者说现在天黑得比较早,或者说我们不信任最高法院新来的法官。

科学调查表明,独居的人会对着自己,对着宠物,对着电视机唠叨不休。我们问猫儿今天该穿蓝色套装还是黄色裙装,问鹦鹉今天晚餐该做牛排还是面条。我们跟自己争论那个花样滑冰选手和这个滑雪运动员到底谁更了不起。这没什么不妥,也对我们有好处,而且不像有些人那么令人尴尬:在超市付款处,排在前面的女人告诉收银员,她的侄女梅莉莎星期六可能会来看她。梅莉莎非常喜爱热巧克力,所以她买了速溶热巧克力粉,虽然她自己从来不喝这东西。

重要的是保持理性。

重要的是不再等待,而是安顿下来,使自己过得舒服,至少暂时要这样。在我们自身的条件下发现一些优雅和乐趣很重要,不要做一个以自我为中心的英国诗人,而要像一个被关在塔楼里的公主,耐心地等待着我们的童话故事进入快乐的结局。

毕竟，事已至此，这或许不是我们所期望的局面，但眼下我们不妨称之为家吧。不管怎么说，没有什么地方比家还好。

VII. 写作指导

以分类法构成段落是常见的写作方法之一。分类法，即把具有某一或某些特征的人或物归入一类。通过分类，可以把篇幅较长的文章分成许多部分或"条块"，使文章结构清晰，便于理解。由于目的不同，归类可以是多方面的。当我们从不同角度考虑问题时就有不同的分类方法，但是作为一个整体，整篇文章的分类的概念必须是一致的。

采用分类法时，以合理的顺序排列也是很重要的。我们可以把较次要的类别排在前面，而把重要的类别排在后面，也可以以时间为顺序，以地点为顺序。总之，让其合乎逻辑而又尽可能将其安排得更加吸引人。

范文：

As for people living alone, we usually find two kinds of them: those who prefer living alone, and those who have to live alone. The former ones desire for inspiration in solitude. Most of them are literary giants, hunters or explorers, and they enjoy the benefits of living alone on purpose. On the other hand, the latter ones are forced to live alone for being divorced or widowed, or because they are never married. Most of them feel bitter and empty while living in solitude. They have no one to talk to and as a result they talk at length to themselves, to their pets and to the television. They even have to ask the cat or the parrot what to do in their daily life.

Section B
I. 阅读技巧

认识段落模式（II）

三、列举式（Simple Listing）

简单列举式中，作者通过列举证据来阐明观点，直接地或用序号列出一系列观点、事实、数据或能支持其论点的其他内容。这种结构内容清晰且较易组织，尤其是当作者要陈述若干要点时。列举的顺序无关紧要，前后调换不影响段落大意。

四、比较与对比式（Comparison and Contrast）

在比较观点或事物时，作者会阐明它们的相似之处；作对比时，则会阐明它们的不同之处。作者常用比较及对比法来分析某问题的正、反面或某件事的利弊。文章内容的组织既可以强调相同点，也可以强调不同点，或两者兼顾。作者往往会运用人们了解或熟知的事物帮助读者了解或区分事物。当出现这种结构时，以下问题有助于理解作者的材料组织：比较或对比的对象是什么？比较对象之间的相似之处或差异表现在哪些地方？这种解释的主要目的是什么？

五、因果关系式（Cause and Effect Relationship）

作者提出观点或描述事件时最常用的段落组织结构之一是因果关系式。作者采用这种结构阐明事件发生的原因、方式极（可能的）结果。劝说或辩论等文章中常用因果式，因为它是推理的主要结构模式。因果式还可以有多种组合方式来表达段落的中心思想。

六、定义式（Definition）

作者在定义式中以解释某一术语或概念的含义为目的。有时候标题、次级标题、段落首句以疑问句形式出现，表明该段可能运用定义式。通常，运用定义式的段落也可以同时配合使用其他形式，尤其是例证式。

七、例证式（Example）

例证式用例子支持论点或中心思想，是写作结构中最常用的方法之一。通常作者运用一个或多个具体事例、图例来支持和展述论点或中心思想，用具体的细节阐明某一概念，或证明某一论据的合理性。好的例证能使宽泛的概念具体化，有助于抓住读者的兴趣。

Ⅱ．词汇与短语详解

1. oral

[词义] *adj.* spoken; not written 口头的

[例句] He passed his English oral examination. 他已经通过了英语口试。

[联想] aural *adj.* 听力的

2. minus

[词义] *prep.* ①零下；②减

　　　　adj. ①负的，零下的；②减

　　　　n. [C] ①负数；②减号

[搭配] minus sign 负号，减号; a minus quantity 负数，负量; minus electricity 阴电，负电; minus material 次品

[例句] The temperature could fall to minus eight tonight.

今晚温度会下降到零下八度。

Seven minus three equals four. 7减去3等于4。

-2 is a minus figure. –2是负数。

I got B minus in the test. 我在测试中得B–。

Two minuses make a plus. 负负得正。

Those pupils are learning to use the pluses and minuses.

那些小学生正在学习使用加减号。

3. vibrate

[词义] *v.* 震动，振动，抖动

[搭配] be vibrated with 被……感动

[例句] The ground vibrated during the earthquake. 地震时地面震动。

[派生] vibration *n.* 震动，摇动; vibratile 能振动的; vibratility *n.* 振动性

4. organic

[词义] *adj.* ① 不用化肥培植的，施用有机肥料的；② 生物体的，有机体的

[例句] Many people believe that organic foods are healthful to them.

许多人认为有机肥料培植的食品对他们的健康有好处。

Peat is decomposed organic matter. 泥炭是已分解的有机物。

[派生] organism *n.* 生物，有机体; organically *adv.* 用有机肥料培植地

5. holy

[词义] *adj.* 神圣的，圣洁的

[搭配] Holy Bible《圣经》; Holy City 圣城; holy water 圣水

[例句] The poem sings the praises of holy love. 这首诗歌颂圣洁的爱。

[联想] holies *n.* 圣地，至圣所

[辨析] divine, holy, sacred

　　　　divine 意为"神的，神圣的"，着重指具有神的本性的，属于神或上帝的;

　　　　holy 是唯一可以用于赞颂上帝的词，着重指内含"神圣的"本质，因而值

得崇拜; sacred 正式用词，所修饰的事物因奉献给宗教而获得神圣性、值得崇敬。

6. stale

[词义] *adj.* ① 没有新意的，过时的；②（食品）不新鲜的，走味的

[搭配] stale air 不新鲜的空气; stale news 过时消息

[例句] He gave a boring speech full of stale jokes.

他的发言很乏味，满是老掉牙的笑话。

You'd better not eat stale bread. 你最好不要吃陈面包。

[派生] staleness *n.* 陈腐，过时; staleproof *adj.* 不腐的; stalemate *n.* 僵局

7. depression

[词义] *n.* ① [U] 沮丧，意志消沉；② [C] 萧条期，不景气

[搭配] financial depression 金融萧条时期; fall into a depression 变得志气消沉

[例句] A holiday will help her out of depression. 一个假期会帮助她不再消沉。

He was unemployed for many years during the depression of the 1930s.

他在20世纪30年代大萧条时期失业多年。

[派生] depress *vt.* 按下，使沮丧; depressing *adj.* 抑压的，阴沉的

8. tolerate

[词义] *v.* ① 忍耐；② 容忍

[例句] Only he can tolerate the noise outside. 只有他能忍耐户外的噪音。

The school cannot tolerate cheating on exams. 学校不容许考试作弊。

[派生] tolerance *n.* 宽容，忍耐力; tolerate *adj.* 宽容的，容忍的

[辨析] bear, endure, stand, tolerate

bear意为"忍受，忍耐"，强调忍受者出于自愿而承受困难、痛苦的力量与心理能力，一般用于疑问句或否定句; endure意为"忍受、容忍、忍耐"，指长期忍受着考验或痛苦而不屈服或退缩，强调持久力与意志坚定; stand多用于口语中的疑问句和否定句，意为"忍受、容忍、经得起"，强调克服自身对讨厌的、敌对的事物等的反感; tolerate所体现的语气较其他几个词弱，所容忍的现象一般不给容忍者直接带来强烈苦难。

9. abstract

[词义] *adj.* 抽象的

n. [C] ① 抽象概念，概括；② 摘要，提要

[搭配] in the abstract 抽象地，理论上; abstract science 理论科学

[例句] Truth and beauty are abstract concepts. 真与美是抽象概念。

Talking about bringing up children in the abstract just isn't enough.

空谈抚养孩子实在是不够的。

He made an abstract of the lecture. 他为讲座写了摘要。

[派生] abstraction *n.* 提取; abstractive *adj.* 具有抽象能力的

[辨析] abstract, digest, outline, summary

abstract通常指学术论文的"摘要、梗概"，一般位于正文前，内容是简要地介绍论文的论题和研究结果，目的是让读者了解论文讲述哪方面的问题; digest 指一篇文章的"简写、选编"，略去不重要的细节，但仍保持原文的顺序、重点和风格; outline 不包括文章、书本或计划的详细内容，只

133

包含主要内容和大致框架，可以是实现拟好的"提纲"，然后加以充实，也可以是为了某个目的分析他人作品的"概要"；summary 指把较长的文字材料的主要内容加以概括而形成的"摘要、概要"，篇幅可长可短，根据需要而定。

10. resort

[词义] *n.* 常去之地，胜地；*v.* 求助，采用

[搭配] a health resort 修养圣地；resort to 求助，诉诸

[例句] There are many summer resorts in the mountains. 在山里有许多避暑胜地。

I had to resort to violence to solve the problem.
我不得不借助暴力来解决问题。

11. disorder

[词义] *n.* ① [U] 混乱状态；② [U] 骚乱，暴乱

[搭配] fall into disorder 混乱，紊乱；throw...into disorder 把……卷入动乱

[例句] The whole room was in a state of disorder. 整个房间乱糟糟的。

The trial was kept secret because of the risk of public disorder.
因为生怕引起公众的骚乱，审判是保密的。

[派生] disordered *adj.* 混乱的，杂乱的；disordering *n.* 无秩序化

12. selection

[词义] *n.* ① [U] 选择；② [C] 可供挑选的东西

[例句] After some discussion, we made our selection.
经过一番讨论，我们做出了选择。

Most schools would have a good selection of these books in their libraries.
大部分学校的图书馆都有许多这样的书供选择。

[派生] select *vt.* 挑选，选择；selective *adj.* 有选择性的，精挑细选的

13. exclaim

[词义] *v.* （由于惊奇、害怕、欢欣等）呼喊，惊叫

[搭配] exclaim against 表示强烈不赞成，指责；exclaim at (on/upon) 对……表示惊奇；exclaim over 感叹

[例句] She exclaimed in delight upon seeing her friends.
她看到她的朋友们高兴地欢呼起来。

[辨析] exclaim, shout, scream

exclaim 指由于惊奇、痛苦、高兴等为表现强烈感情而高声叫喊；shout 指予以警告、注意或表达愤怒的叫喊；scream 指因为恐怖、痛苦等而近乎歇斯底里的突然尖叫。

[派生] exclamation *n.* 惊呼；exclaimer *n.* 大声叫的人

14. paw

[词义] *v.* ① 翻找，笨拙地触摸；②（用脚爪等）抓，扒

n. [C] ① 脚爪，爪子；② 手

[搭配] in the lion's paw 在致命的危险之中；velvet paw hide sharp claws 笑里藏刀，口蜜腹剑；make a cat's paws of sb. 利用某人做爪牙或工具

[例句] She pawed through her purse for keys. 她在手提包里乱翻一气找钥匙。

The dog began pawing (at) the ground in excitement.

这狗开始兴奋地用爪子抓地。

The cat lifted its paw and put it on my knee. 猫抬起爪子放在我的膝上。

Take your filthy paws off my nice clean washing!

把你的脏手从我洗得干干净净的衣物上拿开！

[联想] hoof *n.* 马蹄；trotter *n.* （猪、羊）蹄；claw *n.* 尖爪

15. chip

[词义] *n.* ① [C] 片屑，碎片；② (usu. pl.) 炸薯条；③芯片

v. (使) 削下碎片

[例句] The ground was covered with wood chips. 地上铺满了木屑。

This restaurant serves excellent steak and chips.

这家餐馆供应上好的牛排和炸薯条。

The silicon chip is said to be the invention that has changed the lifestyles in the 20th century. 人们认为硅片是改变了20世纪生活方式的发明。

This plate chips easily. 这个盘子很容易碰碎。

[辨析] chip, fragment, piece, scrap

chip 指从木头、玻璃、石头等物质上削下来的碎片，体积很小；fragment 常以复数形式出现，指整体物质破碎后而形成的碎片，体积可大可小，一般已失去原来整体所具有的价值；piece 常用词，应用范围广，可指任何从整体物质上分离开来的小块物质，未必失去整体所具有的价值；scrap 意为"碎片、零屑、小块"，常含有"废品、破烂"的意思。

16. slap

[词义] *v.* ① 用巴掌打，拍打；② 啪啪地撞击，拍击

n. [C] 掴，掌击

[搭配] slap one's face 打某人的耳光；slap sb. on the back 拍某人的背，鼓励；slap around 打击，粗暴对待；slap on (随便地) 涂上一层

[例句] She slapped his face when he put his hand on her knee.

当他将手放在她的膝盖上时，她打了他一记耳光。

He slapped the book down on the desk. 他把书啪的一声往桌上一扔。

He gave the child a slap on the back. 他在孩子的背上打了一巴掌。

17. strike out 独立闯新路，独立开创

[例句] He decided to leave home and to strike out on his own.

他决定离开家，自己去闯天下。

[联想] strike off 删去，除名；strike up 开始（谈话，相识）等

18. range from...to 在从……到……范围或幅度内变动或变化

[例句] Prices range from $25 to $75. 价格从25美元至75美元不等。

19. give up on 对……表示绝望

[例句] His parents seem to have given up on him. 他的父母看来已对他绝望。

[联想] give in 屈服，上交；give away 赠送，泄露；give off 发出，散发

20. turn up 发觉，发现；出现，露面；开大，调高（火焰、声音等）

[例句] The police searched the house hoping to turn up more clues.

警方搜查了房子，希望找到更多的线索。

If he doesn't turn up soon, we shall have to go without him.

如果他不马上露面的话，我们就不带他去了。

Please turn up the radio. 请把收音机开响些。

21. end up 结束，告终

[例句] Wasteful people usually end up in debt. 挥霍浪费者最后往往负债。

22. spring from 源于，从……产生出来；突然从……冒出；出身于

[例句] The river springs from a lake. 这条河的源头是一个湖。

The inspiration springs from his mind. 灵感一下子蹦了出来。

He is sprung from the common family. 他出身于普通家庭。

23. tear apart 使……分裂

[例句] It was the misunderstanding that tore them apart. 是误解导致了他们的分离。

[联想] tear away（使）勉强离去；tear down 拆掉，拆除；tear up 撕毁

24. resort to 凭借，求助，诉诸；光顾，常去（某地）

[例句] If persuasion won't work, we may have to resort to force.

如果说服工作不见效，我们可能只得诉诸武力。

They resorted to the shop for desserts. 她们常去那家店买甜点。

25. in case 以防万一；假使

[例句] Be quiet in case you wake the baby. 轻点儿，免得弄醒孩子。

In case she comes back, give me a call. 假如她回来了，打电话给我。

26. head off 阻止，拦住

[例句] He will get into trouble if we don't head him off.

如果我们不阻拦他，他会遇到麻烦。

[联想] head on 迎面；head over heels 头朝下，完全地，深深地

27. fill in 把……填进去，把（表格等）填好

[例句] He was required to fill in a form before the interview.

面试前，他被要求填一张表格。

[联想] fill out 填写；fill up 填补，淤积

28. sum up 总结，概括

[例句] The lawyer summed up the evidence presented. 律师总结了呈堂证据。

[联想] in sum 总而言之

29. against all (the) odds 尽管有极大的困难，出乎意料地

[例句] Against all (the) odds, he made a full recovery. 他出乎意料地完全康复了。

III. 难句解析

1. Sarah's ability to solve her dilemma by rooming with her identical twin is unusual, but the conflict she faced is not. (Para. 3)

[释义] **room** vi. 居住，寄宿

e.g. I roomed with Smith in college for two years.

我和史密斯在大学里同房间（住过）二年。

[分析] 后面的分句是省略形式，省略了与前面分句一样的表语unusual。

2. When personalities don't mix, the excitement of being away at college can quickly grow stale. (Para. 4)

[释义] **mix** v. 与人相处融洽

e.g. He is such a friendly person that he mixes well in any company.

他为人和气，跟任何人都能相处得很融洽。

3. **Many schools have started conflict resolution programs to calm tensions that otherwise can build up like a volcano preparing to explode, ultimately resulting in physical violence. (Para. 7)**

[分析] "to calm tensions that..."是不定式短语作目的状语，that引导定语从句，修饰先行词tensions； 在这个定语从句中，现在分词短语 "preparing to explode"是作宾语volcano的伴随状语，"ultimately resulting in physical violence"作结果状语。

4. **Some schools try to head off feuding before it begins by using computerized matching, a process that nevertheless remains more of a guessing game than a science. (Para. 8)** .

[释义] **more of...than** 更……而不是……

e.g. He is more of a poet than a musician. 他更像一个诗人，而不是音乐家。

5. **The matching process is also complicated by a philosophical debate among housing managers concerning the flavor of university life...(Para. 8)**

[释义] **flavor** *n.* 特性，特色

e.g. The film remained much of the novel's exotic flavor.

这部电影保留了原著的许多异国情调。

[分析] "concerning the flavor of university life"是现在分词作定语修饰housing managers。

IV. 重点语法讲解

省略句

为了避免重复，句中有某些部分常可省略。

1. 省掉主语（多限于少数现成说法）

Thank you for your help.

See you tomorrow.

2. 省掉谓语动词和表语等

① 省掉谓语动词。

Some of us study English, **others French**.

He got up later **than her today**.

② 省掉联系动词

My brother is a lawyer, **my sister a doctor**.

She is **as tall as I**.

③ 省掉表语

—Are you ready? —Yes, **I am**.

3. 同时省掉句子几个部分

有时好几个句子成分都被省掉，特别是在表示比较的状语从句中，在对疑问句的简略回答中，以及在反义疑问句或选择疑问句中。

In winter it is much colder in Beijing **than in Nanjing**.

You are a policeman, **aren't you?**

Will you go home **or not?**

—Have you ever been to Tibet? —**Never**.

Ⅴ. 课文赏析

1. 文体特点

文章首先以具体的事例讲述了在校园内很普遍的现象，即室友间的冲突，引出主题。正文部分分析了造成这种现象的原因及一系列不良后果，最后提出为解决这一问题所采取的措施。文章主题明确，事例真实生动，论证充分有力。

2. 结构分析

Part Ⅰ (Para. 1-2) Room conflicts the identical twin Katie and Sarah met in the school.

Part Ⅱ (Para. 4-7) Reasons and bad effects of room conflicts.

Part Ⅲ (Para. 8-9) The measure taken by the school in order to solve it.

Ⅵ. 课后练习答案及解析

Reading Skills

XV.

1. A. d)

   B. The author makes a lot of comparisons between different needs, different hobbies and different beliefs to bring out the main idea that the conflict among roommates are not uncommon.

   C. It is a general statement supported by comparisons and contrasts. The word is "while", which appeared three times.

2. A. d)

   B. The writer starts with identifying the problem: roommate conflict can lead to serious violence with an example presented. Then he offers some solutions: conflict resolution programs to calm tensions with details specified. And at last he evaluates the conflict resolution programs: Through roommate contracts or behavioral guidelines are not legal documents, these would at least give the school permission to talk about the issues with the students.

   C. A general statement supported by a problem-solution-evaluation pattern.

Comprehension of the Text

XVI.

F T T F F   T T F

Vocabulary

XVII.

1. vibrate 译文：像砖和石头那样的重材料不容易摇动，因此很快能减少噪音。

2. holy 译文：所有这些节日都被当成神圣的日子，每当这个时候，所有的日常工作都会暂停。

3. tolerate 译文：他们喜欢彼此的陪伴，并乐意容忍一些不便。

4. stale 译文：他从事第一份工作之前得到一条建议：不要连续干一份工作超过十年，因为你会厌倦的。

5. disorder 译文：饥饿、疾病和内乱破坏社会文明。

6. chew 译文：如果食物又干又硬，我们会自动咀嚼，直到它容易下咽。

7. abstract 译文：人们普遍认为工程学是一种极为抽象和理论化的科学。

8. exclaimed 译文：当一个年轻人手拿着枪突然从苏珊后面出现的时候，他吓得大叫起来。

XVIII.

1. When he received the admission notice from the university, he knew it was time he struck out on hid own.

   译文：当他受到大学录取通知书时，他知道是他开始独立的时候了。

2. His roommate always turns up the CD player to highest point, which makes him miserable.

   译文：他的室友总是把CD的音量开到最大，这使他很痛苦。

3. Every time she tried to argue with her identical twin Katie, she ended up crying her eyes out.

   译文：每次她和她的双胞胎妹妹凯蒂争吵的时候，结局总是以她痛哭流涕为终。

4. Serious violence has sprung from the conflict over insignificant, irritating differences.

   译文：严重的暴力来源于毫无意义的、恼人的分歧引起的冲突。

5. There are many people who believe sincerely that you can train children for life without resorting to punishment.

   译文：许多人认为教育孩子不需要诉诸于武力。

6. Alan signed a dorm contract with his roommate to head off possible conflicts.

   译文：艾伦和他的室友签了一份宿舍协议来避免可能发生的冲突。

7. He was required to fill in a form before the job interview.

   译文：面试前他被要求填一个表格。

8. Her husband used to slap her around, which led to the breakup of her marriage.

   译文：她丈夫过去经常打她，这导致了她婚姻的破裂。

VII. 参考译文

室友间的冲突

同卵双胞胎卡蒂和萨拉·莫纳汉去年来到宾夕法尼亚的葛底斯堡大学，决心闯出一条独立之路。虽然这对18岁的姐妹曾要求住在不同的宿舍楼，但宿管处还是把她们安排在同一栋楼的第8层，中间只隔着一条过道。卡蒂与室友相处融洽，但萨拉却十分不快。她因许多事情而与室友暗地里不和，诸如什么时候熄灯啦，家具应如何摆放啦，等等。最后她们将房间一分为二，彼此不再讲话，主要通过写便条进行交流。

这段时间里，萨拉不断跑到过道对面卡蒂那儿寻求慰藉。不久两人又想住在一起了，而萨拉的室友最终也同意搬出。"从重新一起住的第一晚开始，我就感到舒服，"萨拉说，"就好像回到家里一样。"

萨拉以和同卵双生姐妹同住的办法走出了她的困境，这种办法倒很少见，但她所遇到的冲突却并不罕见。尽管许多学校已做了广泛的努力来为学生安排合适的室友，但常常有不如人意的结果。一位室友感觉很冷，而另一位却往往不想调高暖气温度，尽管气温计上显示室外温度已达零下5度。一个人喜欢安静，而另一个却每天练习两个小时的小号，或将音响开得很大，声音响得连整个房间都振动了。一个只吃天然蔬菜产品，认为所有生物都是神圣的，即使是蚂蚁、蚊子也如此，而另一位却爱穿皮草，喜欢在生物课上将青蛙开膛破肚。

彼此性格不合时，离家上大学的那种兴奋感就会立刻变得索然无味。而且，室友会互相影响对方的心理健康。根据最近的研究，大学生室友的忧郁症往往会从一个人传给另一个人。

学会容忍陌生人的习惯，可使大学生学会灵活应变和妥协的艺术，但这往往是一个十分痛苦的过程。21岁的朱莉·诺埃尔是大四学生。她回忆道，她一年级时与室友无法沟通，彼此整整一年都很不自在。"我曾从早到晚用CD机播放同一张碟,就是为了试试她,因为她太羞怯了,"诺埃尔说,"直到那天晚饭时,她才终于改变了她的羞怯。"虽然她们没有将房间一分为二,但是到了年末,她们还是大吵一场分手了。"回想起来,我真希望当时能跟她谈谈我的感受,"诺埃尔说。

大多数室友的冲突都起因于小小的令人不快的分歧,而不是由抽象的哲学原理上的重大争执引起的。"都是具体的事情弄得室友四分五裂,"俄亥俄州一所大学的宿舍管理处主任助理如是说。

在极端的情况下,室友间的冲突可能引发严重的暴力。去年春天哈佛大学发生的就是这种情况:一位学生将她的室友杀害后自杀。许多学校都已经启动了化解冲突的工作项目,以舒缓紧张形势,要不然它们就会像火山一样蓄势待发,最终导致侵犯人身的暴力行为。有些大学采用了"室友合同"的做法:所有新生在参加有关室友关系的讨论会之后,都要填写签署该份合同。学生们订下了详细的宿舍行为准则,包括可以共同接受的学习时间、睡眠时间,动用彼此物品的原则,以及如何处理留言。虽然合同不具有法律约束力,也永远不会诉诸法庭,但合同副本都送到宿舍指导员处,以防日后发生冲突。宿舍管理处主任说:"合同允许我们处理一些同学们没有想到或不愿谈及的问题。"

有些学校试图用电脑配对安排住宿,以期防止争吵发生。不过这种做法更像推测游戏而非科学。这是根据学生对住宿表格上一系列问题的回答而将他们组合在一起。这些问题包括是否容忍抽烟,选择什么样的作息时间,以及对个人习惯是整洁还是凌乱做自我描述。有时家长会拿走表格,填入不真实的、一厢情愿的数据来反映他们孩子的习惯,特别是在吸烟问题上,这就削弱了这种做法的作用。此外,宿舍管理人员中关于大学生活应有什么特色的理论争论也使这一安排过程复杂化。他们争论:"到底让相同的人还是不同的人住在一起,才能使他们取长补短呢?"一幅漫画道出了许多学生对这一做法的感受:面对一大堆的资料,宿舍工作人员随便拿出两张待选的表格,叫道:"这位喜欢象棋,那位爱好足球,两位住在一起是最理想的了!"

一位二年级的学生艾伦·萨斯曼回忆道:"我觉得他们肯定是了解了我们的性格,然后就选性格相反的。"萨斯曼喜欢整洁,学习认真,而他的室友却邋里邋遢,而且喜欢通宵聚会直至凌晨。"我一进房间,往往会发现他在我的桌子上到处乱翻,想找一张邮票去寄信。还有一次,我回来就看到他在吃我的最后一块巧克力曲奇饼,那是我妈妈带给我的。宿舍楼里的人都在打赌我们什么时候打起来,"他说。但是出乎人们的意料,他们却最终成了朋友。萨斯曼说:"我们彼此从对方学到了许多东西——但我也决不想再有这样的经历了。"

Section C

I.语言点讲解

1. ...why not give this arranged-marriage thing a shot? (Para. 7)

[释义] **give sth. a shot** 尝试一下

> e.g. I'll give skiing a shot in this winter holiday. 今年寒假我会尝试一下滑雪。

2. **Stupid and dangerous as it seems looking back, I went into my marriage at the age of 25 without being in love. (Para. 8)**

[分析] "Stupid and dangerous as it seems looking back"是as引导的让步状语从句,是"形容词+as"结构,需要把从句的表语或状语提前;"looking back"在句中作时间状语,相当于 when I looked back.

3. **Whether or not this is true, the high rate of arranged marriage in different cultures——90 percent in Iran, 95 percent in India, and similar high percentage among Hasidic Jews in New York and among Turkish and Afghan Muslims——gives one pause. (Para. 12)**

[释义] **give sb. pause** 使某人做事前犹豫，让人有理由再想一下

　　e.g. The increasingly growing unemployment gives us pause.

　　　一直增长的失业率使我们深思。

4. **No strings attached, and both of us decide where this goes, if anywhere. (Para. 21)**

[分析] "no strings attached" 是一个过去分词构成的独立结构，作为句子的状语; this指代的是两人的关系。

Ⅱ. 课文赏析

1. 文体特点

　　这是一篇记叙文，讲述了一位在美国留学的印度女性相亲结婚的经历及对这种印度包办婚姻的看法。文章通过作者的亲身经历引入主题，结构清晰流畅，选材真实可信，语言简明易懂，使我们更加深入地了解了印度的婚姻制度。

2. 结构分析

Part Ⅰ (Para. 1-8) Topic introduction by the author's own experience on arranged marriage.

Part Ⅱ (Para. 9-13) The details and characteristics of arranged marriage in India.

Part Ⅲ (Para. 14-23) The author's own successful marriage.

Ⅲ. 课后练习答案及解析

XIX.

Reading Skills

1. A. What are arranged marriages in India? The main idea of the paragraph is implied rather than stated.

　B. Arranged marriages in India begin with matching the horoscopes of the man and the woman. They look for balance so that the man and the woman are complimentary to each other. Besides, the man and the woman are of the same religion and social level.

　C. The paragraph is about the details of arranged marriage in India that help us to understand what arranged marriages are.

2. A. The high success rate of arranged marriage in different cultures.

　B. The author starts with the practice and theory concerning arranged marriages but she does not make any comments of her own. Instead, she quotes some figures to illustrate the high percentage of success for arranged marriages.

　C. A general statement supported by statistics. Even though the author does not state her own viewpoint, she quotes the figures to make us believe that arranged marriages are very successful in different cultures, which is supported by convincing statistics.

Comprehension of the Text

XX.

1. felt confused about　　　　2. fell in love with　　　　3. herself

4. complementary to each other　　5. what kind of people they are

6. good models of achieving   7. considerate and easy-going   8. helpful

IV. 参考译文

<u>印度式包办婚姻</u>

我们围坐在饭桌边，我的家人和我。又是一顿自家做的南印度风味晚饭，把我们都撑坏了。是我弟弟提出了这个问题。

"莎巴，你干吗不回印度来住几个月呢？这样我们可以帮你找对象结婚。"

三双眼睛从餐桌的那边盯着我。我叹了口气。现在已到了我研究生院毕业的那个假期的尾声，我买好了10天后从印度飞往纽约的机票。我已经接受了一份在美国一个艺术家聚居区的工作。我的汽车，还有大多数的个人物品都在美国的朋友那儿。

"没那么简单，"我说。"我的车……怎么办？"

"我们可以在美国给你找一个，"我爸爸回答说。"你可以回美国。"

他们全安排好了，这是个阴谋，我恼怒地皱着眉瞪着父母。

噢，另一种想法却辩解道，何不尝试一下这种包办婚姻呢？好像并没有很多事情等着我回美国去做，而且，随时都可以离婚啊。

现在回忆起来似乎是有些愚蠢、危险，但我当时真的是在25岁时，未经恋爱就结婚了。三年后的今天，我发现自己与这位出色的男人之间的关系十分愉快。他谈论着投资收益曲线及其他的财经统计资料；我开车时他祈祷；我所崇拜的现代艺术家的名字，他都尽力去记住。

我对包办婚姻的热忱是最近才发生的转变。不错，我是在印度长大的，包办婚姻在这儿十分普遍。我父母的婚姻是包办的，我的姑妈、堂兄妹、朋友的婚姻也都如此。但我一直认为我与他们不同。作为一个外国留学生，我在美国的一所大学里过得不错。在那里，个性发展得以鼓励，妇女权利也倍受尊重。在试着当一个美国人的同时，我也进入了美国的价值体系。

于是我决心要与一个非印度人恋爱、结婚。然而，不知怎么的，我总也做不到。噢，恋爱倒是容易，而要维持这种关系才是困难的。

包办婚姻在印度往往是先从匹配男女双方的星座开始。为人匹配星座的人试图找到一种平衡，使女方的强项弥补男方的弱项，而男方的长处也抵销女方的不足。一旦星座配上了，双方家庭就会见面看看他们是否合得来。一般认为双方都应有同一宗教信仰，属于同一社会阶层。

虽然这种做法排除了风险，也有助于确保男女双方有相同的背景和观点，但从理论上来说，是夫妻个性方面的差异才使得婚姻关系引人入胜。不管这种说法是否正确，不同文化中包办婚姻的成功率之高，却不由得使人驻足沉思：伊朗90%，印度95%，在纽约的哈西德派犹太教徒中，以及在土耳其和阿富汗的穆斯林教徒中，也有同样高的成功率。

我们两家是通过一位共同的朋友认识的，但许多印度家庭则是通过全国性报纸上刊登的广告而相识的。

我的父母正式拜访了我未来丈夫的家，看看拉姆的家人是否会善待我。我妈妈坚持认为"从上咖啡的方式，就能了解这个家庭的许多情况。"这家人有一个可爱的花园，他们喜欢园艺。很好。

拉姆的母亲以前为联合国工作过，是关于妇女权利问题的工作。她还为多家印度杂志写风趣的专栏。她会成为一种支持的力量。她不用瓷杯，而用传统的钢杯给我们上浓烈的南印度咖啡；她可以平衡我由于年青而产生的激进思想。

拉姆的父亲属于期望妻子在家呆着的那代印度人。即使如此，他仍然很支持妻子的职业生涯。拉姆有良好的行为榜样。他姐姐是美国的一位医生。或许那意味着他已经习惯于面对有成就的女强人。

1992年11月20日，有人喊道："他们来了！"我表姐轻轻地用肘推我，示意我从卧室走进客厅。

"你为什么不坐？"有人说。

我抬头看到了一张四方脸，微笑的眼睛热切地想使我放松下来。他示意我坐到一张椅子上。不知怎么的，我喜欢他那样。这个人敏感而又自信。

他看起来挺好，当然可以再减几磅体重。我喜欢他嘴唇向上弯曲的样子。他头发浓密，声音威严，笑声爽朗。令我感到意外的是，与他的对话进行得十分轻松。我们有许多共同点，但他的职业与我的却大相径庭。我得知他从美国一所大学取得了工商管理硕士学位（MBA）并在华尔街工作过，后来到了一家金融顾问公司。

两个小时后，拉姆对我说："我想更好地了解你，可惜我得回美国干我的工作了，但我可以隔天给你打一次电话。不存在什么约束，我们两个人都可以决定这件事该怎样发展——如果能有所发展的话。"

我没有不喜欢他。

10天后他给我打了电话，大约一个月后他向我求婚，我接受了。我确信我们成功的关系与两个词有关：容忍和信任。

五、知识链接

In modern Japan, more than 70% of all marriages are referred to as "love marriages," the rest are the more traditional arranged marriages. When an arranged marriage is desired, the man and woman, who are seeking a marriage partner, enlist the help of a go-between. This allows the couple to meet and get to know each other and decide if a marriage is suitable. It is quite common for the parents of the man and woman to be present at the first meeting. Afterwards the couple meets socially over a period of time and then decides, if both acceptable, to marry. This may seem a little clinical in the west, but in Japan, with its high work ethic, and large population, it is hard for some people to meet someone of the opposite sex.

Unlike matchmakers, or dating services in the west, the go-betweens are not professional matchmakers, they are usually people that like to help out of goodwill. Sometimes a go-betweens will be given a percentage (10%) of the wedding preparation money that the groom gives the bride. This money allows the bride to prepare for, and pay, all the costs of the wedding.

Are there any noticeable advantages to this system? Yes. The go-between with his/her knowledge and familiarity with both parties can bring together couples that should be suitable. Even after the marriage the go-between can act as a marriage counselor to help the new couple with their problems. As a result, the number of arranged marriages in Japan that fail is very small.

在现代日本，百分之七十以上的婚姻被称为"爱情婚姻"，而其余的则是更加传统的包办婚姻。当需要包办婚姻时，正在寻找婚姻伴侣的男方和女方，会寻求媒人的帮助。这会使得这对男女见面，互相了解对方，以及决定彼此是否适合结婚。通常第一次会面时男方和女方的家长也会在场。此后这对男女会经过一段时间的交往，然后，如果双方都合意的话决定结婚。这在西方人看来似乎不近人情，但在日本，由于工作道德标准高，人口众多，人们很难遇到某个不同性别的人。

与西方的婚介人员或约会服务不同，媒人通常不是专业的婚介人员，他们通常是出于好心愿意帮助别人的人。有时，媒人会得到新郎给新娘的聘礼的一部分（百分之十）。聘礼是足够支付新娘准备出稼及婚礼的所有费用。

这种制度是不是有其明显的优势呢？是的。媒人凭借他或她的经验和对双方家庭的了解能够使应该适合的一对男女走到一起。即使在婚后，媒人也可以作为婚姻顾问帮助这对新人解决问题。因此，在日本包办婚姻失败的数量很少。

六、自测题

1. The young painter had the example of Shakespeare to _____ and guide himself.
   A. motivate   B. inspire   C. stimulate   D. excite

2. I prefer to receive information in an _____ manner rather than in visual means.
   A. audible   B. oral   C. aural   D. aerial

3. _____ elephants are different from wild elephant in many aspects, including their tempers.
   A. Cultivated   B. Regulated   C. Civil   D. Tame

4. Winning an Olympic gold medal was the _____ moment of her life.
   A. summit   B. supreme   C. senior   D. superior

5. Her New York concert will feature famous _____ from American and European operas.
   A. pickings   B. choices   C. selections   D. collections

6. Some old people don't like pop songs because they can't _____ so much noise.
   A. resist   B. sustain   C. tolerate   D. undergo

7. Open the window and get rid of the _____ air.
   A. stall   B. stake   C. stale   D. stalk

8. It's a pleasure for him to _____ his energy and even his life to research work.
   A. dedicate   B. dictate   C. decorate   D. direct

9. I would never have _____ a court of law if I hadn't been so desperate.
   A. turned up   B. sought for   C. accounted for   D. resorted to

10. I know the place is a _____, but make yourself at home.
    A. disorder   B. mess   C. paradise   D. palace

答案与解析

1. B inspire 鼓励，激励；motivate 激发，常用于被动态；stimulate 刺激，后接宾语sb./sth.；excite 使兴奋

2. C oral 口头的；audible 听得见的；aural 听觉的；aerial 空气的，航空的

3. D tame 驯服的；cultivated 有教养的；regulated 调节的；civil 文明的

4. B supreme 最高的；summit 峰顶，顶点；senior 资深的，年长的 superior 较高的，高级的

5. C selection 精选品；pickings 剩余的零星用品；choice 选择；collection 收藏品

6. C tolerate 容忍；resist 抵抗；sustain 支撑；undergo 经历

7. C stale 不新鲜的；stall 货摊；stake 木桩，利害关系；stalk 茎，梗

8. A dedicate 献身，致力于；dictate 口述；decorate 装饰；direct 指导

9. D resort to 诉诸于；turn up 出现；sought for 寻找；account for 解释

10. B mess 凌乱；in disorder 混乱；paradise 天堂；palace 宫殿

Unit 6

1 学习重点和难点

词汇和短语、语法项目、写作技巧

2 文化知识

课文大背景、课文知识点

3 课文精讲

词汇与短语详解、难句解析、重点
语法讲解、课文赏析、课后练习答
案及解析、参考译文、写作指导

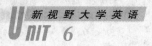

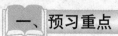

一、预习重点

1. Do you think it is necessary for business students to study professional ethics?
2. Why do people in the motor industry have to give bribes or extra discounts?
3. Why are practices such as paying agents and purchasers and exaggerated commission, and offering additional discounts described as "questionable"?
4. Can you give some examples mentioned in the text to show that "industry is caught in a web of bribery"?
5. What might a foreign company do if they want to sell arms or ammunition to a country?

二、学习重点和难点

Ⅰ. 词汇和短语

Section A: bribe, ethics, substantial, moral, accuse, questionable, account, reject, withdraw, category, consist, donation, distinguish, enforce; on the increase, a way of life, pay up, stand by, in practice, accuse of, in private, a fact of life, consist of, in support of, under investigation, throw out, close a deal, speed up, hit upon/on, distinguish between, amount to, behave oneself, be caught in, on the take, square...with

Section B: journalist, regular, imitate, surrender, innocent, impressive, available, retirement, disable, favor, spray, recovery, resident, priority, prosperous; crop up, act out, nothing more...than..., up to scratch, be on the wrong end of, law and order, throw up, on sick leave, derive...from..., lose count of, come up to, carry out, take up

Ⅱ. 语法项目

① It + is + adj. + infinitive (inf.) /that clause 句型
② "Suppose ＋（that）clause"结构
③ 选择疑问句（Alternative Question）
④ "many + a (an) + 可数名词单数"结构

Ⅲ. 写作

三、文化知识

Ⅰ. 课文大背景

Bribery, in law, the illegal influencing of any person in the exercise of a public duty through the payment of money or anything of value. In the code set down by the Babylonian king Hammurabi（巴比伦国王汉谟拉比的《法典》）, bribery was a punishable offense. By modern common law and statute, the tenderer（偿还人，投标人）and the solicitor of bribes are equally culpable（有罪的）.

In the United States bribery and attempted bribery are defined by the federal government and by most of the states as felonies（重罪）, punishable in many states by imprisonment. Many states also forbid the bribery of labor union agents（工会人员）, business representatives , athletes, jury witnesses, and voters.

Ⅱ. 课文知识点

1. Chrysler Corporation (克莱斯勒汽车公司)

Chrysler Corporation, founded in 1924, used to be one of the three largest American automobile manufacturers whose brands include both passenger and commercial vehicles such as Chrysler, Jeep®（吉普）and Dodge（道奇）. The other two largest American automobile manufacturers are General Motors（通用汽车公司）and Ford（福特汽车公司）. In addition to auto making, Chrysler is also engaged in financial services, providing loan services (mostly) to car buyers. In 1998 it merged with Daimler-Benz AG (of Germany)（戴姆勒-奔驰）(best known for its Mercedes-Benz brand name) to become part of the DaimlerChrysler Corporation（戴姆勒克莱斯勒公司）, which is jointly owned by European, U.S. and other international investors.

2. International Chamber of Commerce (国际商会)

The aim of the International Chamber of Commerce (ICC) , founded in 1919, is to serve world business by promoting trade and investment, open markets for goods and services, and the free flow of capital. Its activities cover a broad spectrum, from arbitration and dispute resolution to making the case for open trade and the market economy system, business self-regulation, fighting corruption or combating commercial crime. ICC is made of a World Council (its governing body) and individual national committees and groups. Individual companies, corporations, professional associations as well as individuals can also join ICC as individual members.

3. Northumbria Police

Northumbria（诺森比亚）Police, based in the North East of England, is the sixth largest police force in England and Wales. It covers over 5,000 square kilometers with a population of 1.5 million people. This includes the cities of Newcastle upon Tyne and Sunderland, other large urban centers of Tyne（泰恩河）and Wear, the coastal areas of North and South Tyneside and the mainly rural county of Northumberland. On a typical day the Northumbria Police can expect to receive 5137 telephone calls, receive/handle 811 "999" calls, deal with 1504 incidents, investigate 381 crimes, make 223 arrests, and they also travel 47,780 miles, attend 13 road collisions, administer 34 breath tests and record 121 sets of fingerprints.

4. Niagara Falls

Niagara Falls（尼亚加拉瀑布）is the name that refers to the American Falls and Horseshoe Falls in Northeast U.S. and Canada. These are among the biggest water falls in the U.S. and Canada as well as the world. Niagara Falls was formed due to glaciers movement（冰河运动）12,000 years ago and now borders both the U.S. (the Niagara Falls County) and Canada (Ontario) via the Great Lakes system.

四、课文精讲

Section A

Ⅰ.短语与词汇详解

1. bribe

[词义] *n.* 贿赂 (尤指钱); *vt.* 向……行贿，买通

[搭配] to take/accept bribes from sb. 接受某人的贿赂; offer a bribe 行贿，bribe sb. into silence 用贿赂封住某人的嘴; be bribed into secrecy 受了贿替人保密

[例句] Margaret was in complete agreement with her husband's refusal to accept the bribe. 玛格丽特完全赞同自己的丈夫拒绝贿赂。

It is a disaster to find your politicians can be bribed, and that your judges and lawyers are neither responsible nor honest. 发现你们的从政者竟然能用金钱买通，你们的法官和律师既不讲理又不诚实，这真是一个大灾难。

[派生] bribery *n.* [U] 行贿，受贿; bribee *n.* 受贿者; briber *n.* 行贿者

[辨析] bribe, bribery

bribe 作名词，表示贿赂时专指用来提供或给予某有地位的人以影响其观点或行为的物体，如钱或好处或贿赂品，即用来影响或说服（他人）的东西，尤其指金钱。

bribery 作名词，表示行贿,受贿时指提供、给予或取得贿赂的行为或实践。如: That country has uncovered 200,000 cases of bribery and corruption this year, said one government officer. 一位政府官员说，该国今年揭露出了20万个行贿受贿和腐败的案子。

2. ethics

[词义] *n.* ① (pl.) 道德准则，伦理标准; ② 伦理学

[搭配] business ethics 商业道德; medical ethics 医德; professional ethics 职业道德

[例句] The principles of good faith reflect professional ethics and general social morality. 信守诺言的原则反映了职业道德准则和普遍的社会道德观。

Ethics is a branch of philosophy. 伦理学是哲学的分支。

[派生] ethicize *vt.* 使伦理化，使变得道德化; ethical *adj.* 伦理的，道德的

3. substantial

[词义] *adj.* ① 可观的，大量的; ② 基本上的，大体上的

[例句] The deal will bring us substantial profits. 这笔生意将给我们带来高额的利润。

I'm in substantial agreement with you. 我大体上同意你的意见。

4. moral

[词义] *a.* ① 道德(上)的; ② 精神上的

n. ① 道德，品行; ② 寓意

[搭配] a moral lesson 公民道德课; a moral victory 精神上的胜利; a moral obligation 道义上的责任; a moral life 合乎道德的生活; a decline in the public morals 共道德的衰落

[例句] She feels responsible for the girl's moral welfare. 她感到应对那姑娘道德上的健康成长负责。

He went along to give moral support. 他前去给予精神上的支持。

The novel reflects the morals and customs of the time.

小说反映了当时的道德标准和社会习俗。

The moral of this story is that crime does not pay.

这则故事的寓意是犯罪是不值得的。

[派生] morality *n.* 道德；道义

[辨析] moral，ethical，virtuous，righteous

这些形容词意为"符合正确或好的行为的原则或规则"。

moral 一词与个人品质及行为有关，特指性行为，依照普遍正确的水准来测量，指"行动上、思想上遵照普遍接受的道德标准的"。如：a moral woman 有道德的女性。

ethical指"伦理的"、"合乎道德的"，尤指"合乎职业道德或规矩的"，强调与理想中的是非标准保持一致，如律师和医生们遵循的准则。如：an ethical lawyer 有道德的律师。

virtuous指"有道德的"、"善良的"、"正直的"，暗示高尚的道德和高贵的品质。如：She was such a virtuous woman that everybody respected her. 她是个道德高尚的女性，人人都尊敬她。

righteous 强调道德方面的正直而且尤指没有罪恶或犯罪的；当它指行为、反应或欲望时，它常暗示有理由的愤怒。如：The effectual prayer is a very righteous man. 能预知未来的祈祷者是非常正直的人。

[联想] immoral *adj.* 不道德的，邪恶的

5. accuse

[词义] *vt.* ① 指控（正式指控某一错误行径）；② 指责

[搭配] accuse sb. of... 指控某人……；the accuseed【律】被告，刑事被告

[例句] The police accused him of murder. 警方指控他谋杀。

Mary was accused as an accomplice. 玛丽被指控为同谋犯。

He was accused of incompetence. 他被指责失职。

[辨析] accuse, charge

accuse 通常表示直接而严厉地指出某人的过错。如：His neighbour accused him of playing the musical instrument too loudly. 他的邻居指责他的乐器弹奏得太响了。

charge在表示"指控"时，仍然包含着这个动词的基本含义，即"使承担责任或任务"，同时强调被指控者的过错相当严重，而且要将这种过错郑重宣布。注意：该词既可用于对罪行很重的人指控，也可用于对于一般过错的人的指控。常用的搭配结构为"charge sb...with..."。如：I won't charge you this time. But you'd not do it again! 这一次我就不告发你了，不过你最好别再这么干了！ The police charged the driver with careless driving. 警察指控那个司机开车粗心。

6. questionable

[词义] *adj.* ① 成问题的，有疑问的，不确定的；② (道德等) 可疑的，有问题的，靠不住的

[例句] The reports conclusions are questionable because the sample used was very small. 那个报告的结论有问题，因为取样太少了。

The desire for wealth lured them into questionable dealings.
他受了发财欲的引诱而被卷入可疑的交易。

[辨析] doubtful, dubious, questionable

doubtful 表示明显的不确定性。如: It is doubtful whether she will be admitted to graduate school. 她能否考上研究生还是个疑问。He is an author of doubtful reputation. 他是一位名声不太好的作家。

dubious 表示的不确定性不那么直接和不那么强, 通常它含有犹豫不决、猜疑、不信任的意思。如: He dubious about agreeing to go. 到底同意去还是不同意去他迟疑不决。It is a painting of dubious value. 这是幅价值没法断定的画。

questionable 意思是 "值得疑问的", 它通常暗指道德、名声或行为等的有问题。如: a questionable stockbroker 不正当的股票经纪人。

7. account

[词义] n. ① 账户; ② 帐目; ③ 考虑, 顾及

v. ① 认为

[搭配] on account 赊账; settle one's account 结帐; take sth. into account 把某事考虑在内

[例句] My salary is paid directly into my bank account.
我的工资直接存入我的银行账户。

The accounts for last year showed a profit of $2 million.
去年的账目显示利润为200万美元。

These figures do not take account of changes in the rate of inflation.
这些数字没有考虑到通货膨胀率的变化。

I account my self well paid. 我认为我得的报酬不少。

[派生] accountable adj. 负有责任的

[联想] accountant n. 会计 (员) , 会计师; accountancy n. 会计行业

8. reject

[词义] v. ① 拒绝 (接受), ② 摒弃; ③ 拒绝 (录用, 雇用等); ④ (因质量不好) 废弃

n. 次品

[搭配] reject an appeal 驳回上诉; reject an offer of help 拒绝别人提供的帮助; a rejected suitor 未被接受的求婚者

[例句] He rejected their invitation point-blank. 他直截了当地拒绝了他们的邀请。

The present generation has largely rejected the beliefs of its parents.
现在这一代人在很大程度上摒弃了父母的观念。

Mr. John, once the reject of the national team, won the championship this year.
曾经被国家队拒绝的约翰先生今年得了冠军。

We have very strict quality control, so anything that is imperfect is rejected.
我们实行非常严格的质量管理, 凡是有缺陷的一概剔除。

The telly is cheap, because it's a reject. 这台电视机很便宜, 因为是次品。

[派生] rejection n. 拒绝

[辨析] decline, refuse, reject

decline 指 "较正式地、有礼貌地谢绝" 或 "婉言谢绝"。如: He declined the nomination. 他谢绝了提名。

refuse 是普通用语，指"坚决、果断或坦率地拒绝"。如: He refused to take the money. 他拒绝接受此款。

reject指"以否定、敌对的态度而当面拒绝"。如: They rejected damaged goods. 他们拒收受损的货物。

[联想] rejecter *n.* 拒绝者，否决者

9. withdraw

[词义] *v.* ① 撤回，撤销，收回；② 不参加，退出；③ 提取 (银行存款)；④ (军队) 撤退

[搭配] withdraw a remark 收回一句话; withdraw the accusation 撤回控诉; withdraw from the competition 从竞争中退出

[例句] She refused to withdraw her application for resignation.
她拒绝收回自己的辞职申请。

More than half of the committee withdrew from the discussion.
半数以上的委员退出了讨论。

He withdrew $500 from a bank account. 他从银行的账户上取了500元钱。

Lots of wounded soldiers withdrew from the battlefield.
许多伤病从战场上撤了下来。

[派生] withdrawal *n.* 收回，取消，撤退

[辨析] retire, withdraw

retire指离开公众场合，退到私人或僻静的地方。如: retire from the political life 退出政治坛。

withdraw除了含有 retire 之意外，还常指军事上的撤退和礼貌性的有意离开。如: withdraw troops from the front 从前线撤军。

10. category

[词义] *n.* ① 种类，类别；② [逻] 范畴

[搭配] wage category 工资级别; weight category 体重级别; conceptual category 概念范畴; abstract category 抽象范畴

[例句] There are different categories of books in our library.
我们的图书馆里有各种不同种类的书籍。

Please arrange the employees under wage categories.
请按照工资级别将雇员们分类。

[派生] categorize *vt.* 加以类别, 分类

11. consist

[词义] *vi* ① 由……组成；② 在于，决定于；③ 一致，符合

[搭配] consist of 组成，构成，包括; consist in 在于; consist with 一致，符合

[例句] His job consists of helping old people who live alone.
他的工作包括帮助无人照顾的独居老人。

The beauty of the artist's style consists in its simplicity.
这位艺术家的风格上的美在于它的简朴。

The information consists with her account. 这消息与她的描述是一致的。

[派生] consistent *adj.* 一致的, 坚固的

[辨析] compose, consist, comprise, constitute, include, involve, compose 表示"由……材料构成"时，通常用系表结构 be composed of, 表示前者由后者组成；在用于主动语态时，一般它所表示的"构成"或"组成"总包含着融合为一，而且主语或者是复数名词或者是集体名词。如：Water is composed of hydrogen and oxygen. 水是由氢和氧组成的。England, Scotland and Wales compose the island of Great Britain. 英格兰、苏格兰和威尔士构成大不列颠岛。

consist 表示前者包含后者，通常用consist of 的主动结构，不能用被动语态。consist of 的含义与被动语态的 compose 相同。如：New York City consists of five boroughs. 纽约市由五个行政区组成。

comprise 在表示"构成"时，其内涵是"包括"或"覆盖"，表示"由许多部分组成"，或"由许多部分构成一个整体"。如：Our curriculum comprises Politics, Chinese, English and History. 我们的课程共有四门:政治、汉语、英语、历史。

constitute 的主语可以是复数名词也可以是单数名词，所"构成"的事物在属性和特征上，或在组织上与组成成分是一致的。如：This growing poverty in the midst of growing poverty constitutes a permanent menace to peace. 在这种不断增长的贫困中正在增长着的贫困构成了对和平的永久的威胁。Seven days constitutes a week. 七天构成一个星期。

include强调"包括作为整体的一部分"。如：The list included his name.这个名单上包括他的名字。

involve 指"由于同主要的有联系而必须含有"。如：Housekeeping involves cooking, washing and cleaning. 家务包括烹饪、洗衣和清扫等。

12. donation

[词义] n.① 捐赠品，捐款；② 捐肋

[搭配] a blood donation 献血；make/give a donation of sth. to sb. 向某人捐赠某物

[例句] Many colonists abroad made a donation of money and substances to the flood-affected areas. 许多海外侨民向洪水灾区捐钱捐物。

He received a letter of thanks for his donation of books to the library. 他收到一封感谢信，感谢她向图书馆捐书。

[联想] donator n.捐赠者

13. distinguish

[词义] v. ① 辨别，区别；② 使有别于……，使有特色；③ 表现突出

[搭配] distinguish good from evil 分辨善恶；distinguish oneself by scholarship 学问超群；distinguish oneself in battle 战功卓著；be distinguished as 辨明为；be distinguished by 以……为特征；be distinguished for 以……而著名

[例句] People who cannot distinguish between colours are said to be colour-blind. 不能分辨颜色的人被称为色盲。

Speeches distinguishes man from the animals. 言语使人区别于动物。

The monitor distinguished himself by his performance in the examination. 班长在考试中成绩优异,因而显得突出。

[派生] distinguished adj. 卓著的, 著名的, 高贵的; distinguishable adj. 可区别的, 可辨识的

14. enforce

[词义] *vt.*① 执行 (法律)，实施，使服从；②（尤指用威胁和武力强迫）实行，把……强加于

[搭配] enforce obedience on/from/upon sb. 强迫某人服从；enforced education 义务教育；enforce an argument/a demand 加强论点（坚持要求）

[例句] The police enforce the law. 警察执法。

The school authority enforced military discipline this term.
校方本学期强制实施军事纪律。

[派生] enforcement *n.* 执行, 强制

[辨析] enforce , implement , invoke

enforce 强调强迫性，强制性，如：enforce the rules 实施规则。

implement 强调使……生效，执行，如: implement the terms of the agreement 履行协议条款。

invoke 强调借助于，调用，如: invoke emergency powers 求助紧急备用部队。

15. on the increase 在增长中

[例句] People become homeless for a wide range of reasons, and sadly homelessness is on the increase, particularly among younger people. 由于各种各样的原因，人们变得无家可归。糟糕的是无家可归者越来越多，尤其是在年青人中。

16. a way of life 生活方式

[例句] All-night parties with music and dancing have become a way of life for a large section of young people. 在很大一部分年轻人中，整夜地在一起唱歌跳舞的聚会已成为一种生活方式。

17. pay up 付款，还钱

[例句] If your parcel is lost or damaged, compensation may be paid up according to the fee paid. 你的包裹如遗失或受损，可能会根据所付的费用来支付赔偿。

18. stand by 遵守，履行

[例句] Washington, he said, stood by its commitment to financially support European countries in their reconstruction after World War II.
他说华盛顿方面信守其承诺，在经济上支持欧洲国家二战后的重建工作。

19. in practice 实际上，事实上，在实践中

[例句] In practice the distinction between the two is not so clear-cut.
在实践中，这两者的区分并不是那么明确。

20. accuse of 指控，指责

[例句] He is accused of making a false statement prior to entering the U.S., which carries a sentence of up to five years in jail.
他被指控在进入美国前做了不实的申报，这要判高达五年的刑期。

21. in private 私下地，秘密地

[例句] Few of his ministers are saying, even in private, that they expect him to lose the next election.
即使在私下，他的大臣们几乎没人说他们预料他在下一次选举中会失败。

22. a fact of life 现实，残酷的事实

[例句] Gradually she had come to accept it as a fact of life, though the grief was still sometimes there. 尽管悲伤有时还在折磨她，但她逐渐将这作为一个残酷的事实接受了。

23. consist of 由……组成

[例句] The library consisted of two rooms, but the only entry to the inner room was through the outer one.
图书馆由两间房间组成，但是进入里间惟一的门得通过外间。

24. in support of 支持，拥护

[例句] This photo is considered to be evidence in support of the theory, which Einstein believed to be the basis of the physical universe. 这张照片被认为是支持这理论的依据，爱因斯坦相信此理论是物质宇宙的基础。

25. under investigation 正在调查中

[例句] It is reported that the company is under investigation by the local inspector of taxes. 据报道，这家公司正在受到当地税务稽查员的调查。

26. throw out 抛弃，扔掉，驱除

[例句] Inspect stored fruit every week and throw out any that has started to go rotten.
每星期检查储藏的水果，把已经开始腐烂的水果都扔掉。

27. close a deal 完成交易，生意成交

[例句] It wouldn't be long before he closed a deal with one of the chain stores.
不久，他与其中一家连锁店达成了交易。

28. speed up（使……）加快速度

[例句] It can be argued that computer communications have simply speeded up the whole process of change enormously.
可以说，计算机通信无疑已加速了整个变化的过程。

29. hit upon/on 碰巧想出，忽然想出

[例句] Ellis, who was unemployed and living on benefit, hit upon the idea that she should go out to work as a waitress. 埃利斯失业了，靠救济金生活，她忽然想出了她应该出去做女服务员的这个主意。

30. distinguish between 区分，辨别，分清

[例句] This distinguished between the temporary unemployment of skilled workers in periods of depression and the permanent underemployment of workers with limited or no skills. 这区分了技术工人在经济萧条时期的暂时性失业和那些具有有限的技术或没有技术的工人的永久性失业两者之间的差别。

31. amount to 实际上，意味着

[例句] To solve the problems, the Committee recommended a number of changes which amounted to an attempt to introduce the modern techniques into business management. 为解决这些问题，委员会提出了一些改革措施，这些改革措施实际上是试图在商务管理中引入现代技术。

32. behave oneself 检点（自己的）行为，（使自己）循规蹈矩

[例句] Ben and his young friends had been told at the start of the meeting to behave themselves and not to get in the way of others, so they did not have a good time. 聚会一开始，本和他的年青朋友们就被告知要行为规矩点，不要妨碍别人，所以他们玩得不痛快。

33. be caught in 陷入，遭到

[例句] Our car was caught in the centre of an enormous traffic jam, and it looked as if we would be lucky to get to the station only an hour or so behind schedule.

我们的车陷入了严重的交通堵塞之中，看来我们要是迟到一个小时左右到达车站就算是挺幸运的了。

34. on the take 受贿

[例句] If the persons on the take are not parroting the opinions of our companies, what can we suppose the money they receive is for? 如果那些受贿的人不鹦鹉学舌般地重复我们公司的观点，我们又能设想他们收的钱是干什么使呢？

35. square...with 符合，相符

[例句] His statement doesn't square with the facts. 他的陈述与事实不符。

II. 难句解析

1. They often do not realize that bribery in various forms is on the increase in many countries and, in some, has been a way of life for centuries. (Para. 1)

[释义] They often don't realize that various forms of bribery are becoming more frequent and that in some countries it is traditional to bribe people in some ways.

[分析] 本句的核心结构为and连接的两个并列的宾语从句。句子的主干为"They often do not realize"。第二个宾语从句省略了引导词that和主语bribery, 在"in some"结构中呈前省略了forms。

2. ...the Minister of Trade makes it clear to you that if you offer him a substantial bribe, you will find it much easier to get an import license for your goods, and you are also likely to avoid "procedural delays", as he puts it. (Para. 2)

[释义] ...the Minister of Trade says clearly to you that if you bribe him with a large sum of money, you will get an import license for your goods more easily and quickly, because some of the procedures will go quickly and smoothly without delay.

put *vi.* 说，表达

e.g. I put my objections bluntly. 我直率地表明了我的反对意见。

[分析] 本句的难点在于结构比较复杂。本句的主干为"the Minister of Trade makes it clear to you"，其中it为形式宾语，真正的宾语为"that if you offer him a substantial bribe, you will find...and you...'procedural delays', as he puts it."在这个宾语从句中，"if you offer...bribe,"为条件句，主句为and连接的两个并列句。在宾语从句的第一个主句"you will find it much easier to get..."中it 为形式宾语，真正的宾语为后面的动词不定式"to get an import license"。as引导方式状语从句, "as he put it"意思是"正如他所说的那样"。

3. Now, the question is: do you pay up or stand by your principles? (Para. 2)

[释义] Now you must decide whether to pay the officials a large sum of money to bribe them or to stick to your principles.

[分析] 在结构上可以冒号表示对后面内容的强调。本句中the question与冒号后的问句为主表结构，表语起到了具体解释主语的作用。

4. It is easy to talk about having high moral standards but, in practice, what would one really do in such a situation? (Para. 3)

[释义] Talking about having high standards of good behavior and honesty is easy. But, in reality, what would one actually do in such a situation?

[分析] 本句为but连接的两个表示转折关系的并列句。在第一句中，使用了it作形式主语，真正的主语为动词不定式 "to talk...moral standards"。第二句中使用了虚拟语气的结构 "would +动词原形"。

5. ...there were people in the motor industry in Britain who were prepared to say in private...(Para. 3)

[释义] ...some people in the motor industry in Britain are willing to say, when there were no other people being present...

[分析] 本句的难点在于使用了限制性定语从句 "who were prepared to say in private..."，先行词为people。在限制性定语从句中，通常把定语从句放在紧靠先行词的位置上。但为了保持结构的平衡和连续性，也可以将定语从句放在离先行词较远的位置，本句就是这种分离的用法。

6. Every year we're selling more than a $1,000 million worth of cars abroad. (Para. 3)

[释义] **worth** *n.* 价值，财产，结构为 "worth of sth"

e.g. stocks having a worth of ten million dollars 价值一千万美元的股票

[分析] 本句为简单句，主语为we，every year为时间状语，谓语部分为现在进行时结构 "re selling"，宾语为 "more than a $1,000 million worth of cars"，地点状语为abroad。本句的结构难点在于理解用现在进行时表示习惯性和发生频率较高的行为，本句意思为 "每年我们都会售出……"。

7. The first category consists of substantial payments made for political purposes or to secure major contracts. (Para. 5)

[释义] The first bribery type includes making payments of large sums of money for political purposes or to make sure that major contracts can be obtained.

[分析] 本句的难点在于宾语 "substantial payments" 带有两个不同形式的宾语。第一个宾语为过去分词短语 "made for political purposes"，第二个定语为动词不定式 "to secure major contracts"。

8. This same company, it was revealed, was ready to finance secret U.S. efforts to throw out the government of Chile. (Para. 5)

[释义] It was made known that it was also this company that was prepared to provide money for the U.S. government so as to help it get rid of the government of Chile.

[分析] 本句的真正主语 "this same company"，谓语部分为 "was ready to finance"。结构的难点在于理解 "it was revealed" 作插入语，起到补充说明的作用。

9. This code would try to distinguish between commissions paid for real services and exaggerated fees that really amount to bribes. (Para. 9)

[释义] This set of moral principles would try to make people recognize the difference between commissions that are paid for real services and exaggerated fees that really are the same as bribes.

distinguish between... and... 把……和……区分开

e.g. distinguish between right and wrong 辨别是非

[分析] 本句的核心结构为 "distinguish between...and...", 意为 "把……与……区分开"。 "paid for real service" 为过去分词短语作后置定语, 修饰commissions; 过去分词exaggerated为前置定语修饰fees。同时, fees本身又是定语从句 "that really amount to bribes" 的先行词。

10. **Unfortunately, opinions differ among members of the ICC concerning how to enforce the code. (Para. 10)**

[释义] It is unfortunate that members of the ICC differ in their opinions about how to make people obey the code.

concerning *prep.* 关于

e.g. I spoke to him concernig his behavior. 我和他谈了他的行为。

[分析] 本句重点在于理解concerning作为介词和带有特殊疑问词的动词不定式共同构成了介词结构作ICC 的定语。

III. 重点语法讲解

1. It + is + adj. + infinitive (inf.)/that clause 句型

It + is + adj. + infinitive (inf.)/that clause 句型中, it为形式主语, infinitive或者that clause才是真正的主语。虽然不定式或that从句可以放于句首作主语, 主语太长而谓语太短会导致句子头重脚轻, 因此使用形式主语的结构可以保持英语句子的结构平衡。

本课中大量使用了这样的结构:

It is difficult to resist the impression that bribery and other questionable payments are on the increase. (Para. 4) 我们很容易产生这样的印象赂贿以及其他可疑开支正日益增多。

Is it possible to devise a code of rules for companies that would prohibit bribery in all its forms? (Para. 9)（疑问句形式）是否有可能设计一套公司法规准则防止各种类型的赂贿呢?

...it is difficult to square his business interests with his moral conscience. (Para. 11)（当今作海外销售的商人）常常很难达到既确保自己的商业利益, 又无愧道德良心的境地。

It's really possible that you can speak English very fluently with lots of practice.

多练习是完全有可能讲出流畅的英文。

It is really astonishing that she refused to talk to her husband.

真奇怪, 她竟然拒绝和她丈夫讲话。

2. "Suppose + (that) clause" 结构

suppose作为连词引导从句, 同时从句的领起词that还可以省略。这一结构可以表达两种含义:

首先, 引导条件句, 表示一种假设或条件, 相当于 "assuming that:" 表达 "what would/will happen if...", 即 "假使...结果会怎样; 万一; 假使"。此时, 该结构和 "supposing/given/provided (都是连词) +（that）clause" 的结构通用。该结构也可独立使用, 省去 "what would......" 部分。如:

Suppose your father saw you now, what would you say?

假设你父亲现在看到了你, 你该怎么说?

Suppose that during a negotiation with some government officials, the Minister of Trade

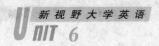

males it clear to you...(Para. 2)

假定在一场与政府官员的谈判中，贸易部长向你明确……。

Suppose (that) you object to carrying out a particular management order and you are afraid of the manager, what would you do.

假设你反对执行一项管理命令，又害怕你的经理，你该怎么办呢？

Supposing it rains what shall you do? 假使下雨，你会怎么办呢？

Suppose a company has a new breakfast cereal that it wants to sell.

假设有个公司想出售一种新的早餐麦片粥。

其次，suppose引导的从句还可以表示祈使语气，相当于 "to consider as a suggestion"，意思是 "让（让我建议）...如何 /...怎么样"。如：

Suppose we go for a walk. 我们去散散步吧。

Suppose we dine together. 让我们一块儿吃饭吧。

Ⅳ. 课文赏析

1. 文体特点

本篇议论文论述了商界普遍存在的一种现象——贿赂。文章以一些具体的贿赂例子引入话题，表明贿赂在世界上许多国家都普遍存在，让读者比较容易接受，具有说服力。文章的主体部分论述了贿赂的主要分类，条理清晰，结构明确。在文章的结尾，作者发出倡议，建议大家应该努力杜绝贿赂现象的发生。

本文运用了例举（listing）、分类别（categorizing）和例证（exemplification）的议论手法，使作者的观点真实可信。文章结构为典型的提出问题——分析问题——解决问题的框架结构，是学习议论文写作的典范。

2. 结构分析

Part Ⅰ (Para.1-4) Concentrating on the point of view that bribery is a common occurrence in many countries.

Part Ⅱ (Para.5-8) Focusing on the three categories of bribery. In this part there are a lot of examples to support the author's points.

Part Ⅲ (Para.9-11) It is about the efforts to prohibit bribery.

Ⅴ. 课后练习答案及解析

Comprehension of the Text

Ⅱ.

1. Because they don't know how serious the problem of bribery is.

2. He will bribe the officials.

3. Because these practices are likely to be morally wrong and may be certain forms of bribery.

4. These companies may be required to reveal such information by the U.S. Securities and Exchange Commission (SEC) , whose duty is to collect certain information about enterprises so as to protect investors.

5. They wanted to avoid an unfavorable conclusion drawn from the investigation of their possible violations of U.S. business laws.

6. They might make large payments to ruling families or their close advisers, or make

donations to party bank accounts.

7. It refers to a rare edition of a book with $20,000 slipped within its pages.

8. It favors a code of conduct and has proposed a council for managing the code, which can distinguish between commissions paid for real services and exaggerated fees that really amount to bribes.

9. No. Because its members have different opinions about the duties of the ICC.

10. Yes. More than 300 U.S. companies, for example, admitted that they had made questionable payments.

Vocabulary

III.

1. Substantial 译文：许多人支持经济体制改革以消除贿赂。

2. procedural 译文：白宫表示在程序上不会有变化，你就等通知吧。

3. negotiation 译文：美国贸易代表卡拉·西尔斯说："我们已经表示出了极大的耐心，而且在决议生效前的30天之内，我们欢迎进一步的磋商。"

4. rejected 译文：我们否决了他要改变汽车生产工序的建议，决定继续采用现有的生产工序。

5. withdrawn 译文：这项起诉因证据不足而被驳回。

6. commissions 译文：这个委员会试图区分真正为服务所付的佣金和实际上等同于贿赂的过高费用。

7. financed 译文：该项目的建设资金来源与政府和公众的捐款。

8. secure 译文：为确保得到武器销售的合同，该组织向它们政党的银行账户上汇了大量款项。

IV.

1. by 译文：他一直坚持说自己书中的内容都是事实，并且他会信守诺言。

2. in 译文：我们现在谈论的一些内容必须保密，所以我们应该私下谈论。

3. of 译文：布什总统担心美国公司日益严重的丑闻会对经济产生影响，因此他指责了一些不负责的公司领导人。

4. to 译文：作为对国家博物馆捐赠的回报，我们将减免其捐赠物价值两倍的税款。

5. up 译文：为了能够直接跨入信息时代，国家正在加速实施其战略计划，向各类信息工程注入大量资金。

6. on/upon 译文：试验过不同的数字组合后，我们终于找到了解决的方法。

7. with 译文：明达的政治观点可以解释这项特定的建议是如何与政府的意图是一致的。

8. in 译文：我们可以想象合并其中的两个观点，但事实上它们是各自独立的。

Collocation

V.

1. commitment 译文：由双方签字的报价信毕竟是一种获得道德承诺的方法。

2. value 译文：他对教授古典或当代现实主义小说和诗歌的价值表示怀疑——阅读这些作品是否能提高人们的道德观。

3. regret 译文：他的话从道义上表达了因辜负别人信任而感到的遗憾，同时也表达了对可能伤害到的人的关心。

4. implications 译文：在此我们可以进一步检验一些信仰与各种生活方式间的相互关系所蕴含的道德意义。

5. strength 译文：没有新思想和新观念这些道义的力量，它又会陷入原来的堕落中。

6. opposition 译文：拳击运动的普及削弱了20世纪末人们对拳击在道义上的反对。

7. decline 译文：与会学者们认为：这只不过是全球范围内道德标准普遍下降的又一个例子。

8. sense 译文：他是非分明，品德高尚，因此受到了大家的尊敬。

Word Building

VI.

1. foresight/forethought 译文：她有先见之明，在房价下跌前就卖掉了房子。

2. forewarned 译文：村里空无一人，很显然，村民们在空袭前事先得到了通知。

3. foreground 译文：虽然因为著作享誉世界，他仍然拒绝把自己放在引人注目的重要位置上。

4. postgraduate 译文：他以研究生的身份进入牛津大学攻读犯罪学博士学位。

5. post-race 译文：比赛结果一公布，立即出现了赛会反应。

6. foresaw 译文：她预见了困难，然后采取措施尽量避免困难的发生。

7. post-Christmas 译文：为了吸引消费者，许多商家采取了常用的打五折的廉价促销方式，希望消费者不要重复以往的习惯——等到圣诞节后才购买特价商品。

8. post-election 译文：根据大选后的一项民意调查，公众对经济复苏的信心急剧下降。

VII.

1. e-shopper 网上消费者
   译文：我鼓励你在网上购物，互联网上可供选择的商品及其价格的范围极大，而且非常方便，只是不要总是盯着明星看，要谨慎行事，在未来的几年里你就会成为一个快乐，安全的网上购物者。

2. e-merchant 网商
   译文：首先，如果你打算在网上购物，就要选择一家信誉好的公司，如果你觉得一家新的网上商店对你有吸引力，还是花几分钟时间做一些调查。

3. e-journal 电子杂志
   译文：你可以从《系统》这本电子期刊里免费下载这些论文。

4. e-classroom 网络课堂
   译文：传统的学校依然存在，但网络教室在现代学习中占据了很重要的作用。

5. e-commerce 网上交易/电子商务
   译文：电子商务，即网上交易的简称，实在令人兴奋，但其税务问题确实是一件令人十分头痛的事。

6. e-mail 电子邮件
   译文：许多人不得不放弃自己的邮件账户，因为他们对垃圾邮件感到生气。

7. e-dictionaries 电子辞典
   译文：有些网站提供电子词典，你可以在上面查这些生词的意思。

8. e-cash 电子现金
   译文：丘比特通信公司的市场研究人员估计，到2000年，智能卡和电子现金可以占到网上销售83亿美元的一半。

Structure

VIII. ▶

1. It's pointless to go there next Monday Mth ere's public holiday.

   译文: 下周一是公共假期，去那里没有意义。

2. It is probable that we'll be late.

   译文: 我们很有可能迟到。

3. It is interesting to see different cultures and ways of life.

   译文: 体验不同文化和生活方式是很有趣的。

4. It is really astonishing that she refuses to talk to you.

   译文: 她拒绝跟你讲话，这真令人惊讶。

5. It is important that she comes straight to me when she arrives.

   译文: 她到了以后要直接来我这里，这一点很重要。

IX. ▶

1. Suppose you object to carrying out a particular management order and you are afraid of the manager, what would you do?

   译文: 假设你执行一项管理命令，又害怕你的经理，你该怎么办？

2. Suppose you have just got married and are employed for three years to work abroad, how would you explain it to your newly married wife?

   译文: 假如你刚结婚，但受聘要到国外工作三年，你怎样去跟你妻子解释？

3. Suppose you don't understand why not to arrest Harry, would you decide to remove any doubts?

   译文: 假如有人不理解你为什么没有逮捕哈利，你怎么去消除这些疑虑？

4. Suppose your tenant fail to pay the rent by accident, is it fair that you would throw him out?

   译文: 假如你的房客只是偶尔欠房租，你就把他赶出去这合理吗？

5. Suppose you are a very heavy smoker and are anxious to break the habit, where could you get the help?

   译文: 假如你抽烟抽的很厉害，想急切地改掉这个习惯，你该到哪寻求帮助？

Translation

X. ▶

1. We would not stand by and let bribery in various forms be on the increase.

2. While lending you the substantial sum of money, I made it clear to you that if you couldn't pay it off in time, you might be accused of taking bribes.

3. Competition of financial power has become a fact of political life; but if you receive questionable political contributions for this reason, you will soon be under investigation.

4. To secure major arms deal contracts, they have made a substantial donation to the bank account of the party in power.

5. He hit upon a good method to speed up the progress of the experiment, but opinions differed among members of the group on it.

6. It's difficult to enforce the new law because people are not ready to act on it.

7. We think it's the business of the United Nations troops to enforce a ceasefire in that area, while the job of the local government is to prepare to restore law and order.

8. Having made the decision, she joined the organization, which is in support of woman's rights.

XI.

1. 他们通常没有意识到在很多国家，形形色色的贿赂行为日益增多。在某些国家，这已经成为人们几百年来的生活方式。

2. 现在的问题是：你是被迫掏钱还是坚持原则？

3. 很容易产生这样的印象：贿赂以及其他可以的开支正日渐增多。的确，这似乎已成为商界的一个事实。

4. 这一事实的披露，使其和与其它三百多家美国公司一样，想美国证券交易委员会承认自己近年曾有过这样或那样的支出，像贿赂、额外打折等。

5. 据闻，其他国家也是如此，向外国公司施压，要他们向党派组织的帐户捐款。

6. 第二大类包括为促使政府对某些工程项目的正式批准而做的支出。

7. 这些准则试图区分真正为服务所付的佣金和事实上等同于贿赂的过高费用。

8. 在一家知名英国报纸上，最近有位作家指出"企业已陷入贿赂的蛛网"，人人都"贪赃枉法"。

Essay Summary

XII.

BACBA   ADDCB   CBCAD   ABACD

Text Structure Analysis

XIII.

1. (1) This same company was ready to finance secret U.S. efforts to throw out the   government of Chile.

   (2) A British company paid £ 1 million to a "negotiator" who helped close a deal for the supply of tanks and other military equipment to Iran.

2. (1) covers payments made to obtain quicker official approval of some projects.

   (2) He bought a rare edition of a book, slipped $20,000 within its pages, and then presented it to the minister.

3. (1) payments made in countries to pay people to help with the passage of a business deal.

VI. 参考译文

贿赂与商业道德

商科学生有时对课程里包括商业道德课略感吃惊。他们通常没意识到在很多国家，形形色色的贿赂行为正日益增多。在某些国家，这已成为人们几百年来的生活方式。

假定在一场与政府官员的谈判中，贸易部长向你明确表示如能给他一大笔贿赂，拿到进口许可证就会容易得多，还可能避免他所说"程序上的延误"。现在的问题是：你是被迫掏钱呢，还是坚持原则？

高尚的道德标准说起来容易，但实际上人们在这种情况下究竟会怎么做呢？早些时候，一家英国汽车制造商被指控经管一笔基金行贿，还有其他一些可疑运作，如给代理商和客户高额回扣、提供额外折扣、向一些在瑞士银行开的匿名账户汇款等。这家汽车公司否认了这些指控，后来也就撤诉了。然而，当时英国汽车业里就有人私下里说："瞧，我们这一行竞争激烈，每年我们汽车的海外销售额超过10亿英镑。如果花几百万英镑能让客户高兴，谁会有损失呢？我们不这样干，别人也会干的。"

很容易产生这样的印象：贿赂以及其他可疑开支正日渐增多。的确，这似乎已成为商界的一个事实。仅举一例：美国第三大汽车制造企业克莱斯勒汽车公司透露，它在1971至1976年间共发生了250万美元的可疑开支。这一事实的披露，使克莱斯勒与其他300多家美国公司一样，向美国证券交易委员会承认自己近年曾有过某种形式的支出，像贿赂、额外打折等等。为方便讨论起见，我们可将这些支出分为三大类。

第一大类是那些为政治目的或为获得大宗合同所付出的大笔款项。比如，有一家美国企业曾因可能触犯美国商业法规而正受调查，此时它捐出一大笔款项支持一位总统候选人。后来发现，正是这家公司打算资助美国推翻智利政府的秘密行动。

这一大类也包括为得到武器销售或重大的石油、建筑等项目合同而向权势家族及其身边顾问所付出的大笔款项。在一桩涉及对伊朗武器销售的案子中，一位证人声称一家英国公司曾付给某"洽谈人"100万英镑。此人帮忙做成了一笔向伊朗提供坦克和其他军事设施的交易。据闻其他国家也是如此，向外国公司施压，要他们向党派组织的账户捐款。

第二大类包括为促使政府加快对某些工程项目的正式批准而作的支出。有个故事是说明这类支出的有趣例子：有个销售经理几个月来一直试图向加勒比地区一个国家的建工部长推销道路工程机械。他终于想出了办法。了解到建工部长收藏珍本书，他买了一本书的珍藏版，在书里夹上两万美元，将其送给部长。部长查看了书的内容，说道："我知道这书有两卷本的。"头脑灵活的销售经理答道："先生，两卷本公司买不起，不过我们可给你弄一本带'前言'的！"不久，这笔生意获准了。

第三大类指某些国家按照的传统做法付给在交易中起作用的人一笔费用。中东的一些国家和某些亚洲国家都属此类。

是否有可能设计一套公司法规准则防止各种类型的贿赂呢？国际商会（ICC）赞成用行为准则来禁止行贿索贿。这些准则试图区分真正为服务所付的佣金和事实上等同于贿赂的过高费用。已成立了一个委员会来实际操作这一准则。

可惜的是，国际商会委员们关于如何实行这一准则意见不一。英国委员们希望这一体系有充分的法律效力以使公司规范行事。而法国代表认为制定和实施法律是政府的事；像国际商会这样的商业团体该做的是表明孰对孰错，而非强制实行什么。

在一家知名英国报纸上，最近有位作者指出"企业已陷入贿赂的蛛网"，人人都"贪赃枉法"。这一说法可能有些夸张。然而，当今做海外销售的商人们经常难以达到既确保自己的商业利益，又无愧道德良心的境地。

VII. 写作指导

描述或记叙一个经过或一个事件的时候，通常需要使用一些表示时间先后顺序的时间短语，连词，从而使继续或描述更具有逻辑性，线索更清晰。例如：last night, then, finally, before, after, afterward, next, firstly, secondly, last等。

范文：

Three Kinds of People who Choose to Live alone on Purpose

Normally there are three kinds of people who choose to live alone on purpose. The first group of people is artists. They believe in the inspiration in solitude. One of my friends is a writer. He enjoys the time when he is alone. He can stay up late to read and above all, concentrate on his writing without fear of being interrupted by others. On his wall he posts a quotation from Thoreau: "I never found the companion that was so companionable as solitude." The second group of people is hunters, who prefer to live by themselves. Hunters are afraid that too many people will frighten away their prey. The third group consists of people who are disappointed from their marriage or family life. Once the newspaper reported a story about a woman who has been living alone since her husband left her five years ago for some better economic opportunities. She is not waiting for his return but she is just disappointed in life.

Section B

Ⅰ. 阅读技巧

英语成语来源于长期的历史生活积淀，有着独特的文化背景，因此它的含义是很难猜测的，有时既使是借助于词典知道其每个单词的意思也无法找到其正确的含义。如何在文章中正确快速理解成语，需要注意以下方面：

1) searching for context clues 寻找上下文线索

2) looking at examples if there are any 寻找文中举例

3) finding explanations if there are any 寻找文中的解释

4) locating opposite or similar phrases. 寻找反义或近义词组

Ⅱ. 词汇与短语详解

1. journalist

[词义] *n.* ① 新闻记者；② 新闻工作者报刊编辑

[搭配] accredited journalist 特派新闻记者；sports journalist 体育记者

[例句] Many war Journalists were sent to the battle fields to report news in the Second World War. 二战中很多战地记者亲赴战场报道新闻。

[派生] journalistic *adj.* 新闻事业的，新闻工作者的

[联想] journalist 的缩写形式为：jour.

2. regular

[词义] *adj.* ① 有规律的；② 平常的；③ 频繁的，正常的

[搭配] a regular verb 规则动词；keep regular hours 过有规律的生活；a regular meeting 例会

[例句] His regular living habits do good to his health.

他有规律的生活习惯对他的健康大有益处。

John's our regular caller. 约翰是我家的常客。

Regular teachers just don't have the training to deal with problem children.

一般的教师只是没有接受过应付问题儿童的训练。

[辨析] regular, ordinary

regular 指有规律的，正规的，定期的

ordinary 强调 "平常的"、"平淡无奇的"，指种类普通且不能从其他中加以区别的，它有时是贬义的。如：A ballpoint pen is adequate for most ordinary purposes. 原珠笔适合最普通的用途。The pianist gave a very ordinary performance marked by an occasional memory lapse. 钢琴家因偶然记忆失误表现平平。His ordinary supper consists of only bread and milk. 他通常的晚餐不过是面包和牛奶。

[联想] irregular *adj.* 不规则的，无规律的

3. imitate

[词义] *vt.* 模仿（模仿或运用……的风格；照搬某人的动作、容貌、特殊习惯和讲话；模拟），仿效（当作一个模范来使用或追随）

[搭配] an imitated industrial concentration area 模拟工业区

[例句] Parrots imitate human speech perfectly. 鹦鹉能维妙维肖地学人语。

The child imitates his father. 这孩子模仿他的父亲。

[派生] imitative *adj.* 模仿的

[辨析] imitate，mimic，mock，ape，copy，simulate

imitate 指"模仿"、"仿效"、"效法"，是按照其他人设立的方式或风格去做。如：The adults drank their tea in a ceremonious manner, and the children imitated them. 大人们客套地喝着茶，孩子们模仿着他们。

mimic 指"模仿"、"模拟"、"细致地模仿"，尤指"为开玩笑而模仿"，是对他人的动作，话语或特殊习惯等作相近的模仿，经常是为了取笑，如：In private the candidate mimicked his opponent's stammer. 私下里那个候选人模仿着对手的口吃。

mock 指"通过模仿进行嘲弄或嘲笑"。如：Some boys mocked the accent of the new boy. 一些孩子嘲弄新来孩子的口音。

ape 是盲目地仿照别人的指导，但经常产生荒唐的结果。如：Use your mind, don't ape those pop singers. 动动脑筋吧，不要盲目模仿那些流行歌手们。

copy 是尽可能精确地复制原作。如：He tried to copy the teacher's cultivated accent. 他尽力地模仿老师的优雅口音。

simulate 是假装某物的表象或特征。如：The little dog lay there simulating death. 那只小狗躺在那儿，假装死了。

4. surrender

[词义] *vi.* 投降，自首；*vt.* 放弃，使投降；*n.* 放弃，投降

[搭配] surrender to sb. 向某人投降；surrender all hope 放弃所有希望

[例句] We shall never surrender. 我们决不投降。

Surrender your arms, or we'll shoot! 缴枪不杀！

The enemy were forced to make an unconditional surrender.

敌军被迫无条件投降。

[派生] surrenderee *n.* 受让与者；surrenderor *n.* 让与者

[辨析] surrender, submission, capitulation

surrender 是最常用的词，表示因为要求或强迫而把所有权或控制权转交他人，"屈服，投降"。如：No terms except unconditional and immediate surrender can be accepted. 除去无条件立即投降，其它条件一概无法接受。

submission 强调已经投降的那一方的低级属性。如：The cruel and unrelenting enemy leaves us only the choice of brave resistance, or the most abject submission. 残酷而无情的敌人留给我们的选择只有勇敢的抵抗或者最奴颜卑膝的投降。

capitulation 暗指在特定的预先安排好的情况下的投降。如：Lack of food and ammunition forced the commander of the rebels to consider a capitulation. 食物和弹药的缺乏迫使叛乱领袖考虑投降。

5. innocent

[词义] *adj.* ① 清白的，无罪的；② 单纯的，天真无邪的

[搭配] be innocent of a crime 无罪; an innocent child 天真的孩子; innocent amusements 无害的娱乐

[例句] Can you provide any evidence that he was innocent of the crime?
你能提供证据证明他没有犯这罪吗？
She was attracted by the child's innocent stare.
她被这孩子直率的目光吸引了。

[派生] innocence *n.* 清白，无辜，单纯，天真

[联想] guilty *adj.* 犯罪的，有罪的

6. impressive

[词义] *adj.* 感人的，令人难忘的

[搭配] an impressive Olympic Games 给人深刻印象的奥林匹克运动会

[例句] The Gettysburg Address is Abraham Lincoln's most impressive speech.
《葛底斯堡演说》是亚伯拉罕·林肯最感动人的演说。

[派生] impressively *adv.* 令人难忘地

7. available

[词义] *adj.* 能得到的；可利用的；有空的

[搭配] available for use 可加以利用; employ all available means 千方百计, 用尽所有办法; make sth. available to/for 使……可以享受某物, 使……买得起某物

[例句] It is required that every driver should keep a fire extinguisher available at all times. 每个司机应该任何时候都要放置即时可用的灭火器
These tickets are available for one month. 这些票有效期一个月。
Attention, please. These tickets are available on (the) day of issue only.
请注意，这种车票仅在发售当天有效。

[派生] availability *n.* 可用性，有效性，实用性

8. retirement

[词义] *n.* 退休

[搭配] a retirement community 退休者社区; go into retirement 退休，退职; live in retirement 过退休或隐居生活

[例句] He was given a gold watch on his retirement. 他退休时得到了一块金表。

9. disable

[词义] *vt.* 使失去能力 (from doing, for)

[搭配] disabled ex-servicemen 残疾退役军人

[例句] He was disabled in the accident. 他在事故中受重伤。
An accident disabled him from playing football.
一场意外事故使他不能踢球。

[派生] disability *n.* 无能，残疾; disabled *adj.* 报废的, 损坏的, 丧失劳动[战斗] 力的

10. favor

[词义] *n.* ① 好感，宠爱；② 恩惠

      vt. 支持，赞成

[搭配] in favor of 支持，有利于; do someone a favor 帮助人; win the favor of sb. 赢得某人的好感

[例句] The boss didn't say "hello" this morning—I think I must be out of favour.

      老板今天上午没有跟我打招呼——我想我一定失宠了。

      May I ask you a favor? 我可以请您帮个忙吗?

      The president is belived to favour further tax cuts.

      大家认为总统将支持进一步减税。

[派生] favorable *adj.* 赞许的；讨人喜欢的；有利的

[联想] favorite *n.* 特别喜欢的人 (或物)，亲信 *adj.* 喜爱的，宠爱的

11. spray

[词义] *n.* 喷雾，飞沫；*vt.* 喷射，喷溅

[搭配] a spray of water 水花飞溅; spray paint 喷漆; a spray can 喷雾器

[例句] He sprayed the flowers with water. 他用水浇花。

      We parked the car by the sea and it got couered with spray.

      我们将汽车停在海边，汽车上溅满了浪花。

[派生] sprayer *n.* 喷雾器，洒水车; spraycup *n.* 喷 (嘴) 头

12. recovery

[词义] *n.* ① 痊愈；②（经济）复苏

[搭配] the recovery of a lost thing 失物的找回; make a quick recovery 迅速痊愈

[例句] She made a quick recovery after her illness. 她病后恢复得很快。

      The past decade has witnessed the economic recovery of Africa.

      最近的十年间非洲的经济复苏了。

[联想] recover *vi.* 痊愈, 复原

13. resident

[词义] *n.* 居民；*adj.* 居住的, 常驻的

[搭配] local residents 当地居民; resident aliens 定居的外国人; a resident doctor 住院医生; the resident population 居民

[例句] City residents worried that migrant workers might threaten to take already scarce urban jobs.

      城市居民担心民工们可能会威胁着本来就很紧张的城市就业机会。

      Many retired people are now resident in the countryside.

      许多退休的人现在住在乡村。

[派生] residence *n.* 居住，住处

[联想] president *n.* 总统，会长，校长

14. priority

[词义] *n.* ① 优先考虑的事；② 优先权

[搭配] establish an order of priority 按重要性确定……的次序; priority of one's claim 优先要求权; priority construction 首期建筑

[例句] The highest priority of governments has been given to the problem of heavy traffic. 政府已经优先考虑交通拥挤的问题。

The government gave (first) priority to those jobless people.

政府把 (最) 优先权给了那些物业人员。

[辨析] superiority, priority

superiority 表示优越性，指状态或质量上优于、大于等。如：superiority in strength 实力方面的优势；superiority to bribery 拒绝贿赂的超 然精神；assume an air of superiority 摆架子。

priority 指优先权，优先考虑的事情。如：top priority 最优先考虑的事；take priority of 比……居先，得……优先权。

15. prosperous

[词义] adj. ① 繁荣的，兴隆的；② 茂盛的

[搭配] a prosperous year 兴旺的一年；a prosperous business 兴旺的事业；prosperous leaves 茂盛的树叶

[例句] At no time has the country been more prosperous than at present.

我国任何时候都没有现在这样繁荣。

[联想] unprosperous adj. 不茂盛的，不繁荣的

16. crop up (问题等的) 突然出现，突然发生

[例句] The political crisis cropped up making the government at a loss.

突然出现的政治危机使得政府措手不及。

17. act out 表演

[例句] They acted out the bank robbery to the policemen.

他们连说带比划地向警察演示了那桩银行抢劫案。

18. nothing more...than... 只不过，仅仅是

[例句] He was quite clear that he was nothing more than a small potato.

他很清楚自己不过是个无足轻重的人物。

19. up to scratch 达到标准，合格；处于良好的状态

[例句] He has to retire because his health is not up to scratch.

因为健康不佳他不得不退休了。

20. be on the wrong end of 承担……的不利后果

[例句] You should be on the wrong end of this accident since you are in charge of this project. 既然是工程的负责人，你就得承担这次事故的过错。

21. law and order 法律和秩序

[例句] Every citizen must obey law and order of its country.

每个公民都得遵守国家的法律和秩序。

22. throw up 产生，出 (人才)；使突出；匆匆建造

[例句] China has thrown up many world-famous scientists.

中国出了很多世界知名的科学家。

Their sudden arrival threw up the international tension.

他们的出现加剧了国际形势的紧张。

The government decided to pull down the shoddy houses that were thrown up in a few months. 政府决定拆毁在短短几个月内建起的劣质房屋。

23. on sick leave 休病假

[例句] She is now on sick leave. 她正在休病假。

24. derive...from...来自，源于，从……中获得

[例句] True happiness derives from hard working. 真正的幸福来自于辛勤的劳动。

I derive a lot of interesting knowledge form reading books.

我从读书中获得了很多有趣的知识。

25. lose count of 数不清，数的过程中忘记……，数不清……的确切数目

[例句] So nervous was I that I lost count of the goods.

太紧张了，我数不清货物的数量。

26. come up to 达到，符合；走近，靠近

[例句] Come up to me whenever you need help!无论何时你需要帮助，来找我吧！

The quality of the products couldn't come up to the standard of environment protection. 这些产品的质量无法达到环保的要求。

27. carry out 实施，展开（计划，试验）；履行（业务，约定）

[例句] They decided to carry out the experiment immediately.

他们决定立即展开这个试验。

Her husband promised that he would carry out his obligation to take care of her all his life. 她的丈夫承诺一定会履行自己的义务照料她一生。

28. take up 占据（时间、空间）

It took up lots of her time to cook everyday. 每日烧饭占了她很多时间。

Ⅲ. 难句解析

1. The journalists also get a chance to shoot a gun on the practice range; none of it seems that difficult, and we put most of the bullets somewhere on the target. (Para. 2)

[分析] 本句为分号连接的两个并列的简单句。难点在于理解 "on the practice range" 意思为在射击场上。range在此专指 "A place equipped for practice in shooting at targets"，即射击场（用来进行射击练习的地方）。that 为副词，修饰形容difficult，相当于 "so/very"，意思为 "那么，非常"。

2. The lights on the range are dimmed and we are stood in front of a large screen...(Para. 2)

[释义] **stand** *vt.* 使立于，使站立

e.g. We had to stand the new desk on end to get it through the office door.

我们得把这张新办公桌竖起来才能抬进办公室。

[分析] 本句为and连接的两个简单句结构。难点在于对"be stood"结构的正确理解。"are stood" 为被动语态，意思为 "我们被安置在……"。

3. I am afraid we killed many an innocent person carrying nothing more lethal than a stick. (Para.3)

[分析] 本句的核心结构为 "I am afraid + 宾语从句"。在宾语从句中，现在分词短语 "carrying nothing more lethal than a stick." 作 "person" 的后置定语。

[译文] 恐怕我们打死了很多无辜的人，这些人手中最致命的武器不过是一根棍子而已。

4. Actually the biggest threat to the traditional image and role of police officers does not come from guns and armed crème but the increase in the tasks we expect the police to carry out. (Para.14)

[分析] 本句的核心结构为 "not...but..." 结构，具体在句中表现为 "does not come from...but the increase...."，其中but 后省略了come from。"we expect the police to carry out" 为定语从句，省略了关系代词that，修饰先行词tasks。

Ⅳ. 重点语法讲解

1. 选择疑问句（Alternative Question）

提供两种（或两种以上）情况问对方选择哪一种的疑问句叫作选择疑问句。这种疑问句常常需要对方用完全句子回答。

选择疑问句的结构为 "一般疑问句+or +一般疑问句（后一个疑问句常用省略结构，省去意义上与前句相同的部分）"。在朗读时，前一个疑问句用升调，后一个疑问句部分有降调。例如：

Shall I go with you or will you go yourself? 是我跟你一起去，还是你自己去？

Will he go on Monday or on Saturday? 他是星期一走还是星期六走？

Is the man apparently preparing to surrender really going to, or is he going to raise the gun in front of him and shoot? (Para.3) 那个看似想投降的人是否真的会投降，还是想举枪射击？

2. "many + a (an) + 可数名词单数" 结构

"many + a (an) + 可数名词单数" 结构的意思为 "许多……"，"不止一个……"。在该结构中不定冠词和可数名词单数中间还可添加形容词作定语。

虽然该结构表达复数的意思，但作主语时在结构上按照就近原则决定谓语动词的单复数形式，因此句子的谓语动词必须用单数形式。例如：

many an innocent person 许多无辜的人

Many a day has passed. 好多日子 (许多天, 长时间) 过去了。

Many a liitle (pickle) makes a mickle. 积少成多（集腋成裘）。

Ⅴ. 课文赏析

1. 文体特点

本篇议论文论述了英国是否应该给更多的警察配枪的问题。文章首先以记者们在射击场上的体验引出主题。文章通过分析当前警察所面临的最大困扰和对比警方和公众对此问题的不同态度来说明通过配备少数特警是不解决问题的。文章的最后提出了一些解决办法。

文章首尾呼应，论点鲜明突出，内容真实可信，具有较强的说服力。

2. 结构分析

Part Ⅰ (Para.1-3) Topic introduction by the journalists' experience on the practice range to put forward the opint of the passage: whether more police should be armed with guns.

Part Ⅱ (Para.4-10) Different viewpoints from the police and the public.

Part Ⅲ (Para.11-13) The current measures taken by the police to protect the policemen.

Part Ⅳ (Para.14-15) The biggest threat faced by the policemen and measures which should be taken to solve the problem.

Ⅵ. 课后练习答案及解析

Reading Skills

XV.

1. Actors imitated various types of conditions to bring the people in the training camp into some real life situation.

2. the journalists are inexperienced in deciding whom to shoot, whether to shoot or not and when to shoot. As a result, they "killed" innocent people because of mistakes of judgment.

3. From our common sense and understanding of the whole reading passage, the police believe that widespread arming of the officers will increase the possibility of their being attacked with weapons.

4. People don't mind seeing the police further armed but they do mind if they can't see police on the street.

5. The policeman has been so much occupied with some extra duties that he would not have the time either for answering questions or being interviewed.

Comprehension of the Text

XVI.

F F T F F   T F F

Vocabulary

XVII.

1. tackle 译文: 难以置信的是，许多经验不足的飞行员并没有真正的考虑过如何处理在田地里降落。

2. imitated 译文: 她对别人服装、礼仪和声音都很感兴趣，并以此模仿。

3. dimmed 译文: 当时，希特勒的掌权使得日内瓦裁军大会前景黯淡。

4. fake 译文: 通常，问题不仅仅是真与假的问题，而是有多少用，随后为达到目的做什么，什么时间，由谁来做和为什么的问题。

5. impressive 译文: 这位生产商年产量超过60万辆汽车，他的努力使其在取得新成果或保持持继不断的成功方面令人瞩目。

6. encountered 译文: 格拉期完整地讲述了他在那个极端困难的地区所遇到的或好或坏的行为，像他这样的讲述并不常有。

7. equivalent 译文: 当意识到我已经所蛋糕吃了一半时，我感到很尴尬。

8. widespread 译文: 这种疾病在美国蔓延，最近根据报告在英国的狗身上有发现了此种疾病。

XVIII.

1. up 译文: 这些研究已经得出了一些有趣的结果。

2. waway 译文: 血迹在早上已经被冲洗掉了，因此没有证据表明这里曾发生过犯罪事件。

3. up 译文: 上午和、下午的会议主要讨论工会的事情，代表们原则上同意了所提出的议案。

4. up 译文: 那个学期的最后一天，毕业班的学生来到我的办公室，向我表示感谢。

5. out 译文: 一个需要立即关注的严重问题突然出现了，这是真的。

6. out 译文: 为和很好地把握剧本，约翰逊不啬辛苦地写出了该剧的表演细则。

7. to 译文: 不管人们的身体状况如何，集中建档都为他们提供了使用大量相同信息的途径。

8. on 译文: 你可以带薪休病假，量显然对此是有些限制的。

VII. 参考译文

对警察职责的最大威胁

每年夏天，总有大约十几名记者聚集在伦敦北部的一个旧军训营，用一整天来观看伦敦特警部队的训练。特警通常要对付日益增多的携带枪支的犯罪分子。

记者们也有机会在练习场射击。射击似乎并不难，我们的子弹几乎都打到靶上了。然后进入训练的下一步：模拟在街道上实际会出现的一些问题。场上的灯暗了下去，我们面对一块大屏幕站着，手中仍有枪，但子弹是假的。屏幕上演员在扮演着各种场面。

那个抓着一名妇女挡在身前的人真拿着枪吗？那个看似想投降的人是否真会投降，还是要举枪射击？我们必须判断是否该开枪，何时该开枪，就像警察真实地面对此情此景时必须做出判断一样。记者们在这一阶段的表现不太出色。恐怕被我们打死的不少人是无辜的，他们手中最致命的东西只不过是一根棍子而已。

多年来，对于英国是否该给更多的警员配枪一直争论不休。目前的做法是在英国所有的43个警局中都配备少数特警，他们定期接受强化训练来保持达标。

但是随着警察遭遇的暴力事件逐渐增多，人们对这一做法是否明智提出了疑问。通常，正是在街上巡逻的普通警察因此遭殃，而不是姗姗来迟的武装特警。

为了了解英国警方面临的局面，可以看一下诺森布里亚郡警局的情况。该局负责英格兰东北部5,000平方公里区域内的治安。辖内的乡村和几个城区居住着150万人口。那里的3,600名警察要应付英国20世纪90年代常见的各类事件。

该警局负责人约翰·史蒂文斯最近发表了他对过去几年工作的述评。例如，1994年，共有61名警员（男性54人，女性7人）由于履行职责时遭受攻击而不得不提早退休。在因健康原因而获准退休前，他们共请病假12,000日，相当于50名警员休假一年。

史蒂文斯这样评论道："警务的人力成本从未如此之高，离职的警员中严重伤残的达三分之一，他们因打击犯罪而将在余生中承受痛苦。"

警察的这种遭遇也发生在英国其他地方。不过警察当局本身仍反对扩大为警员配备武器的范围。去年进行的最新调查表明，赞成者只占46%。

但是普通老百姓赞成这一做法，他们中的67%赞成扩大配发枪支的范围。但他们自己当然不想带枪，甚至不必用枪。回想一下我自己在练习场射击的经历，我肯定也不想负这个责任。

人人都清楚警察需要更多的保护，以防刀枪。他们现在所携的警棍较以前的要长。他们也有了防利器的上衣、手套。

下一步可能的做法是政府同意试验胡椒喷雾剂，一种从胡椒中提取的有机物质。如果喷在脸上，它能使袭击者丧失行动能力。运用得当的话，所产生的不适只是暂时的，尽管很强烈。只要用水冲洗，几个小时内应可彻底恢复。这当然是难受的，但比挨枪子要好。

很多英国人不反对警察携带加长的警棍或胡椒喷雾剂。他们实在很愿意警察这样做。不知多少次，当我们在街上拍摄警察镜头时，总有当地居民向我们走来告诉我们说这是几周以来他们在此地第一次看到警察。

实际上，对传统警察形象、职责的最大威胁并非来自枪支和武装犯罪，而是来自我们要求警察做的日益增多的工作。新的法令和重点警务工作占去了大量时间，结果使得很多警队就是派不出警员上街巡逻。官员们要求民众守街。在一些繁华地区，居民们雇请私人保安公司。

很多警员认为正是这些额外工作，而不是担心被枪击，才改变了他们的职责。今后，如果想知道时间，去问警察恐怕会没有用。要么你连见都见不到他，要么他没有时间回答。

Section C

Ⅰ. 语言点讲解

1. **These two countries share a common border that runs for thousands of kilometers, with not a single soldier along the way. (Para. 1)**

   [分析] 本句在结构上的重点为介词短语结构引导的独立主格结构，即"with not a single soldier along the way"作补语，逻辑主语为a common border。

2. **For many years he put up with this nuisance, but he planned to get even. (Para.2)**

   [分析] 本句的难点在于对get even with固定词组的理解，相当于"to repay with an equivalent act, as for revenge"，意思为"报复，为了复仇"。

3. **Most of the officers ended up believing that the truck driver was simply pulling their leg. (Para.8)**

   [分析] 本句的难点在于对固定词组的"pull one's leg"的正确理解。不能按字面想当然理解为"拖某人后腿"。这个词组的意思为"作弄，愚弄，取笑某人；哄骗某人的钱"，相当于"to play a trick on someone"。"拖某人后腿"的正确表达方式为"hinder (or impede) sb.; be a drag on sb.; hold sb. back"。

Ⅱ. 课文赏析

1. 文体特点

本文是一篇记叙文，向读者讲述了一位退休的卡车司机如何巧妙地通过海关走私自行车的故事。文章首先描述了在美国与加拿大的共同边境上，海关在打击走私方面的认真负责。然后，文章用较大篇幅描写了一位卡车司机在退休后如何瞒过认真的海关人员，成功走私自行车的经过。

本文语言生动幽默，条理清晰，扣人心弦。在文章结尾部分才揭示谜底的写法更让文章悬念重重，更加具有趣味性。

2. 结构分析

Part Ⅰ (Para.1) Introduction about the import role that the customs on the border between American and Canada nowadays.

Part Ⅱ (Para.2-9) The retired truck driver tired to play tricks on the responsible customs officer by everyday riding a bike with a bucket of sand, leaving the officer checking it without finding anything to be smuggled.

Part Ⅲ (Para.10-17) When the officer retired, he got the answer to his doubt how the truck driver smuggled, which is that he smuggled bikes.

Ⅲ. 课后练习答案及解析

Reading skills

XIX.

1. This implies that the driver purposely made his appearance noticed by the customs officers so that they would check him.

2. From the next sentence we find that "pulling their leg" means playing a joke on them.

3. Because the customs officer failed to find out what the driver smuggled.

4. When the driver came he was riding a beautiful racing bicycle whereas when he went back he was riding a bicycle, which was not the previous one, a beautiful racing bicycle.

5. The customs officer always takes his job seriously.

Comprehension of the Text

XX.

1. customs officers

2. taking illegal items

3. took their jobs seriously

4. delayed

5. noticed

6. only playing a joke on them

7. asked the truck driver

8. same

Ⅳ. 参考译文

狡猾的走私者

你可能认为国境线没有什么了不起的。然而加拿大和美国却很为两国的边界自豪。两国有几千公里的共同边界，在这条边界线上没有一个巡逻的士兵。虽然没有巡逻兵，却有海关工作人员。有时，有货车藏着毒品企图过境，有时也有普通的旅游者试图偷带一瓶酒出境。在海关官员看来，这些事没什么不同，所有的走私者都一样是走私，只不过数额有大有小而已。他们的工作就是阻止任何人非法运送货物出入境。

走私者与海关官员之间经常发生的冲突影响了人们对这件事的看法。这不太公正，但很多人还是会忽略海关官员所作的宝贵贡献。发生这种情况的时候，尽管海关官员始终恪尽职守，冲突会略显滑稽。据说在著名的尼亚加拉瀑布大桥那儿就发生过这样一次冲突。有一个卡车司机，他的工作需要他经常穿越边境。每次到达大桥，他就得停车，向海关官员出示各种证件，有时还得等上老半天。间或海关官员还要他卸车检查。因为他从未携带过非法物品，这种种耽搁尤其使他恼火。他不明白，别人违法，为何自己也要受烦扰。这么多年来，他一直忍着这种麻烦，但他决定报复。等到终于退休了，他便开始实行这一计划。

他最后一次驾着卡车过境之后三四天，他又出现在海关人员面前。这回他没有开车，而是骑着辆自行车! 那是辆漂亮的赛车。那个卡车司机身体很棒，他骑得很快，在过境处的停车场绕了几大圈。他确信所有的海关官员都看到了他，然后来到了过境处。

"喂，老朋友，"一个海关官员说，"你已退休了，还有什么要效劳的吗? "

"跟以前一样，"他答道，"我要过境，请检查证件，让我过去。"

这里该提一下的是，这辆车有个独特之处: 车把两边各挂着满满一桶沙。这太奇怪了! 海关官员当然马上就注意到了。司机被叫了过去。

"你可以过去，"他说，"但先得检查你的货。"他翻看了这些沙，却没发现什么。海关官员有点失望，就让这退休司机过了境。

海关官员们对司机的这一奇怪举动感到好笑，后来也就忘了。但才过了一小时，这司机又返回来了。他要过边境回去。他仍然骑着一辆车，带着两桶沙。另一海关官员检查了沙，还是没发现什么。司机高兴地骑车回了家。此后的一年里，这一同样的古怪现象每天出现两次，天天如此。海关官员用尽了一切手段。他们把沙浸入水中看看里面是否混有什么东西。他们每次都要搜查司机的衣袋，最后甚至还用X光检查自行车，想看看是否在车内藏着什么。他们始终未发现任何东西。最终大多数海关官员认为这司机不过是想捉弄他们一番。他并没走私，只是跟他们开个玩笑而已。

然而有一个海关官员始终不信。他认为司机的行为一定有秘密。他明知如此，却猜不透。一次次检查都找不出什么，这挺令人尴尬的，他也就不再在那司机过境时检查了。不过他仍留意着这司机，相信自己总有一天会明白的。

最后，这个海关官员也到了退休年龄，也要停止工作了。与卡车司机不同，他没有开始骑车运动，但他也没远离大桥，他喜欢钓鱼。大多数日子的下午，他在距自己工作了一辈子的地方不远的尼亚加拉河里钓鱼。该发生的事情终于发生了。司机沿河骑着车来到了他钓鱼的地方，下了车。有一小会儿，两人都望着河上的大桥。海关官员说："好了，我认输，不管怎样，这事过去了，现在你可以告诉我了。你那沙中到底有什么？"

"什么也没有，"退休卡车司机说。

"你是说你这样做就只是为了烦扰我们？"

"才不是呢，我一直在走私。不过你们不够聪明，从未抓住我。"

"这太过分了，"海关官员叹道，"我知道的！我知道的！但你的违法东西是怎么藏的？"

"藏？算你问到点子上了。我什么也没藏。"

"不可能！我们什么都查了。你走私什么？"

"自行车。"

五、知识链接

U.S. Securities and Exchange Commission (SEC)

SEC is a government commission created by Congress to regulate the securities markets and protect investors. At present the SEC is comprised of five presidentially-appointed Commissioners, four Divisions and 18 Offices, with a total of about 3,100 staff. The five members of the SEC are appointed by the President and confirmed by the Senate for terms of five years.

U.S. government agency, whose mission is to protect investors and maintain the integrity of the securities markets. The Commission was set up in response to the aftermath of the "Black Monday", the Great Stock Market Crash of 1929. Its purpose was to restore investor confidence in the U.S. capital markets by providing more structure and government oversight. It is based on the concept that all investors, whether large institutions or private individuals, should have access to certain basic facts about an investment prior to buying it.

To achieve this, the SEC requires public companies to disclose meaningful financial and other information to the public, which provides a common pool of knowledge for all investors to use to judge for themselves if a company's securities are a good investment. It is believed that only through the steady flow of timely, comprehensive and accurate information can people make sound investment decisions.

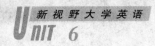
美国证券交易委员会

美国证券交易委员会是由国会创立的管理证券市场，保护投资人利益的政府机构。目前，该委员会包括5位总统任命的委员，4个分会，18个办事处，共3100名工作人员。该委员会的五个由总统任命委员、参议院批准，任期为五年。

作为美国的政府机构之一，它的任务是规范证券市场，保护投资者的利益。由于1929年纽约股市大崩溃，为了抵制股市"黑色星期一"的恶果，该委员会应运而生。它的作用在于通过提供更多的经济建构和政府监督，重建投资者对美国资本市场的信心。它诞生在这样的理念之上：所有的投资者，无论是大投资机构还是私人投资者，在投资前都有权掌握可靠的基本事实。

为了实现上述保证，证券交易委员会要求上市公司公开有价值的财经信息和其它情况。这对于投资者而言，这样可以为他们提供信息的储备，以便他们对公司证券是否绩优做出判断。人们相信，只有依据及时的、翔实的和准确的信息，他们才能做出正确的投资决定。

六、自测题

Directions: In the following passage there are altogether 10 mistakes, one in each numbered line. You may have to change word, add a word or delete a word. If you change a word, cross it out and write correct word in the corresponding blank. If you add a word, put an insertion mark (∧) in the right place and write the missing word in the blank. If you delete a word, cross it out and put a slash (/) in the blank.

One of the three major commercial networks, CBS were
organized in l928 which its founder, William Paley, acquired
ownership of a group of radio stations. As the Columbia
Broadcasting System expanded its operations, soon become
the largest radio network in the United States, it precociously
recognized the potential for the rapidly evolved television
broadcasting technology.

1. _____
2. _____
3. _____
4. _____

On July 13th, 1931, it began experimentally television
broadcasting in New York, and ten years later began regular
black and white week broadcasts over its WCBW TV station in
the same city, that became WCBS TV in November 1946. With
Television City in Hollywood, CBS launched the industry's first
full scale production studio. Today CBS owns television stations,
radio stations, and home video production and distribution
interests. The CBS\Broadcasting Group composed of six
divisions: television network, entertainment, sports, news, local
television stations, and radio.

5. _____
6. _____
7. _____
8. _____

For most of commercial television history, CBS has been the leader in prime time ratings, having the highest rated shows in almost every year from the mid 1950s through the mid 1980s. During the late 1980s, however, CBS lost its top position from NBC. CBS has traditionally been strong in the TV news area. The network began the first regular TV news program in 1948 with Douglas Edwards as anchor, Journalism legends such as Edward R. Murrow and Walter Cronkite gave CBS its reputation as quality news broadcaster.

9. _____

10. _____

答案与解析

1. 将were改为was。作为美国三大商业广播电视网之一，哥伦比亚广播公司成立于1928年。本题辨析谓语动词单复数的误用。本句的主语为CBS (哥伦比亚广播公司)，而不是networks。因此，将were organized改为was organized。

2. 将which改为when/in which。那年，它的创始人威廉·佩利获得了数家广播电台的所有权。本题辨析定语从句引导词的误用。作"年代"的定语从句，其引导词可以是that, which, in which或when。这须判断定语从句缺少什么成分，"its founder William Paley, acquired ownership of a group of radio stations"中，缺少时间状语，故引导词应为when或in which。

3. 将become改为becoming。随着哥伦比亚广播公司业务范围的拓展，它很快成了美国的最大广播网。本题辨析谓语动词与分词状语的误用。故意将分词短语设计错误，这是六级考试辨错题的一个常考类型。"As the Columbia Broadcasting System expanded its operations"是一个由as引导伴随状语，与"soon become the largest radio network in the United States"之间有一种逻辑上的因果关系，而不是并列关系，而且soon become...在句法上也与并列句子不合。(由and连结)，因此，用become是不合适的，由于become的逻辑主语是the Columbia Broadcasting System，因而将become变为becoming，使这个句子成为结果状语后，就使整个句子符合逻辑连贯性了。

4. 将evolved改为evolving。它一开始就认识到了未来广播电视技术迅猛发展的趋势。本题辨析作前置定语时分词的误用。作前置定语时，现在分词表示"正在或将要发生"，过去分词表示"已经成为过去"。根据句意，发展趋势是未来的，因此，evolved是不合适的。要将evolved改为evolving。

5. 将experimentally改为experimental。1931年7月13日，它开始在纽约试播电视节目。本题辨析形容词，副词的误用。副词作状语时，通常在实义动词之前，助动词之后。那么，experimentally放在began之后，是不合适的，那么，experimentally应修饰television broadcasting。但修饰名词应用形容词experimental，而不是experimentally。

6. 将week改为weekly。10年后，开始在纽约通过其WCBW TV电视台每周播放一定的黑白电视节目。本题辨析定语的误用。名词也可以作定语，但一定要符合句意。week意为"周，星期"，与broadcast的搭配，没有什么合乎逻辑的含义，若将之换为weekly，"每周播放"则合乎句意。

7. 将that改为which。1946年11月，WCBW TV电视台改为WCBS TV。本题辨析非限定性定语从句的误用。从逻辑意义上讲，that became WCBW TV in November 1946是非限

定性定语从句，that代替WCBW TV。但非限定性定语从句的引导词，只能用which。

8. 将composed改为is composed。该广播电视集团有六大组成部分：电视网、娱乐、体育、新闻、地方电视台以及广播电台。本题辨析动词语态的误用。"在表示由……组成"时，一般用be composed of。

9. 将from改为to。然而，到了80年代末，哥伦比亚广播公司失去了其领先地位，由全国广播公司取而代之。本题辨析介词的误用。from，表示"从……来"。本句因from的误用，使句子失去了逻辑意义，则将from改为to，就表示了"将位置丢给了NBC"，to表示的意义刚好和from相反。

10. 将quality前加一个"a"。新闻界的传奇人们爱德华·默罗和沃尔特·克朗凯特给哥伦比亚广播公司带来了盛誉，使其被称为信得过的新闻广播电视台。本题辨析不定冠词的漏用。quality news broadcaster的中心词是broadcaster (广播电视台)，是可数名词的单数形式，所以，应在quality前加上不定冠词a。

Unit 7

① 学习重点和难点

词汇和短语、语法项目、写作技巧

② 文化知识

课文大背景、课文知识点

③ 课文精讲

词汇与短语详解、难句解析、重点语法讲解、课文赏析、课后练习答案及解析、参考译文、写作指导

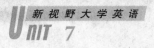

一、预习重点

1. What does *The History and Geography of Human Genes* conclude?

2. Why did people assume that Australia's native people were closely related to black Africans?

3. Apart from the human origins, what else does genetic information contribute to human beings?

二、学习重点和难点

Ⅰ. 词汇和短语

Section A: superior, bias, prime, assemble, resemble, distinct, exploit, mission; to date, nothing less than, serve as, be confined to, as of/from , in effect , adapt to, in combination with, shed/throw light on, be descended from

Section B: supervise, fascinate, fatigue, identify, steer, assess, alert, peer; spring up, out of nowhere, look into, go out of one's way, make a not of, pick up, in question, have an advantage over, in a (good) position to do, far from

Ⅱ. 语法项目

① "more than + noun /adjective phrase"结构

② "nothing less than + noun /adjective phrase"结构

③ "not just...but...as well"结构

④ "not only/just...but also"结构

Ⅲ. 写作技巧

主旨句+例证（the statement supported by examples）

三、文化知识

Ⅰ. 课文大背景

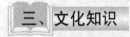

The world is filled with nearly 6 billion people, but each of us is different from everbody else. Only you have your combinations of looks, personality, and behavior. At the same time, you have your combinations of looks, personality, thinking, and being that you share with some other people, such as your parents. For instance, you may look like your father or share your mother's sense of humor. One way that scientists know this to be true is by studying our genes. Genes are units of information inside the cells of your body.

They contain the instructions for making cells and for doing the work that goes on inside them. It is through the genes that traits are handed down from parents to children. Genes help decide your size, build（身材，体型）, skin color, personalities, and other features. They decide you a male or a female. Scientists also believe that genes also play a role in how you think and behave and in your body's health. The ultimate goal of studying genetics however, is not just scientific: it hopes to have a social effect by proving that there is no biological basis for racial prejudice.

II. 课文知识点

1. Luca Cavalli-Sforza 路卡·卡瓦里–斯福尔扎

Cavalli-Sforza, born in Genoa（热那亚）, Italy, was educated at the University of Pavia where he gained his MD（医学博士）in 1944. After working on bacterial genetics at Cambridge (1948—1950) and Milan (1950—1957) he has held chairs in genetics at Parma（帕尔马）(1958—1962) and Pavia（帕维亚）(1962—1970). In 1970 he was appointed professor of genetics at the University of Stanford, California, a position he held until his retirement in 1992. Cavalli-Sforza has specialized mainly in the genetics of human populations（人口遗传学）, producing with Walter Bodmer a comprehensive survey of the subject in their *Genetics, Evolution and Man*（《遗传学、进化与人类》）(1976). He has also done much to show how genetic data from present human racial groups could be used to reconstruct their past separations.

2. Columbus 哥伦布

Christopher Columbus, an Italian-born master navigator (born in Genoa（热那亚）, Italy in 1451 and died in Spain in 1506) who sailed in the service of Spain, is commonly described as the discoverer of the New World—America. His four transatlantic voyages（四次横渡大西洋）(1492—1493, 1493—1496, 1498—1500, and 1502—1504) opened the way for European exploration, exploitation（开发，剥削）, and colonization of the Americas. Columbus's real greatness lies in the fact that having found the West Indies—making major errors in his navigational computations（航海计算）and location in doing so—he was able to find his way back to Europe and return to the Indies. It is as the result of Columbus's "discovery" that the New World became part of the European world.

3. human genetic map 人类基因图谱

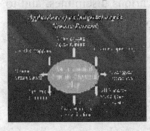

Our bodies are comprised of trillions of microscopic units called cells. Cells in turn are built up from many specific types of molecules, both large and small. The large molecules or macromolecules include polysaccharides（多糖）, nucleic acids（核酸）and proteins（蛋白质）. Proteins are the workhorses of our cells. There are about 40,000 different types of proteins in our bodies. Each protein is present in many, many copies. An adult, for example, carries about 1021 (a billion trillion) hemoglobin（血色素）molecules. The flow of genetic information is from DNA（脱氧核糖核酸）to RNA（核糖核酸）to Protein. Each protein is a linear polymer（线性聚合物）of a specific sequence of 20 different amino acids（氨基酸）. DNA is also a linear polymer comprised of 4 types of nucleotides（核苷）. The sequence of amino acids in each protein is encoded by a segment of DNA called a gene. Three consecutive（连续性的）nucleotides in a gene encode a single amino acid in the corresponding protein. The genetic code is universal among all living things.

4. Khoisan 科伊桑人

Khoisan is the name by which the lighter skinned indigenous peoples of southern Africa. These people were the earliest inhabitants of Africa and dominated the sub-continent for millennia before the appearance of the Nguni（祖鲁人）and other black peoples. There were probably about 120,000 living in South Africa around 1500.

5. Basques 巴斯克人

The Basques are a people who mainly live in a small region that straddles the border of Spain and France from the sea in the west into the Pyrenees in the east. This area comprises seven provinces, historically: four on the Spanish side;the other three on the French side. The Basque name for their language is Euskara，which has a number of dialects.

6. Mozart 莫扎特

born on January 27, 1756 in Salzburg（萨尔茨保，奥地利城市），Austria and died on December 5, 1791. Wolfgang Amadeus Mozart（莫扎特，乌夫冈·阿马戴乌斯）is probably the greatest genius in Western musical history. Mozart began writing minuets（米奴哀小步舞曲）at the age of 5, and by the time of his death at age 35, he had produced 626 cataloged works including nearly 50 symphonies（交响乐），20 operas, and 23 piano concertos（钢琴协奏曲）. His beautifully constructed works, including the famous last symphonies and the operas *The Marriage of Figaro*（《费加罗的婚礼》）(1786)，*Don Giovanni*（《唐·乔万尼》）(1787)，and *The Magic Flute*（《魔笛》）(1791)，are ranked among the most perfect compositions.

7. Society for Research in Child Development

This Society is a multidisciplinary（多学科的）, not-for-profit（非盈利的）, professional association with a membership of approximately 5,500 researchers, practitioners, and human development professionals from over 50 countries. The purposes of the Society are to promote multidisciplinary（有关各种学科的）research in the field of human development, to foster the exchange of information among scientists and other professionals of various disciplines, and to encourage applications of research findings. Their goals are pursued through a variety of programs with the cooperation and service of their governing council, standing committees（常务委员会），and members.

四、课文精讲

Section A

I. 短语与词汇详解

1. superiority

[词义] *n.* [U] 优越 (性)，优等

[搭配] superiority over sth. 比……优越; superiority in sth. 在某方面有优势

[例句] There is a feeling of our own superiority and our pride that lie at the root of our response to them.

我们对他们的反应从根本上存在一种自我优越性和骄傲的感觉。

It was believed that the country already had superiority in conventional armies and weapons. 据信，这个国家已在常规军队和常规武器方面占有优势。

[联想] inferiority *n.* 劣势，低等

2. bias

[词义] *vt.* 使有偏见；*n.* 偏见，偏袒，偏爱

[搭配] bias sb. against sth. 使某人对……有偏见；without bias and without favor 不偏不倚，大中至众

[例句] We argued that the broadcasting was biased towards the right wing and the government of today. 我们认为广播对右翼和现政府有偏见。

His birth background biases him against businessmen.
他的家庭背景使他对商人抱有偏见。

He had a bias toward the plan. 他对该计划有成见。

[联想] biased *adj.* 有偏见的

[辨析] bias，prejudice

bias 指依个人好恶或成见提出有偏差的意见或判断。

prejudice 指除了私人感情以外毫无根据的判断或成见，常带有恶意，如：
He had a prejudice against farmers. 他对农民有偏见。

3. prime

[词义] *adj.* 首要的，主要的；*n.* 青春，壮年，全盛时期

[搭配] a matter of prime importance 最紧要的事情；in the prime of life 正在壮年，正在年富力强时期；past one's prime 过了年富力强的时期

[例句] Spring is the prime time for planting trees. 春天是植树的最好时间。

[辨析] prime, principal, primary

prime 指与其它事物相比较处于第一位的或质量最好的事物，如：a theory of prime significance 极具重要性的理论。

principal 适用于在等级、权力或意义上处于第一位的人或物，如：the principal rivers of a country 一个国家的主要河流。

primary 强调在起源、结果或者发展的意义上的第一位的，如：a matter of primary importance 头等重要大事。

4. assemble

[词义] *vi.* 集合，聚集；*vt.* 集合，聚集

[例句] In a school without a hall, the whole school usually assembles in the playground for meetings.
在没有礼堂的学校，开大会时，全校师生员工通常在操场上集合。

He assembled a radio set. 他装配了一台收音机。

[联想] disassemble *vt.* 解开；assemble *n.* 集合，装配（= gather together）

5. ensure

[词义] *vt.* 保证，担保，确保

[搭配] ensure success/safety/supplies 保证成功/安全/供应；ensure sb. against/from danger 保护某人免受危险

[例句] If you want to ensure that you can get the diploma, you'd better not choose too many classes. 如果你想确保拿到文凭，最好别选太多的课。

[辨析] assure, ensure, insure

assure 用来指人，有"使某人放心"的意思，如：He assured the leader of his loyalty. 他使领导确信他的忠诚。

ensure 和 insure 在一般情况下可以互换，现在只有insure 广泛用于美国英语中，商业中意指"给人或财产保险以防意外"。

6. resemble

[词义] *vt.* 像，类似于

[例句] She resembles her mother in the way she moves her hands when she talks.
她说话时打手势的动作像她妈妈。

[联想] resembling *adj.* 相似的，模仿的

7. distinct

[词义] *adj.* ① 有区别的，清楚的；② 显著的

[例句] There has been distinct improvement of people's life in the last twenty years.
20年来，人们的生活有了明显的改善。

[派生] distinction *n.* 区别，差别；distinctive *adj.* 与众不同的

[联想] extinct 熄灭的，灭绝的；distinct 区别的，不同的

8. exploit

[词义] *vt.* ① 剥削；② 开采

n. (常 *pl*) 业绩，功勋

[例句] Factories here are coming under criticism for exploiting workers.
这儿的工厂因剥削工人而遭到批评。

They exploited its rich resources in wheat and soil.
他们开发这个地区丰富的小麦和石油资源。

Their heroic exploits will go down in history.
他们的英雄业绩将被载入史册。

[派生] exploitable *adj.* 可开发的，可利用的

9. mission

[词义] *n.* 使命，任务，天职

[例句] It seemed to be her mission to care for her brother's children.
照顾她弟弟的孩子似乎是她的使命。

10. to date 至今，直到现在

[例句] To date, research on the application of the genetic map is very limited.
至今，对基因图应用的研究工作还是非常有限的。

11. nothing less than 简直是，同……一点也不差

[例句] Our aim is nothing less than to make China the best trained and educated nation in the world. 我们的目标就是要使中国成为世界上受到最好培训和教育的国家。

12. serve as 起……作用，当成

[例句] His remarks should have served as an encouragement to the authorities to develop this important aspect of community care. 他的一席话应当视作是对当局发展社区保护中这一重要方面的一种鼓励。

13. be confined to 限制于，局限于

[例句] Criticism and debate are to be welcomed and should not be confined to academic circles. 批评和辩论应受到欢迎，并且不应该仅局限于学术界。

14. as of/from 从……时候起

[例句] As of now, cigarettes are banned in my house and all the offices.
从现在起，我的屋子和所有的办公室都禁止吸烟。

15. in effect 事实上，实际上

[例句] In effect, the influence of this government was going down gradually.
事实上，这个政府的影响力正在逐渐下降。

16. adapt to（改变……）使适应

[例句] Only when your approach to good health can be adapted to all your own requirements, will you really succeed in obtaining your goals of health care.
只有当你对待健康的方法能适应所有你自己的要求，你才真正能成功达到你的保健目标。

17. in combination with 与……合作，共同

[例句] The firm is working on a new product in combination with several overseas partners. 公司正在联合几家海外合伙人制造新产品。

18. shed/throw light on 使（某事）更为清楚，阐明（某事）

[例句] In addition, the research is expected to shed more light on the social consequences of cities' changing economic roles. 另外，这项研究会更为清楚地说明城市变化的经济作用所产生的社会影响。

19. be descended from 为……的后裔，是……的后人

[例句] Wherever they are now, black people are descended from Africans.
无论黑人在哪儿，他们都是非洲人的后裔。

Ⅱ. 难句解析

1. **While not exactly a top selling book, The History and Geography of Human Genes is a remarkable collection of more than 50 years of research in population genetics. (Para. 1)**

[释义] Although the book is not, in a real sense, a best seller, The History and Geography of Human Genes is a special and unusual book, which reflects 50 years' effort in the research work on population genetics.

a top selling book 畅销书，相当于 "a best seller".

e.g. The novel *Gone With the Wind* has been a top selling book for three weeks.

[分析] while在句中作从属连词，引导让步性状语。状语从句中省略了主谓结构 "it is"，只保留了表语 "not exactly a top selling book"，这在语法上被称之为带从属连词的短语结构。

2. **In fact, there is no scientific basis for theories pushing the genetic superiority of any one population over another. (Para.1)**

[释义] Actually, theories suggesting that one race of people is superior to another have no scientific basis.

[分析] 本句的核心结构为 "there be" 句型，其中现在分词结构 "pushing the genetic

superiority of any one population over another"作定语，修饰theories。同时，在该定语结构中，another后承前省略了"population"。

3. Result: the closest thing we have to a global family tree. (Para.2)

[释义] As a result, we've got something extremely close to a global family tree—how the world populations are related to each other.

[分析] 本句的难点在于使用了倒装结构，把需要强调的宾语 "the closest thing" 直接提到句首。这是英语中一种常用的倒装结构，其作用就是突出强调。通常而言，可以将英语句子中任何一个需要强调的成分放在句首，其他成分语序不变。本句的正常结构为 "we have the closest to the global family tree"。

4. And to ensure the populations were "pure", the study was confined to groups that were in their present locations as of 1492, before the first major movements from Europe began—in effect, a genetic photo of the world when Columbus sailed for America. (Para.3)

[释义] And to make sure the survey participants were not mixed with outsiders, the study was limited to districts where people had been living since 1492 and were not affected by the first major movements from Europe due to Columbus's discovery of America. In fact, what the scientists drew was a genetic map of the world in 1492.

[分析] 本句中不定式短语 "to ensure the populations were 'pure'" 为目的状语，主句中套用了定语从句 "that were in their present locations as of 1492," 修饰先行词 "groups"。从句为before引导的时间状语从句。破折号部分采用了省略结构，省略了 "it was"。

5. One of them jumps right off the book's cover: a color map of the world's genetic variation has Africa at one end of the range and Australia at the other. (Para.5)

[释义] One of the discoveries was right on the book's cover—a color map of world's genetic change, showing that Australians are most distant from the Africans in genes.

[分析] 短语 "jump right off the book's cover" 非常生动形象地表述了书封面上的内容醒目跳入读着眼帘的动作，意思为"赫然出现在书的封面上"，相当于 "one of the discoveries jump off the book's cover into our eyes"。

6. The same map, in combination with ancient human bones, confirms that Africa was the birthplace of humanity and thus the starting point of the original human movements. (Para.6)

[释义] The same genetic map, together with the study of ancient human bones, firmly proves that Africa was the origin of human races and therefore the starting point of human migration.

the starting point 出发点，起跑点，始发地

e.g. The article provides a good starting point for discu ssion.

这篇文章为讨论提供了一个很好的出发点。

[分析] 本句的主干为 "the same map confirms that..."。在宾语从句中，使用了副词thus + noun phrase 的省略结构，相当于 "thus it is the starting point of..."。

7. **In addition to telling us about our origins, genetic information is also the latest raw material of the medical industry, which hopes to use human DNA to build specialized proteins that may have some value as disease-fighting drugs. (Para.9)**

[释义] **in addition to** 除了……还有

e.g. In addition to money, it also costs lots of time.

[分析] 短语 "in addition to" 中的to 为介词，后接名词或动名词。本句中 "which hopes to use human DNA...disease-fighting drugs." 为非限制性定语从句，先行词为前面的整个句子。在这个非限制性定语从句中又套用了一个限制性定语从句，即 "that may have some value as disease-fighting drugs"，修饰先行词proteins。

8. **Activists for native populations fear that the scientists could exploit these peoples: genetic material taken from blood samples could be used for commercial purposes without adequate payment made to the groups that provide the DNA. (Para.9)**

[释义] Activists for native populations worry that the scientists could take advantage of these peoples, getting DNA information from their blood samples to gain profit without paying them enough.

[分析] 本句的核心结构是 "Activists...fear that..."。为了解释宾语从句，在宾语从句后使用冒号使用了宾语从句的同位语从句。在同位语从句中，过去分词短语 "taken from blood samples" 作后置定语，修饰 "genetic material"。"that provide the DNA" 为定语从句修饰先行词the groups。

Ⅲ. 重点语法讲解

1. "more than + noun/verbal/adjective phrase" 结构

短语 "more than" 意思是 "having greater value or importance than sth. else"，相当于 "not only..., not just..."。请注意，此时的 "more than" 不与比较状语从句连用。其中的more 为形容词比较级的替代词，可以用任何具体形容词的比较级替代。

该短语有如下三种常用结构：

1) More than + a noun phrase 不只是……

The variation among individuals is much greater than the differences among groups. (Para. 1) 个体间的差异远远明显大于群体间的差异。

The book, however, is much more than an argument against the latest racially biased theory. (Para.2) 然而，此书不仅仅是对当前的种族歧视理论的反驳。

Learning English is more than attending the classes and taking notes. 学习英语不只是来上课和记笔记。

He's more than a coach; he's a friend. 他不只是一个教练，他更是一位朋友。

2) More than+ a verbal phrase 不只是……，不仅仅……

We more than waited from morning till night; we were worried. 我们不只是从早一直等到晚，还担心受怕。

She more than suffered from the disease; she was penniless. 她不仅仅是饱受疾病之苦，而且穷得身无分文。

He more than scolded me; he told me what to do next.

他不只是责怪我，还告诉我以后该怎么做。

James more than shouted; he threw the glass at the waiter.

詹姆斯不只是大声喊叫，还把玻璃杯扔向侍者。

3) More than + an adjective phrase 非常…… 极度……

She was more than glad to hear the news. 听到这个消息她非常高兴。

His house is more than large and beautiful. 他的房子非常大也非常漂亮。

I was more than frightened when I saw the terrible man.

当我看见那个可怕的人时，感到极度害怕。

The jokes you told me the other day are more than funny. 那天你给我讲的笑话非常有趣。

2. "nothing less than + phrase" 结构

短语 "nothing less than" 相当于 "exactly the same as"，意思是 "简直，正是……"，对后面的修饰成分的重要性或不受欢迎起到强调，加强语气的作用。请注意，在表示上述含义时，该短语通常不与比较状语从句连用。该短语有如下常用结构：

1) Nothing less than+ a noun phrase

The prime mover behind the project, Luca Cavalli-Sforza, a Stanford professor, labored with his colleagues for 16 years to create nothing less than the first genetic map of the world. (Para.2)

该项目的主要倡导者，斯坦福大学的卢卡·卡瓦里·斯福尔扎与同事经过16年的研究，编著了这部相当于世界上第一部基因分布图谱的书。

You're nothing less than a murderer! 你简直是一个杀人犯!

A co-educational school offers children nothing less than a true version of society in miniature.

男女同校的学校正是向孩子们提供了一个真实社会的缩影。

The setting up of this plant in three months is nothing less than a miracle.

三个月就建成了这个工厂简直就是一个奇迹。

2) Nothing less than + an adjective phrase

The present trend is nothing less than alarming. 当前的这种趋势确实令人担心。

His experience is nothing less than magical and I am moved to tears.

他的经历简直太具魔幻色彩，我被感动得流下眼泪。

3. "not just...but...as well" 结构

"not just...but...as well"结构连接两个并列成分，相当于 "not only...but also..."，意思为"不仅……而且……"，在该结构中，更强调but后面的内容。

Cavalli-Sforza stresses that his mission is not just <u>scientific</u> but <u>social</u> as well. (Para. 10)

卡瓦里·斯福尔扎强调他的工作不仅有科学意义，而且也有社会意义。(连接两个并列的表语)

Some parents are not only <u>concerned with safety</u> but <u>skeptical of the educational value of such strips</u> as well. 有些父母不仅关心这些连环画的安全性，还对它们的教育价值表示怀疑。(连接两个并列的表语)

The government radio not only <u>reported the demonstration</u>, but <u>announced it in advance</u> as well. 政府电台不仅报道了这次示威游行，而且事先做了预告。(连接两个并列的谓语部分)

IV. 课文赏析

1. 文体特点

写作风格

本文以说明为主，兼有议论性质的说明文。作者运用了列举和例证法，列举四个重要发现：

1）发现了非洲人与澳洲人并不是如以前所认为的那样基因接近，相反，他们之间差距最大（34-35）；

2）证实了非洲是人类的起源地（42-43）；

3）揭开了长期以来困扰科学家的某些人种的起源问题（46）；

4）基因信息是新型医药工业的原材料之一（62）。简要地说明了人类基因的发展与地理分布为人类基因研究所做出的卓越贡献。文章首先以这本书的一大功绩，即世界上首张人类基因分布的图谱，引入话题；然后对这一图谱的价值进行了详细得分析；最后以这本书作者的话结束，进一步说明了种族之间是平等的，没有孰优孰劣的区别。

注意对段落主题句的运用：除第一段的主题句位于段末，其余都位于段首，有助于很快抓住文章的重点，从而达到将复杂的科学概念和研究用浅显易懂的语言表达出来的效果。

2. 结构分析

Part I (Para.1-2) The significance of the remarkable book The History and Geography of Human Genes.

Part II (Para.3-4) The difficulties in conducting the research.

Part III (Para.5-9) Scientists made some remarkable discoveries through the research.

Part IV (Para.10) The conclusion: The research on Human Genes is not just scientific but social as well.

V. 课后练习答案及解析

Comprehension of the Text

II.

1. The book concludes that despite surface features, the "races" are remarkably alike under the skin.

2. Luca Cavalli-Sforza, a Stanford professor, and his colleagues.

3. In human blood: various proteins that serve as markers to reveal a person's genetic makeup.

4. Because they share such superficial characteristics as skin color and body shape. But the discoveries indicate that Australians are most distant from the Africans and most closely resemble the Southeast Asians.

5. It confirms that Africa was the birthplace of humanity and thus the starting point of the original human movements.

6. Their genes show the Khoisan may be a very ancient mix of west Asians and black Africans, rather than being directly descended from the most primitive human ancestors.

7. All Europeans are thought to be a mixed population, with 65% Asian and 35% African genes.

8. It is the latest raw material of the medical industry. And in addition, it can be used to weaken conventional notions of race that cause racial prejudice.

Vocabulary

III.

1. discounted 译文：一些医学专家认为，不能忽视这种疾病在欧洲，包括英国爆发的可能性。

2. biased 译文：这篇报告有偏见，因为它的作者持一种造成种族偏见的传统观念。

3. variation 译文：在花园里种植不同品种的玫瑰是个好主意，因为这样可以使花园更加富有变化和吸引力。

4. feature 译文：但是有一些书是专门介绍这个国家在社会、文化或者职业生活方面的信息的。

5. Confronted 译文：在证据面前，他们承认整个人类中澳大利亚人与非洲人的基因差异最大。

6. migrated 译文：这本书中的妇女主要分为两类：一类是从印度和巴基斯坦的农村来英国的妇女，另一类是同样来自于这两个国家的农家妇女，但她们首先移民到东非，然后才到了英国。

7. descended 译文：现有的信息表明，每一个现代国家都是多个民族的后裔，更不用说那些已延续多年的民族了。

8. exploiting 译文：他们担心一些组织以科学研究为名来利用当地人，将他们所收集的基因材料用于商业用途。

IV.

1. The scientists announced last year that one of the genes that played a determining intelligence had been identified, but to date the results have yet to be confirmed.
   译文：科学家去年宣布他们已经识别了一种对智力起一定作用的基因，但是到目前为止，这一结论还没有得到进一步的证实。

2. They seem to think that building a new road will improve the traffic problem, but in effect, it will make it worse.
   译文：他们似乎认为修一条新路将会改善交通问题，但事实上，那样做将会使问题更糟。

3. The scientists created nothing less than the first genetic map of the world.
   译文：科学家成就了这一相当于世界上首幅人类基因组分布的图谱。

4. As of today Dr. Carey will be in charge of a long-term study of children who are unusually good at math.
   译文：从今天起，Carey 博士将负责对那些擅长学习数学的孩子进行长期研究。

5. The best way to lose weight is proper diet in combination with regular exercise.
   译文：减轻体重的最好办法是合理的饮食和长期的锻炼。

6. Many women in the city have taken low-paid, so-called part-time work in addition to their child-rearing and community care activities.
   译文：在这个城市中，很多妇女除了抚养孩子以及提供社区服务外，还从事低薪的工作，即所谓的兼职工作。

7. Their research into better parenting and educational techniques sheds new light on the fact that more boys have unusual mathematical abilities than girls.

译文: 他们对于如何更好地抚养孩子与教育孩子所做的技巧方面的研究为男孩的数学天赋总是高于女孩这事实提供了新的解释。

8. It is now known that this illness is not confined to any one group in society.

译文: 人们现在了解到这种疾病并非仅限于社会的某个群体。

Collocation

V.

1. secret 译文: 她笑得有些古怪, 好象她与她信任的为数不多的几个人中的一个在一起分享一个秘密, 而我却被他们蒙在鼓里。

2. experiences 译文: 那些加入的人可以分享经验, 得到有关肺病的最新资料、治疗方法和服务。

3. characteristics 译文: 因此, 尽管他们也具有独特的特征, 但人们还是希望他们具有由那些共同祖先所传承下来的特点。

4. idea 译文: 他们都认为奖不太有可能充分解释这种行为。

5. information 译文: 据说不愿分享共同情报导致了意外, 因为情报没有及时地传送给适当的人。

6. success 译文: 新的管理体系实施后, 投资方同意与管理方共同分享成功。

7. prejudices 译文: 有些人曾指出出于一些美国本土居民对于外国移民都存有偏见, 以及不同的宗教信仰使得20世纪20年代产生了3K党。

8. equality 译文: 帮助落后民话这一目标必须要基于人权面前人人平等的真诚愿望。

Word Building

VI.

1. privacy 译文: 用户网站是很趣的, 但同样也有瓶颈, 因为在付账退出这些网站时你不得不牺牲你的隐私。

2. intimacy 译文: 虽然保持了一定的距离, 但是在他们之间还是存在着亲密的友谊和深深的相互理解。

3. frequency 译文: 近来这个国家遭受空恐怖袭击的频率似乎呈上升趋势。

4. fluency 译文: 该工作的要求之一是要掌握两门或以上的非洲语言。

5. secrecy 译文: 囚犯被关押的情况外人一无所知, 他们与外界完全隔离。

6. urgency 译文: 科学家们认为应该尽快削弱导致种族偏见的传观念。

7. consistency 译文: 第一天有很多事情做, 第二天又无所事事, 这并不好, 我们需要一定的连贯性。

8. dependency 译文: 随着年龄的增长, 能力的丧失就意味着会过多地依赖他人, 正如文章中清楚描述的那样。

VII.

1. politics 译文: 她的观点十分偏激, 在1980年至1990年被禁止参政, 并被软禁了十年。

2. classics 译文: 她在研究古典文化方面很有成就, 能流利地说罗马语与希腊语。

3. electronics 译文: 事实上, 在电子学领域里, 很少不涉及数字技术与计算的

4. economics 译文: 欧洲政府强调货币不仅仅是经济学的概念。法国财政部长多明尼

克·施特劳斯-卡恩说: "从里斯本到赫尔辛基, 从巴黎到维也纳, 欧元是整个欧洲共同体的象征。"

5. psychology 译文: 他对有关人思维的方式及如何影响行为的研究十分感兴趣, 所以上大学时, 他决定主修心理学。

6. methodology 译文: 社会科学不象自然科学, 讨论时往往以结论开始而忽略了研究方法, 社会科学则需要对研究的具体做法进行详尽的讨论。

7. technology 译文: 我们尽力提供最新的技术与优质的环境。

8. biology 译文: 因此, 生物科学对于我们如何理解人类的进化产生了深远的影响。

Structure

VIII. ▶

1. Being healthy is more than a question of not being ill.
   译文: 健康远不是不生病的问题。

2. I was more than a little put out; I was totally shocked.
   译文: 我岂止是有点不知所措, 简直是非常吃惊。

3. This story is more than interesting; it is educational as well.
   译文: 这个故事不仅趣, 还富有教育意义。

4. Hepworth is much more than a filmmaker; he had learnt to find stories that would have genuine popular appeal.
   译文: 赫普沃斯不止是制片人, 而且他还能够发现受观众欢迎的剧本。

5. It was more than a misjudgment: it revealed the extent to which the religious intellectuals' theory of the church was outdated.
   译文: 那不仅仅是一次误判, 它还表明了宗教人士的教会理论已经过时了。

IX. ▶

1. What was needed was nothing less than a new industrial revolution.
   译文: 所需要的就是一次新的工业革命。

2. This is nothing less than a call to arms to restore the vitality of the American dream.
   译文: 这简直就是在呼吁军队重新恢复美国梦的生命力。

3. Their dream was nothing less than a revolutionary project to bring computers and ordinary people together.
   译文: 他们的梦想不亚于是一个计算机和普通人连在一起的革命性的方案。

4. The experience of sightseeing in the wonderful island is nothing less than exciting and I am moved to tears.
   译文: 在这个美丽的岛屿上观光简直是令人太兴奋了, 我激动得落了泪。

5. He was much concerned that she should not be tired, or bored and he wanted to make sure that the holiday would be nothing less than perfect for her.
   译文: 他非常关心她是否会感到疲倦, 或者无聊, 因为他想确保他能度过一个相当完美的假期。

Translation

X. ▶

1. We have received three anonymous letters from Palestine to date, in addition to one

suspicious package.

2. Their dream was nothing less than a more equal society where there is no racial prejudice.

3. He read more than Shakespeare's plays; he liked modern music.

4. His fate in the last election, she said, would serve as a reminder to all politicians that popularity does not last.

5. In effect, only hard work in combination with proper methods will always give you an advantage over others.

6. Technology itself, and its effective use, is not to be confined to the traditional science subjects.

7. Since the truth of this report was discounted, I was not in a position to publish it for you.

8. Many software companies have adapted their general programs to the new operating system.

XI.

1. 它对人类在基因层面上的差异做了迄今为止最广泛的调查。

2. 实际上，那种认为某一种群比另一种群的基因更优越的理论是毫无科学根据的。

3. 为了确保种群的"纯正"，这项研究将对象限定于其目前的生活区域仍与1492年以来相同的那些群体，即在来自欧洲最初的大规模迁移之前。这实际上就是一幅真实的哥伦布驶向美洲时期的世界人口基因分布图。

4. 我们眼中看到的人种差异，例如欧洲人与非洲人的差异，主要是人类从一个大陆向另一个大陆迁移时为适应气候所产生的。

5. 结合对远古人骨的研究，这一图谱证实了非洲是人类的诞生地，因而也是人类迁移的始发地。

6. 这些发现，再加上现代非洲人与非非洲人之间的巨大基因差距，说明了从非洲人种群开始的分支是人类家谱上最早的分支。

7. 除了揭示人种的起源以外，基因信息也是医学界可用的最新原材料。医学界希望能用人类脱氧核糖核酸（DNA）制成特别的蛋白质，这些蛋白质具有某种抗病药物的价值。

8. 保护土著人权益活动家们担心科学家可能会利用土著人谋利：从当地人血样中提取的基因物质可被用于商业目的，却不给DNA提供者以足够的报酬。

Essay Summary

XII.

C B A D A   C D C C B   A D B D A   C A D B B

Text Structure Analysis

XIII.

A statement: (1) the origins of populations

Example 1: (1) that the Khoisan may be a very ancient mix of west Asians and black Africans

Example 2: (1) to be the most direct relatives of the Cro-Magnon people, among the first modern humans in Europe

(2) 65% Asian and 35% African genes

VI. 参考译文

对人种遗传学的研究

尽管不完全是畅销书，《人类基因的发展与地理分布》是一本汇集了50多年来人种遗传学方面的研究成果的好书。它对人类在基因层面上的差异作了迄今为止最为广泛的调查，得出了明确的结论：如果不考虑诸如影响肤色、身高等外部特征的基因，不同的"种族"在外表之下令人吃惊地相似。个体之间的差异大于群体之间的差异。实际上，那种认为某一种群比另一种群的基因更优越的理论是毫无科学根据的。

然而，此书还不仅仅是对目前的种族偏见理论的反驳。这一项目的主要倡导者，斯坦福大学教授路卡·卡瓦里-斯福尔扎与同事一起经过16年的努力，成就了这一相当于世界上首本人类基因分布图谱的书。此书的一大特点是提供了500多幅图，显示相同的遗传基因所处的区域。这很像其他地图上用同样的颜色表示同样海拔高度的地区。通过测定当前人类种群间的亲缘关系，作者们弄清了地球上早期人类迁移的路线。他们的工作结果相当于一份全球家谱。

他们在人类血液中找到了绘制这一家谱所需的信息：不同的蛋白质就是显示一个人的基因构造的标志。作者们用几十年来科学家们收集的数据，汇编成了2,000多个群体中成千上万个个体的数据图。为了确保种群的"纯正"，这项研究将对象限定于其目前的生活区域仍与1492年以来相同的那些群体，即在来自欧洲最初的大规模迁移之前。这实际上就是一幅真实的哥伦布驶向美洲时期的世界人口基因分布图。

收集血样，特别是到偏远地区的古老人种中去收集，并非总是易事。可能的供血者通常不敢合作，或产生宗教上的担心。有一次在非洲乡下，正当卡瓦里-斯福尔扎要从儿童身上采血时，一个愤怒的农人手执斧头出现在他面前。这位科学家回忆道："我记得他说，'如果你从孩子们身上抽血，我就要放你的血。'那人是担心我们可能用这些血来施魔法。"

尽管碰到了困难，科学家们还是有了一些引人注目的发现。其中之一就醒目地印在此书封面上：人类基因变异彩图表明非洲与澳洲分别位于变化范围的两端。因为澳洲土著和非洲黑人之间有一些共同的外表特征，如肤色、体型等，所以普遍认为他们有较近的亲缘关系。但是他们的基因却表明并非如此。在所有人种中，澳洲人与非洲人的关系最远，而与其邻居东南亚人非常接近。我们眼中看到的人种差异，例如欧洲人与非洲人的差异，主要是人类从一个大陆向另一个大陆迁移时为适应气候所产生的。

结合对远古人骨的研究，这一图谱证实了非洲是人类的诞生地，因而也是人类迁移的始发地。这些发现，再加上现代非洲人与非非洲人之间的巨大基因差距，说明了从非洲人种群开始的分支是人类家谱上最早的分支。

这一基因分布图谱对长期以来困绕着科学家的人种起源问题也做出了新的解释。南部非洲的科伊桑人就是一个例子。很多科学家认为科伊桑人是一个独立的非常古老的人种。他们语言中那种独特的短促而清脆的声音使得一些研究者认为科伊桑人是最原始的人类祖先的直系后裔。然而他们的基因说明了不同的结果。基因研究表明科伊桑人可能是古代西亚人与非洲黑人的混血，图谱上显示的遗传轨迹表明这一混血人种的发生地可能就在埃塞俄比亚或中东地区。

人类家谱图上欧洲人分支的非常特殊的成员就是法国和西班牙的巴斯克人。他们有几组少见的基因型，包括一种罕见血型的发生率在巴斯克人中也是最高的。他们的语言起源不明，也无法根据任何通常分类来归类。他们居住的地区紧挨着发现早期欧洲人壁画的几个著名的洞穴的事实使卡瓦里-斯福尔扎得出这样的结论："在欧洲最早的近代人中，巴斯克人极有可能与克罗马努人关系最直接。"人们认为所有的欧洲人都是混合人种，有65%的亚洲人基因,35%的非洲人基因。

除了揭示人种的起源以外，基因信息也是医学界可用的最新原料。医学界希望能用人类脱氧核糖核酸（DNA）制成特别的蛋白质，这些蛋白质具有某种抗病药物的价值。保护土著人权益活动家们担心科学家可能会利用土著人谋利：从当地人血样中提取的基因物质可被用于商业目的，却不给DNA提供者以足够的报酬。

卡瓦里-斯福尔扎强调他的工作不仅有科学意义，而且也有社会意义。他说研究的最终目的是"削弱"造成种族偏见的"传统的种族观念"。他希望这一目的会得到土著民族的接受。长期以来，他们一直在为同样的目的进行抗争。

VII. 写作指导

例证法 Exemplification

本单元练习例证的作文写作方法。例证法（exemplification）也是一种常见的段落扩展方法，即用事例表达文章和段落主题，向读者展开，并使读者具体感受到主题中尚未展开的内容和细节。例证法强调用具体的个例（examples）来证明或支持文章的观点或段落的主题句（statement），要注意到例证必需生动、可信。

常用的表示举例的词组有：for example, for instance, such as,...and so on/forth.

常用的表示举例的句型用：Here is a good case in point.

Let's take...as an example.

...is a case in point.

A case in point is that...

范文：

Sticking to high moral standards is easier said than done. Some time ago, a young British car manager had just been finishing the courses on business ethics. He was sent to sell hundreds of cars to the Minister of Transportation of an African country. The negotiation had been going on for months without any real results. He was at his wits end. Finally, he hit upon the answer. One day he just bought a popular novel without even glancing at the book title, slipped a check of ￡20,000 within its pages, and then presented it to the minister. This man examined its contents, but he pretended not seeing anything at all. Then he said with a smile: "Young man, I hear London is in its best in May?" The sales manager, who was quick-witted, replied: "My company in London will be most honored to welcome your visit!" A short time later, the deal was approved, in London!

Section B

I. 阅读技巧

本单元复习和练习浏览（scanning）这一快速阅读技巧。在《新视野大学英语读写教程》第一册的第八单元和第三册的第一单元我们都做过详细讲解。广义上来说，快速浏览就是快速地扫描文章，其目的在于找到某一待搜索信息在文章中的位置，并且理解这一信息，不需要全文或全段阅读。这种阅读的特点在于读者可以跳过许多与该特定信息不相关的许多内容，一方面可以减收不必要的阅读量，另一方面还可以回避某些生词对理解的干扰，从而实现快速准确理解信息的目的。

Ⅱ. 词汇与短语详解

1.prodigy

[词义] *n.* ① 奇迹，奇事；② 奇才

[搭配] child prodigy 神童 (= infant prodigy)

[例句] This apple is a prodigy, it's 5 times the usual size.

这个苹果真是奇物，有一般苹果的5倍大。

He is a prodigy who had learned several foreign languages when he was five.

他是个五岁时就学会了几门外语的天才。

2.supervise

[词义] *vt.* 监督，管理，指导

[例句] I supervised the workers loading the lorry. 我监督工人把货物装上卡车。

[派生] supervision *n.* 监督，管理

[联想] supervisor *n.* 监督人，管理者;（研究生）导师

3.fascinate

[词义] *vt.* 强烈地吸引，迷住

[搭配] be fascinated with sth. 对……着迷的

[例句] Anything to do with old myths and legends fascinates me.

任何与上古神话传说有关的东西都会使我着迷。

[派生] fascination *n.* 魔力，入迷; fascinating *adj.* 迷人的

[辨析] fascinate, charm, enchant

fascinate 指使人非常感兴趣，以致于要继续下去，如：The children were fascinated by all the toys in the shop windows. 那些孩子被商店橱窗里所有的玩具迷住了。

charm 指使人喜悦的迷醉，如：Her beautiful voice charms everyone. 她优美的声音迷醉了每个人。

enchant 通常为由于喜悦而着迷，如：She was enchanted by the flowers you sent her. 她着迷于你送给她的花。

4.fatigue

[词义] *n.* 疲劳，劳累; *vt.* (使) 疲劳

[搭配] pale with fatigue 疲惫的苍白

[例句] He was pale with fatigue after his sleepless night.

经过不眠的一夜，他疲劳的脸色苍白。

The ill child fatigued his parents very much. 那个生病的孩子把父母累坏了。

[派生] fatigueless *adj.* 不会疲劳的，不知疲劳的

[辨析] fatigue, exhausted, tired

fatigue表示体力和心力非常疲乏，如：I was fatigued with sitting up all night. 我坐了一夜，感到很疲倦。

exhausted 表示体力完全或几乎完全耗光，如：Her strength was exhausted, and she fell back on the pillow. 她筋疲力尽，一头倒在枕头上。

tired 一般用语，疲劳。

5.identify

[词义] *vt.* ①认出，鉴定；②把……等同于

vi. 与（某人）在感情上认同，与（某人）有同感(with)

[搭配] identify with sb. 同情、理解某人

[例句] Can you identify your umbrella among this lot?

你能在这些伞中认出你自己那一把吗？

He identifies beauty with goodness. 他认为美与善是一致的。

I didn't enjoy the movie because I couldn't identify with any of the characters 我不喜欢那部电影，因为我对里面的任何人物都不能认同。

[派生] identification n. 认同，辨认，鉴定

[联想] identity n. 同一性，身份，特征

6.steer

[词义] vt. ① 驾驶，为……操舵；② 引导

vi. 驾驶

[搭配] steer clear of 绕开，避开

[例句] He steered the car skillfully through the narrow streets.

他熟练地驾驶着汽车穿过狭窄的街道。

He steered me to a table and sat me down in a chair.

他把我领到一张桌子前，让我在椅子上坐下。

You steer and I'll pash. 你来掌握方向，我来推。

[辨析] steer, guide

steer 常表示引导，暗示，指导着某人、某物度过难关，如：Soon the country will be steered to peace and prosperity. 这个国家很快会被带入和平与繁荣之境。

guide 常指为别人带路、指导暗示避免走弯路或遇到危险，如：guide a ship through a channel 引领轮船通过海峡。

7. assess

[词义] vt. 对……进行估价

[例句] He's so lazy that it's difficult to assess his ability.

他懒惰得难以对他的能力做出评估。

[派生] assessment n. 估价，被估定的金额

[辨析] assesses, estimate, evaluate

assess原义是对某商品进行估价以决定税，如：My crop is assessed at fifty pounds a year. 我的收成估计每年50磅。

estimate 根据个人知识、经验或认识做出的判断，如：You estimate his worth too highly. 你高估了他。

evaluates 强调评价人或物的价值，如：She evaluate people by their clothes. 她根据衣着来评价一个人。

8.alert

[词义] adj. 警觉的，留神的；vt. 向……报警

n. ① 警戒（状态）；② 警报

[搭配] on the alert 警戒，随时准备着，密切注意着; alert sb. to sth. 警告某人当心某事危险

[例句] The government is alert and will take necessary steps to maintain security and stability. 政府时刻警惕着，并将采取必要措施以确保安全和稳定。

197

The doctor alerted me to the dangers of smoking.
医生警告我注意吸烟的危险。
Bird watchers on the alert for a rare species. 看守人密切注意稀有鸟类。
Sirens sounded the alert for an air raid. 空袭警报的警笛响起。

[派生] alertly *adv.* 提高警觉地，留意地

9. peer

[词义] *n.* 同龄人，同等地位的人；*vi.* 费力地看

[搭配] peer into/through 凝视，盯着看

[例句] He doesn't spend enough time with his peers. 他不大与同龄人交往。
The mew postman peered through the mist, trying to find the right house.
新来得邮递员在雾中仔细张望，设法寻找到他要找的那一家。

[派生] peerless *adj.* 出类拔萃的，无可匹敌的

[辨析] peer, glare, peek, gaze
peer 指费力地细看，如: He was peering down the well. 他费力地向井里看。
glare 指恐吓、凶狠或愤怒的眼光。
peek 指偷看、通过孔隙窥视。
gaze 指目不转睛地看。

10. spring up 涌现，发生，迅速长出

[例句] His success doesn't spring up out of nowhere. As he self-studied College English in high school, he has had a head start over his peers. 他的成功不是凭空而来的。他在中学就自学了大学英语，所以比其他同学领先了一步。

11. out of nowhere 不知打哪儿来，突然冒出来

[例句] The thought swam into her mind out of nowhere and she realized it was a great relief to have this as an excuse. 这想法不知从何处涌入她的脑海，她意识到有了这种理由心里觉得大大地宽慰了。

12. look into 调查，仔细检查

[例句] The union representative is looking into the case to see if the company is responsible, but at the moment it rather looks as if it was entirely Len's fault. 工会代表正在调查这起案子，察看公司是否负有责任，但是目前看上去好像完全是莱恩的过错。

13. go out of one's way 特别费心（做某事），千方百计

[例句] He could have complained to the top about my basic lack of professionalism but instead he went out of his way to try and help me. 他原本可以向上层领导埋怨我缺乏基本的职业技艺，可相反，他千方百计地试图帮助我。

14. make a note of 把（某事）记录下来

[例句] While reading, make a note of any page of special importance.
阅读时，任何有特别重要意义的那一页都要记下。

15. pick up 学到，获得

[例句] As a mail boy, he had picked up the habit of addressing people by their Christian names, whoever they were.
作为一个邮递员，他养成了用教名称呼任何人的习惯，不管他们是谁。

16. have a head start 有先起步的优势，领先

[例句] If you are lucky enough to have your own land, you have a head start over those of us who have to rent facilities. 如果你有幸拥有自己的土地，比我们中那些不得不租用设施的人一开始就有利了。

17. in question 谈论中的，考虑之中的

[例句] If the restaurant in question adds a service charge, then there would be fewer customers. 要是那家谈论中的餐馆增收服务费，那么顾客就会比较少了。

18. pass on 把……传给……

[例句] Genetics deals with how genes are passed on from parents to their offspring and a great deal is known about the mechanisms governing this process.
遗传学涉及的是基因是如何从父母亲遗传给其后代的，人们对控制这一过程的机理已经了解了许多。

19. step by step 一步步，逐渐地

[例句] Step by step, they are approaching the crux of the problem.
一步步地，他们正接近问题的关键。

20. have an advantage over 比……处于有利地位，比……有优势

[例句] His recent research finds that older learners have an advantage over the very young in learning rule-governed aspects of the language. 他最近的研究发现在学习语言的有规则的方面，年龄较大的学习者比年龄非常小的有优势。

21. in a (good) position to do 能够（做某事），有条件（做某事）

[例句] As a minister, judge and professor, I feel I am in a good position to speak about the history of marriage, its importance in society, and the duties of the married couple to each other and the wider community.
作为一名牧师、法官和教授，我感到我能够来谈论婚姻的历史、婚姻在社会中的重要性，以及已婚夫妇对双方和社区的责任。

22. far from 远远不，一点也不

[例句] Far from damaging the environment, the expanded road program will improve the quality of life of thousands of people. 扩展道路计划非但不会对环境造成破坏，反而将改善成千上万人的生活质量。

Ⅲ. 难句解析

1. It is a popular myth that great geniuses—the Einsteins, Picassos and Mozarts of this world—spring up out of nowhere as if touched by the finger of God. (Para.1)

[释义] Most people mistakenly believe that great geniuses such as Einstein, Picasso and Mozart appear suddenly and unexpectedly and they seem as if they were created by God.

[分析] 本句的核心结构是 "It is a popular myth that..."。It 为形式主语，真正的主语为后面的that 从句为主语从句。在主语从句中，as if 引导了使用虚拟语气的省略方式状语从句，省略了 "they were"。

2. There is plenty of evidence that, too often, pressure from parents results in children suffering fatigue rather than becoming geniuses. (Para.4)

[释义] Much evidence points to the fact that, quite often, parental pressure leads not so much to a child's intelligence as to his tiredness.

[分析] 本句的核心结构为 "There is plenty of evidence..."。其中that从句为 "evidence" 的

同位语从句。

3. **Supportive parents were those who would go out of their way to help their children follow their favorite interests and praised whatever level of achievement resulted. (Para.5)**

[释义] Supportive parents were those who would make a special effort to help their children do whatever they find great interest in and praise even very small progress ever made.

[分析] 本句的核心结构为 "supportive parents were...and praised..."。本句中的三个their 指代不同的内容，"their way" 与 "their children" 指代Parents'，而 "their favorite interests" 中的their指代的是children's。

4. **...when these made a sound, they had to make a note of what they were doing and assess how happy and alert they felt. (Para.6)**

[释义] **make/take a note of** 记录，记下

e.g. Please make a note of my new address.

请记下我的新地址。

[分析] 本句为带有when引导的时间状语从句的主从句结构。在主句中的核心结构为 "they had to make...and assess..."。本句的难点在于区分两个易混淆的词组 make/take a note of 意思是记录，记下，相当于 " record (sth. that one wishes to remember)"；而 "take note of" 意思是注意到，留意，相当于 "pay attention to"。

5. **The children who fared best were those whose parents were both supportive and stimulating. (Para.7)**

[释义] **fare** *vi.* 进行，进展，相当于 "to get along"

e.g. How are you faring with your project?

你怎样进行你的计划？

[分析] 本句的核心结构为 "The children...were those..."。定语从句 "who fared best" 作主语children的定语。定语从句 "whose parents...stimulating" 作表语those 的定语。

6. **One reason why prodigies such as Picasso and Einstein had a head start in life was that they had parents who demonstrated how to think about subjects like art or physics at a very early age. (Para.9)**

[释义] One reason why exceptionally gifted people such as Picasso and Einstein had an advantage over others was that they had parents who show them how to think about subjects like art or physics since they were very young.

[分析] 本句的核心结构为 "one reason...was that..."。句中共包含了三个从句：why引导的定语从句 "why...others"，that 引导的表语从句 "that they had parents" 以及who 引导的定语从句 "who...age"。

7. **So what is the outlook for parents who do everything right, those who manage to be both supportive and stimulating, who are good at demonstrating thinking skills to their children and successful at cultivating a self-motivated approach to learning? (Para.13)**

[分析] 本句的核心结构为 "what is the outlook for parents...?"。句中共使用了三个定语从句："who do everything right" 修饰先行词parents；"who...stimulating" 和 "who are...learning" 这两个并列的定语从句修饰先行词those。在本句中 "those" 作 "parents" 的同位语。

8. **The most significant implication would seem to be that while most people are in a good position to fulfill their biological potential—barring serous illnesses or a poor diet during childhood—it is far from certain that they**

will grow up in an environment where that capacity will be developed. (Para.14)

[释义] **barring** *prep.* 除……之外，相当于 "except"

e.g. Barring strong headwinds, the plane will arrive on schedule.

如果不是猛烈的顶头风，飞机会准点到达的。

[分析] 本句的核心结构为 "The most significant implication would seem to be that...". "while...developed" 为表语从句，引导词为that。在表语从句当中，"that they will grow up in an environment...developed." 为主语从句，指代形式主语it。

IV. 重点语法讲解

"not only/just...but also" 结构

在正式写作中 "not only...but also" 结构应这样用：每一个成分后都跟一个相同形式的结构，即连接两个并列的句子成分。例如，应把She not only bought a new car but a new lawnmower 写成 She bought not only a new car but a new lawnmower；在第二个句子里，not only 和 but also 后都跟名词短语。

请注意：1）该结构中的only可以用just带替；2）当第二部分只是强调第一部分时，在 not only 结构里 also 通常省略。

She is not only smart but brilliant. (连接两个并列的表语)

她不仅聪明过人而且才华横溢。

He not only <u>wanted</u> the diamond but <u>wanted</u> it desperately.(连接连个并列谓语动词)

他不仅想要钻石，而且非常想要。

It is not just <u>the time</u> spent that counts, but also <u>the way</u> in which a parent talks. (Para.11)

重要的不仅仅是花了多少时间，而且还有与孩子交流的方式。

V. 课文赏析

1. 文体特点

本文是一篇说明文，通过例子和实验，说明了天才与遗传有关，但正确和良好的家庭教育也很重要。文章先通过高斯等几个杰出人物说明了他们的成功和童年时期良好的教育有关。然后通过实验对比了三种不同教育方式的父母对孩子的影响。最后强调了良好的家庭教养和教育技巧的重要性。

2. 结构分析

Part Ⅰ (Para.1-3) Topic introduction by an example of gauss to show that good parenting plays an important role.

Part Ⅱ (Para.4-8) It mainly discusses which type of parental stimulation is the most effective, supportive parents, stimulating parents or parents with both.

Part Ⅲ (Para.9-12) It discusses that another crucial factor is the need for parents to have proper conversations with children.

Part Ⅳ (Para.13-15) It stresses that though genuine biological differences exist, better parenting is very important.

VI. 课后练习答案及解析

Reading Skills

XV.

1. The author holds a doubtful attitude towards to popular myth.

2. Two kinds of parent style—the supportive and the stimulating.

3. Four groups of children: one with supportive parents, one with stimulating parents, one

whose parents combined both qualities and a final group who offered neither.

4. Eleven seconds a day in Holland an less than a minute a day in the United States.

5. The environmental factors such as better parenting and educational techniques.

Comprehension of the Text

▷▷ XVI. ▶

1. B (Please refer to Para1, 2, 3.)

2. C (to the last sentence of Para.3.)

3. A (A is the right choice according to the first sentence of Para.8.)

4. B (B is the right choice according to the last but one sentence of Para.7.)

5. B (B is the correct choice as parents can help children cultivate an open and creative thinking style.)

6. C (C is the correct answer according to Para.12, 13.)

7. B (Please refer to Para.13.)

8. C (Please refer to Para.14Because there are biological differences between individuals.)

Vocabulary

▷▷ XVII. ▶

1. supervised 译文: 他们指导并帮助守林人寻找、抓捕以及盘问毁坏森林的人。

2. fatigue 译文: 调查表明，父母激励孩子却又不给予孩子支持很可能会使孩子感到疲劳厌倦。

3. guarantee 译文: 进一步的安排和良好的沟通是保证艾滋病患者做出最好的选择及继续享受高质量生活的两大基石。

4. explore 译文: 应该鼓励孩子探索各种想法，这样能培养他们开放、有创见的思维方式。

5. sophisticated 译文: 科学家们普遍认为，需要一种更复杂的方法来搞清一个难题，即伟大的天才是天生的还是后天培养的。

6. identified 译文: 罗伯特·普罗明博士的研究表明，基因被认为是决定智力的重要因素，但这一结论还没有得到进一步的证实。

7. steer 译文: 这位高层执行官在工作上总是向前看，而不向后看，它可以把公司引导到盈利、节约的轨道上。

8. beneficial 译文: 我认为我们早就认识到了良好人际关系的重要性，所以现在我们制定的政策对生意双方都有益。

▷▷ XVIII. ▶

1. up 译文: 政府鼓励在农村建立拥有轻工业的新城镇。

2. out 译文: 她报了警，告诉警察她的恐惧，然后他们就仔细检查了她的花园，并向她保证他们会提高警惕。

3. up 译文: 水利管理部门将农业部的大笔资金投入到降低河流水们的工程设计计划中。

4. in 译文: 这些正在被讨论的土地大部分从自然条件上看都不适合种水稻。

5. over 译文: 电视剧的导演比作者更有优势，因为拍电影比写小说更加灵活。

6. up 译文: 认你的孩子看到你伤心的样子，这样在他们成长的过程中，就有形成这样的认识: 生活中遇到一些不愉快的事情是很平常的。

7. in 译文: 至少有17种"癌症基因"已经得到了证实，而且在每种情况下，它们似乎相同的或者是与在健康细胞中发现的一般基因很相似。

8. into 译文: 她觉得同样重要的是检察员应该调查孩子与老师之间的关系。

VII. 参考译文

天才与良好的家庭教养

有一种流行的说法，世界上的伟大天才——爱因斯坦们、毕加索们、莫扎特们，不知从什么地方突然冒了出来，似乎都是造物主的神功使然。卡尔·弗里德里克·高斯就是一个典型，据说他出身在一个体力劳动者家庭，后来却成了现代数学之父。

一位研究早期学习的教授驳斥了这一 说法，称他研究了高斯的童年，发现在他两岁时，母亲就教给他数字。他的父亲是个体力工种的监工，本人不是工人，并常和高斯玩计算游戏。而且高斯还有个受过教育的叔叔，他在高斯很小的时候就教他复杂的数学。

其他天才们的情况也同样。爱因斯坦的父亲是个电气工程师，他表现出的物理知识使儿子很着迷。毕加索的父亲是个美术教师，他要八岁的小帕布罗画一碗又一碗的水果。莫扎特的父亲是个受雇于贵族宫廷的音乐家，他在儿子还不会走路时就教他唱歌、弹奏乐器。"在每一个例子里，仔细研究一下天才的成长背景，都可以发现父母或教师给予早期激励这样一种模式，"这位教授说。

但是父母应该给予怎样一种激励呢？大量证据表明，家长的压力常会导致孩子疲劳厌倦而不是成为天才。有一项研究分出了两种风格的家长——支持型的和激励型的。

支持型的家长会尽全力帮助孩子发展兴趣爱好，赞扬其获得的成就，不管那有多么微小。一般来说，这样的家长创造出一个有规矩的、令人愉快的家庭环境。激励型的家长会更主动地参与到孩子们的活动中去，在某些领域里带领他们前行，推动他们努力，通常起着导师的作用。

这一研究跟踪研究了四组儿童：一组儿童的家长是支持型的，一组是激励型的，一组是支持激励相结合的，最后一组儿童的家长既不支持也不激励。孩子们拿到一些电子装置。当发出声响时，他们就要记下当时孩子们正在干什么，并评估孩子们从中所感受到的快乐和反应的敏捷程度。

结果并不太意外。支持型父母的孩子所感到的快乐程度高于平均水平，但学习或做事时却不是那么高度集中精力。表现最好的孩子是那些其父母为既支持又激励型的。这些孩子显示了相当不错的快乐感，在学习过程中反应也很敏捷。

激励型却缺乏支持的父母，他们的孩子很可能会疲劳厌倦。这些孩子确实能长时间努力，但他们在学习过程中的敏捷程度和快乐感大大低于生活在能兼顾激励和支持的家庭环境中的孩子。

另一关键因素是父母应该与孩子进行适当的交谈。通过与成年人的交流，孩子学会的不仅是语言技巧，而且还有成年人的习惯与思维方式。像毕加索、爱因斯坦这样的神童之所以能在生活中率先起跑的一个原因就是他们的父母在他们很小的时候就教给他们如何思考如艺术或物理这样的科目。

在荷兰进行的调查表明，父亲们一般每天用于与孩子交谈的时间只有11秒钟。新近在美国作的研究显示了稍好的结果，但这些父亲每天与孩子的交谈时间仍不到一分钟。

重要的不仅仅是花了多少时间，而且还有与孩子交谈的方式。对孩子的问题只做出简单的回应，或是只给出乏味的回答，这样的父母传给孩子们的是一种消极的、偏狭的思维方式。从另一方面来说，乐意与孩子作一步一步深入的论证，鼓励子女探索各种想法，这样的父母会培养出开放的、有创见的思维方式。

一名研究人员试图通过实验论证这一观点。在他的研究里，几组家长学着如何与自己的幼小子女作有益的交谈。他说这些孩子在语言能力、智力，甚至领导才能上都比同龄孩子要强。尽管这一研究尚未结束，这些孩子已显出具备了长期的优势。

那么，对那些模范家长，那些做到了对孩子既支持又激励，善于教给孩子思考的方法，成功地培养孩子学习上的主动性的家长，前景如何呢？能否确保他们的孩子成为天才？

人们普遍认为，个体之间存在着生理差异，要成为天才必须幸运地既拥有天才的基因，又拥有能造就天才的父母。最重要的启示似乎是：尽管大多数人都有条件很好地发挥他们的生理潜能——即除非童年时得了严重疾病，或饮食太差，他们肯定能充分发展自己的基因遗传能力——但是，他们是否能生长在一个能开发其能力的环境中则远非一个确定因素。

因此，虽然了解天才人物的生物特征非常令人感兴趣，但对良好的家庭教养和教育技巧的研究才真正具有长远的意义。

Section C

I. 语言点讲解

1. At present, it is believed that genes account for at least half of what researchers call "g"—the general thinking ability that IQ tests are supposed to measure-while environmental influences account for the other half. (Para.5)

[释义] **at present** 现在，马上，相当于 "at the present time, right now"

e.g. You should Ceave at present. 你应该现在就离开。

[分析] 本句的核心结构为 "it is believed that..."。"that genes...the other half." 为主语从句，指代形式主语it的具体内容。在主语从句中，"what...'g'"为名词性从句作介词of 的宾语。连词 "while"相当于 "whereas"，"but"，起到与前面比较，转折的作用。

2. But so far the only evidence for a genetic component has been through statistics, the relationship being inferred mathematically from comparisons of twins and other such studies of close relatives. (Para.6)

[分析] 本句的核心结构为 "the only evidence...has been through statistics"。"the relationship"为同位语，补充说明statistics。现在分词短语 "being inferred...relatives"为定语，修饰relationship。

3. This identification of even one gene does, however, have immense implications for the genetics/environment debate. (Para.6)

[分析] 该句为强调句型中强调谓语动词的一种形式，即助动词+动词原形的结构。在本句中具体表现为 "does + have"。使用这种形式的强调句型，时态和数的变化是通过助动词的变化体现的，即do/does/did。对句子的其他成分强调则用 "It is/was...that/who..."的句型结构。

II. 课文赏析

1. 文体特点

本文是一篇议论文，论述了创造天才的遗传和环境因素。文章通过加德纳博士对儿子的培养方式引入话题——天才是后天培养还是先天形成的，选材贴近生活，具有说服力；主体部分通过两个实验结果，论证了天才和遗传有很大关系，最后作者也肯定了环境因素在创造天才时所起的作用。

2. 结构分析

Part I (Para.1-3) It puts forward the main point that is about the debate over the issue of which is more important ,environment of genetics.

Part II (Para.4-11) It reveals Plominaand Benbow's finding that seem to give support to the argument that outstanding mental abilities are largely the result of genetics.

Part Ⅲ (Para.12) The author adds that the role that environmental factors is also very important in creating genius.

Ⅲ. 课后练习答案及解析

Reading skills

XIX.

1. Dr. Howard Gardner of Harvard University believes that geniuses are largely made.
2. Dr. Sandra Scarr of Virginia University believes geniuses are largely born.
3. Genes account for at least half of one's thinking ability.
4. The majority of talented children good at math are boys.
5. The radio between talented boys and girls in the U. S. is thirteen to one according to Professor Camilla Benbow's finds.

Comprehension of the Text

XX.

F T F F F   T T F

Ⅳ. 参考译文

创造天才的遗传和环境因素

哈佛大学的霍华德·加德纳博士认为天才主要是后天造成的。他的家里不看电视，因为他担心电视会破坏家人的思考能力。他每天都挤出时间来听7岁的儿子弹钢琴，既使在他外出开会时，也要通过电话听几分钟。

弗吉尼亚大学的桑德拉·斯卡博士，儿童发展研究会主席，认为天才主要是天生的。她说该带孩子去看球赛还是参观博物馆，对此家长不必过多担心。才华终将显示出来。

哪个更重要，环境还是遗传？对这个问题似乎专家们一向都有分歧。然而，这一情况可能会有所改变。在今年早些时候组织的一次会议上，论战双方的知名人物聚于伦敦，一些未曾公开发表的令人惊讶的结果被公之于众——双方的趋同已初见端倪。

研究个体生理差异的科学家带来了最令人兴奋的结果。宾夕法尼亚州立大学的罗伯特·普罗明博士已经找到了影响智力的一种基因的踪迹，他希望能在几个月内公布结果。这样一种基因已经被发现，但结论还有待证实。

人们目前认为，对于研究人员称为"g"的能力——即智力测验所要衡量的综合思维能力——基因至少起了一半的作用，而环境影响则起到了另一半作用。但迄今为止，遗传基因所占比重的仅有的证据只是一些统计数据，即，从对双胞胎的比较，以及对其他血缘接近者的研究中得出的数学统计关系。普罗明的方法利用新的基因图谱技术，有望对基因所起的作用提供直接证据。

普罗明强调，发现第一个基因并不意味着解开了智力之迷。一个基因仅仅为构成大脑的众多分子和细胞蛋白中的一个指定遗传密码。这就是说，智力涉及的基因没有几千也有几百个。不过，哪怕辩出一个基因对于遗传与环境之争也是意义重大的。

另一进展，一台计算机控制的脑部扫描仪，使得寻找思维能力的生理因素的研究人员有了第二个发现。爱荷华州立大学的卡米拉·班博教授领导着一项对具有数学特长的儿童的长期研究。多年来，她对为何她的研究中有那么多的男孩感到困惑——高级组中男孩女孩之比为13比1。在即将发表的论文中，班博表明，天资好的男孩的脑子处理物体方位信息的过程好像与一般的男孩非常不同，甚至与天资好的女孩也不同。

研究中，给孩子们看一道简单的视觉难题，同时对其脑部进行扫描。智力一般的男孩与天资好的女孩在解题时脑子的两半球都活跃。但是天资好的男孩却表现出极大的不同。他们的左半脑——与语言能力相关的那一半——的活动急剧下降，而右半脑，擅长思考物体方位的那一半，却做出强烈的反应。看来，具有数学天赋的男孩的大脑在生理方面的活动相当独特。

班博说，天资好的女孩居然没有这种反应模式，这使她很吃惊。惟一的解释就是：男性的大脑在发育过程中有分工更明确的趋势，大脑的两半球各有不同的功能。这种分工到了极致，就产生了不寻常的数学能力。

因为女性不具备这种趋势（人脑的这种分工已知是男性激素影响的结果），数学好的女孩是因为她们的整体智力发育很好。又因为这样全面的能力并不常见，这就解释了为何有数学天赋的女孩较为少见。

不过，班博又迅速补充说，文化传统上人们对孩子的期望可能更扩大了这一差别。在中国，人们往往更鼓励女孩学数学，那儿有天赋的男孩与女孩的数量之比为4比1，而不像美国是13比1。

普罗明和班博的研究结果似乎都支持了出众的智力主要是遗传的结果这一论断。但是那次会议也提出了同样充分的证据支持环境因素在创造天才上的作用。发言者们多次提到的一个主题就是不同寻常的孩子身后一定有不同寻常的家长。

五、知识链接

Pablo Picasso

Spanish artist, Pablo Picasso, was born in Malaga, Spain on October 25, 1881. By the age of 15 he was already technically skilled in drawing and painting. Picasso's highly original style continuously evolved throughout his long career, expanding the definition of what art could be. In addition to painting, Picasso excelled in sculpture, etching, stage design, and ceramics, and became one of the most the most prolific and influential artists of the 1900s. Paintings from Picasso's Blue Period (1901—1904) depict forlorn people painted in shades of blue, evoking feelings of sadness and alienation.

After his move to Paris in 1904, Picasso's Rose Period paintings took on a warmer and more optimistic mood. In 1907 he and French painter George Braque pioneered cubism and he introduced the technique of collage. By 1912 Picasso was incorporating newspaper print, postage stamps and other materials into his paintings. This style is called collage. By the late 1920s he turned toward a flat, cubist-related style.

During the 1930s his paintings became militant and political. *Guernica* (1937), a masterpiece from this period depicts the terror of the bombing of the town of Guernica during the Spanish civil war. Following World War II, Picasso's work became less political and more gentle. He spent the remaining years of his life in an exploration of various historical styles of art, making several reproductions of the work of earlier artists.

Picasso died on April 8, 1973 at his home France. Among Picasso's masterpieces are *Les Demoiselles d'Avignon* (1907) and *Guernica* (1937).

帕布罗·毕加索

西班牙画家帕布罗·毕加索1881年10月25日出生于西班牙小城马拉加。十五岁时他已经在素描和油画方面技艺娴熟。毕加索高度独创性的风格贯穿于他整个艺术生涯，丰富了艺术的理念。除了绘画，他还擅长雕刻、蚀刻、舞台设计、陶艺等其它艺术形式，成为20世纪最多产和最有影响力的画家之一。毕加索"蓝色时期"（1901-1904）的作品以兰色调刻画了被遗弃的人，表达一种悲伤和孤独。

1904年他迁居巴黎后，他的"玫瑰时期"作品表达一种温暖乐观的情绪。1907年，他与乔治·布拉克开创了立体主义画派 (1906-1925年)，并引入了拼贴艺术。1912年他的作品中开始出现报纸插图、邮票等现实的物品。这种风格就是拼贴艺术。到20世纪20年代末，他的绘画转为平面与立体相结合的风格。

他二十世纪30年代的作品展现战争和政治主题。代表作之一《格尔尼卡》(1937年) 刻画了西班牙内战中格尔尼卡小城受到炮弹轰炸的恐怖。而二战后的作品政治意味淡化了，较为温和。晚年他致力于对各种历史艺术形式的研究，复制一些早期艺术家的作品。

1973年4月8日，毕加索在法国的家中与世长辞。在他杰作中，最具代表性的还当数1907年的《阿维尼翁的小姐》和1937年的《格尔尼卡》。

六、自测题

Directions: In the following passage there are altogether 10 mistakes, one in each numbered line. You may have to change word, add a word or delete a word. If you change a word, cross it out and write correct word in the corresponding blank. If you add a word, put an insertion mark (∧) in the right place and write the missing word in the blank. If you delete a word, cross it out and put a slash (/) in the blank.

Few football grounds boast a more prestigious address than the Bernabeu, lies as it does on the Castellana, the three lining highway that runs through the heart of Madrid.

1. _____
2. _____

As Real date back to 1902, when the Sociedad Madrid Football Club was formed, it was not until 1920 when the club was granted permission to use the Real (royal) prefix. Work began on the current stadium in October 1944. The land had been purchased on three million pesetas; construction costs totalled a further 38 million, a staggered sum for the time. The cost of the new stadium led to claims, never proving, that Real had received financial aid from General Franco's government. Under Bernabeu's patronage, Real Madrid became the greatest club side ever, won the European Champions Cup a record five times in a row between 1956 and 1960, a remarkable feat that is unlikely to be challenged.

3. _____
4. _____
5. _____
6. _____
7. _____
8. _____

Madrid lies, quite literally, at the heart of Spain. This is no small coincidence that the capital's leading football club is seen like a symbol of all things Spanish, just as FC Barcelona is a beacon for the independent Catalan spirit.

9. _____
10. _____

答案与解析

1. 将lies改为lying。没有别的体育场位置能与伯纳贝乌体育场位置相媲美了，它位于卡斯特拉纳，位于穿越马德里市中心这条高速公路的三叉路口。本题辨析主句与分词状语关系的误用。lies as it does on the Castellana，虽然主语应该是Bernabeu，但由于前面Few football grounds boast a more prestigious address than the Bernabeu是比较级的句子，而且比较对象很明确：是Few football grounds 与the Bernabeu，而lies的误用，导致了句子结构的混乱。鉴于lies as it does...是对the Bernabeu的补充说明，故将lies改为lying，使之与后面的句子变成状语，就解决了问题。

2. 将three-lining改为three-lined。本题辨析分词作定语时的误用。three-lining与其修饰词highway的逻辑关系是被动的。而现在分词往往是与其修饰词的关系是主动的。因此，将three-lining改为three-lined。

3. 将As改为Though。尽管皇家马德里队的历史可追溯到1902年索西达德马里足球俱乐部队成立之时，但是直到1920年，俱乐部才被允许在其名字之前冠以"皇家"二字。本题辨析连接词的误用。Real date back to 1920与it was not until 1920 that the club was granted permission to use the Realprefix之间的逻辑关系应是转折关系，而as的误用导致了关系的混乱。改为表示转折的Though/Although。

4. 将when改为that。本题辨析连接词的误用。强调句与定语从句的区别主要有两点：引导词与引导词前后的句子的结构。强调句的连词除了强调人可以是who 以外，都用that。另外一点，强调句前半部分是"It is..."，句意不完整，that后面的部分也不完整，只有将It is...that中间的成分移到后面才完整。本句是强调句，而不是定语从句，故when属误用，须将when改为that。

5. 将on改为for。购买体育场地皮花去300万比赛塔，建造费用总共达3800万比赛塔。本题辨析介词的误用。介词的作用在英语中的作用是不容忽视的，每一个介词都有其独特的用途。on除了表示时间，空间位置外，还可以表示"在……方面"，不表示花费多少钱。故句中on属误用，将之改为表示数目多少的介词"for"。

6. 将staggered改为staggering。在当时，这是一笔令人惊愕的数目。本题辨析同源的形容词的误用。以"ed"结尾的形容词主语一般修饰人，表示"感到……的"，以"ing"结尾的形容词一般修饰非生命的"物"，表示"令人……的"，句中sum是staggered逻辑主语，故staggered属误用，将之改为staggering。

7. 将proving改为proven。新建体育场的巨大耗资引起了许多传言，还说皇家马德里队曾接受过佛朗哥政府的资助，但从未得到证实。本题辨析作状语时，分词的误用。never proving是主句The cost of the new stadium led to claims的分词状语，proving的逻辑主语是that Real had received financial aid from General Franco's government，在关系上与proven属被动，因此，proving属误用，改为proven。

8. 将won改为winning。在伯纳贝乌的资助下，皇家马德里最终成为最优秀的一支俱乐部足球队，在1956年至1960年期间，这支球队五连冠夺得欧洲足球冠军杯。本题辨析分词在作状语时的误用。由won开始的状语短语，逻辑主语是Real Madrid，主语和won的逻辑关系是主动的。won是误用，因此改为winning。

9. 将This改为It。这支首都著名足球俱乐部队被视为西班牙民族精神的象征，就像巴塞罗那足球俱乐部队是独立的加泰罗尼亚精神的标志一样，这绝不是巧合。本题辨析作形式主语时代词的误用。本句是长句子，真正的主语是that后面的部分。为了保持句子的平衡，将较长的主语放在后面，而将 it放在句首，作形式主语，是英语惯用的手段。而本句用this作形式主语是不合适的，故改为it。

10. 将like改为as。本题辨析将介语用作连词的误用。在作"像……"这一意思时，like虽与as词意看似相似，但用法区别很大。like是介词，连接名词或代词，as是连语，连结句子，而FG Barcelona is a beacon for the independent Catalan spirit是个句子，故like属误用，应改为as。

Unit 8

1 学习重点和难点

词汇和短语、语法项目、写作技巧

2 文化知识

课文大背景、课文知识点

3 课文精讲

词汇与短语详解、难句解析、重点
语法讲解、课文赏析、课后练习答
案及解析、参考译文、写作指导

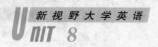
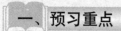

一、预习重点

1. What are the effects of wrinkles on women?
2. What is meant to women when becoming old?
3. Why do women feel obliged to look young and wrinkle-free?
4. What, in your opinion, are the most essential things for a woman to keep from aging?

二、学习重点和难点

Ⅰ. 词汇和短语

Section A: prop, exclusive, caution, generous, tendency, register, thrill; up to, peer at, in passing, break off, in that, give of (one's money/time, etc.), disapprove of, belong to, at one's elbow, pay a/the price for, in the main, prop up, in company with, more or less

Section B: wrinkle, abnormal, extract, texture, vacant, diagnose, interact, prompt; beat back, pour out, have/be to do with, when it comes to sth., attach to, on the surface, interact with, in...then..., do the trick, in no way, in particular, be tied up with, invest in

Ⅱ. 语法项目

① "mind + if clause/doing sth." 介意/不喜欢……
② "no + noun" 位于句首结构
③ "if...then..." 句型

Ⅲ. 写作技巧

举细节+归纳总结观点

三、文化知识

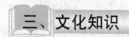

Ⅰ. 课文大背景

Slavery as an issue in America was in constant conflict with the founding Democratic principles of this nation. Slavery therefore became the ultimate test of disunity within the union of states which were already at odds in a democracy espousing freedom for its people. At the center of this conflict were the Africans who were bought, sold, and used as workers on American soil. The use of slave labor was a well known practice for years in the world community. Documented accounts of slavery as a world-wide practice are covered in hundreds of books and articles on the subject reaching as far back to the ancient region of Mesopotamia around 3500 BC.

For the Africans on American soil, that horrible journey started with the developing territorial colonies at a time when workers were needed to keep the economy of this new country solvent. Therefore, by 1619, the use of indentured servants brought the first Africans to America at Jamestown, Virginia. Poor whites also worked during this period as indentured servants. A "contract" said that this service would last from four to seven years—thereby the said would then become free. During this early period, some of the first enslaved Africans worked their way out of this system and became free tradesmen and property owners on American soil. The quest for more land and an economy based upon profit were two of the major points that escalated the demand for more slaves in America. Therefore, Black slave workers became highly prized commodities in a system dependent upon lots of manual labor. The entire southern American economy and the states in that warm region needed laborers to work on the plantations dealing with rice, indigo, tobacco, sugar cane, and cotton. Other slaves labored as dock workers, craft workers, and servants. Slaves in the northern American region labored on small farms and as skilled and unskilled workers in factories and along the coast as shipbuilders, fishermen, craftsmen, and helpers of tradesmen.

Slavery on American soil grew at such a fast rate that, by 1750, over 2,000,000 African slaves were here. Fifty years later, that number grew to 7,000,000. In South Carolina alone, African slaves outnumbered the white population, and they made up more than one half of the populations in the states of Maryland and Virginia. The free Black American population did expand to about 40,000 throughout the colonies by 1770.

The system of slavery was so entrenched in the daily routines on American soil that it had to be dealt with as a National issue. Lengthy debates, political compromises, moral dilemmas, slave rebellions, and a Nation divided against itself suddenly had to face the issue of enslaved Africans existing on American soil. America condoned the "peculiar institution" of slavery from 1619 up until the passage of the 13th Amendment to the Constitution which abolished "slavery and involuntary servitude" on December 18, 1865.

This period in American history left behind some of the most unbearable scars on the African-Americans as a people, but the free thinking decent people and countless allies envisioned a broader, more humane society.

Ⅱ. 课文知识点

1. Eatonville 伊顿维尔

It is a small community of great significance to African-American history and culture. Located just north of Orlando（奥兰多）, Florida between Winter Park and Maitland, it is historically recognized as the first incorporated African-American municipality in the United States（第一个被收入美国的黑人自治镇）and one of the oldest surviving African communities in the U.S（迄今保留下来历史最久远的全部由黑人组成的小镇）. Following the Civil War, "free" Africans settling in the area worked primarily as farm hands clearing land or helping in the construction of nearby Maitland, a white township. Eatonville is culturally important for its renowned native daughter, Zora Neale Hurston（左拉·尼尔·赫斯顿）(c.f. Note 3 below), author, anthropologist（人类学家）and folklorist（民俗学家）. Her words captured forever the culture of the community and painted an image of an environment typical of the rural Southern working-class African-American. Each January, Eatonville plays host to the Zora Neale Hurston Festival of the Arts and Humanities.（每年一月份，伊顿维尔的人们都举办左拉人文艺术节）。

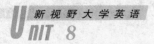

2. Orlando 奥兰多

It is the fifth-ranking U.S. destination of overseas travelers—after San Francisco, Miami, Los Angeles and New York City—and it claims the second highest number of hotel rooms in the U.S., lagging just behind Las Vegas in the bedroom stakes. The city has also established itself as part of Florida's high-tech corridor, boasting not only the space technology industries focused on the Florida Space Coast (also keen on "booms"), but a healthy dose of bits and bytes makers as well. There wasn't much to Orlando until Walt Disney started buying up property at the city's southwestern edge in the 1960s and the property he bought became Disney World in 1971. Since then, waterslides (滑水), roller coasters (过山车), fairy tale palaces and costumed characters have made Disney World one of the world's most visited tourist attractions.

3. Zora Neale Hurston 左拉·尼尔·赫斯顿

Hurston (1891-1960) was American writer, folklorist and anthropologist. Born in Eatonville, Florida, Hurston was educated at Howard University, at Barnard College, and at Columbia University, where she studied under German-American anthropologist Franz Boas. Eatonville was the first incorporated all-black town in the United States, and Hurston returned there after college for anthropological field study that influenced her later output in fiction as well as in folklore (民间传说). Hurston also collected folklore in Jamaica (牙买加), Haiti (海地), Bermuda (百慕大), and Honduras (洪都拉斯). *Mules and Men* (《骡与人》) (1935), one of her best-known folklore collections, was based on her field research in the American South. *Tell My Horse* (《告诉我的马》) (1938) described folk customs in Haiti and Jamaica.

As a fiction writer, Hurston is noted for her metaphorical language, her story-telling abilities, and her interest in and celebration of Southern black culture in the United States. Her best-known novel is *Their Eyes Were Watching God* (《仰望上帝》) (1937), in which she tracked a Southern black woman's search, over 25 years and 3 marriages, for her true identity and a community in which she can develop that identity. Hurston's work was not political, but her characters' use of dialect, her manner of portraying black culture, and her conservatism created controversy within the black community. Throughout her career she addressed issues of race and gender, often relating them to the search for freedom. In her later years Hurston experienced health problems, and she died impoverished (穷困的) and unrecognized by the literary community. Her writings, however, were rediscovered in the 1970s by a new generation of black writers, and many of Hurston's works were republished. In 1995 a two-volume set of her writings, some previously unpublished, was released.

4. Jacksonville 杰克逊维尔

It is 134 miles northeast of Orlando, Florida. Once infamous for its smelly paper mills (造纸厂), it is now one of the South's insurance and banking capitals. Although Jacksonville claims to be the capital of Florida's historic "First Coast", the city dates its beginnings from an early-1800s settlement named Cowford, because cattle crossed the St. Johns River here. Cowford changed its name to Jacksonville in 1822 to honor General Andrew Jackson, the provisional (临时的) governor who forced Spain to cede (放弃) Florida to the United States 2 years earlier.

5. Ageism 对老年人的歧视

Ageism is a negative and/or stereotypic perception of ageing and aged individuals, readily apparent in such areas as language, media, and humor. This stereotypic and often negative bias against older adults is "ageism". Ageism can be defined as "any attitude, action, or institutional structure which subordinates (服从) a person or group because of age or any assignment of roles in society purely on the basis of age". As an "ism", ageism reflects a prejudice in society against older adults.

四、课文精讲

Section A

Ⅰ. 短语与词汇详解

1. prop

[词义] *vt.* ① 支撑，支持；② 把……靠着
　　　 n. ① 支撑物；② 后盾，靠山

[搭配] prop sth. against sth. 把……靠着，使保持在某一位置上

[例句] It is not the government's policy to prop up declining industries.
资助不景气的工业不是政府的政策。
The mailman propped his bicycle up against the wall and put the mail into the mailbox. 邮电员把自行车靠在墙上把邮件放到信箱里。
Props were used to prevent the roof collapsing.
用了一些支柱以防止屋顶塌落。
Her daughter was the only prop to the old lady during her illness.
她女儿是老太太病中唯一的依靠。

2. exclusively

[词义] *adv.* 独特的，排他地

[例句] This sample room is exclusively for women. 这试衣室仅供女士使用。

[派生] exclusive *adj.* 独占的，唯一的；exclusion *n.* 排除，除外；exclude *vt.* 把…… 排除在外

[联想] inclusive *adj.* 包含的，包括的

213

3. tendency

[词义] *n.* 趋向，趋势

[例句] There is a growing tendency for people to work at home in office.

倾向于在家工作而不在办公室工作的趋势在不断增长。

[辨析] tendency，trend，drift，inclination

tendency指向某一方向移动或在确定的趋向中行动，暗含着以某一特定方式进行的倾向，如：The tendency of our socialist construction is towards firm and solid society. 我们社会主义建设的趋势是走向一个稳定、坚实的社会。

trend经常指普遍的或流行的方向，尤指在某一特定领域总的趋向或倾向，如：a recent trend in literature 最近的文化中的倾向。

drift指事情进行的趋势或动向，如：The drift of opinion was against war. 意见的动向是反战。

inclination 通常指个人爱好或喜欢此物甚于彼物的倾向，如：Man's capacity for justice makes democracy possible, but man's inclination to injustice makes democracy necessary. 人类对公平的接受能力使民主成为可能，但人类对不公平的倾向却使民主变得必需。

4. register

[词义] *v.* ① 现出，露出（表现）；②（机器）显示记录；③ 登记，注册

n. 记录

[例句] Her face registered anxiety. 她脸上出现焦虑的表情。

The earthquake registered 3 on the Richter scale. 地震为里氏三级。

A student must register at the beginning of every term.

学生必须在每学期开学前注册。

The teacher kept a register of the names of the children.

这个老师保留了一份孩子们的名册。

[派生] registration *n.* 注册，报道

5. up to 直到

[例句] These schools up to 1998 were financed for capital expenditure by the local church as part of the church's determination not to lose control of them.

这些学校的资金支出直到1998年都是由本地教堂承担的，这是教堂为了继续控制它们所做决策的一部分。

6. peer at 仔细看，凝视

[例句] My study is the perfect place for an author, especially if he doesn't object to being occasionally peered at through the windows by curious visitors.

我的书房对一个作家来说是个完美的地方，特别是如果他不反对偶尔被好奇的来访者透过窗子端详的话。

7. in passing 顺便

[例句] These points have been mentioned in passing in the previous class, but they are summarized here for the sake of convenience and for added emphasis. 这几点在上堂课已经顺便提过了，但是为了方便和加以强调，这里再归纳一下。

8. break off（使……）中断

[例句] Yesterday's meeting resumed talks broken off 8 years ago; this event has been taken as a new start in the relationship between the two countries.

昨天的会议恢复了八年前中断的会谈，这一事件被看作两国关系新的开始。

9. in that 因为，在于

[例句] Your behavior is extremely important in that it conveys your attitude much more effectively and directly than the words you use. 你的行为是极为重要的，因为它比你的言语更有效、更直接地传达你的态度。

10. give of (one's money/time, etc.) 给，提供，献出

[例句] But talent can be developed and trained and provide a sound basis for you to give of the best inside you. 但是才能是可以挖掘和训练出来的，它为你提供了展现最精彩自我的一个可靠基础。

11. disapprove of 不赞同，不喜欢

[例句] Even when other people around us do things we disapprove of, we don't have to laugh at them.

即使周围的人做一些我们不赞同的事情，我们也无须嘲笑他们。

12. belong to 是……的一员，属于

[例句] Although they belonged to different generations, they shared many thoughts in common. 尽管他们不是一代人，但是有很多共同的想法。

13. at one's elbow 在（某人）手边，在（某人）近旁

[例句] They set the table for dinner, but before they started, the telephone at their elbow rang. 他们摆好了餐桌，但是刚打算开始吃，手边的电话就响了。

14. pay a/the price for 为……付出代价

[例句] Doubtlessly he paid a price for that too, but if he had not felt that misery he could never have created the works he did. 毫无疑问，他也为此付出了代价，但是如果不经受这样的痛苦，他就决不可能创造出这样的作品。

15. in the main 基本上，大体上

[例句] But, in the main, the teachers were very satisfied that they could make the new arrangements work to the advantage of the students.

但是，大体而言，能够从学生的利益出发安排新的教学工作，老师们对这一点十分满意。

16. prop up 支撑，支持

[例句] He was propped up on one elbow, his dark hair sweat-curled and his eyes gleaming with desire.

他用肘撑着脑袋，黝黑的卷发上满是汗，眼里闪烁着渴望的光芒。

20. in company with 与……一起

[例句] Retirement allowed him the time to enjoy music, often in company with his children and grandchildren. 退休让他有时间享受音乐，和儿孙共享天伦之乐。

> **21. more or less 在某种程度上，或多或少地**
>
> [例句] In most common diseases of Western society, we know more or less what has gone wrong, even if we do not know why it has gone wrong. 就西方社会最普遍的弊病来说，我们多多少少知道什么出了差错，即使搞不清它的原因。

Ⅱ. 难句解析

1. Up to my thirteenth year I lived in the little Negro town of Eatonville, Florida. (Para. 1)

[释义] I had been lived in the little Negro town of Eatonville, Florida until I was thirteen years old.

[分析] 本句的难点在于对Negro这个词的理解。Negro 意为"黑人"，因含有贬义"黑鬼"，现在少用，可以用 "black" 或 "African-American" 代替。Colored 指 (人种) 有色的，也具有贬义。

2. When I got off the riverboat at Jacksonville, she was no more. (Para.1)

[分析] 本句的主句为省略结构的简单句 "she was no more"，省略了 "Zora"，从句为when引导的时间状语从句。本句中的 "she" 指的是来自伊顿维尔的那个黑人小姑娘，即 "I"。这样替换人称是为了暗示自己的人生已经不同于昨天。

3. They were peered at cautiously from behind curtains by the timid. (Para. 1)

[释义] The shy people would looked out through their curtains at the Northerners carefully.

[分析] 该句为简单句的被动结构，但涉及到了较多的语法：

① 双介词连用是英语中常见的表达方式，即在本句中使用了 "from behind"。

② 本句结构上表现为被动句，但在翻译成汉语时改成主动句比较符合汉语的表达习惯。

③ "the timid"指胆小的人，相当于 "the shy and nervous people"。在英语中常使用"定冠词the + 形容词"，表示一类人或事物。

4. I would probably "go a piece of the way" with them,...(Para. 2)

[释义] I would most likely travel a short distance together with them.

[分析] 本句的难点在于 "go a piece of the way" 这一习惯搭配（local expression）的理解，意思是"跟随一段距离"，相当于 " to follow for a distance"。

5. They liked to hear me "speak pieces" and sing and wanted to see me dance, and gave me generously of their small silver for doing these things, which seemed strange to me for I wanted to do them so much that I needed bribing to stop. (Para. 3)

[释义] They liked to hear me say something to them and sing and wanted to see me dance, and were willing to give their small coins more than expected for doing these things. This (They...gave me generously of their silver for doing these things) seemed unusual and unexpected to me as I liked very much to talk to them, and to sing and dance for them to the degree that if they were to ask me to stop doing so they would have to pay me.

[分析] 本句的核心结构为 "They liked to hear...and wanted...and gave...these things"。非限制性定语从句 "which seemed...stop" 的先行词为前面的句子。在该定语从句中包

含了for引导的原因状语从句，并且在原因状语从句中包含了 "so...that..." 的结果状语从句。

6. I became a permanent brown—like the best shoe polish, guaranteed not to rub nor run. (Para.4)

[释义] The writer is saying that her color is fast or fixed and will not come off on anything adjacent, as the best brown shoe polish might do. What she intends to say is that she is now a person mature enough to stand between the white and the black.

rub *v.* 擦掉，去掉，相当于remove, erase

e.g. a blackboard that rubs clean easily. 很容易擦干净的黑板

[分析] 本句的核心结构为 "I became...brown..."。破折号后的介词短语 "like...polish" 起到举例说明的作用，适用了明喻 (simile) 的修辞格。过去分词短语 "guarantee...run" 作定语修饰 shoe polish。本句的难点在于理解句子的暗含意义：作者认为自己现在在思想上已经成熟，因此不必在意自己是个黑人。

7. The operation was successful and the patient is doing well,...(Para. 5)

[释义] Here the author compares the American Civil War to an operation. Slavery was officially ended at the end of the Civil War.

[分析] 本句的难点在于运用了暗喻（metaphor）的修辞格，即把解放黑奴（emancipation of slaves）的斗争比喻为一个手术（the operation），把美国比喻成病人（patient）。

8. The world to be won and nothing to be lost. (Para. 5)

[释义] This is saying that this is a very good bet: if I enter upon this bet I can win everything, the world, and if I lose, I lose nothing (or at least not anything important).

[分析] 这是个省略主语和谓语的省略句，完整的结构应为 "we will have the world to be won and nothing to be lost"。"the world"指世界上的一切。

9. We enter chatting about any little things that we have in common and the white man would sit calmly in his seat, listening to me with interest. (Para. 6)

[释义] The white man and I would naturally start to talk about the trifles we have in common and the white man would sit there peacefully, listening to me without any signs of feeling bored.

have in common 共同拥有

e.g. I have a lot in common with my parents. 我与父母有许多共同之处。

[分析] "that we have in common"为限制性定语从句，修饰先行词things，现在分词短语 "listening to me with interest"作sit的伴随状语。

10. On the ground before you is the pile it held-so much like the piles in the other bags, could they be emptied, that all might be combined and mixed in a single heap and the bags refilled without altering the content of any greatly. (Para.7)

[分析] 本句使用了暗喻（metaphor）的修辞格，即 "it"指代前文的 "the brown bag"。"could they be emptied"为省略if的倒装虚拟语气，完整结构应为 "if they could be emptied"。过去分词短语 "refilled without altering the content of any greatly"为后

置定语，修饰bags。本句将不同种族的人比作不同颜色的袋子，而人的内涵则是袋子里所装的东西，从而表明人都是大同小异，无显著差别的。

11. A bit of colored glass more or less would not matter. (Para. 7)

[释义] This implies that in this world it does not matter to have some colored people living together.

[分析] 本句使用了暗喻（simile）的修辞格，即将colored people比喻成"colored glass"。

Ⅲ. 重点语法讲解

1."mind + if clause/ doing sth."介意，不喜欢……

mind 作及物动词时，意思是"反对，介意，不喜欢"，相当于"to object to，dislike，be annoyed by"。此时，mind通常与疑问句、否定句、或者if是否句型连用。当mind与动词连用时，动词需用动名词形式。

But I didn't <u>mind the actors knowing</u> that I liked it. (Para.2)

但是我并不在意那些演员们知道我喜欢看。

He <u>doesn't mind doing</u> the chores. 他不介意做家务。

<u>Would you mind changing</u> places with me so that I can be nearer the fire?

你能不能与我换一换位置，这样我可以离炉火近一点。

I don't <u>mind if it takes time to wait for my husband's arrival</u>.

我不在乎花时间等我丈夫归来。

2."no + noun"位于句首结构

"no + noun"位于句首作主语，意思是"没有任何的，毫无，没有一个"，相当于"not a + noun"或"not any + noun"，"not one"。限定词（determiner）既可以与可数名词连用，也可与不可数名词连用。

<u>No one</u> on earth ever had a greater chance for glory. (Para.5)

世界上再没有什么人有过比这更大的机会争取荣耀的了。

<u>No friends</u> came to see her. 没有任何朋友来看她。

<u>No cookies</u> are left. 一块饼干也没剩下。

No task is so difficult but (that) we can accomplish it.

不管任务怎样困难，我们都能完成。

Ⅳ. 课文赏析

1. 文体特点

本文是一篇记叙文，以第一人称的方式叙述了种族问题，作者的笔端没有常见的愤世嫉俗，而是从一个全新的角度，以幽默、轻快、温暖的笔触讲述了自己作为一个黑人的亲身经历和感受，提出了与人们对种族歧视的普遍理解截然不同的观点：作为美国有色公民，她从未有过被孤立的感觉。本文最重要的一个特点就是以细节开始，然后给出概括性的句子或结论，与以往我们接触到的一般——具体的模式不同。以第一人称来叙述，显得十分亲切可信。生动的语言和丰富的修辞手法是本文的一大特色，运用了大量的暗喻。

在篇章组织上，作者先通过陈述自己的亲身经历等细节，再带出自己鲜明的观点，运用了归纳法的写作模式，有助于通过细节帮助读者酝酿情绪，走入情境之中，然后再顺理成章地给读者灌输观点，行文流畅，水到渠成。

2. 结构分析

Part Ⅰ (Para.1-3) My impressions of the white people when I was a child.

Part Ⅱ (Para. 4) The time I became aware of being colored.

Part Ⅲ (Para. 5-7) My feeling about being colored.

Ⅴ. 课后练习答案及解析

Comprehension of the Text

Ⅱ.

1. They hid behind their curtains and looked through them at the travelers cautiously.

2. The small town was a stage where actors were the different travelers who passed by and revealed themselves to the audience—the villagers in different aspects. In a child's eye, it was a play, bringing to her a lot of pleasure.

3. Probably there were different ways of greetings between them, so there might be some misunderstandings or some inappropriate responses.

4. She wanted to sing and dance so much that she thought the money should be given as a discouragement instead of an encouragement.

5. After she was thirteen and left her hometown of Eatonville, and then she experienced a huge change. She was aware that she was black.

6. It expresses the author's attitude or the status of mind that she was not emotionally disturbed by the fact that she was a descendent of slaves. She felt good about herself.

7. The author felt like a brown bag of mixed items propped up against a wall.

8. As is described, the contents revealed are nothing but common objects. It suggests that for ordinary people, no matter whether they are white or black, they share something in common.

Vocabulary

Ⅲ.

1. cautiously 译文: 那个间谍小心谨慎地向四周看了看，然后走进电影院，消失在黑暗中。

2. bribing 译文: 那个人被控向一名高级银行官员行贿，被判了十年监禁。

3. disapprove/disapproves/disapproved 译文: 那个黑人女孩的家人强烈反对她在公共场合表现出兴高采烈，特别是在陌生人面前。

4. tendency 译文: 因此，晚上当体温开始下降时，我们很自然地就会进入梦香，而在早上体温开始上升时，我们就会醒来。

5. registered 译文: 当他看到在那个黑人女孩身上发生的一切时，他的脸上显露出极其反对和不满的神色。

6. depression 译文: 当裁员的消息在办公室宣布时，大家都觉得非常失望。

7. propped 译文: 他的衣服穿得好好的，背对着墙靠坐在床头。

8. guaranteed 译文: 尽管强调有这些机会不一定就能成功，但是以市场为导向的企业还是觉得它们值得关注。

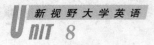

IV.

1. peering at 译文：霍华德坐在那边，透过眼镜看着街上来来往往的车辆。

2. be broken off 译文：那个演员从舞台上掉下来摔断了左腿，不得不中止演出。

3. disapproved of 译文：反对香烟广告的人会比那些赞成的人更有可能把烟戒掉。

4. propping up 译文：贿赂政客以及支持腐败政府的行为使得美国在世界贫苦与落后国家中的声誉变得更为糟糕。

5. In the main 译文：总得来说，广告中一些美容产品不断夸大的用辞都是些空洞的许诺。

6. in company with 译文：因为他们与陌生人在一起时会害羞，所以这些胆小的人选择从窗帘后面偷偷窥视那些北方人。

7. in that 译文：对我来说，那时白人与黑人是不相同的，因为他们的语言听起来很奇怪。

8. at her elbow 译文：她周围的人反复提醒她说她的外貌的确是发生了变化。

Collocation

V.

1. experiencing 中国市场在过去的十年中经历了飞速的变化，给外国投资者带来了更多机会。

2. resist 译文：在所谓的民主社会中，当我们无法抵制政府未经同意就强加到我们头上的任何政策变化时，积极的公民身份就失去意义了。

3. advocate 译文：人类的本性就是对所发生在他人身上的事情上总是持肯定态度，而对自己需要在方面改变的必要性，却持强烈的否定态度。

4. indicate 译文：这个词 是一个表示意义改变的标志词。

5. notice 译文：尽管那段时间，杰克在语言上谨慎，但他的朋友们还是开始注意到了他的变化。

6. undergo 译文：因为这些植物被吸引到现在这个地方，所以它们必须经受住环境改变而带来的考验。

7. welcome 译文：银行欢迎这些变化，但是一些评论家担心它弊多利少。

8. caused 译文：这些专家们产生了分歧，有人认为是炎热、干燥的气候导致了这些植物繁殖系统发生了变化。

Word Building

VI.

1. devalued 译文：在这个领域里最近新冒出来的一些专家在市场上的影响力已经逐步下降。

2. demobilized 译文：据报道，那些抢劫集团主要是由一些复员军人组成的。

3. deregulated 译文：日本政府在过去三十年中，极大地放松了对货币市场的管制，使市场对价格的变化更加敏感。

4. decentralized 译文：去年他们分散业务范围，并在那个国家重新开了几家地方性的办事处。

5. destabilizing 译文：人们普遍认为这场冲突导致了整个地方的不稳定。

6. depersonalized 译文：大多数父母说他们认为穿校服会使他们的孩子失去个性。

7. deskilled 译文：在工厂车间里，机械技术的进步使得大量工人的工作不再以技术为主。

8. decoded 译文：诗的确是用来传达信息的，但为了更好地理解它所表达的意思，我们必须对它加以诠释。

VII. ▶

1. retirees 译文: 该国几乎三分之二当前的退休者超过一半的生计是靠社会福利系统维持的。

2. interviewees 译文: 在面试过程中, 我们尽量使那些应聘者感到放松些。

3. trainee 译文: 我仍然记得我的第一份工作是在那家报社做一名实习记者。

4. employees 译文: 在过去的几十年里, 那个公司雇员的数量增加了十倍。

5. escapees 译文: 通过对整个地区三天的搜查, 他们最终逮捕了那两名逃犯。

6. addressee 译文: 因为邮资将由收件人支付, 因此你无须巾邮票。

7. devotees 译文: 对音乐爱好者, 以及那些专心致力欲音乐的人们来说, 阿尔塞纳的音乐会将会是一个满足自我的很好的机会。

8. divorcee 译文: 英国国王爱得华八世放弃王位, 只想娶一名离过婚的美国女人为妻。

Structure

VIII. ▶

1. I know she isn't really interested in window-shopping, but she doesn't mind waiting while I have a look.
   译文: 我知道她对逛街不感兴趣, 但她不介意在我看东西的时候等我一会儿。

2. If people don't mind my having no degrees, I could give a few music lessons!
   译文: 如果人们不介意我没有学历的话, 我能教一些音乐课。

3. People don't mind paying much more for good software because they can see the benefits of using it.
   译文: 人们不介意花一些钱去买好的软件, 因为他们知道用它的好处。

4. I am big for my age and I didn't mind if he thought I was a young man.
   译文: 就年龄而言, 我已长大了, 但我不介意他以为我是年轻人。

5. We don't mind if it takes time for people to express their hopes and goals and their fears and needs in their lives.
   译文: 我们不会介意花一些时间倾听人们讲述生活中的希望、目标、恐惧以及需要。

IX. ▶

1. No friends came to see her; she shut herself off, in the old familiar world of bedroom and drawing room, and her only amusement, for weeks on end, was the reading of her set texts.
   译文: 没有任何朋友来看她, 她把自己封闭在她的卧室和画室这些她所熟悉的环境中, 连续两个礼拜, 她唯一的消遣就是阅读她那些指定的教科书。

2. No cigarette end could give us any clues to or signs of anyone having ever been there.
   译文: 并无任何烟头能给我们提供有人曾到过这里的线索。

3. No gas, no water and no electricity in the hospital! How could you expect the children to survive this?
   译文: 这所医院没有气, 没有水, 没有电! 你能指望这些孩子在这里生存下去?

4. No other information is given about the book itself, although there is a brief biographical note about the author.
   译文: 除了作者的生平简历外, 就没有这本书的任何资料了。

5. No effort has been made to investigate the tens of thousands of murders and "disappearances" that have occurred over the past three years.

译文: 没有做任何的努力去调查过去三年来所发生的一系列的谋杀和失踪案。

Translation

X. ▶

1. Up to yesterday, we had no idea whether the war would break out or not.

2. Someone is always at my elbow reminding me that I am a descendent of slaves, but it fails to register depression with me.

3. I do not want to tell you that story; I have just mentioned that in passing.

4. I prefer his plan to yours in that I think it is more practical.

5. The disapproval registered on her face was so real that even I would have thought it genuine.

6. They broke off the business relations with that company as it suffered huge losses in the last financial year and went bankrupt.

7. Perhaps this was the price that has to be paid for the progress in the first place—who knows?

8. When she was preparing her luggage, the bag was emptied and refilled several times.

XI. ▶

1. 本地的白人骑着风尘仆仆的马匹，而北方来的旅游者则驾着汽车沿着乡下的沙土路一路驶来。

2. 小镇的人胆小的就躲在窗帘后小心翼翼地偷看他们，胆大的则会走出屋外看着他们经过，感到很开心，就像这些旅游者看到这村庄也感到很有乐趣一样。

3. 不仅在镜中，也在内心深处，我变成了永远不黑不白的棕色人——就像那最好的鞋油，不会被抹掉，也永不褪色。

4. 他们对我表现出的任何一点欢乐的苗头都不赞同。但我仍然是他们的佐拉，我是属于他们，属于周围的旅馆，属于那个地方，属于每一个人的佐拉。

5. 我似乎已发生了巨大的变化，我再也不是伊顿维尔的佐拉了，我现在成了个小黑妞。

6. 占据国内舞台的中心可真刺激，而台下的观众则不知是喜是忧。

7. 我没有老是感到自己是有色人种。甚至现在我感觉自己还是在伊顿维尔小镇上的懵然无知的佐拉。

8. 也许当初上帝这个装袋者往我们各自的皮袋子中填塞时正是这么做的，谁知道呢?

Essay Summary

XII. ▶

B D A D C   A B B C D   A C A B D   C B A C D

Text Structure Analysis

XIII. ▶

Para. 1

(1) on horses or in automobiles

(2) watched them

(3) as they got out of the village

Para. 2

(1) watching and waving at the white

(2) greeting to them

Para. 3

(1) they rode through town and never lived there

(2) to hear me speak and sing and wanted to see me dance

VI. 参考译文

黑奴的历史对我没有什么损失

我清楚地记得我成为黑人的那一天。13岁之前我一直住在佛罗里达州的一个黑人小镇伊顿维尔。小镇的居民全是黑人。我所接触过的仅有的白人都是来自佛罗里达的奥兰多或是去往奥兰多的过客。本地的白人骑着风尘仆仆的马匹，而北方来的旅游者则驾着汽车沿着乡下的沙土路一路驶来。小镇的人见惯了南方人，因此他们经过时小镇的人照旧大嚼甘蔗。但是看到北方人则又是另一回事了。小镇的人胆小的就躲在窗帘后小心翼翼地偷看他们，胆大的则会走出屋外看着他们经过，感到很开心，就像这些旅游者看到这村庄也感到很有乐趣一样。

上门前平台去可能会吓坏镇上其他人，但对我来说，那儿就像前排座位一样。我最爱坐在门柱上。我不仅喜欢在那儿看人们来来往往，也不在乎让那些人知道我喜欢看，顺便还与他们搭几句话。我向他们挥手，如果他们也向我挥手，我还与他们打招呼。对此，骑马或驾车的人通常会停下来，我们不可思议地互打招呼之后，我可能会随着他们"颠儿几步"，这是我们佛罗里达最南边的说法，意思是跟着他们走上一小段路。如果正赶上家里人碰巧来到房前见到我，他们当然就会毫不客气地打断我们的交谈。

那段日子里，在我看来，白人和黑人的不同只不过是他们路过镇上，但从不住在镇上。他们喜欢听我"说几句"，听我唱歌，想看我跳舞，并为此大方地给我小银币。这倒使我感到奇怪，因为我太愿意跟他们"说上几句"，为他们唱歌跳舞了，得给我钱才能使我停下来。只是他们不知道这一点。黑人不会给我钱，对我表现出的任何一点欢乐的苗头，他们都不赞同。但我仍然是他们的佐拉，我是属于他们，属于周围的旅馆，属于那个地方，属于每一个人的佐拉。

但我13岁时，家里发生了变故，我被送到杰克逊维尔的学校去了。离开伊顿维尔时我还是我，佐拉。可在杰克逊维尔下了船后，原来的佐拉不复存在了。我似乎已发生了巨大的变化，我再也不是伊顿维尔的佐拉了，我现在成了个小黑妞。在好几方面我都发现了自己的这种变化。不仅在镜中，也在内心深处，我变成了永远不黑不白的棕色人——就像那最好的鞋油，不会被抹掉，也永不褪色。

身边总有人不断提醒我自己是个奴隶的后代，但这并没有使我沮丧。奴隶制是60年前的事了。解放黑奴这场手术很成功，病人的情况也不错，谢谢。这场使我从黑奴变为美国公民的可怕战争对我叫道"各就各位！"内战后的那段时期说"预备！"我的上一代人喊道"跑！"就像一场赛跑一样，我飞速起跑，决不可中途停步，回望伤心。黑奴的历史是我为文明生活所付的代价，而做出这一选择的并不是我。世界上再没有什么人有过比此更大的争取荣耀的机会了。想想将要获得的新生活，而且我们没有任何损失。不管我做什么，都可能得到双倍的嘉奖，或是双份的责难。想想这一点，知道这一点都令人激动不已。占据国内舞台的中心可真刺激，而台下的观众则不知是喜是忧。

我没有老是感到自己是有色人种。甚至现在我感觉自己还是在伊顿维尔小镇上的懵然无知的佐拉。比如，我可以在餐馆和一位白人坐在一起。我们闲谈一些平常的琐事，白人会安静地坐着，兴味盎然地听着。

有时候我不属于任何人种，我就是我自己。但我大体上还是感觉自己像一只靠墙立着装满各种杂物的棕色皮袋子。靠墙立着的还有其他颜色的袋子，白色的，红色的，黄色的。倒出袋中物，可以发现一堆或有用或无用的小杂物：碎玻璃块；小线头儿；一扇早已朽败的门上的钥匙；一把锈蚀的刀；一双为某条从来没有、将来也不会有的路而准备的旧鞋；一颗弯折的钉，它所承受过的重量足以弄折任何钉子；一两支干花，仍散发出几许花香。你手中拿的是棕色的袋子，面前的地上则是袋中所装的那堆东西的——它与其他袋子中所倒出的一堆堆东西几乎一模一样，如果把它们混成一大堆，再重新装回各自的袋中，也不会有多大的不同。多少有点有色玻璃片也没有什么关系。也许当初上帝这个装袋者往我们各自的皮袋子中填塞时正是这么做的，谁知道呢？

VII. 写作指导

概括法通常要求先写出具体的内容和细节，然后得出结论。也可以首先概括出观点，然后再详述细节。这种写作方法有些类似举例法，两者都是用事例说明主题句，但区别在于概括是指结论是建立在几个所给的例子作为事实或观点的基础上的得出的，这一结论是明显的或者能被读者认可的。读者的注意中心在概括或总结归纳出的结论或观点上。

范文：

I would never forget the days when I was a small black girl in my little Negro town of Eatonville. Every day I sat in front of my house, watching the white people passing through the town, some on horses and some others in automobiles. I usually spoke to them in passing. I'd wave at them and when they friendly returned my wave, I would say a few words of greeting. Usually the automobile or the horse stopped at this, and after a few exchange of greetings, they would like to hear me sing and wanted to see me dance. They enjoyed the joyful tendencies in me. During this period, it seemed to me that I never felt the differences between the white and the black. The only difference to me was that we were born with different skin colors.

Section B

I. 阅读技巧

本单元复习与联系区分事实与作者观点的阅读技巧。阅读时，首先需要确定的是文章中是向读者表达了什么观点还是提供了事实，以及这些事实与观点的可信度。这就要求读者必须能够区分清楚观点和事实。通常，事实（fact）就是一种真实存在的事物或情况，是可以通过观察或者实验检测的。观点（opinion）简单而言指的是一个人对某事的判断（judgment），belief（信仰）或feeling（感觉），具有较强的主观性，可能是正确的，也可能是片面的。例如，一些形容词常常可以表示观点；而一些动词或者表示时间、地点的短语结构用来表示事实。但就一个句子而言，是由侧重点的，需要读者判断该句的核心是为表达观点还是陈述事实。

例如：They were peered at cautiously from behind curtains by the timid. 尽管本句中的 cautiously和timid表达了观点，也有陈述事实：peered at，from behind curtains。但此句的核心是为了陈述事实：The Northerners were being peered at from behind curtains. 因此，此句从根本上而言是陈述事实的（factual）。

Ⅱ. 词汇与短语详解

1.wrinkle

[词义] *n.* 皱，皱纹；*vt.*（使）起皱纹；*vi.* 皱眉

[搭配] wrinkle one's nose in disdain 皱鼻子表示不屑

[例句] Grandfather has many wrinkles on his face. 祖父脸上有许多皱纹。

With the time gone, the skin round her eyes wrinkled when she smiled.
随着时间的流逝，她一笑，眼角边上就起了皱纹。

He wrinkled his forehead at her. 他向她皱起了眉头。

2. abnormal

[词义] *adj.* ① 反常的；② 异乎寻常的，例外的；③ 变态的，畸形的

[例句] We do not think such an abnormal phenomenon will last long.
我们认为这样的反常现象不会持续很久。

An abnormal amount of snow fell here last week.
上周这里下了异常大的雪。

It is important to make a study of abnormal psychology.
研究变态心理学是重要的。

[联想] normal *adj.* 正常的，正规的，标准的

3. extract

[词义] *n.* 提炼物；*v.* 提取，提炼

[例句] Add a teaspoon of vanilla extract to the milk. 在牛奶中加一茶匙香草精。

This substance is extracted from seaweed. 这种物质是从海藻中提取的。

[联想] attract *vt.* 吸引；distract *vt.* 使分心；contract *vt.* 收缩

4. texture

[词义] *n.* ①（织物的）质地；②（材料等的）结构

[例句] The material has a silky texture. 这种料子的手感像丝绸。

the orderly texture of matter can be seen through an electron microscope
通过电子显微镜可以看到的物质的有序结构。

5. vacant

[词义] *adj.* ① 空着的；②（职位、工作等）空缺的

[搭配] a vacant room 空房间；a vacant position 空缺职位

[例句] Are there any rooms vacant in this hotel? 这家旅馆有空房吗？

He wanted to apply for a vacant position in an office.
他想申请一个空缺的职务。

[派生] vacancy *n.* 空，空白

[辨析] vacant，blank，empty

vacant指没有人居住或占据，如：The house was vacant. 这房子无人居住。

blank表面的空白，如：My window faces a blank wall. 我的窗正对着一面空白的墙。

225

empty 是常用语，指其中无人无物的，如：The house was empty when the fire broke out. 火灾发生时，屋子是空的。

6. diagnose

[词义] *vt.* 诊断，判断

[搭配] diagnose sth. as sth. 把……诊断为……

[例句] The general practitioner diagnosed the illness of the baby as pneumonia.
全科医生把小孩儿的病诊断为肺炎。

[派生] diagnosis *n.* 诊断

7. interact

[词义] *vi* 相互作用，相互影响

[例句] All things are interrelated and interact with each other.
一切事物都是相互联系又相互影响的。

[派生] interaction *n.* 相互作用

8. prompt

[词义] *vt.* 促使，推动
adj. ① 敏捷的；② 及时的，迅速的

[搭配] prompt payment 即刻付款；prompt answer 迅速答复

[例句] The man confessed that poverty prompted him to steal.
这个男子承认是贫穷促使他偷窃的。
The drowning child was saved by Dick's prompt action.
那个溺水的孩子被迪克的及时行动救了。
Prompt payment of bills greatly helps our company.
迅速付款给了我们公司很大的帮助。

[派生] promptly *adv.* 敏捷地，迅速地

9. beat back 击退，逐回

[例句] With a strength Isabel had not known she possessed she had beaten back panic.
伊莎贝尔凭着一股自己也不知道哪来的力量击退了恐惧。

10. pour out 倾吐，诉说

[例句] In six letters he poured out to her his hopes, his feelings, and his frustrations.
在六封信里他向她倾诉了他的希望、感受和经受的挫折。

11. have/be to do with 和……有关系

[例句] But some of these projects clearly also have to do with the problem of conserving cultural tradition. 但是一些方案很清楚是和保护文化传统的问题有关。

12. when it comes to sth. 当涉及到，当谈到

[例句] The British can write novels and plays, even produce an occasional world-class painter but, when it comes to cinema, they might as well forget it.
英国人能写小说和戏剧，甚至偶尔出现一位世界级的画家，至于电影，他们似乎没有什么建树。

13. attach to 认为有（重要性等）；把……附加于

[例句] The importance attached to every other issue rose sharply when the campaign began, but the importance attached to defense hardly changed. 战役爆发后，人们越发强烈地重视起其他问题，而防御的重要性却几乎没有改变。

Life has always had some risks attached to it. 生命总是附带了一些冒险色彩。

14. on the surface 面上，表面上

[例句] Whatever their difference on the surface, their company was excellent for business. 不管他们表面上有多么不同，合开的公司却生意兴隆。

15. interact with 与……互相作用，与……互相影响

[例句] What is more, these factors interact with one another and different combinations and sequences will determine what eventually happens.
此外，这些因素互相作用，不同的组合和顺序会决定最终的结果。

16. if...then... 如果……，那么就……

[例句] If you don't make a will, then the distribution of what you possess when you die may not be as you would wish. 如果你不立下一份遗嘱，那么你死后财产的分割就可能不会按照你的意愿进行。

17. do the trick 有效，达到目的

[例句] Becoming better at what we do and widening the gap between selling price and manufacturing cost is the only target that will do the trick for us.
把工作做得更好，扩大产品的出售价格和生产成本之间的差距，对我们而言是惟一有效的方法。

18. in no way 决不，无论如何不

[例句] In no way had she ever been prepared for the hard life she was leading on the campus. 她根本没有对校园里的艰苦生活做好准备。

19. in particular 尤其，特别

[例句] She could well understand how women in particular wanted to get away to the West where daily life was so much more convenient.
她很能理解妇女尤其想去西方国家，因为在那里日常生活要方便得多。

20. be tied up with 与……有密切关系，与……有联系

[例句] The result is entirely tied up with the intensity of interest or desire which you apply to the various things you do.
你在所从事的各种事情上投入的兴趣和热情将和结果有着密切的关系。

21. invest in 投资于，花钱买

[例句] It will be necessary to decide on the amount of resource to be invested in management development, and what mechanism should be used to allocate these resources.
有必要决定在管理开发上投入的资源量，以及用于分配这些资源的机制。

III. 难句解析

1. ...I was looking into skin cream that claimed to beat back the destruction that comes with age,...(Para. 1)

[释义] ...I was investigating skin cream that was said to be able to resist against the wrinkles resulting from the ageing process,...

[分析] 本句的核心结构为 "I was...cream"。本句包含了两个that引导的定语从句。第一个定语从句 "that claimed...destruction"，修饰先行词cream；第二个定语从句 "that comes with age"修饰先行词destruction。

2. **Fingering her beautiful but finely-lined features, she explained that, although she knew her discovery had more to do with the shock resulting from the sudden end of a six-year relationship than early ageing, she just had to do something about it. (Para. 1)**

[释义] While touching her beautiful but slightly-wrinkled face with her fingers, she explained that she knew these wrinkles were more connected with the shock caused by the sudden end of a six-year relationship than with early ageing, but she just had to take some measure for it.

finger *v.* 用手指拨弄或摩挲。

e.g. she fingered the rich silk happily. 她高兴地用手触摸那华美的丝绸。

[分析] 本句的核心结构为 "she explained that...", "fingering...features" 为现在分词短语作伴随状语。that引导的宾语从句中又套用了 "although...aging" 让步状语从句。

3. **Fuelled by the immense value attached to youth, it has made millions out of vacant promises of renewing faces and bodies. (Para. 3)**

[释义] The importance that youth is believed to have has made the beauty industry develop rapidly and it has made millions of dollars out of empty promises of renewing faces and bodies.

vacant *adj.* 空洞的，空闲的，空缺的

e.g. vacant promise 空洞的许诺; vacat hours 空闲的时间; a vacant position 空缺的职位

[分析] 句中的过去分词短语 "fuelled by...youth," 作原因状语，相当于原因状语从句 "as it is fuelled"。

4. **To give skin care scientific authority, beauty counters have now stolen a thin covering of respectability from the hospital clinic. (Para. 3)**

[释义] In order to make skin care scientifically authorized, beauty counters have imitated the way the hospital clinics conduct their business.

respectability *n.* 可尊敬之人或物，值得尊敬之性质或品格

e.g. As a doctor, his respectability in his nature is integrity.

[分析] 本句的难点在于对句子讽刺意味的理解。动词不定式 "to give...authority" 作目的状语，"respectability" 指的是医院诊所的良好声誉和一套使人信任的诊疗程序，"a thin cover of" 用来讽刺那些美容品专柜通过抄袭一些皮毛和形式来唬人。

5. **Sales staff in white coats "diagnoses" skin types on "computers" and blind customers with the science of damaged molecules and DNA repair. (Para. 3)**

[释义] Sales clerks wearing white coats identify the customers' skin types on computers and fool customers unaware of the truth with the science of damaged molecules and DNA repair.

[分析] 本句的难点在于理解两个带引号的词都带有讽刺意味，由于护肤品销售员不是医生，因此她的行为不能算作 "diagnose"，用来 "诊断" 的机器也算不上 "computer"。"blind" 在句中作及物动词，意思是 "蒙骗"。

6. **Providing the "drugs" for this game, the industry has created new skin**

therapies...(Para. 3)

[释义] By giving the "drugs" in its plan to attract more customers, the beauty industry has invented new skin treatments...

[分析] "providing...game" 为现在分词方式状语。本句的难点在于对 "game" 的理解，意思是 "策略；计谋"，相当于 " a way of behaving in which a person uses a particular plan, usually in order to gain an advantage for himself or herself"。

7. If normal cells can be stimulated to divide, then abnormal ones could also be prompted to multiply, so causing or accelerating skin cancer. (Para. 5)

[释义] If the statement that normal cells can be stimulated to divide is accepted as true, then the statement must also be accepted as true that those cells that are not normal could also be caused to reproduce and increase, so causing or quickening skin cancer.

[分析] 在 if...then...句型中，如果 if 条件句所述是正确的，那么 then 句所述也应该认为是正确的。"副词 so+现在分词短语" 结构作结果状语，表示得出了与期待的相反的结果。

8. Such controversy is familiar ground to Brian Newnan,...(Para.10)

[解析] 本句的难点是对 ground 词义的正确理解。在本句中，ground 是名词，意思是 "话题，方面"，相当于 "area of reference or discussion, a subject"。例如：The professor covered new ground in every lecture. 教授在每次讲座中都涉及新的领域。

9. The value of age and experience is denied, and women in particular feel the threat that the visible changes of ageing bring. (Para. 11)

[释义] When the value of age and experience is no longer taken into consideration, and people, especially women, feel that the apparent changes caused by growing old will threaten them.

[分析] 在这个长句是由 and 连接的两个并列的简单句组成，即 "the value...denied"+", and"+"women...bring"。在第二个简单句中，"that the visible...bring" 是限制性定语从句，修饰先行词 "the threat"。

Ⅳ. 重点语法讲解

"if...then..." 句型

"if +句子，then +句子"，the structure is used to say when the first of the two statements is accepted as true, then the second statement must also be accepted as true. 也就是说，在 if...then...句型中，如果 if 条件句所述是正确的，那么 then 句所述也应该认为是正确的。

If normal cells can be stimulated to divide, then abnormal ones could also be prompted to multiply,....(Para. 5)

如果正常的细胞可以受刺激而分裂，那么不正常的细胞业户加速繁殖……。

If the answer is "yes", then we must decide on an appropriate course of action.

如果回答是肯定的，那么我们必须决定恰当的做法。

"John is the best basketball player in our club." "Nonsense! If John is our best player, then I'm Yao Ming!" "约翰是我们俱乐部里最好的篮球选手！" "胡说！如果约翰是我们的最好选手，那么我就是姚明了。"

V. 课文赏析

1. 文体特点

本文较好的回答了女人为什么怕皱纹这一问题。首先以与同事的谈话引出主题，然后从两个方面说明这一问题，一方面女人使用护肤品是为了美丽，从另一个较深的层次上来说要归结于什么原因使女人看上去年轻并且没有皱纹。由于女性的本领仍在很大程度上被看作与生育能力密切相关，年龄的增长向世人显示的是她的衰老。最后作者提出应该理解年龄的真正价值。

2. 结构分析

Part I (Para.1-2) The talk between the author and her colleague about wrinkles.

Part II (Para.3-10) The surface reason and an example of skin cream Imedeen.

Part III (Para.11) The deep reason for this.

Part IV (Para.12) Conclusion.

VI. 课后练习答案及解析

Reading Skills

XV.

F O O F F

Comprehension

XVI.

F T T F F   F T T

Vocabulary

XVII.

1. appeal 译文: 这种食品现在作为一种健康食品受到越来越多有健康意识顾客的青睐。

2. poured 译文: 至于她, 在买衣服和娱乐上她花钱简直如流水。

3. denied 译文: 在年龄和经验不被重视的社会里, 女人们衰老的迹象出现时在就很难做任何事了。

4. renew 译文: 害怕他再次袭击自己, 贝蒂拿起枪打死了那个陌生的壮汉。

5. stimulated 译文: 公众在安全与环境问题上态度的变化进一步激起了人们对这些大多与能源有密切关系问题的关注。

6. perceived 译文: 物价上涨是对生活水平的一种威胁, 因此, 物价增长越快, 工人们就越有可能加入工会来维持他们的损失。

7. accelerate 译文: 如果工人相信通货膨胀可能加速, 他们将会要求加薪来补偿可以预料到的价格增长带给他们的损失。

8. controversy 译文: 他们的目标是确保英国电影避免有关政治、宗教和社会争论的各种问题, 并且不做任何可能引起麻烦的事情。

XVIII.

1. look into 译文: 同时, 共同经济委员会将努力寻求公司之间的经济与工业合作的方式。

2. poured out 译文: 斯温顿·爱德华在给她的六封信中, 倾诉了他的希望、感情和挫折, 还给她写了许多诗。

3. beat back 译文: 这台小仪器可以轻柔地活动你细小娇嫩的面部肌肉, 使皮肤紧绷, 抚平皱纹。

4. When it comes to 译文：当谈到年龄的价值问题时，女性尤其感受到由于年龄明显变老所带来的威胁。

5. have to do with 译文：在某些此类的研究中，研究结果之所以会产生争议，其原因可能是与其他一些无法控制的变量有关。

6. specialize in 译文：有些专门研究肺癌的医生对这种新药的效果提出了质疑。

7. was tied up with 译文：在我们结婚的初期，我知道由于忙于生意，不得不让你独自度过了许多时光。

8. symbolic of 译文：女人把长发剪成了短发以表明她想改变自己的生活。

VII. 参考译文

女人为什么怕皱纹

我无意中向同事提起我正调查那种自称可以消除岁月之痕的护肤霜时，她向我倾吐烦恼。她告诉我，一个月前，她突然注意到脸上布满皱纹。她一边用手指抚摸着漂亮的，但有些细小纹路的面部，一边解释说，尽管她知道这一发现主要是因为那段历时六年的感情关系突然结束给她带来了打击，而不是由于早衰，但她还是得采取些措施。

在向她说明岁月无情，要改变现实可能性不大之后，我告诉她我认为这些灵丹妙药所宣传的都很荒谬。但不管我说什么，她求我告诉她去哪儿能做我所说的那些护理。只要说是美容，谁还管真相如何？

人们对自己想要的东西的信任在过去使得美容业容易生存。青春具有巨大的价值，这大大刺激了美容业，使其得以从它的那些使我们面容、身体焕然一新的空洞许诺中赚了数百万元。为了使皮肤护理具有科学的权威，销售美容品的柜台现已从医院诊所盗用了体面的外表。推销人员穿着白大褂，在"电脑"上给消费者"诊断"皮肤类型，用修复受损分子和DNA这些技术来蒙蔽消费者。美容业给这一花招提供"药物"，以此创造了新的皮肤疗法，还说这种疗法并不是仅停留在表面，它实际上作用于细胞层。

但这真的是一个无害的花招吗？制造商越来越夸张地宣称其产品的除皱能力，这使得医生们感到很担忧。广告声称那些活性因子能刺激皮肤深层的细胞分裂，以此来替换旧细胞，并有效地更新皮肤。

如果真是这样，其效果会有害吗？如果正常的细胞可以受刺激而分裂，那么不正常的细胞也会加快繁殖，引起或加速皮肤癌的发生。抗皱行列的一个新产品声称可以用一种更自然的方法来避免讨厌的皱纹。那是一种叫做"伊美婷"的药丸，不是外搽的霜。它由内到外发挥作用，提供皮肤所需的营养和化学物质，促进人体的自体修复过程。

这一产品最初是斯堪的纳维亚地区开发出来的。它含有鱼类、海洋植物、虾壳等的提取物，组成了一个包括蛋白质、矿物质和维生素在内的配方。根据一份已公开的研究，使用该疗法两三个月后皮肤肌理看得出有所改善。皮肤更柔软、更光滑，皱纹虽非全部去除但已减少，斑点和细小的棕色纹路消失。

一位女士承认自己在试用"伊美婷"之前是有怀疑的。她认为女性有必要保持体内自然的化学平衡。她说，小心维护好人体的化学平衡不仅能改进外貌，而且也能增加活力，甚至能扩大意识和思维能力。"伊美婷"通过提供皮肤所需的养分而做到了这一点。但虾壳等物真能对皱纹产生这样的奇妙效果吗？

一位研究过"伊美婷"的英国外科医生布赖恩·纽曼提出了一个更为科学的解释。他说随着食物的消化这种复合物会起一种特别的作用，防止食物中的基本蛋白质被破坏，使其能以一种更易为皮肤所用的状态被吸收。

而另一方面，另一位专门从事皮肤研究的医生对这些数据不以为然，并对这一研究中所用的方法提出了质疑。而且，发表研究"伊美婷"的那份医学刊物是一份"收费"刊物——任何研究结果只要交费都可发表。据这位医生说，任何企图玩弄医学研究规律的做法都是徒劳的。

这样的争论布赖恩·纽曼已习以为常了。他用的一种从花中提取的油多年后才被普遍接受。他毫不气馁，坚持说要确立的最重要的一点就是"伊美婷"实际上是有效的。

但是，从根本上说，真正的问题首先是我们究竟为何那么害怕皱纹。可悲的是，青春、美貌已成了我们这个社会的货币，可以买到人心和机会。年龄和经验的价值被否定了。女性尤其感受到因衰老而致的外在改变所带来的威胁。据一位心理学专家说，男人头发有点花白通常增添了他们的魅力，因为对他们而言，年龄意味着权力、成功、财富及地位。但由于女性的本领仍在很大程度上被看作与生育能力密切相关，年龄增长向世人显示的是她的衰老，就她的首要作用而言她已无用了。皱纹就象征着她生育能力的衰退。

除非我们能够理解年龄的真正价值，否则的话，当出现年老的迹象时，除了恐慌以外就很难有其他办法了。只要媒体继续将成功的形象表现为各年龄层的男性身边伴着皮肤光滑的年轻女性，妇女们就会继续花钱去买一瓶又一瓶毫无价值的垃圾。让我们期待更多成熟的有皱纹的妇女成为有魅力、成功的、幸福的角色，也让我们期待男士们纷纷争先恐后与她们为伍。

Section C

Ⅰ. 语言点讲解

1. I found most young friends expected me—automatically—to "be" a certain way. (Para. 4)

[分析] 本句的核心结构为"I found + 宾语从句"，其中宾语从句的引导词that省略。破择号中的成分为插入语，起到补充信息的作用。

2. I must admit that I am now a devoted grandmother, but being put in a particular category about that bothered me, as though all of my reactions could be known in advance and belonged to the general group "grandmother" rather than to me. (Para.4)

[分析] 本句中被动语态的动名词结构"being put...that"作主语，代词"that"指代前面提到的grandmother。"as though"引导了虚拟语气的方式状语从句，从句中的主语是"all of my reactions"，"could be known"与"belonged to"为并列谓语。需要注意的是"belong"不能使用被动语态结构。

3. When spend their lives accepting the idea that to be beautiful one must be young, and only beauty saves one from being discarded. (Para.10)

[释义] Through women's whole lives, they are forced the thoughts that beautiful women must be young, and to be beautiful is the only way to prevent them from being rejected.

save... from... 抢救，挽救，拯救

e.g. I saved the animals from the flood. 我把动物从洪水中救出来。

[分析] 本句中"that to be...young"是同谓语从句，作"idea"的同谓语。

4. But who would not when, be to with younger people is so often to be

invisible, to be treated as irrelevant, and sometimes even as disgusting. (Para. 11)

[分析] 本句的核心结构使用的省略结构，完整结构应该是 "But who would not say they like better when..."。在when引导的时间状语从句中，主语是不定式 "to be...people"，系动词is后面接了三个并列表语：to be invisible, to be treated as irrelevant, (to be treated) as disgusting。

5. **We have made old women invisible so that we do not have to confront our society's myths about what makes life valuable or dying painful. (Para. 12)**

[分析] 本句为包含了 "so that" 目的状语的主从句结构。"what makes...painful" 为介词 about 的宾语，其中dying painful为省略结构，承前省略了make。

Ⅱ. 课文赏析

1. 文体特点

本文选材贴近生活，讲述了一个妇女变老的经历以及社会是如何对待年老妇女的。文章以别人对我的关于年龄的评价引入话题，接下来多方面说明 "我" 正在变成年老的妇人。最后分析了产生对老年妇女的看法的原因，较好的回答了年老到底意味着什么。

2. 结构分析

Part Ⅰ (Para.1) Other's comment on my age and my feeling of this.

Part Ⅱ (Para.2-8) Realization of the fact that I'm becoming old.

Part Ⅲ (Para.9-13) The reason for unfair treatment to old women.

Part Ⅳ (Para.14) The real meaning of growing old to me.

Ⅲ. 课后练习答案及解析

Reading skills

XIX.

O O O O F

Comprehension of the Text

XX.

1. uneasy
2. lowered
3. dislike
4. unable
5. Because some of my family members and close friends died or are suffering from disease
6. escape
7. invisible and powerless
8. fewer

Ⅳ. 参考译文

年迈到底意味着什么

先是在我五十八九岁时，后来在六十多岁时，人家对我说 "真不相信你有那个年纪了。你看上去没有那么老。" 起初我会感到那是赞扬，后来觉得有点不安。它使我想起女权运动兴起之前的情况。那时男士们恭维我时说我比 "其他的" 女人 "更精明" 和 "更独立"。

渐渐地愈来愈多的其他经历都在提示我：我的生命状态已真的出现变化了。

首先，我搬家了。在新的环境里我很容易融入到年长者中去，而当年青人与我说话时，他们总会说"你使我想起我外婆"之类的话，外婆?! 我觉得自己被贴上了标签，地位也有点下降了。

我最近的确当外婆了。我发现大多数年青朋友都理所当然地认为我"会"这样或那样。这样的期望很多都与我的感受一致，但有些可不同。我并没有一下就喜欢上了我的外孙。我倒是更牵挂我的女儿，关心她当时的感受。我得说我现在已是一个慈爱的外祖母，但是就此而被归于某一特定的类别却使我不快，好像我所有的反应人们都能预见，也都为一般的"祖母"类的人所有而不是属于我自己似的。

最近我由于判断失误而损失了一些钱，我突然意识到我可能再也无法重获那笔钱了。我已没有足够的时间去再挣那么一笔钱了。

我看到镜中的我有了很多皱纹，感到很难使那外在的我与内在的我相吻合。我觉得自己还是原来的我，可是外观上我却有了变化。我去挂了号整容，但是感到十分忧虑不安。那个诊所里就像在开展营销活动! 医生跟我说他能使我不对自己感到陌生，我会看上去就像我感受到的那样! 整个这一过程使我感到害怕。做完后我是谁? 这张脸? 我内心会怎样感觉? 内外两个形象怎么就联系不起来? 我自己对年老的看法告诉我，自己的外表是难看的。但是我感受到我的内心一点也没有变，那可一点也不难看。

最后，死亡这个直白的现实进入了我的生活。我最年长的一位朋友三年前死于癌症。我父亲在经历了一场后来证明是毫无必要的手术后于两年前去世。另一个好朋友在与癌症搏斗了一年之后也于上个月去世。我的母亲得了严重中风，现正缓慢而痛苦地朝着死亡走去。我顿时意识到我与死亡的接触会越来越频繁。

不仅是年龄，就是生活本身也在告诉我：我正在变成一个年长的，或是年老的妇人。

想想社会上所用的那些非常不尊重人的形容词，它们都是年龄歧视主义用来说老年妇女的：无用，无能，爱抱怨，多病，体弱，保守，僵化，无助，成不了事，满脸皱纹，丑陋不堪，魅力无存，等等，等等。

这种对老年妇女的看法是怎么产生的? 为了弄清这个现象，我们必须看到这个社会一直坚持认为女性只有能吸引男人，对男人有用时才有她们自身的价值。女人毕其一生接受了这个观点，那就是要想漂亮就得年青，只有漂亮才不致被弃。女人的生存，不论是生理的还是心理的，都与其取悦于男人的能力有关。难怪进入老年的前景对于女人来说是那么可怕。我们想用否认衰老来逃避年老所要受的苦难。

老人被送去待在他们自己的牢笼里。他们常说他们更喜欢那样。可谁会不喜欢呢，尤其是当他们与比自己年轻的人相处往往使得自己显得无足轻重，被看作不相干，有时甚至会被讨厌的时候。

我们一贯从各方面瞧不起老年妇女，不让她们参加生产活动，主要从其日渐衰落的能力和作用上去评价她们，还要说她们很可怜。我们把老年妇女送进养老之"家"，那儿没有丝毫促进思考动脑的活动，远离人间的温暖和交往，然后指责她们丧失了思维能力。我们不尊重老年妇女，漠视她们，然后说她们乏味而排斥她们。我们使老年妇女退出社会，销声匿迹，这样我们就不用面对这个社会里关于何以使生命如此宝贵，死亡如此痛苦的问题了。

我们这样地对待她们，然后将对于衰老的种种不幸和恐惧统统归因于衰老过程本身。可怕的并不是衰老，也不是伴随着衰老而来的各种身体上的疾患。可怕的是社会对待老年妇女和她们遇到的各种问题的方式。我们接受并容忍这样的对待，就是接纳了默许这种做法的年龄歧视。

那么年老到底意味着什么呢？对我来说，首先，年纪大了，我仍然是我。不管社会怎样认为我已无足轻重，无能无力，我仍然存在。我是一个人，一个有性别的生命，一个努力奋斗的人，她要探索重大问题，要学习新的东西，要迎接新的挑战，要有新的开端，要担当风险，要考虑结局。即使我的选择已不多了，但前方总还有新路要走。

五、知识链接

The Civil War

The American Civil War was the only war fought on American soil by Americans. 3 million fought and 600,000 died. It was fought in the United States of America between the northern states, popularly referred to as the "Union", and the seceding southern states (in the U.S., The South), calling themselves the Confederate States of America or the "Confederacy" between 1861 and 1865. There is considerable debate about causes that may have motivated the states to war, such as state's rights with respect to the federal government, taxation, and imbalance of trade. But there is no question that the salient issue in the minds of the public and popular press of the time, and the histories written since, was the issue of slavery. Slavery had been abolished in most northern states, but was legal and important to the economy of the Confederacy, which depended on cheap agricultural labor.

The Union was led by President Abraham Lincoln and the Confederacy by President Jefferson Davis. Significant Southern military leaders included Robert E. Lee, Thomas Stonewall Jackson, James Longstreet. Northern leaders included Ulysses Grant, William Sherman, and George Meade.

It started with Lincoln's victory in the presidential election of 1860, which made South Carolina's secession from the Union a foregone conclusion. The state had long been waiting for an event that would unite the South against the antislavery forces. Once the election returns were certain, a special South Carolina convention declared "that the Union now subsisting between South Carolina and other states under the name of the 'United States of America' is hereby dissolved." By February 1, 1861, six more Southern states had seceded. On February 7, the seven states adopted a provisional constitution for the Confederate States of America. The remaining southern states as yet remained in the Union.

Less than a month later, on March 4, 1861, Abraham Lincoln was sworn in as president of the United States. In his inaugural address, he refused to recognize the secession, considering it "legally void". His speech closed with a plea for restoration of the bonds of union. But the South turned deaf ears, and on April 12, guns opened fire on the federal troops stationed at Fort Sumter in the Charleston, South Carolina harbor. The war ended in 1865 with the surrender of Confederate forces. General Lee surrendered his Army of Northern Virginia on 9 April 1865. The Civil War ended with the emancipation of all slaves held in the Confederate States. Slaves were not freed in the remaining states until the passage of the Thirteenth Amendment to the Constitution by 3/4 of the states, which did not occur until December of 1865, 8 months after the end of the war.

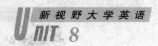

美国内战

美国内战是美国历史上唯一一场美国人在本土打过的战争，共有三百万人卷入到这场战争，60万人丧生。在1861-1865年这场内战中，美利坚合众国分成了两派：被习惯上称作"联邦"的北方各州和由脱离"联邦"的南部州，他们自称为"美国南部联邦"或"南部联邦"。关于导致这场战争的原因有很多争论，例如各州在联邦政府中以及税收和贸易上的权力不均。然而，民众，媒体和历史学界当时最敏感的焦点还是奴隶制的问题。当时，大部分北部诸州都已经废除了奴隶制，然而奴隶制在"南部联邦"不仅是合法的，而且对于依赖廉价农业劳动力的南部经济也是至关重要的。

当时联邦是总统亚伯拉罕·林肯率领尤利西斯格兰特，威廉·谢尔曼，和乔治弥德与"南部联邦"由"总统"杰斐逊·戴维斯率领军时要员罗伯特·E· 李将军，托马斯·斯通沃尔·杰克逊，詹姆斯·朗斯特里特对决。

1860年林肯成功竞选总统成为这场战争的契机，这促使了南部的卡罗来纳州如人们所料的那样脱离了联邦。卡罗来纳州一直在伺机脱离联邦以加入到反废奴制的南部势力当中。当竞选结构已成事实时，南卡罗来纳州特别大会就宣布"美利坚合众国名下包括南卡罗来纳州和其他诸州的'联邦'就此解体"。到1861年1月1日又有其他6个州脱离了联邦。2月7日，这七个州通过了"美国南部联邦"的临时宪法。其他南部州仍然属于联邦。

不到一个月后，1861年3月4号，亚伯拉罕·林肯宣誓就任美国总统。在他的就职演说中，他拒绝承认这些州的脱离，宣布是"无效脱离"。他呼吁重新建立联邦体制。然而"南部联邦"对此置若罔闻，他们在4月12日向联邦在南卡罗来纳港查理斯顿的驻军开火，挑起战事。1865年战争以南部联邦军队的投降而告终。李将军率领他的北弗吉尼亚军于1865年4月9日投降。内战解放了南部联邦的所有奴隶。战争结束八个月后，在1865年12月全国四分之三的州终于通过了第13条宪法修正案。到此，美国所有州的奴隶才都获得了自由。

六、自测题

Directions: In the following passage there are altogether 10 mistakes, one in each numbered line. You may have to change word, add a word or delete a word. If you change a word, cross it out and write correct word in the corresponding blank. If you add a word, put an insertion mark (∧) in the right place and write the missing word in the blank. If you delete a word, cross it out and put a slash (/) in the blank.

American law regards a partnership as an association of
two or more persons who have agreed to combine their labour,
property, and skill, or some or all of them, for the purpose
of engaging in lawful business and shared profits and losses   1. _____
between them.

The parties forming such an association is known as   2. _____
partners. Partners may create a name and use a real family name   3. _____
or names for a partnership. The agreement to form a partnership
is known as an article of co-partership or partership contract. The
importantest provision of the agreement is the one stipulating the   4. _____
manner of distributing profits.

Any number of persons may contract to forming a partnership, and firms of partners may enter into partnership with one another. However, most corporations have not power to enter into partnership if such power is expressly given in the corporate charter or article of association. New members may be admitted into an existed partnership only with the consent of all the partners. The agreement of a partnership has a definite term of years in general. If no duration is specified, it is said to be a partnership at will and can legally terminate at any time by any partners. A partnership can be dissolved or terminated and the terms of the partnership agreement modified at any time.

5. _____

6. _____

7. _____

8. _____

9. _____

10. _____

答案与解析

1. 将shared改为sharing。该组织联合几方或全部的劳动、财产或技术，以从事合法的商业活动为目的，共享利润，共担损失。本题辨析分词作定语时的误用。句中，engaging in lawful business和shared profits and losses between them，作the purpose的定语。engaging与shared是并列的，他们的共同的逻辑主语是an association of two or more persons，在逻辑关系上，都是主动的，而且，share business本应该是动宾关系，而过去分词shared的误用却改变了这种关系，使shared profits成为一个由过去分词修饰的名词短语：共享的利润。从而使句法混乱，因此，将shared改为sharing。

2. 将is改为are。构成这种组织的各方称为合伙人。本题辨析谓语动词单复数的误用。本句的主语是The parties，故谓语动词应该用are，在使用时，不要受an association的干扰。

3. 将and改为or。合伙人可以给合伙企业起一个名字，也可以使用一两个真实的姓名作为合伙企业的名称。本题辨析并列连词的误用。表示并列关系常用的连词有两个：即and和or。and表示"和……"表示兼而有之，or表示"或……"，表示选择。句中的意思是：可以起一个名字，或者可以使用一个或几个真实的姓名。因此，不用and，而该用or。

4. 将importantest改为most important。其中最重要的条款就是对如何分配利润做出的规定。本题辨析形容词最高级形式的误用。形容词的最高级有两种构成方法，一般情况下，加"est"，但多音节词则是most+形容词原形。句中，important属多音节词，正确的最高级形式应为most important。

5. 将forming改为form。形成合伙企业的人数不限。合伙企业之间也可以形成合伙企业。本题辨析非谓语动词形式的误用。contract动词，意为"签订合同"，后面跟动词不定式作宾语contract to do sth.。故文中，应为contract to form,而不应为forming。

6. 将not改为no。然而，除非公司章程明确赋予该公司拥有达成合伙企业的权力，否则大多数公司不可以与他人达成合伙企业。本题辨析否定词词类的误用。句中常用的否定词有not和no。not为副词，用来修饰动词；no是形容词，修饰名词。句中，power是名词，故用not是不正确的。

7. 将if改为unless。本题辨析连接词的误用。全句因if (如果) 误用，而失去了逻辑连贯性。应将if改为unless引导的条件状语从句。

8. 将existed改为existing。新合伙人只有得到全体合伙人的同意才能被接纳为合伙人。本题辨析作定语时分词的误用。分词在作前置定语时，现在分词表示"现在"，过去分词表示"过去"，主要是时间上的差异。根据句意，partnership指的是"现在存在的合伙关系"，并非指"合伙关系已成为过去"。因此，应将existed改为existing。

9. 将terminate改为be terminated。如果未对此进行规定，则该合伙称为任意合伙，可按合伙人的要求随时予解散。本题辨析动词语态的误用。本句是一个长句子。can terminate的主语为it，代指agreement，因此，主语和谓语构成事实上的被动关系。terminate这一主动的用法显然与句法不合，故改为be terminated。

10. 将partners改为partner。合伙企业可以随时予以解散。终止修改合伙协议。本题辨析名词单复数的误用。any在表示"任意"，"任何的"这一含义时，后面可跟不可数或者可数名词的单数形式。本句any不是"一些"，而是"任何"的意思，因而partners的用法是错误的。

Unit 9

一、预习重点

1. What is the French government's attitude towards Euro Disneyland near Pairs?
2. What advantages does Euro Disneyland have in attracting tourist?
3. What criticism of the Disney management on the issue of the Euro Disneyland project is implied in the passage?
4. What should we do towards foreign cultural invasion?
5. What are your opinions about having a foreign recreation moved into your country?

二、学习重点和难点

I．词汇和短语

Section A: contend, attendance, legend, offend, delicate, invade, stretch, sensitive, prominent; shave off, take sb. to court, put before, for all, come into, so far, in response to, focuse on, in a flash

Section B: analysis, analyse/-yze, analyst, franc, elaborate, sustain, reverse, amid; gear up, warn against, react to, be superior to, on a/an...basis, in the long term, hang over, account for, in line with

II．语法项目

① "For all + a noun phrase" 尽管，虽然
② "rather than" 连接并列结构
③ 介词 "given" 的用法

III．写作技巧

总分写作法扩展段落

三、文化知识

I．课文大背景

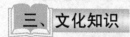

Theme Park 主题公园

Known as amusement park, it is an outdoor area containing amusements , such as games of skill and big machines to ride on, which are sometimes all based on a single subject, for example, space travel. The first theme park was Disneyland, at Anaheim (阿纳海姆，加州西南部城市) , California, opened in 1995 and based on Walt Disney's cartoon characters. Walt Disney, American animator, showman, and film producer noted for his creation of the cartoon characters Mickey Mouse（米老鼠）and Donald Duck（唐老鸭）, he produced the first animated film with sound (有声动画片) , *Steamboat Willie*（《威利号汽船》)(1928) , and the first full-length animated feature, *Snow White* (1938)。The name of the first theme park is Magic Kingdom in Cailifornia sometimes used instead of Disneyland in California. Euro Disneyland is another extremely large amusement park, run by the Walt Disney Company, just outside Paris in France. It is based on Disneyland and Disneyworld in the U.S.

II. 课文知识点

1. TGV 法国高速电气列车

The name "Train à Grande Vitesse (TGV)" translated into English means high speed train. The TGV is a system which comprises train, track, and signaling technologies that when combined make high speeds (typically 300 km/h, or 186 mph) possible. The TGV system is owned and operated by SNCF (法国国营铁路公司), the French national railways, and is an integral part of French rail travel.

The TGV program was launched in the late 1960s. In its early stages, the program was considered a technological dead end. Conventional wisdom at the time held that steel wheel on steel rail technology had been explored and understood to its fullest, and it was time to move on to more innovative technologies like magnetic levitation (磁悬浮力) and jet-powered hover trains (喷气式翱翔列车). As a result, the project did not originally receive any government funding.

Today, there are three major trunk lines radiating out of Paris, the most recent one being the Nord-Europe line, opened in 1993 and connects Paris to Lille (里尔，法国北部城市), Belgium, the Netherlands, Germany, and Britain through the Channel tunnel. Extensions continue to be built, although budgetary constraints have slowed the momentum (势头) of the TGV expansion.

2. Sleeping Beauty 睡美人

Sleeping Beauty is a fairy-tale heroine who slept for 100 years until wakened by the kiss of a prince. The story of *Sleeping Beauty* formed the subject of a ballet by Tchaikovsky (柴可夫斯基).

3. Snow White 白雪公主

Snow White is the main character in an old fairy tale. Snow White is a beautiful princess who has a jealous stepmother. The stepmother owns a magic mirror which when asked "Mirror, mirror, on the wall, who is the fairest (最美丽的) of us all?" always answers that she is the most beautiful, until one day it says "Snow White". The stepmother is very angry and sends Snow White into the forest to be killed. Snow White does not die, but lives with seven Dwarfs (侏儒，小矮人). Her stepmother tries to kill her with a poisoned apple, but instead of dying she goes to sleep until a prince kisses her and wakes her, and they live happily ever after.

4. Peter Pan 彼得·潘

Peter Pan is the main character in a story titled *Peter and Wendy* by James M. Barrie (詹姆斯·马修·巴里) (Scottish playwright and novelist, 1860-1937), a young boy who never grows up but lives in a magic land called Never-never Land (想象中的地方，故事中指虚无岛). In the story, three children, Michael, John, and Wendy, go with Peter Pan and Tinkerbell to stay in the Never-Never Land, where they have many adventures. Peter Pan's enemy in the story is Captain Hook, an evil pirate (海盗) who has a metal hook in the place of one of his hands. Captain Hook lost his hand in a fight with Peter Pan, and Peter Pan threw the hand into some water. It was eaten by a crocodile, who liked the taste so much that it then followed Captain Hook around trying to catch and eat the rest of him.

5. Pinocchio 皮诺曹

The international classic of childhood literature *Pinocchio* was written by Carlo Lorenzini (Italian journalist and writer, 1826-1890), under the pen name of C. Collodi, and first published in Rome in 1881. Its hero Pinocchio is the little wooden puppet who walks and talks, and whose nose grows every time he tells a lie.

6. Mickey Mouse 米老鼠

Mickey Mouse is probably the most famous of the Disney cartoon characters. Making his debut (初次登场) in *Steamboat Willie* at the Colony Theatre in New York City on November 18, 1928, Mickey went on to star in over 120 different cartoons. He also starred in "The Mickey Mouse Club" television show of the 1950s.

Mickey Mouse's original drawings used circles for his head, body and ears. 1939's *The Pointer* saw a bold, new design for Mickey as his body became more pear-shaped and pupils were added to his eyes to increase his range of expression. Later on, animators (漫画家) of the 1940s would add a perspective aspect to his ears, giving them a three-dimensional effect. This change, however, was short-lived. The Mickey Mouse of today appears much as he did in the early days with the exception of a costume change here and there.

Originally, Mickey was voiced (配音) by Walt Disney himself. Later, those duties were assumed by Jim Macdonald and today Wayne Allwine provides Mickey's distinctive voice.

Mickey Mouse has appeared on thousands of merchandise items, and currently holds the esteemed title of Chief Greeter at the Disney theme parks.

7. Jules Verne 儒勒·凡尔纳

Jules Verne (1828-1905) was a French writer and a pioneer of the science fiction genre (类型). His most famous books are *Journey to the Centre of the Earth* (《地心之旅》), *Twenty Thousand Leagues Under the Sea* (《海岛两万里》), and *Around the World in Eighty Days* (《八十天周游世界》).

Verne was born in Nantes (南特，法国西部港口城市) to attorney (律师) Pierre Verne and his wife Sophie. The oldest of the family's five children, he spent his early years at home with his parents, on a nearby island in the Loire River (卢瓦尔河). This isolated setting helped to strengthen both his imagination and the bond between him and his younger brother Paul. At the age of nine, he and his younger brother were sent to boarding school (寄宿学校) at the Nantes. Verne's fascination with adventure asserted itself at an early age, inspiring him at one point to stow away on a ship bound for the Orient. His voyage was cut short, however, as he found his father waiting for him at the next port.

About 1848, in conjunction with Michel Carre, he began writing librettos (歌剧、音乐剧等的歌词或剧本) for operettas (小歌剧). For some years his attentions were divided between the theatre and work, but some of his travellers' stories seem to have revealed to him the true direction of his talent: the telling of delightfully extravagant voyages and adventures to which cleverly prepared scientific and geographical details lent an air of verisimilitude (逼真).

When Verne's father discovered that his son was writing rather than studying the law, he promptly withdrew his financial support. Consequently, the author was forced to support himself with the income from his work, which he found to be a difficult proposition with his limited contacts. During this period, he met the authors Alexandre Dumas (大仲马) and Victor Hugo (维克多·雨果), who offered him some advice on his writing.

It was during this period that Verne met and married Honorine Morel, a widow with two daughters. At his father's urging, Verne took a job as a stockbroker (股票经纪人), though with his wife's encouragement he continued to write.

The stories he wrote were an enormous success, and was republished in a number of languages. Verne became wealthy and famous.

四、课文精讲

Section A

Ⅰ. 短语与词汇详解

1. contend

[词义] v. ① 声称；② 竞争；③ 斗争

[例句] She contended that the report was deficient. 她声称该报告有欠缺。

Several teams are contending for the prize. 有几个队在争夺锦标。

John has to contend with great difficulties. 约翰得与那些艰难困苦做斗争。

[辨析] contend, compete

contend 指不断努力以求克敌，如：Our basketball team is contending with one from the next town for the championship. 我们篮球队正与邻镇的篮球队争夺冠军。

compete 是指在竞争环境中与人相争并设法获胜，争得名次、奖品，不含有将对手征服的意思，如：Only two boys are competing for the cup. 只有两个男孩争夺奖杯。

2. attendance

[词义] n. ① 出席人数，出席者；② 出席

[例句] There was a small attendance at the meeting. 出席这次会议的人很少。

You have missed several attendances this term. 这学期你有几次缺席。

[辨析] attendance，presence

attendance, presence 表示"出席"之动作，attendance=presence，如：attendance/presence at the meeting 出席会议。

attendance 还表示"出席人数，出席者"。

3. legend

[词义] n. ① 传说，传奇故事；② 传说中的人（或事）

[例句] The dance was based on several Chinese legends.

这舞蹈是根据一些中国传说编的。

Both men were legends in their own time. 这两个人当时都是传奇人物。

4. contemplate

[词义] vt. ① 对……周密考虑；② 凝视

[搭配] contemplate on/upon 深思默想，深思熟虑

[例句] He contemplated what the future would be like without the children.

他思忖要是没有这些孩子未来会是什么样子。

She stood contemplating herself in the mirror. 她站着，凝视着镜中的自己。

5. offend

[词义] *vt.* ① 冒犯，得罪；② 违犯

[搭配] offend sb. 冒犯某人；be offended with/by/sb. for sth. 因某事对某人生气；offend against custom 违反习惯；offend against the law 违法

[例句] I'm sorry to have offended you with so many questions on such an occasion.

在这种场合问了你这些问题，不便之处请多原谅。

Some criminals are likely to offend again when they are released.

这些罪犯被释放后有可能重新犯罪。

[辨析] offend，insult

offend 是在另一个人心里引起不愉快、受伤的感觉或强烈的反感，如：Her words offended me. 她的话伤了我的感情。

insult 暗含全然的不敏感、傲慢或轻视的粗鲁或导致羞辱或窘迫，如：He insulted her by calling her a stupid fool. 他叫她笨蛋来侮辱了她。

6. delicate

[词义] *adj.* ① 棘手的，微妙的；② 精巧的，精致的，精美的；③ 娇弱的，体质差的

[搭配] delicate subject 微妙的主题

[例句] The negotiations are at a delicate stage. 谈判正处于微妙的阶段。

The scientist needs some delicate instruments.

这位科学家需要一些精密的仪器。

Her delicate health needs great care. 她娇弱的身体需要小心照料。

7. invade

[词义] *vt.* 侵略，侵袭

[搭配] invade sb's rights 侵犯某人的权利

[例句] Famous people often find their privacy is invaded by the press.

名人总是发现他们的隐私被报界侵犯。

[派生] invasion *n.* 入侵

8. stretch

[词义] *vi.* 伸展，延伸，延续

[搭配] at a stretch 不停地，连续地

[例句] The desert stretched away into the distance. 沙漠一直延伸到远方。

She stretched herself to provide for the family. 她竭尽全力养家糊口。

[辨析] stretch, elongate

stretch 与 elongate 通常都表示空间的"延长"，差异仅在于前者不正式，后者正式且多见于科技语言，如：A piece of rubber can be elongate by stretching. 一块橡皮可以拉长。

9. prominent

[词义] *adj.* ① 突出的，杰出的；② 突起的

[例句] The beautiful star's big mouth is the most prominent feature of her.

那个漂亮明星最显著的特征是大嘴。

Having a lean, gaunt frame with prominent bones.
骨瘦如柴的身材又细又瘦，骨骼突出。

10. shave off 剃（胡须、毛发等）

[例句] Most professional male swimmers shave off their body hair to make them more streamlined and thus swim faster. 大部分男性职业游泳运动员把体毛剃了，使自己身体更具流线型，以游得更快。

11. take sb. to court 对某人提出起诉

[例句] The buyer signed the contract, but then did not carry it out, so the seller took him to court.
购买者签了合同，但是没有执行，所以销售者把他告上了法庭。

12. put before 认为……比……更重要

[例句] He puts his health before all other considerations.
他认为他的键康比别的什么都重要。

13. for all 尽管

[例句] For all her privilege and wealth, life had not been easy and the experiences of childhood had left an indelible mark on her mind.
尽管总她享有特权和财富，可是她的生活一直是很不容易，童年的经历在她的脑海中留下了一个抹不去的印记。

14. come into 开始进入（某种活动或状态）

[例句] The planned cable will also link to other cable systems and give direct connections to the rest of the world, and is set to come into service by the end of 1999. 计划中的电缆也将连接到其他电缆系统，以便能与世界其他地方直接相连，并定在1999年底前投入使用。

15. so far 到目前为止，迄今为止

[例句] Meanwhile, health campaigns have largely failed so far to change their behavior. 同时，健康运动到目前为止总体上没能改变他们的行为。

16. in response to 作为对……的答复，作为对……的反应

[例句] This scheme started in the 1980s, in response to the demand from older people who were unable to find an appropriate insurance company. 这计划是在20世纪80年代开始的，是对那些无法找到合适保险公司的老年人的要求的回应。

17. focus on 把（注意力等）集中在

[例句] Since their work focused on certain topics it was natural that they particularly looked for evidence relating to these topics. 由于他们的工作是集中在某些话题，很自然，他们要特别寻找与这些话题相关的证据。

18. in a flash 转眼间，一眨眼

[例句] It happened in a flash, although in retrospect everything seemed to occur in slow motion.
尽管回想起来一切似乎都是慢慢地出现的，可是这却是眨眼间发生的。

Ⅱ. 难句解析

1. Does this mean that French men seeking work with the Disney organization must shave off their moustaches too? (Para. 3)

[释义] Does this mean that French men who want to work with the Disney organization must also remove their moustaches?

245

[分析] 本句的主干是 "Does this mean that French men...must shave off their moustaches too?" 句中的现在分词短语 "seeking work...organization" 作定语修饰 "French men"。本句的难度在于理解本句暗含的意思。通常法国人喜欢留胡须，而美国人则恰恰相反。从文章下面的内容可以知道，欧洲迪斯尼乐园的员工们都得刮去胡须以增加主题公园的美国味。这就是欧洲迪斯尼乐园造成的文化冲突。

2. **A labor inspector took the Disney organization to court this week, contending that the company's dress and appearance code—which bans moustaches, beards, excess weight, short skirts and fancy stockings—offends individual liberty and violates French labor law. (Para. 5)**

[释义] A labor inspector forced the Disney organization to answer charges in a court of law this week. The inspector stated that the company's rules—according to which its employees are not allowed to have moustaches or beards, their body weight should not exceed its standards and they are not allowed to wear short skirts and fancy stockings—disregard individual liberty and fail to comply with French labor law.

[分析] 本句的核心结构为 "A labor inspector...this week"。现在分词短语 "contending that...labor law" 作伴随状语。在该分词结构中有that引导的宾语从句 "the company's dress and appearance code...offends...labor law"。宾语从句中的破则号部分相当于非限性定语从句 "which...stocking" 作宾语从句主语的定语。

3. **The case is an illustration of some of the delicate cultural issues the company faces as it gets ready to open its theme park 20 miles (32 kilometers) east of Paris in five months...(Para. 6)**

[释义] This case provides a good example of some of the cultural issues the company is now faced with and these issues need to be treated carefully or sensitively in order to avoid causing offence or failure when it starts off opening its theme park which is 20 miles (32 kilometers) east of Paris in five months...

[分析] "the company faces" 为定语从句，省略了引导词that/which。as 引导的时间状语从句。

4. **Anyway, a company spokesman says, no one has yet put his moustache before a job. (Para. 7)**

[释义] A company spokesman said that people believed that a job was more important than their moustaches.

put... before/over... 把……看得……更重要，比……更优先考虑……

e.g. As a scientist, he always put his discovery before/over the award. 作为一个科学家，比起奖励而言，他更看重自己的发现。

[分析] 本句使用了插入语（parenthesis）结构，将 "a company spokesman says" 当作插入语。

5. **Financial experts say that Euro Disneyland, the first phase of which is costing an estimated $3.6 billion, is essential to Disney's overall fortunes, which have been hit by competition and declining attendance in the United States. (Para. 11)**

[释义] Financial experts said that the first stage of building Euro Disneyland was costing an estimated \$3.6 billion and Euro Disneyland was extremely important to the whole Disney organization financially because it had been severely affected by competition and the number of the people who visited Disneyland and Disney world in the United States was declining.

[分析] 本句的主干是 "Financial experts say + that宾语从句"。宾语从句的主干为 "that Euro Disneyland is essential to Disney's overall fortunes"。在宾语从句中使用了两个非限制性定语从句。第一个为 "the first phase of which is...billion" 修饰 "Euro Disneyland"；第二个定语从句为 "which have been...States" 修饰先行词 "fortunes"。

6. The Disney management is stressing this tradition in an apparent response to suggestions that it is culturally insensitive. (Para. 13)

[释义] The Disney management is giving special importance to this tradition as a clear reply to suggestions that it does not take into consideration the fact that each country has its own unique cultural tradition.

[分析] suggestion 在本句的意思是 "暗示，不明说"，相当于"a subtle pointing out"。"that it...insensitive" 为suggestions 的同位语从句。

7. "The legends and fairy tales which come from Europe figure prominently in the creative development of the theme park."(Para. 13)

[释义] "The legends and fairy tales which originate from Europe are important and are included noticeably in the creative development of the theme park."

figure *vi.* 扮演角色，起到举足轻重的作用，相当于 "be or play a role or part of or in..."

e.g. Roger figured as chief guest. 罗杰以主客姿态出现。

[分析] 本句的主干为 "the legends...figure...park"。"which come...Europe" 为限制性定语从句修饰主语。本句的难点在于掌握动词figure，意思是"扮演角色"，"起到举足轻重作用"，相当于 "be or play a role or part of or in..."。

8. In this way, he said, people who might otherwise have contemplated a vacation in the United States will be happy to stay on this side of the Atlantic. (Para. 15)

[释义] He said that in this way people who might otherwise have considered spending a vacation in the United States would be ready to have their vacation in Europe.

[分析] 本句中 "who might...the Unite States" 为定语从句修饰people。"might otherwise have considered" 结构表示语气不肯定的推测判断。"side of the Atlantic" 指的是欧洲。

III. 重点语法讲解

1."for all + noun phrase/clause" 结构

"for all" 结构中 "for all" 相当于despite，意思是 "尽管，虽然"，作让步状语。相当于though/although 引导的让步性状语从句。其后面即可以语名词性短语连用，也可接短句。

For all his knowledge and experience, he is not conceited.

尽管他有丰富的知识和经验，可他并不自满。

For all the talk of "cuts", state spending on health has increased by nearly a third in real terms since 1979.

247

尽管一直在谈"削减"，但实际上政府在健康问题上的开支从1979年以来上涨了三分之一。

For all its concern about foreign cultural invasion and its defense against the pollution of the French language by English words, France's Socialist government has been untroubled about putting such a huge American symbol on the doorstep of the capital. (Para. 9) 尽管对外国文化入侵感到不安，尽管要保护法语不受英语的污染，法国的社会党政府对将这么庞大的美国文化的象征放在首都门口却一点都不担忧。

"for all someone knows/cares"通常为口语用法，相当于"that even if something was true, a particular person would not know/care about it"，意思是"尽管/即使……是真的，也没有人会知道或者在意的"。

He might be a murderer, for all we know. 反正我们不知道，即使他可能是杀人犯。

I might as well be dead, for all you care. 即使我可能会死，反正你也不会在意的。

2."rather than" 连接并列结构

"rather than"作为连词词组，在句中连接两个语法成分相同（或并列）的结构。意思"是……而非……"，"胜于"，相当于"one thing is preferred to another or happens instead of another"。

Dick chose to quit rather than admit that he had made a mistake.

迪克选择放弃而不是承认自己犯了错误。（连接两个动词不定式宾语，其中后一个to省略）

Financial support will be offered by private companies rather than the government.

是私人公司而非政府提供财政支持。（连接两个介词的宾语）

We want the matter settled sooner rather than later.

我们希望这件事尽快解决而不以后解决。（连接并列时间状语）

Ⅳ. 课文赏析

1．文体特点

本文最突出的特点是综合运用演绎法（从概括到具体）和归纳法（从具体到概括）来阐述观点。这样组织材料，使读者对这一文化问题有全面透彻的了解，使文章颇具说服力。文章幽默简洁的开头也是独树一帜，通过幽默的设问对答，把读者的好奇心调动起来。

本文是一篇记叙文，以迪斯尼公司面临的一个案件引出主题，吸引读者继续读下去，条理清楚、层次分明。

2．结构分析

Part Ⅰ (Para.1-7) A law case reflecting the cultural clash the Disney organization faces.

Part Ⅱ (Para.8) A transitional paragraph linking the first part with the third.

Part Ⅲ (Para.9-18) The different concerns from the French government towards the Euro Disney near Paris, from the French intellectuals and kids and from the Disney organization.

Ⅴ. 课后练习答案及解析

Comprehension of the Text

Ⅱ.

1. Because he believed that the company's dress and appearance code offended individual liberty and violated French labor law.

2. To show that the company faces some of the delicate cultural issues like this while it gets ready to open its theme park near Paris.

3. It argues that all employees have to obey the company's code about appearance and it believes that an employee should think a job is more important than his moustache.

4. It made an extraordinary series of tax and financial concessions in order to attract it.

5. They have had a negative attitude towards the project and have criticized it.

6. The Disney management has been criticized as being culturally insensitive.

7. The Disney management has tried to make Euro Disneyland unique in a manner appropriate to its European home. For example, European legends and fairy tales figure prominently in the creative development of the theme park. What's more, the direction signs will be in French as well as in English and some performers will chat in French, Spanish and English.

8. Its short distance to Paris.

Vocabulary

III. ▶

1. violated 译文: 司马特说，"如果政府能证明我们所有的报道都是不恰当的，那意味着人权不会再受到侵犯，那么我只会感到欣慰。"

2. stretch 译文: 凭借报纸的发行，当地媒体的潜在客户可能会多达数千万。

3. contended 译文: 律师声称，他的当事人是无辜的，该公司关于外表的规定没有侵犯到个人自由。

4. invasion 译文: 法国政府号召人民抵御外来文化的入侵，捍卫本国语言的纯洁性。

5. figured 译文: 在达成协议的过程中，他们否认他们的让步起了重要作用。

6. attendance 译文: 在最初的几年中，尽管游客数量非常多，可是欧洲迪尼斯乐园的支出仍然超过了收入。

7. concessions 译文: 去年，政府通过一系列减税政策来为宾馆和旅游部门引进个人资金。

8. unique 译文: 为了使欧洲迪尼斯乐园具有自己独特的风格，主题乐园的开发涉及了欧洲传说和童话故事。

IV. ▶

1. made some concessions 译文: 冲突双方在昨天的会谈中都做出了让步。

2. putting...before 译文: 众所周知，母亲们把家庭利益放在个人利益之上。

3. be untroubled about 译文: 政府似乎对在其首都建立一个美国文化的象征——迪尼斯乐园一点也不感到担忧。

4. take it to court 译文: 工人们要求公司放弃在衣着方面的要求，否则，他们将把其告上法庭。

5. came into service 译文: 第一条高速电气铁路开通20年，在法国就有了关于高速列车的想法。

6. in response to 译文: 为了回应当地知识分子对于其文化盲目性的批评，公司已经改变了关于主题公园的最初的设计方案。

7. rather than 译文: 迪尼斯乐园的一些员工宁愿遵从公司的规定，宁愿剃掉胡须，也不愿丢掉工作。

8. focused on 译文: 作者认为迪尼斯公司在头发问题上太在意了。

Collocation

V. ▶

1. peace 译文：难怪那些寻求国家间和平的人们应该依靠法律法规，来调节和减少国家间使用武力。

2. attention 译文：骄傲是一种状态，指人们对自身及其行为的关注和认可。

3. solution 译文：约翰多布尼并不是傻子，他已经找到了解决途径，因为他发现了凌晨3点出现的不明噪音的来源。

4. advice 译文：尽管员工们进行了全面的培训，但他们仍可以就一些复杂的问题向专家请教。

5. opportunity 译文：他们寻求机会在安全的地方重建家园，并希望有一天能重返故土。

6. guidance 译文：买方通常会通过电话寻求指导，解决他们的疑问。

7. permission 译文：为给孩子请假，家长必须要提前写信以征得校长的同意。

8. challenge 译文：此刻，他变得更加好斗，眼睛不停地转来转去，似乎在寻找新的机会。

Word Building

VI. ▶

1. endurance 译文：身体的耐力可以通过爬山来增强。

2. tolerance 译文：他一贯信守自己的原则——无论人民的宗教教信仰如何，他都会尊重和容忍那些按照自己的信条追求美好生活的人。

3. defiance 译文：为表示对陌生人的敌意，她握紧着拳头，嘴巴紧闭。

4. attendance 译文：参加大会的人数逐年增加，吸引了越来越多的国际代表。

5. acceptance 译文：她强调，这样调查不会妨碍发展或阻碍公司的进程，相反，会促进公众接纳新科技。

6. admittance 译文：对任何想进入你家的来访者的身份，你都要认真检查。

7. Reliance 译文：对父母的依赖不是引起儿童成长问题的惟一因素。

8. Observance 译文：习俗的遵守通常是由社会的认可并加以鼓励，而没有必要用法律来强制执行。

VII. ▶

1. unanimous 译文：这需要得到全体成员国的一致同意。但显然爱尔兰和卢森堡会强烈反对。

2. unify 译文：自私会导致分裂，关爱会达成和平与统一。

3. unicycle 译文：舞台上，一位年轻人骑着一辆挂满气球和装饰物的独轮车。

4. unique 译文：这些窗户给予她全方位的视角来观赏这个地方。

5. uniform 译文：据说，他们被强行穿上了监狱的制服，并且被铐在密室的门闩上至少长达17天之久，以防他们脱掉制服。

6. unite 译文：那些人企图用武力来统一欧洲，但却失败了。

7. union 译文：该学者向他的朋友抱怨说，进入这个协会很难，而且在这行业谋生也很难。

8. unity 译文：为了应对这一挑战，必须不仅在语言上，在行动上也要奠定坚实的基础。

Structure

VIII. ▶

1. For all the concept of the theme park closely based on the original Magic Kingdom

in California and Walt Disney World in Florida, Euro Disneyland will be unique in a manner appropriate to its European home.

译文: 尽管主题公园的概念将严格以加利福尼亚洲的奇妙王国和佛罗里达州的沃尔特·迪斯尼乐园为基础，但欧洲迪斯尼乐园将具有欧洲的独特风格。

2. For all its American name, the theme park looked European.

译文: 尽管主题公园有一个美国名字，但看起来很欧洲化。

3. For all the high attendance levels, the company sustained a net loss for the financial year.

译文: 尽管游客很多，公司在这个财政年度里还是遭受了净亏损。

4. For all the changes, the prime emphasis in the retail market, so far as movies are concerned, still seems to be on the past, and predominantly on the mainstream Hollywood past.

译文: 尽管变化很快，但在电影业，零售市场的重点似乎还得放在过去，主流是好莱坞往事。

5. For all sharp criticism of it, the article was widely read and well appreciated.

译文: 尽管这篇文章遭受到了一些批评，但还是被广泛阅读和受到欣赏。

IX. ▶

1. He was compelled to spend most of the time talking to Mrs. Harlowe rather than to his daughter.

译文: 他不得不花大量的时间与哈劳沃夫人谈话，而不是与她女儿。

2. I believe it is important to invest in new machinery rather than to deposit the money in banks.

译文: 我认为重要的是要把钱投资在新机器上，而不是把它存在银行里。

3. We ought to check up the results of the research project rather than just accept what he says.

译文: 我们应该核对研究项目的结果，而不是仅接受他的一面之辞。

4. He always prefers starting early and making necessary preparations rather than leaving everything to the last minute.

译文: 他总是喜欢提前动手做好必要的准备工作，而不是把一切都留到最后一分钟才做。

5. It ought to be your boss to sign the contract rather than you.

译文: 应该由你的老板来签这个合同，而不是你。

Translation

X. ▶

1. When he shaved his beard off, he looked ten years younger.

2. The delay is a perfect illustration of why we need a new computer system.

3. For all her privilege and wealth, life had not been easy and the experiences of childhood sufferings had left a deep mark on her life.

4. So far, 150 have been tested, and the full statistical results will be available soon.

5. The company has changed some of its working practices in response to criticism by government inspectors.

6. Tonight's program focuses on the way homelessness affects the young.

7. It happened in a flash, although in retrospect everything seemed to occur in slow motion.

8. The issue was expected to figure importantly in their discussion.

251

XI.

1. 迪斯尼公司正准备五个月后在巴黎以东20英里（32公里）的地方建造一个主题公园，而这一案子正说明了公司面临的一些文化方面的棘手问题。

2. 迪斯尼管理层正在为这一主题公园组织一支他们称为"演职人员"的12,000人的队伍。管理方说所有的雇员，从刷瓶工到总裁，他们的工作都类似于演员，都得服从关于仪表的规定。

3. 公司发言人说，不管怎样，至今还没有人把胡子看得比工作还重要。正如一个新来的"演职人员"所说："你必须相信你这份工作的意义，不然的话日子不好过。"

4. 主题公园本身只不过是这一巨大综合项目的一部分。综合项目包括住房、办公楼，以及将一直延续到下一世纪、包括影视拍摄设施在内的度假胜地开发。

5. 如果欧洲迪斯尼乐园获得成功—— 迄今为止在法国开设的主题公园都不成功——到本世纪末很可能会再建第二甚至第三个主题公园。

6. 迪斯尼管理层强调这一传统，显然这是对有人暗示迪斯尼管理层在文化传统方面麻木不仁的回应。

7. 欧洲迪斯尼乐园距巴黎不远，这肯定颇具吸引力。任何人厌倦了那里的美式或仿冒的欧式文化，就可乘快速列车，不到一小时就可到达罗浮宫，一瞬间就从米尼老鼠身边来到了蒙娜? 丽莎面前。

8. 东欧的开放对迪斯尼来说又是一大收获，他们认为几百万人将会把迪斯尼乐园作为其首次西欧之旅的首选之地。

Essay Summary

XII.

ACBBC　DBBDC　ADDAB　CABDC

Text Structure Analysis

XIII.

Paras. 13—14

(1) figure prominently in the creative development of the theme park

(2) features well-known European actors

(3) French as well as English, and some performers will chat in French, Spanish and English

Paras. 15—16

(1) a basically American experience

(2) "messy hair and hairy chins"

(3) even offending mustaches

VI. 参考译文

使欧洲迪斯尼乐园更欧洲化

米老鼠有胡须吗?

没有。

这是不是说法国人要想在迪斯尼工作就必须剃掉胡子才行?

这得看情况了。

一位劳工问题督察员本周将迪斯尼公司告上了法庭，他声称公司的着装规定——不准蓄胡须，不准体重超标，不准穿超短裙和花哨的袜子——侵犯了个人自由，也违反了法国的劳工法。

迪斯尼公司正准备五个月后在巴黎以东20英里（32公里）的地方修建一个主题公园，而这一案子正说明了公司面临的一些文化方面的棘手问题。

迪斯尼管理层正在为这一主题公园组织一支他们称为"演职人员"的12,000人的队伍。管理方说所有的雇员，从刷瓶工到总裁，他们的工作都类似于演员，都得服从关于仪表的规定。公司发言人说，不管怎样，至今还没有人把胡子看得比工作还重要。正如一个新来的"演职人员"所说："你必须相信你这份工作的意义，不然的话日子不好过。"

然而人们怎样看待欧洲迪斯尼乐园？各处的人们想知道欧洲人是否会欢迎美国式的消遣活动。

尽管对外国文化的入侵感到不安，尽管要保护法语不受英语的污染，法国的社会党政府对将这么庞大的美国文化的象征放在首都门口却并不担忧，而是更多地关心其社会效果。为了将这一主题公园留在这里，而不是建在充满阳光的西班牙，法国政府做出了税收和财政方面的一系列重大让步。

主题公园本身只不过是这一巨大综合项目的一部分。综合项目包括住房、办公楼，以及将一直延续到下一世纪、包括影视拍摄设施在内的度假胜地开发。作为与迪斯尼公司合作协议的一部分，政府正在铺设新的公路并支付建设款项，它是巴黎地区快速轨道交通的延伸，甚至可直接连接到通往英吉利海峡隧道的高速电气铁路（TGV）。欧洲迪斯尼乐园的正门前正在建设高速电气铁路火车站，预定于1994年交付使用。

如果欧洲迪斯尼乐园获得成功——迄今为止在法国开设的主题公园都不成功——到本世纪末很可能会再建第二甚至第三个主题公园。欧洲迪斯尼乐园的第一期工程预计将花费36亿美元，财政专家说这一项目对迪斯尼的总体财富非常重要。迪斯尼在美国已遭遇到了竞争，游客量正在下降。

法国的知识分子们对这个项目并无好感，然而孩子们却不管这些。睡美人、白雪公主、彼得·潘和匹诺曹都是欧洲童话故事里的人物，这里的孩子对他们的熟悉程度丝毫不亚于美国的孩子。在法国孩子眼里，米老鼠是法国人；在意大利孩子眼里，米老鼠是意大利人。

迪斯尼管理层强调这一传统，显然这是对有人暗示迪斯尼管理层在文化传统方面麻木不仁的回应。尽管主题公园这一概念是以加利福尼亚州的奇妙王国和佛罗里达州的沃尔特·迪斯尼世界为基础的，但"欧洲迪斯尼乐园将具有欧洲的独特风格，"公司说。"主题公园的创造性发挥突出地表现了欧洲的传说和童话故事，"公司的行政人员指出，例如，睡美人的城堡这个主题公园的中心建筑不是像一些人所想的那样根据好莱坞的作品创造的，而是根据一本欧洲中世纪的书中的插图建造的。同样，根据儒勒·凡尔纳所写的冒险故事拍摄的360度环形电影是由著名的欧洲演员主演的。

当问及还有什么其他措施来使主题公园更欧洲化时，一位发言人提到，公园的指示牌会既用英语，也用法语，一些表演者会以法语、西班牙语和英语表演。这位发言人说："难的是要将人们已熟知的事说得让它听起来不同。"

而另一方面，主题公园也不会过分欧洲化。迪斯尼的另一位发言人早些时候说主题公园的目的就是为那些追求美式生活的人带来基本上是美国式的体验。他说，这样，那些本已考虑去美国度假的人就会高兴地留在大西洋的此岸了。

迪斯尼公司似乎对须发特别在意。它称将在欧洲迪斯尼乐园的中心"美国大马路"建一个旧时的"和谐理发店"来处理"乱糟糟的头发和胡子拉碴的下巴"，也许还要管管唇上髭须。这一乐园与加利福尼亚州和佛罗里达州的乐园有一个不同之处：这条"美国大马路"的部分地区，以及入内游玩的等候区将会有遮棚，以对付巴黎的多雨季节。

欧洲迪斯尼乐园距巴黎不远，这肯定颇具吸引力。任何人厌倦了那里的美式或仿冒的欧式文化了，就可乘快速列车，不到一小时就可到达罗浮宫，一瞬间就从米尼老鼠身边来到了蒙娜·丽莎面前。

交通因素在迪斯尼公司做出将其第四个主题公园选址于巴黎附近这一决定中起了重要作用。这一地址距3亿2,000万欧洲人不超过两小时飞行距离。东欧的开放对迪斯尼来说又是一大收获，他们认为几百万人将会把迪斯尼乐园作为其首次西欧之旅的首选之地。

VII. 写作指导

总分写作法 the General-to-Specific Pattern

从总体的抽象性陈述（general statement）到具体事例（specific details/illustrations）的总分写作法也是一种常用的段落扩展方法。这种方法可以使抽象，笼统或者概括性极强的陈述具体有趣味性，生动形象化，清晰易懂，更加具有说服力。

需要注意的是，具体的解释性内容可以是一个或几个事例（examples），也可以是描述性的细节信息（descriptive details），既可以是具体的个案（a case）也可以是具体代表性的事物（specimen）。

范文：

Euro Disneyland is sure of its success at the beginning.

In Euro Disney actors present *Sleeping Beauty*, *Snow White*, *Pinocchio* and other European legends and fairy tales in French and the direction boards also in French. And the American Mickey Mouse learns to say "welcome" to the excited children, in French, too. Europeans coming here will feel at home with the prominent French environment.

And the easy communication also accounts for its success. People in Paris can reach Euro Disney by express railway in less than an hour—from Mona Lisa to Mickey Mouse in a flash. And it takes people from any parts of Europe only about two hours by flight to enjoy Euro Disney with a European accent.

Section B

I . 阅读技巧

学习理解文章中单词的直接意义：一个词最特定的或最直接的意义（denotation），与它的喻意或相关意相对；和在特定语境（context）中所表示的言外之意（connotation），即：包括单词字面意思之外普通意义的全部内涵的意义。

Denotation指的是可以直接从字典中查到的意思（literal meaning），不受到上下文的影响。而connotation则指的是单词在文章中所表达的暗含的意思（implied meaning）。例如die 的denotation指的是"死亡，停止呼吸"，相当于stop living。然而在句子"Some die at 30 but are not buried until they are 70"中，die 的connotation指的是"stop living spiritually, stop growing intellectually"，即"精神上的死亡"。

Ⅱ. 词汇与短语详解

1. analysis

[词义] *n.* 分析，分解

[搭配] on/upon analysis 经分析; make an analysis of 分析 (= analyze)

[例句] Close analysis of sales figures shows clear regional variation.
对消售额的仔细分析显示出明显的地区差别。

2. analyse/—yze

[词义] *vt.* 分析

[例句] We must try to analyse the causes of the strike. 我们得研究一下罢工的原因。

3. analyst

[词义] *n.* 分析家，分析员

[搭配] a chemical analyst 化学分析家

[例句] A football coach has to be a good analyst of his play's abilities.
足球教练必须擅长分析队员的长处。

4. franc

[词义] *n.* 法郎

[例句] France is the monetary unit of Switzerland. 法郎是瑞士的货币单位。

5. elaborate

[词义] *adj.* ① 精心计划的; ② 详尽的; ③复杂的

[搭配] an elaborate design 精心的设计; elaborate directions 详尽的指示

[例句] The elaborate festivities for the 200th anniversary of the town's founding will
begin at 8 o'clock this evening.
精心计划的庆祝建城200周年的庆典将于今晚8点拉开帷幕。
The sectetany made elaborate notes of the meeting.
秘书对会议做了详细的记录。
What an elaborate machine. 多复杂的机器呀！

[派生] elaboration *n.* 苦心经营

[辨析] elaborate, illustrate
elaborate 强调具体说明细节，如: The chairman just wanted the facts, you don't
need to elaborate on them. 主席只想了解事实，你不必做详细说明。
illustrate 只用图或例子"说明、阐明"，如: The book was illustrated with color
photographs. 这本书配上了彩色照片。

6. sustain

[词义] *vt.* ① 保持; ② 供养; ③维持（生命等）

[例句] The sea wall sustains the shock of the waves. 海堤能抵挡海浪的冲击。
The teacher tried hard to sustain the children's interest.
老师努力去保持孩子们的兴趣。
A good breakfast will sustain you all morning.
丰富的早餐会使你整个上午都精力充沛。

[扩展] sustainment *n.* 支持，维持; sustainable *adj.* 可以忍受的，足可支撑的

[辨析] sustain, support
sustain 常指支撑，维持，如: His hope for future sustained him. 对未来的希望支持了他。

255

support系支撑常用词，强调给某人（物）以积极援助或支持，如：We should support each other. 我们应互相支援。

7. reverse

[词义] *vt.* ① 撤销，推翻；② 使位置颠倒

[搭配] in reverse 反过来；与……相反

[例句] He reversed the judgment and set the prisoner free after all.
他最终撤销了原判，释放了囚犯。

The first of the year Peter did well in school, but then he started moving in reverse. 学年之始彼得学业成绩很好，但后来就开始倒退了。

[辨析] reverse, invert

reverse 指完全转变至相反的位置，如：He reversed the car. 他倒车。

invert 指把事物倒置或里面转到外面，可意指以相反顺序放置某物，如：Invert and air the mattress. 倒转并为弹簧床垫充气。

8. amid

[词义] prep. 在……中间，在……之中，被……围绕

[例句] Amid all the haste and confusion the bridegroom didn't remember giving the ring to the best man before leaving for the church.
忙乱中新郎忘记他在出发去教堂前已经把戒指交给了男傧相。

Amid warm applause the honored guests mounted the rostrum.
在热烈的掌声中贵宾们登上了主席台。

9. gear up（使）准备好，作好安排

[例句] If the industry had taken the advice that we put forward three or four years ago, it would have been well geared up to meet the present challenge. 如果这行业在三、四年前就采纳我们提出的建议，它就完全能准备好应付目前的挑战。

10. warn against 告诫，提醒（某人）以防备（……的危险等）

[例句] But at the same time the president warned against mass movements of people which will create pressures and could bring instability.
但总统同时告诫要防备会造成压力，带来不稳定的大规模人群迁移。

11. react to（对……）做出反应

[例句] If companies had reacted to early signs of slowdown with large cuts in production and investment, the situation would have been different.
要是公司对经济放缓的早期迹象做出大幅度削减生产和投资的反应，形势就会不一样了。

12. be superior to 优于

[例句] He has the unshakeable faith in women's ability to organize, to be caring and to be, just in so many ways, superior to men.
他坚信妇女的组织能力、关心别人的能力等许许多多方面都优于男人。

13. on a/an...basis 以……方式

[例句] Most of the workers in the factory are paid on a piece-work basis.
这家工厂的大部分工人计件领取报酬。

14. in the long term 从长远来说，长期来说

[例句] But in the long term he opened the way to the great revolution in industry that came with the advances on his original idea.

但从长远来说，他打开了通向这场工业上的伟大革命的道路。这场革命随着他的独创性思想的发展而来到了。

15. hang over（威胁、危险等）临头，笼罩，迫近

[例句] The threat of war hung over this country for almost one year.

战争的威胁在这个国家持续了近一年。

16. account for（指数量等）占; 解释，说明（原因等）

[例句] Overseas earnings of the country accounted for 9 per cent of the total last year and could reach 30 per cent this year.

这个国家的海外收入去年占总收入的百分之九，今年能达到百分之三十。

Money was being spent every day, but how it was spent could not be accounted for. 每天都在花钱，可是又解释不清这些钱是如何花掉的。

17. in line with 与……一致，符合，按照

[例句] We hope that in line with our recommendations, the government will change its procedures. 我们希望政府能按照我们的建议改变其做法。

Ⅲ. 难句解析

1. The Euro Disney Corporation, acknowledging that its elaborate theme park had not performed as strongly as expected, announced Thursday that it would sustain a net financial loss of unpredictable scale in its first financial year. (Para. 1)

[释义] The Euro Disney Corporation admitted that its carefully planned and complicated theme park had not achieved what was expected and announced on Thursday that it would suffer an unexpectedly heavy net financial loss in its first financial year.

[分析] 本句的核心结构为 "The Euro Disney Corporation...announced Thursday that..."。现在分词结构 "acknowledging that its...expected" 作伴随状语，其中的that分句作 acknowledge 的宾语，"as strongly as expected"使用了省略结构，在expected之前省略了it was。

2. The company said that 3.6 million people had visited the park from April 12 to July 22, a performance superior to that of comparable start-up periods at other theme parks (Para.8)

[释义] **superior to** 比……更高级，高等，相当于better than, 没有比较级的结构，反义词为 inferior。

e.g. Thia western restaurant is superior to the one we went to last week.

这家西餐馆比我们上星期去的那一家好。

[分析] 本句的主干为 "the company said + that 宾语从句"。句中的第二个that指代performance。

3. But it warned investors against expecting profits soon from Euro Disney, of which it owns 49 percent. (Para. 5)

[分析] 本句的主干是 "but it warned...from Euro Disney "，"of which it owns 49 percent" 为介词提前的非限制性定语从句，结构上可理解为 "it owns 49 percent of which"，which 指的是Euro Disney。

4. The announcement amounted to an extraordinary reversal for Euro Disney, which opened amid immense celebration and widespread predictions of immediate success. (Para. 6)

[释义] The announcement seemed in fact to say that Euro Disney experienced a surprising loss/failure while it was warmly welcomed and many people predicted it would succeed very soon when it opened.

amount to 等于，相当于，相当于 "be equivalent to"

e.g. The purchases amounted to 50 dollars. 买东西总共花了50美元。

[分析] 非限制性定语从句 "which opened...success" 修饰先行词Euro Disney。

5. Clearly, costs have been geared to a revenue level that has not been achieved, and the company is beginning to drop hotel prices that have been widely described as excessive. (Para. 10)

[释义] It is clear that costs to run Euro Disney have been estimated and planned in line with a revenue level that has not been achieved, meaning that their cost levels have surpassed the current revenue level, and the company is beginning to reduce hotel prices that most people have considered too high.

gear to 调整，适应

e.g. Education should be geared to children's needs. 教育应适合学生们的需要。

[分析] 本句中包含了两个由that引导的限制性定语从句。第一个 "that has not been achieved" 修饰level，第二个 "that have been widely described as excessive" 修饰prices。

6. For its third quarter ending June 30, the first in which the park had been operating, the company announced revenues of 2.47 billion francs ($492 million), but gave no profit or loss figures in line with the French practice of only giving such figures at year's end. (Para. 15)

[分析] 本句中 "the first in which the park had been operating" 为 "its third quarter" 的同位语，其中包含了一个介词in提前的限制性定语从句，修饰先行词the first，在first之后省略了quarter。动名词短语 "only giving...end" 作介词的宾语。

Ⅳ. 重点语法讲解
介词 "Given" 的用法

given 为介词，相当于 "because of a particular fact/considering/knowing about"，意思是 "假设，考虑到……"，其后既可以跟名词短语连用也可以与that 宾语从句连用，其中that 还可以省略。

But it warned that, given the likely strong seasonal variation in attendance, it was not possible to predict future attendance or profits. (Para. 8)

但公司也提醒说，考虑到游客量可能有相当大的季节性变化，所以无法对今后的游客量和收益做出预测。

Given the condition of the engine, it is a wonder that it even starts.

倘若这发动机能发动的话，可真是不可思议

I'd come and see you in New York, given the chance.

如果有机会,我就到纽约来看你。

Given that conflict is inevitable, we need to learn how to manage it.

假如冲突不可避免，我们就得学习如何解决它。

V. 课文赏析

1. 文体特点

本文是篇议论文，开篇开门见山地提出主题公园经营亏损，接下来分析存在和面临的问题包括成本、股票等方面的因素，用事实来说话，辅以大量数据说明，真实可信。最后提到了迪斯尼公司采取的措施。

2. 结构分析

Part I (Para.1) The fact that the theme park's performance was not as good as expected.

Part II (Para.2-13) Some problems that the park encountered.

Part III (Para.14-15) Some possible solutions.

VI. 课后练习答案及解析

Reading Skills

XV.

1. Denotation: carry out a duty; act or show

   Connotation: work or operate

   (解析：根据文章内容，主语为the theme park)

2. Denotation: strike; come against with force

   Connotation: meet; face with

   (解析：根据文章内容，与problem 的搭配通常表达"遇到困难"的动词应该为meet，face with)

3. Denotation: come to; reach to

   Connotation: be equal to; be same as

   (解析：根据句意)

4. Denotation: points or facts about something

   Connotation: unimportant small points

   (解析：根据文章内容，由事实或详情引出的涵义)

5. Denotation: succeed in doing; run or take charge of

   Connotation: control

   (解析：根据文章内容，manage 与cost 连用，可以表达control 之意。)

Comprehension

XVI.

F T F T T   F T F

Vocabulary

XVII.

1. adjustment 译文：然而，如果你感觉进展过慢，那就需要调整饮食结构和锻炼计划，以便达到你的期望。

2. acceptance 译文：在城市附近兴建一座主题公园的想法很快就得到大家的普遍认可。

3. acknowledged 译文：迪斯尼公司在它的年度报告中承认自己遇到了竞争，在美国的游客量也一直在下滑。

4. sustained 译文：正经历着向社会民主党转变的保守党在全国损失惨重，与1995年相比，它的总票数已下跃了6个百分点。

5. Preliminary 译文：初步结果显示，油箱并未漏油，但这一结论还要经过详细的证实。

6. reversal 译文：与他最初的决定完全相反，他同意开始实施这项计划。

7. variation 译文：调查发现游客量随季节变化很大，即使可能，也很难对未来的游客量和利润做出预测。

8. temporary 译文：欧洲迪斯尼公司相信，主题公园目前的财政亏损只是暂时的，从长远的角度来看，它们会盈利的。

XVIII.

1. According to the survey, students and children accounted for more than 50% of the visitors to Euro Disneyland last year.
   译文：据调查，学生和儿童占去年欧洲 斯尼乐园的游客数的50%以上。

2. There employees thought banning moustaches and beards amounted to violating their individual rights.
   译文：这些员工认为禁止留胡须侵犯了他们的个人权利。

3. Most of the student guides work for the theme park on a voluntary basis.
   译文：大多数学生导游是自愿为主题公园工作的。

4. The theme park is gearing up for the invasion of tourists in the coming summer vacation period. 译文：主题公园正在为即将到来的夏季旅游高峰做准备。

5. uncertainty again hangs over the company's current financial conditions and many stockholders are selling its shares.
   译文：公司目前的财政状况仍无法确定，很多股民都在纷绥地抛售股票。

6. Manufacturing companies spend millions of pounds trying to convince customers that their products are superior to those of other companies.
   译文：生产厂家花上百万英镑试图说服客户们，他们的产品的质量要好过于其他的厂家。

7. The union representative argued that the practices of banning moustaches excess weight and short skirts were not in line with French labor law.
   译文：工会代表声称，不准留胡须，不准体重超标，不准穿超短裙都是不符合法国劳动法的规定。

8. The stock prices of the company are too high now, but they are going to be alright in the long term.
   译文：现在这家公司的股票价格过高，但从长远看来，它会恢复正常的。

VII. 参考译文

不要期待欧洲迪斯尼会很快盈利

　　欧洲迪斯尼公司承认，其精心建造的主题公园并未如预期般表现出色。该公司星期四称在首个财政年度里公司将继续蒙受难以预料的净亏损。

　　主题公园位于巴黎以东30公里（20英里）处，占地4,800英亩。在它四月份开张时，欧洲迪斯尼行政人员说他们希望在9月30日结束的这个财政年度中能小有盈余。但那以后，这个主题公园遇到了一些问题。

"我们已为充分的运作做好了准备，"公司的财务总管约翰·佛斯格伦在电话采访中说。"运作是相当充分，但尚未达到我们预期的程度。"

"尽管游客数量相当大，"他说，"可我们的成本支出的确需要根据当前的收益状况做出调整。"

它的母公司沃尔特·迪斯尼公司星期四说欧洲迪斯尼的收入本季度上升了33%。该公司拥有欧洲迪斯尼49%的股份，但它提醒投资者不要期待欧洲迪斯尼会很快赢利。

欧洲迪斯尼公司说尽管游客量一直相当大，"公司预计在1992年9月30日结束的财政年度里会有净亏损。"还说"亏损的程度将取决于关键的欧洲夏季假期里剩余日子所能带来的游客量和宾馆入住率。"这一宣布等于是说欧洲迪斯尼的情况出现了罕见的逆转。当初它在一片欢呼声中开张，并被普遍看好会立即获得成功。

4月12日公司开张时，公司的股票价为140.90法郎（28.07美元），今年初曾高达170法郎。本周四股票下跌了2.75%，收盘价为97.25法郎。佛斯格伦先生说，他认为股票市场"对初期消息的反应有点情绪化了。"他补充道，"从任何客观标准来看主题公园都是很成功的。公众对它的长期接受程度相当高，而其他情况只是枝节而已。"

公司说从4月12日至6月22日期间，有360万游客入园，这比其他迪斯尼主题公园开放初期的情况要强。但公司也提醒说，考虑到游客量可能有相当大的季节性变化，所以无法对今后的游客量和收益做出预测。

对此番话，股票市场行家，帕里巴斯资本市场集团发布了一份"出售"欧洲迪斯尼股票的建议，指出这一阶段的游客量比预期的低15%，食品及其他商品的消费额比预期的低10%。它预计欧洲迪斯尼公司在本财政年度会损失3亿法郎，并且还将继续亏损两年。

欧洲迪斯尼所面临的主要问题似乎是控制成本，和为它的5,000多间宾馆客房合理定价。很明显，当初定成本曾依据的收益水平并未达到，公司开始下调曾被普遍认为过高的宾馆房价。

佛斯格伦先生说员工人数现为17,000人，"今后两个月内公司员工数量会显著下降，这主要是因为季节工的减少。"他说目前的员工中5,000人是临时雇佣的。

他也承认，度假地的最低房价已从开张时的750法郎降为550法郎（110美元），一些房间的冬季价已降至400法郎。分析家们认为宾馆入住率一直约为全部接待能力的68%，尽管眼下超过了90%。

"关键的问题是成本，"一位财务专家说。"他们不知道冬季的游客量会达到什么水平，他们正在努力使成本降到恰当的水平。股价仍然过高，但我认为长期来看，他们会使其恢复正常的。"

公司计划主题公园在欧洲寒冷的冬季仍然开门迎客，此举是否可行仍有疑问——欧洲其他主题公园从未这样做过。上个月，公司说现已难以吸引巴黎地区的游客。佛斯格伦先生说法国游客量有所上升，占了360万游客中的100万，而其余的游客大部分来自英国和德国。只有百分之一的游客是美国人。

6月30日结束的第三季度是主题公园正式运作的第一个季度。公司说这个季度的营业收入达24亿7,000万法郎（4亿9,200万美元）。但公司未提利润或亏损数字。这是法国的一贯做法，只在年底才统计利润或亏损。在前半年里，公司共赢利7,500法郎，主要是投资收入和出售公司地盘上的建筑权所得。

Section C

Ⅰ. 语言点讲解

1. **Balanced at the edge of a narrow white platform, I'm about to jump head first into a hot new phase of Japan's leisure boom: indoor sky diving, without a parachute. (Para.1)**

   [分析] 本句中主干为 "I'm about to jump...boom"，过去分词短语 "balanced at...platform" 作伴随状语，其逻辑主语与主句的主语是一致的。冒号后的内容为 "a hot new phase of Japan's leisure boom" 同位语。

2. **To get out, I would have to climb back down the narrow ladder from the tower and walk past the long row of "salarymen" and "office ladies" lincd up behind me at an amusement park named "Tokyo Roof". (Para. 2)**

   [分析] 本句中位于句首的不定式 "to get out" 作目的状语，句子的主干为 "I would have to climb...and...walk..."。过去分词短语 "lined up behind...park" 作后置定语，修饰 row；"named..." 也是过去分词短语作后置定语，修饰 park。

3. **Designing cities according to the traditional concept that hard work is a moral duty, those who rebuilt Japan after World War II left almost no room for recreation. (Para. 6)**

   [分析] 现在分词短语 "designing...duty" 作原因状语，其逻辑主语与句子主语是一致的。在分词结构中的 "that hard work...duty" 为 concept 的同位语从句。限制性定语从句 "who...II" 的先行词为 those。

4. **Golf driving ranges layered four stories high in the heart of the city, with towering green nets to keep the balls from smashing windows in neighboring office buildings. (Para.7)**

   [分析] 本句只是一个带有复杂成分的名词短语。核心成分为 "Golf driving ranges"。连个后置定语分别为 "layered four...the city" 为过去分词短语作后置定语；"with...buildings" 为介词短语作后置定语。

5. **With my blood pressure going crazy but my pride intact, I excited the tower, only slightly shaken after thrilling encounter with the Japanese concept of leisure. (Para. 15)**

   [释义] **intact** *adj.* 完好的，完整的，未经触动的，原封未动的

   e.g. He lived on the interest and keep his capital intact. 他靠利息生活，本钱不动。

   [分析] 本句的难点在于理解 "with my blood...intact" 为介词引导的独立主格结构，其中分词的逻辑主语为 "my blood pressure"，而全句的主语是 I。

Ⅱ. 课文赏析

1. 文体特点

本文以自己的亲身体验室内蹦极跳开始，设下悬念，引起读者兴趣。由这一体验引出主题：日本掀起了休闲热。在谈论了出现这种现象的原因之后，又列举了休闲市场上出现的新项目。文章结尾和开头照应，更详细地介绍了这次体验，语言生动，使人有身临其境的感觉。

2. 结构分析

Part Ⅰ (Para.1-2) Generalization of my experience of indoor sky booming.

Part Ⅱ (Para.3-6) Reasons for leisure boom's appearance.

Part Ⅲ (Para.7-9) Examples of some new entries in leisure market and introductions of amusement parks.

Part Ⅳ (Para.10-15) My experience of indoor sky booming in details.

Ⅲ. 课后练习答案及解析

Reading skills

XIX. ▶

1. Denotation: much loved

   Connotation: precious; expensive

2. Denotation: a division of a house

   Connotation: space

3. Denotation: a sudden strong feeling of excitement; or joy

   Connotation: thrilling entertainment items

Comprehension of the Text

XX. ▶

B C B C A   C C A

Ⅳ. 参考译文

日本掀起了休闲热

我的双膝发抖，心狂跳不止，头戴的防撞头盔看上去似乎太单薄了。我在一块窄窄的白色跳板前端站稳，准备头朝下跳出去。这一跳将跳进日本休闲热中的一个崭新的热门项目：室内蹦极跳，不带降落伞的。

我得再好好想想，但现在已没有退路了。要出去，就得顺着窄窄的梯子从高塔上往下爬，走过排在我后面的长长的一列"薪水阶层"、"办公室女郎"。这一切发生在一个叫做"东京屋顶"的游乐园里。

几百家游乐园、体育中心、度假地在日本各地相继开张，"东京屋顶"就是其中之一。日本这个勤劳的民族近来把游乐作为一件认真的事来做，体现了其典型的高效和激情。

日本掀起了休闲热，就像这里的很多全国性潮流一样，这也是在政府倡导下出现的。美国以及日本其它的贸易伙伴抱怨日本劳工过分辛苦，在他们的压力下，日本正努力推出干活不要那么拼命的观念。

据日本劳动省的数据，日本工人每年要比一般的美国工人多干200小时的活。日本学校的上课时间为每周五天再加星期六上午，每年10个月，这样，日本学生每年的上课日比他们的美国同龄人几乎多60天。

但现在，政府和大企业都在大力提倡"休闲"这个概念。一些公司要求雇员休较长的假期，另一些正在朝取消传统的星期六工作日努力，以便人们可以出外放松。但是在一个人口拥挤，土地昂贵的国家，有了闲暇的人们却遇到了这样一个问题：没有多少地方可供游玩。二次大战之后重建日本时城市规划所依据的仍是传统的勤奋工作的道德观念，没有为娱乐活动留下空间。今天，据建设省说，东京居民人均拥有约2.5平方米的活动场地。

为了弥补公共活动场地的短缺，在休闲市场上私营企业正发明出各种各样的新项目，包括：室内滑雪胜地，那儿有在大楼内用压碎的冰做成的山，还配有送滑雪者上山的升降椅，以及滑雪学校；室内登山中心，那儿有人造山峰与悬崖；通宵高尔夫球场，那儿的球色彩明亮，旗杆顶上还有闪烁的小红灯；高尔夫练球场，它位于市中心，高达四层楼，上罩绿色的网以防球砸坏周围办公大楼的窗户。

自从1983年建成东京迪斯尼乐园以来，已有几十家游乐园开张，还有200家已提出计划或正在建造。很多游乐园推出的惊险项目不仅以儿童为目标，还瞄准了已有工作的年青单身族。东京的一家游乐园里有6个环滑车道，能在沿着轨道快速滑行时，作360度旋转。

还有这家我玩室内蹦极跳的"东京屋顶"。它建在市中心的一个停车场上，入口处有一巨大的招牌，上面用英文写着"在世界线上从你心底发出的优美音乐"（Good Music from Your Body Heart on the World Line）。"东京屋顶"是各种新颖游乐园想法的试验场。那儿有录像模仿的高尔夫球场，有赛车道供游客驾驶按比例缩小的赛车，还有一个电影院，里面的座椅可随着银幕上的场景而颠簸晃动。不过那儿最吸引人的还是这个我排队登上的高塔。

蹦极跳每次收费15.60美元，"东京屋顶"租给我一套飞行服、特殊的鞋子、手套、耳塞、头盔、面罩、护牙套、还有一套安全装备（但是没有降落伞）。

我包裹在这一身装束里，与其他的历险者一起排了一小时队。他们大多是20多岁的办公室职员。终于轮到我爬上梯级，踏上狭窄的跳板了。

我的前方是一个六米高的网状圆柱形空间，底部是金属丝编成的网。"教练"站在高塔下面指点，我照着他的话，紧了紧头盔，闭上双眼，纵身一跃。

我发现自己悬在了空中——高塔底部一架工业用强力风扇吹出时速达130公里的风柱将我拖起。这就是室内无伞蹦极跳得以进行的诀窍。还真成了，这使我放下心来。

在这震耳欲聋地呼啸轰鸣的风柱上我翻腾了三分钟，感觉真像蹦极跳，只是没有下跳而已。在这惊心动魄的整个过程中，我在高塔内几乎差不多的高度上飘动。

高塔上垂下一根竿，我抓住它以求平衡。教练的喊声盖过风扇的轰鸣，告诉我如何屈折各肢体来乘着风柱上下左右地飘动，我照着他说的毫无结果地折腾了一番。最后，我总算掌握了一点控制要领，移到了退场的平台上。我出了高塔，血压升高，不过保住了自尊。在惊心动魄地见识了日本式的休闲后，多少有些发怵。

五、知识链接

Mona Lisa

Mona Lisa by Leonardo da Vinci, is perhaps the most famous painting in the world, going so far as to be iconic of painting, art, and even visual images in general. No other work of art is so romanticized, celebrated, or reproduced.

The work, which was accomplished between 1503 and 1506, measures 77 x 53 cm and is an oil painting on wood. It was brought to France by Leonardo when King Francois I invited the great painter to work near the king's chateau. As a result, the Mona Lisa today hangs in the Louvre in Paris, and is the museum's star attraction.

The identity of the lady in the painting is not known for certain, except that she was a wealthy

Florentine. Although it is definitely difficult to view the painting critically and ignore all the mythology behind it, it does display a technical mastery that more or less unquestionably seats it amongst Leonardo's masterworks (although some count The Last Supper as a greater work).

The compelling nature of the image has been the subject of reams of discussion. In general, it can be stated that the vividness and ambiguity of the facial expression is due to Leonardo's use of sfumato[1] (a term coined by Leonardo da Vinci to refer to a painting technique which overlays translucent layers of colors to create perceptions of depth, volume and form), blurring the most expressive portions of the face (the corners of the eyes and mouth) to give the picture greater mystery. Indeed, the eyes appear to follow the viewer around the room, and the enigmatic smile is the picture's most famous feature (giving us the expression, "a Mona Lisa smile").

The painting was also one of the first portraits to depict the sitter before an imaginary landscape. One interesting feature of the landscape is that it is uneven. The landscape to the left of the figure is noticeably lower than that to the right of her. This has led some critics to suggest that it was added later.

The painting has been restored numerous times: unfortunately, several details have been lost in the process, including Lisa's eyebrows and (possibly) a pearl necklace she was wearing.

On August 22, 1911, Louvre employee, who at first believed the Italian painting belonged to Italy and shouldn't be kept in France, stole the painting by simply walking out the door with it hidden under his coat. However, greed got the better of him and the Mona Lisa was not returned to the Louvre until 1913 when he attempted to sell it to a Florence art dealer. The Guinness Book of Records counts the painting as the most valuable object ever insured.

注：Sfumato：渲染层次，莱奥纳多自创的绘画术语，指通过覆盖半透明的颜色层次来达到深度感，量感和形式感。

《蒙娜·丽莎》

莱昂纳多·达·芬奇的《蒙娜·丽莎》也许是世上最著名的油画作品，通常来说，它既是油画也是艺术甚至视觉像的代表。它是迄今世界上最富有传奇性，知名度最高和最广泛被复制的艺术作品。

这幅木版油画完成于1503年至1506年，尺寸为77 x 53厘米。当年达·芬奇受国王弗朗科伊斯一世邀请到国王的城堡附近创作，这幅画就被画家带到了法国。因此，《蒙娜·丽莎》现如今就挂在巴黎的卢浮宫内，成为最吸引人气的作品。

没人知道画中这位女士的身份，大家只知道她是佛罗伦萨的富人。尽管人们很难去评判这幅画和不去考究这幅画背后的种种传说，然而这幅画的确展现了画家的高超绘画技艺，毋庸置疑地成为莱昂纳多的代表作之一（尽管有人认为《最后的晚餐》较之更胜一筹）。

画中人物突出的性情一直以来是人们广泛探讨的话题。总的来说，人物鲜活的面部表情与模糊不定的神情是由于画家采用了渲染层次的画技，将面部最富有表情的部位（眼角和嘴角）模糊化处理，从而添加了作品的神秘感。的确，画中蒙娜丽莎的眼睛仿佛在跟随着观画者，迷一般的微笑是这幅画最突出的特征（人们称之为"蒙娜丽莎式的微笑"）。

这幅画曾被无数次复制：不幸的是在复制的过程中一些细节性的东西缺失了，其中就包括丽莎的眉毛，可能还有她颈上戴的珍珠项链。

1911年8月22日，卢浮宫的一个雇员把这幅画藏在了衣服里并带了出去。起初，这个雇员认为，意大利的油画应该属于意大利而不应留在法国，于是他把它偷走了。然而，贪婪占了上风。直到1913年当他企图将画兜售给佛罗伦萨的一个艺术品经销商时，这幅画才被送还卢浮宫。《吉尼斯纪录》纪录表明这幅画是迄今投保物品中价值最高的。

六、自测题

Directions: In the following passage there are altogether 10 mistakes, one in each numbered line. You may have to change word, add a word or delete a word. If you change a word, cross it out and write correct word in the corresponding blank. If you add a word, put an insertion mark (∧) in the right place and write the missing word in the blank. If you delete a word, cross it out and put a slash (/) in the blank.

Cannes Film Festival, the most prestigious motion picture
festival in the world, held each May in the resort city of Cannes,
in southeast France. The Cannes Film Festival was conceived   1. _____
at the end of 1938 as a reaction of reports that the Venice Film
Festival became a platform for fascist propaganda. Due to World   2. _____
War II (1939-1945) however, the first Cannes Film Festival   3. _____
was not held till 1946. Internationalism and postwar optimism
characterized the first festival, although organizers placed less   4. _____
emphasis on competition as on mutual creative stimulation   5. _____
between national productions. In later years the selection, by   6. _____
juries, of entrires for prizes was reflected more commercial
interests and the festival soon acquired its current reputation as a 7. _____
fashionable professional event, more concerning with advancing
the film industry than the art of film . French director Francois   8. _____
Truffaut addressed these issues in 1956 which he exposed the
Festival's political intrigues and promotional deals, and predicted 9. _____
its commercial demise. The festival survived, however and in
1959, Truffaut himself was awarded the prize for best screenplay
for Les Quatre Cents Coups (The Four Hundred Blows, 1959) .
In spite its ever present financial interests and political overtones, 10. _____
the Cannes Film Festival remains an essential showcase for
international cinema.

答案与解析

1. 将held改为is held。戛纳电影节是世界上最有声望的电影节。每年5月在法国南部的旅游胜地戛纳举行。本题辨析非谓语动词用作谓语的误用。英语中动词不定式，现在分词与过去分词都属非谓语动词，不能单独构成谓语，但都可以用作状语。所以，在改错时应特别当心，注意判断其与主句的关系，到底是主谓关系，还是句子与状语的关系，本句是长句子，关系复杂，主语是Cannes Film Festival,但除了过去分词held所构成的状语外，并没有谓语出现。故，将held改成is held.

2. 将of改为to。1938年底，威尼斯电影节已蜕变成了法西斯的宣传舞台。针对这一情况戛纳电影节应运而生。本题辨析介词与名词搭配的错误。reaction后若有后置定语时，固定的介词应该用"to"而不是"of"，类似这一用法的名词还有"key ,answer"等。

3. 将became改为had become。本题辨析动词时态的误用。英语的长句中，若出现两个动词，都发生在过去，发生在前的应用过去完成时。句中，was conceived和became都发生在过去，而威尼斯的蜕变(became)明显在前，因此，应用had become。

4. 将till改为until。然而，由于第二次世界大战，第一届戛纳电影节直到1946年才得以举办。本题辨析连词的误用。本句表达的意思应是"直到……才"。表示肯定的意思，而前面已用了not,因此，应该和有否定意义的until一起，才构成肯定的意思，而till的误用，使本句在语法上发生了混乱。

5. 将although改为as/because。第一届电影节洋溢着国际主义和战后乐观主义的情绪，因为组织者们侧重于民族作品间的相互创造激情而不是竞争。本题辨析连词的误用。句中Internationalism and postwar optimism characterized the first festival与organizers placed less emphasis...之间关系，应该是因果关系，结果在前，原因在后。而although却表示的是转折关系。故属误用，应改为表示因果关系的连词as或because。

6. 将as改为than。本题辨析连词的误用。less一词是little的比较级，故此句不是同级比较，所以，as是误用，应改为"than"。

7. 将was删去。在以后的几年，由评审团评选的入围作品则带有更多的商业利益。本题辨析动词语态的误用。本句的主语是the selection，它与reflect的关系是主动的，是入围的作品反映出商业利益，而不是入围作品由商业利益反映出，而介词by在句子里，仅表示与juries一起，构成selection的定语，与被动语态没有任何关系。故将reflect由被动语态改为主动，将was去掉。

8. 将concerning改为concerned。戛纳电影节很快以其时髦的专业形象而声名大震。它更注重推动电影业的发展，而不是电影艺术本身。本题辨析作定语时分词的误用。本句，concern with意思为："使……关心"。concerning with短语是句子的状语，而其逻辑主语是the festival，很明显，the festival与concern之间的关系，应该是被动的，concern应该用被动式conceced，故concerning属误用。

9. 将which改为when或in which。法国导演特吕福特在1956年就指出了这些问题。他揭露电影节带有政治阴谋和推销伎俩，并预言其在商业上的崩溃。本题辨析定语从句关系引导词的误用。在定语从句，指代年代的词可以有when，可以是which或in which只要判断出定语从句中，到底是缺什么成分。若缺的是状语，应用when,或in which,若缺主语或宾语，则用which或that，而句中，be exposed the festival's political intrigues and

promotional deals, 缺的是时间状语, 故引导词该是when或in which, 那么, 将which前加in 或改为when则可以了。

10. 将In spite改为In spite of或Despite。尽管有商业利益及政治高调贯穿始终, 戛纳电影节依然是国际电影的一个重要的展示机会。本题辨析连词的误用。in spite有"尽管"的意思。后面可跟句子, 也可跟名词, 但跟名词, 必须加个of, 相当于despite。句中, In spite后不是句子, 而是一个名词词组。故在后面加上of, 或将in spite改为despite。

Unit 10

① 学习重点和难点
词汇和短语、语法项目、写作技巧

② 文化知识
课文大背景、课文知识点

③ 课文精讲
词汇与短语详解、难句解析、重点语法讲解、课文赏析、课后练习答案及解析、参考译文、写作指导

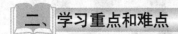

一、预习重点

1. Do you know what EQ is? Does it play any role in one's all-around development?
2. What are the major qualities that make up emotional intelligence according to author?
3. What's the author's suggestion for people who want to develop their emotional intelligence?
4. What does the author mean by saying "without the software of emotional maturity ad self-knowledge, the hardware of academic training alone is worth less and less"?
5. What is the theory proposed by Emotional Intelligence by Daniel Goleman?

二、学习重点和难点

Ⅰ. 词汇和短语

Section A: incorporate, mature, trigger, embrace, adapt, conscious; make a contribution to, sort through, aim at, on purpose, in the act of doing (sth.), take note of, set aside, reflect on/upon, away from, keep at

Section B: upbeat; turn out, interact with, hold out, shy away from, show up, end up, on sight/at sight, be about to do sth., thanks to, at first glance, have authority over, substiute for, break out, be blessed with, count for

Ⅱ. 语法项目

① "No matter + 特殊疑问词（who, when...）引导的小句"结构
② "so that"句型的倒装结构
③ "neither"否定副词位于句首的倒装结构

Ⅲ. 写作

列举法（the structure of Listing supported by details）

三、文化知识

Ⅰ. 课文大背景

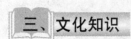

EI 情感智能

The expression "emotional intelligence" is used to indicate a kind of intelligence that involves the ability to perceive, assess and positively influence one's own and other people's emotions. To be exact, emotional intelligence refers to the ability to perceive accurately, appraise and express emotion; the ability to access and/or generate feelings when they facilitate thought; the ability to understand emotion and emotional knowledge; and the ability to regulate emotions to promote emotional and intellectual growth.

Intelligence is the "ability to adapt effectively to the environment, either by making a change in oneself or by changing the environment or finding a new one". According to this definition, being intelligent entails much more than having strong cognitive abilities（认知能力）—the kind of abilities that are typically measured by an intelligence test.

To address some of the further abilities possessed by intelligent people, Elliot Solloway coined（编造）the term emotional intelligence. He considered that being able to direct one's emotions, as well as being able to understand and influence other people's emotional responses, went a long way towards effective adaptation to an environment. The term was picked up in 1995 by Daniel Goleman in his best-seller book of the same title: *Emotional Intelligence*.

Ⅱ. 课文知识点

1. Daniel Goleman 丹尼尔·戈尔曼

A psychologist who for many years reported on the brain and behavioral sciences for *The New York Times*, Dr. Goleman previously was a visiting faculty member（客座老师）at Harvard. Dr. Goleman's 1995 book, Emotional Intelligence, argues that human competencies like self-awareness, self-discipline, persistence and empathy（移情）are of greater consequence than IQ in much of life, that we ignore the decline in these competencies at our peril, and that children can—and should—be taught these abilities. The best selling author of several books like *Emotional Intelligence: Why it can matter more than IQ* (1995), *Working with Emotional Intelligence* (1998), *Destructive Emotions: How We Can Overcome Them* (2003) that describe Emotional Intelligence.

2. people skills 与人相处的能力

People skills are the ability to understand and communicate with others.

3. Bell Labs 贝尔实验室

A research institution in the U.S.A. founded in 1925. It is well known for its invention of transistors（晶体管）. Other inventions include stereo recording, sound motion pictures（有声电影）, the first long-distance TV transmission（首次远程电视转播）, the first fax machine, the touch-tone phone（按键式电话）, etc. The Bell Labs also developed Unix operating system（多用户操作系统）which made large-scale networking of diverse computing systems—and thus the Internet—practical. It also developed the computer programming languages C and C++ which are the world's most widely used programming languages.

4. Carnegie-Mellon University 卡内基–梅隆大学

Carnegie-Mellon is a private research university of about 7,500 students and 3,000 faculty, research and administrative staff. The institution was founded in 1900 in Pittsburgh, U.S.A. with private funds from Andrew Carnegie, an industrialist.

四、课文精讲

Section A

Ⅰ. 词汇与短语详解

1. incorporate

[词义] *vt.* 使合并，使并入

[搭配] incorporate...with 与……合并; incorporate...in/into 把……吸入，并入

[例句] They incorporated the new plans with the old. 他们把新老计划合而为一了。

They incorporated your proposals into their new plan.
他们把你的建议纳入他们的新计划中。

2. maturity

[词义] *adj.* ① 成熟；② 成熟期

[搭配] mental maturity 心智成熟；physical maturity 生理成熟；reach maturity 达到
成熟期；

[例句] My plan has gradually come to maturity. 我的计划逐渐成熟。

These insects reach maturity after a few weeks. 这些昆虫几周后就达到成熟期。

[派生] mature *v.* 变成熟 *adj.* 成熟期

3. trigger

[词义] *vt.* 触发，引起；*n.* ①（枪等的）扳机；② 引起反应的行动

[例句] The tragic chain of events was triggered off. 引发了一连串的悲惨事件。

I pulled the trigger and the gun went off. 我一扣板机，枪就响了。

The odour of food may be a trigger for salivation.
食物的香味可能会引起流涎反应。

4. embrace

[词义] *vt.* ① 采用，接受；② 拥抱，搂抱；③ 包含，涉及；④ 包围

[搭配] loving embrace 深情的拥抱；embrace sb. in one's arms 拥抱某人

[例句] He embraced my offer to employ him. 他接受我的建议雇用他。

In the past, Chinese lovers were too reserved to embrace or kiss each other in
public. 过去中国的情侣太过含蓄，不会当众拥抱或亲吻。

The article embraces many important points of the government reconstruction
plan. 文章中包括着政府重建计划的许多要点。

We allowed the warm water to embrace us. 我们让温水包围我们。

5. adaptive

[词义] *adj.* 适应的

[例句] Plant behaviour is often adaptive. 植物的习性常常显示出它的适应性。

[派生] adapt *v.* 适应；adaptable *adj.* 能适应的；adaptability *n.* 适应性

6. make a contribution to 对……做出贡献

[例句] Everyone in the area had made a contribution to the family restaurant
market, which enabled people to have a very good value meal in enjoyable
surroundings, for less money.
这个地区的每个人都对家庭式餐馆市场做出了贡献。这市场使得人们能在
愉快的环境中享受到真正物有所值的膳食，花的钱也不多。

7. sort through 整理，捡出

[例句] They sorted through the books and divided them into two lots.
他们整理了书籍，把它们分成两份儿。

8. aim at 旨在，追求

[例句] But that is the effect, he wrote, that is the effect I am aiming at.
但那就是结果，他写道，那是我追求的结果。

9. on purpose 故意，特意

[例句] Whether on purpose or by mistake, Andrew was exchanged for the baby who
came to be known as Steve.
不管是故意的还是由于差错，安德鲁换成了后来叫史蒂夫的那个男孩。

10. in the act of doing (sth.) 正在做某事时

[例句] He turned and, in the act of rising, felt his hat being swept off his head.

他转过身，正要站起时，感到他的帽子从头上被吹走了。

11. take note of 注意，注意到

[例句] But the names mean nothing to me because I only take note of the roles actors take in the play.

可是名字对我来说无所谓的，因为我只注意演员们在戏中的角色。

12. set aside 拨出，留下以备将来使用

[例句] Thus if you set aside 500 dollars per month, it would take two years to accumulate the minimum sum needed for your kid. 这样，如果你每月留出500美元，要两年才能攒到你小孩所需要的那笔钱的最低数目。

13. reflect on/upon 思考，考虑，沉思

[例句] He reflected on the options which had been open to him, one of which had led to his downfall.

他反省那些自己以前一直可以有的选择，其中有一选择导致了他的垮台。

14. pull away from 使脱身，使脱离

[例句] Harvey elbowed his way through and, grasping Lisa by the hand, pulled her away from David, and escorted her out of the room. 哈维挤过人群，抓住利萨的手，把她从大卫那儿拉开，并护送她走出了房间。

15. keep at 继续做，坚持干

[例句] We know it's easy to say, but you'll soon start to see and feel the benefits of dieting, providing you keep at it. 虽然我们知道说起来容易，但是只要你坚持，你不久就会看到并体会到节食的益处。

II. 难句解析

1. As Daniel Goleman suggests in his new book Emotional Inteligence, the latest scientific findings seem to indicate that intelligent but inflexible people don't have the right stuff in an age when the adaptive ability is the key to survival. (Para. 2)

[释义] As Daniel Goleman suggests in his new book *Emotional Inteligence*, the latest scientific findings seem to show that people who are intelligent but not flexible to respond to changes don't possess the right ability in an age when the adaptive ability is important to survival.

[分析] 本句的主干为 "the latest scientific findings seen to indicate that..."。句中的that引导的是宾语从句，"when the adaptive...survival" 定语从句，修饰先行词age。"as...Intelligence" 为提前的非限制性定语从句，先行词为后面的整个句子。Key 后面的to为介词，为固定搭配，类似的结构还有：answer to the question，问题的答案，access to all information 使用全部资料的权利，new approach to language teaching 语言教学新方法。

2. The basic significance of the emotional intelligence that Time called "EQ" was suggested by management expert Karen Boylston: "Customers are telling businesses, 'I don't care if every member of your stall graduated

273

form Harvard. I will take my business and go where I am understood and treated with respect.'"(Para.3)

[分析] 本句的主干为 "the basic significance of the emotional intelligence was suggested by management expert Karen Boylston"。冒号后面的内容起到具体解释的作用。"that Time called EQ" 为定语从句，修饰the emotional intelligence。在引用的原话中，"where I am understood and treated with respect" 为名词性从句作状语，意思是"……的地方"。

3. If the evolutionary pressures of the marketplace are making EQ, not IQ, the hot ticket for business success, it seems likely that individuals will want to know how to cultivate it. (Para. 4)

[释义] With the development of business, the pressures from the market are becoming higher and higher and this causes EQ, rather than IQ, to be the key to business success. In this case, individuals are very likely to want to know how to develop and improve EQ.

the hot ticket 通行证，相当于 "what is needed or suitable to be successful and eeryone wants it"

e.g. Mastery jof operating computer skills is the hot ticket to hunt a good job.
掌握电脑操作技能是找份好工作 的通行证。

[分析] 本句中主句结构为 "it seems likely that + 主语从句"，其中it为形式主语，真正的主语为后面的that主语从句。

4. I think of this as thinking differently on purpose. (Para. 5)

[释义] In my opinion, raising consciousness means thinking in a different way intentionally.

[分析] 本句中的动词结构为 "think of...as..."，意思是"把……看作（为）……"，相当于 "view...as..."，"consider...as..."。注意，类似的 "vt.+as" 的结构还有choose...as 选择……作为，strike...as 给……以……的印象，appoint...as 任命……为，dismiss...as 把……作为……草草处理; consider...as 把……视为; label...as 把……称为,regard...as 把……视为, look at...as 把……看作为, view...as 把……看作为, describe...as 把……说成。

5. It's about noticing what you are feeling and thinking and escaping the conditioned confines of your past. (Para. 5)

[释义] It involves becoming aware of what you are feeling and thinking and getting free from the limitations brought about by your past experiences.

[分析] 本句的主干是 "It's about noticing...and...escaping"。动名词 noticing和escaping作介词about 的宾语。"what you are feeling and thinking" 为特殊疑问词引导的名词性从句作noticing的宾语。过去分词 "conditioned"作形容词，修饰confines。

6. The next time someone interprets something differently from you—say, a controversial political event—pause to reflect on the role of life experience and consider it a gift of perception. (Para. 8)

[释义] The next time someone has a different interpretation of something from ours, for example, a political event that causes disagreement or discussion, we should think about the role of life experience in enlarging our senses and consider his or her different interpretation as a gift to broaden our perception.

[分析] 本句中 "the role of life experience" 暗含的意思是 "People have different life experiences and they look at something based on their own life experiences and, as a result, their interpretation of something may be different from ours.",即不同生活经历的人们对事物的看法也不同。短语 "a gift of perception" 在此指的是 "The fact that people's different interpretation or the way of thinking is taken as a gift for us to broaden our own perception.",即他们不同的理解和思考方式帮助我们扩展视野。

7. Keep at it, however, because they are based on what we're learning about the mechanism of the mind (Para. 9)

[分析] 本句中使用了三个代词。it指的是前句中的 "practicing these skills" 整个动作,即 "要坚持操练这些技能"; they指的是 "these skills",即前文中提到的 "raising consciousness, using imagery, considering and reconsidering events to choose the most creative response to them, integrating the perspectives of others" 这四项技能。"what we're...the mind" 为特殊疑问词引导的名词性从句,作介词on 的宾语,意思是 "······的东西。"

8. That done, we are "biologically wired" with what one of the nation's leading brain researchers calls our own "world view". (Para. 11)

[释义] When that is finished, what one of the nation's leading brain researchers calls "our view of the world" has been shaped /has become fixed biologically.

[分析] 本句中的 "That done" 为独立主格结构,that 指的是前句中所提到的 "chemical activity in the brain is cut in half" 这个动作。"what one of the nation's leading brain researchers calls our own 'world view'" 为特殊疑问词引导的名词性从句作介词 with 的宾语,意思是 "被······称之为······的东西"。

Ⅲ. 重点语法讲解

1. "No matter + 特殊疑问词(who,when...)引导的小句" 结构

"no matter" 意思是 "无论/不论······",相当于 "regardless of..."。与no matter连用的特殊疑问词通常有who,what,why,when,how,相当于whoever(不论是谁),whatever(不论什么),wherever(无论哪里),whenever(无论何时),however(无论如何)。

Don't trust him, no matter who (=whoever) repeats it.

不论是谁说的,你都不要相信他。

Don't cry, no matter how he scold you.

无论他如何责备你,你都别哭。

2. "so that" 句型的倒装结构

"so that" 句型的倒装结构是部分倒装结构,具体结构位 "So + adj./adv. + 部分倒装结构 + that 从句"。其中that引导的结果状语从句的语序保持陈述句的语序。把状语部分或者表语部分提到句首,起到强调的作用。

So unique is the personal experience that people would understand the world differently. (Para. 11)

个人的体验都是独一无二的,以至于人们对外界的理解都不同。

So successful was her business that she was able to retire at the age of 50.

她的生意非常成功，因此她在50岁就可以退休了。

So unlikely did his story sound that no one believed him.

他说的事情听起来非常不可能，没人相信他的话。

试比较正常语序：His story sounded so unlikely that no one believed him.

IV. 课文赏析

1. 文体特点

本文最突出的写作特点是运用了列举法来谋篇布局。作者用小标题的形式把培养情商的四个技巧列举出来，使读者一目了然。本文是一篇论文，以一个问题开头，然后提出论点：情商是企业走向成功的通行证，接着给出四点建议，最后指出情商可以培育并得出结论：没有情商纯学术性的培训是没有用的。

2. 结构分析

Part Ⅰ (Para.1-3) an argument that EQ is the hot ticket for business success

Part Ⅱ (Para.4-9) raising and solving problem: how to cultivate EQ

Part Ⅲ (Para.10-12) an argument that EQ can be cultivated

Part Ⅳ (Para.13) the conclusion of the essay

V. 课后练习答案及解析

Comprehension of the Text

Ⅱ. ▶

1. Because he believes that knowledge is useless until it is applied. And application of knowledge takes judgment.

2. The ability to adapt./The adaptive skills.

3. Accept a highly personal practice to improve the four adaptive skills: raising consciousness, using imagery, considering and reconsidering events to choose the most creative response to them and integrating the perspectives of others.

4. Thinking differently on purpose. It involves noticing what you are feeling and thinking and escaping the conditioned confines of one's past.

5. Because by doing this they can improve their performance.

6. Because your view of the world is limited by your genes and experiences you've had and by integrating the perspectives of others you can enlarge your senses.

7. The author believes that our ability to think and reason is not confined to the brain but is distributed throughout the body's universe of cells and we think with our hearts, brains, muscles, blood and bones.

8. By saying this, the author means without cultivating emotional intelligence, the academic training is useless.

Vocabulary

Ⅲ.

1. incorporate 译文：以计算机为基础的通信，即网络，可以提供很多的教育机会。因此，教育家们应该在课堂上利用这些新的媒体，来改变当前的教育方法。

2. triggered 译文：自戈尔曼博士著的《情感智能》这本书发表以来，引起了人们关于情商对个人事业和生活取得成功的重要性方面热烈的争论。

3. perspectives 译文: 由于生活阅历和社会背景的不同，人们对同一件事情的可能会有不同的看法。

4. ultivating 译文: 戈尔曼博士相信在新的千年里，经济和通信都将有不断的发展，因此对于情商的培养将会越来越重要。

5. confine 译文: 当心理学开始思考并写作有关智力的书籍时，他们往往会局限在认知能力方面，比如说记忆和解决的能力等。

6. capacity 译文: 购买500辆坦克是"未来五年内把现有的军事力量增强25%"这一战略目标的一部分。

7. Controversial 译文: 尽管情商具有争议性，但公司还是非常重视培养员工的情商。

8. consciousness 译文: 在难民营的工作使他亲眼目睹了战争受害者所遭受的苦难帮助他提高了自身的政治觉悟。

IV.

1. to 译文: 他相信运用情感智能这种方法，研究智商心理学家们可以对他们未来的客户给予相当重要的帮助。

2. at 译文: 我们知道说起来容易，但你很快就会发现并感觉到节食的益处。坚持下去，你就会成功。

3. to 译文: 在小乔娜四岁的时候，为了做手术她在医院里待了两年。

4. aside 译文: 为了进行检查，应该专门留出一段时间来。

5. to 译文: 他的自杀有可能是因为在大学生活中缺乏解决感情问题的能力。

6. on/upon 译文: 想想我们过去在情感上受的伤害，我们就可以理解他何以会坚持这一重大的原则性问题。

7. away 译文: 那个小孩试图离开母亲舒适的怀抱，但被母亲抱得很紧。

8. of 译文: 他们显然已经注意到校园里的所见所想，所以才能为你们带来如此精彩的教育节目。

Collocation

V.

1. atmospheric 译文: 用胶带将他们全部封闭起来是不明智的。因为气压的变化会破坏一些器械。

2. blood 译文: 你如果再喝的比这个多的话，你就会有血压升高的危险，而血压升高则会进一步导致心脏病发作或窒息。

3. intense 译文: 正是在国会民主党的强压下，白宫于昨日宣布布什总统要求国会给波兰增加2亿美金的援款，这几乎是他以前要求的两倍。

4. public 译文: 前情报局长巴德恩先生已经在公众压力面前低下了头，决定实施民主改革措施，并对给国家造成经济危机的人进行调查。

5. financial 译文: 这个实验室是科学工程研究会下属的四个实验室之一。因为年预算很明显地大幅下降，该实验室已面临越来越大的财政压力。

6. enormous 译文: 因为最近所发生的贝弗利•刘易斯的悲剧，阿德里安娜•贝克开始为自助团体辩护为减轻残疾儿童的母亲所感受到的孤独感和巨大的压力。

7. outside 译文: 此外，自主的真正含义就是一个国家不接受任何外部力量对其所施加的压力。

8. personal 译文: 在接受采访期间，她对这些年来她的工作中所承受的个人压力只字未提。

Word Building

VI.

1. multicolored 译文：明亮的路灯和五颜六色的标牌在漆黑寒冷的夜中隐约闪现。

2. multicultural 译文：同时也有一部分讨论是关于对那些多文化背景的老年人提供服务的未来计划。

3. multimedia 当今的多媒体指的是使用不同媒体的计算机，如激光影碟、光盘驱动器、有线电视等以及我们目前还想不到的其他媒体。

4. multinational 译文：联合国已决定为了维持该地区的和平派遣多国部队。

5. multi-dimensional 译文：犯罪是个涉及面很广的问题，寻求该问题的解决方案需要教育家、家长及社会工作者的共同努力。

6. multimillion 译文：根据《时代周刊》的报道，印度软件业将会赢得几百万美金的合同。

7. multiparty 译文：在这些国家里，政党必须在多党间的比例选举制度下竞争，而且这些党派通常在政府机构中分享权力。

8. multipurpose 译文：他们刚把这个大厅改成多功能的运动厅，在此可做各种室内活动，如：篮球、乒乓球和排球等。

VII.

1. semi-permanent 译文：他又回到了格拉斯哥，这次要在这呆上一段时间。

2. semi-finals 译文：人们预计公开半决赛将会是两场势均力敌的比赛，结果没有让我们失望。

3. semi-automatic 译文：接下来我们获得的情报是邻国的士兵已经配备了半自动步或全自动步枪。

4. semi-detached 译文：那栋房子会花你一大笔钱，那是一幢半独立式的住宅，面朝美丽的海湾，位于该优良社区的中心位置。

5. semi-darkness 译文：孩子们充满恐惧地朝昏暗的灌木丛前进。

6. semi-official 译文：他在伦敦作为期三天的非官方上午访问，主要是为了促进两国间的汽车贸易。

7. semi-skilled 译文：如果公司不能尽快拿到新订单的话，一些不熟练的和半熟练的工人将不得不被解雇。

8. semi-retired 译文：约翰逊在过去40年间为4个不同的老板工作过，他现在即将退休，退休工资是以前工资的三分这二。目前他还得花几个月来帮助新的销售人员熟悉业务范围。

Structure

VIII.

1. They smiled almost continuously, no matter what was said.
   译文：无论别人说什么，他们几乎一直保持着微笑。

2. I told him to report to me after the job was completed, no matter how late it was.
   译文：我告诉他不管多晚完成工作，都要向我汇报情况。

3. No matter where you go, you'll find Coca-Cola.
   译文：无论你走到哪里，都可以看到可口可乐。

4. No matter when you die, whether you're a hundred and twenty or whatever, you can get the sum that you're assured of according to the legal document.

译文：无论你什么时候死亡，不管活到多少岁，根据法律文件你都会得到你所投保的保险金额。

5. He is a very skilled and brilliant player and also a proper gentleman on the tennis court. No matter whom he plays with, whether a low ranked or high ranked player, he has great respect for them.

译文：在网球场上，他既是一个技术好，充满智慧的运动员，又是一个很有风度的绅士。他对所有的对手，无论是排名靠前的还是靠后的，都给予足够的尊重。

IX.

1. So advanced was his method that no one could match him.

译文：他的方法如此先进，没有人可和他相比。

2. So rapid is the rate of progress that advance seems to be following on almost a monthly basis.

译文：发展的速度如此之快，似乎每个月都有新进步接踵而来。

3. So successful was he that offers flowed in from publishers and editors on both sides of the Atlantic.

译文：他是一个非常成功的作家，大洋两岸的编辑和出版商都纷纷向他约稿。

4. So effective was their network that workers were able to organize two unusual nationwide protests.

译文：他们的团队是如此有效，工人们能够组织起两次非同寻常的全国范围内的抗议。

5. So serious was the famine that the United Nations sent food and water supplies to the area.

译文：饥荒非常严重，以至于联合国向该地区的提供了食物和水。

Translation

X.

1. I have been sorting through these old papers to see what can be thrown away.

2. They went on working, taking no note of the passage of time.

3. He had been speaking nothing less than the truth when he put down what he had seen.

4. As you get older you begin to reflect on the uncertainty of life.

5. You are asked to confine your use of telephone to business calls alone.

6. I kept at it and finally finished at 3 o'clock in the morning.

7. In the act of bending down, he slipped and hurt his back.

8. Day centers for the elderly make a valuable contribution to overall public service.

XI.

1. 提高意识程度。我把这看作是思考中有目的的独辟蹊径。这是指注意自己感受到什么，在想什么，摆脱掉往日带给自己的种种限制。

2. 这就是奥林匹克滑雪赛手在进入起跑门之前所做的：他们闭上眼，摆动身体，在头脑中先把整个滑雪道跑一遍，这能提高他们在实际比赛中的表现。

3. 每当发生重要事情时，要尽可能多方面地看问题，甚至作超乎寻常的理解，然后照着最有利于自己理想的那种理解去做。

4. 学会吸纳他人有用的观点就等于是一种扩大自己的见识的方式。

5. 习惯的力量——严格说就是头脑里已建立的思维方式——会妨碍你操练这些技能。

6. 我们现在知道，思想活动并不局限在脑部，而是遍布全身范围的细胞中。

7. 他说任何两个人都不可能对外界有完全一样的看法，人们"认识"世界的手段受到经验的影响，而这种经验都是独一无二的。

8. 但最新的研究似乎表明，缺乏情感成熟和自我了解这一软件，单靠纯学院式的培训这一硬件是没有用的。

Essay Summary

XII. ►

CBADA   CDCBA   BDDAB   CABCD

Text Structure Analysis

XIII. ►

1. **Raising consciousness:**

   what you are thinking and feeling

2. **Using imagery:**

   what you want to achieve

3. **Considering and reconsidering events to choose the most creative response to them:**

   have as many interpretations as possible

4. **Integrating the perspectives of others:**

   is a way of enlarging your senses

VI. 参考译文

> 如何培育"情商"

员工对公司最有价值的贡献是什么，是知识还是判断力？我说是判断力。不管知识面有多宽，如果得不到应用，那就毫无用处。而知识的应用需要判断力，判断力涉及某种第六感觉——是思维的高度运用。

这就提出了现今关于企业界人士最佳培训课程的有趣问题。正如丹尼尔·戈尔曼在他的新书《情感智能》中所说，最新的科研结果似乎表明，在一个适应能力是生存关键的年代，聪明但缺乏灵活性的人并不具备这种适应的才能。

《时代周刊》最近的封面故事列举了关于智能的一些流行看法，报道说，"新的人脑研究表明，情感，而不是智商，可能是衡量人的智能的真正尺度。"《时代周刊》称之为"情商"的情感智能的根本意义，在企业管理专家凯伦·波尔斯顿的话中可见一斑："顾客对企业说'我可不在乎你的每个员工是否都毕业于哈佛，我只愿与能理解我、尊重我的企业打交道。'"

如果说市场的进化发展所造成的压力使得情商，而不是智商，成为企业走向成功的通行证，那么，人们似乎很可能希望懂得如何培养情商。我有个小小的建议：积极进行自我训练，努力提高以下四项适应性技能：

提高意识程度。我把这看作是思考中有目的的独辟蹊径。这是指注意自己感受到什么，在想什么，摆脱掉往日带给自己的种种限制。尽可能多地注意到思考时的自己，以此来提高意识程度。要习惯性地注意自己的情感，问问自己是在面对事实还是逃避事实。

利用意象。这就是奥林匹克滑雪赛手在进入起跑门之前所做的。他们闭上眼，摆动身体，在头脑中先把整个滑雪道跑一遍，这能提高他们在实际比赛中的表现。我们也可以这样做，每天留出时间来带着激情想像一番自己想要获得的成就。

反复考虑各种事件，并对它们做出最富创意的反应。2,000年前的一位希腊哲学家说过，重要的不是事件本身，而是我们对事件的看法，他说的正是此意。每当发生重要事情时，要尽可能多方面地看问题，甚至作超乎寻常的理解，然后照着最有利于自己理想的那种理解去做。

综合考虑他人的看法。大脑研究表明，人们对外界的看法受到遗传基因及个人经历的局限。学会吸纳他人有用的观点就等于是一种扩大自己的见识的方式。下次如果有人对某件事与你有不同的看法，比如某个有争议的政治事件，停下来想想这其实是生活阅历使然，应把它看作一种感知能力的馈赠。

习惯的力量——严格说就是头脑里已建立的思维方式——会妨碍你操练这些技能。然而要坚持下去，因为它们是以对思维机制的认识为基础的。

人脑的容量在生命开始的最初六周增长了一倍，到四岁时又增长一倍，其后大脑的容量迅速发展直到性成熟为止。人体有大约1,000亿个神经细胞，每一次经历都会激发脑部的反应，而这种反应实际上影响着我们的感知。我们现在知道，思想活动并不局限在脑部，而是遍布全身范围的细胞中。是的，我们的确是在用心、用脑、用肌肉、用血液和骨骼来思考。

我们的青少年阶段有一个为期三周的关键时期，此时脑部的化学反应活动一分为二。完成了这一变化，正如国内一位重要的大脑研究人员所说，我们"对外界的看法"就"在生理上定型了"。他说任何两个人都不可能对外界有完全一样的看法。个人的体验都是独一无二的，以至人们对外界的理解都不相同。

然而，他说，人们对外界的看法不仅有可能改变，而且实际上这比克服毒瘾要容易。但是，要想做到这一点需要训练。因此我们推荐了上述做法。

这并不是像MBA那样的课程。但最新的研究似乎表明，缺乏情感成熟和自我了解这一软件，单靠纯学院式的培训这一硬件是没有用的。

Ⅶ. 写作指导

Listing 列举法

列举法也是一种常见的段落扩写方法。在主题句后列举出具有代表性或逐一出具体相关事例来阐述主题，丰富具体主题，是主题句更加易懂。该方法简洁。直接了当，是考试作文常见的方法之一。

Probably the four most essential attributes are flexibility, honesty, creativity and perseverance.（本句中的 four 是使用列举法的提示。）

也可以在行文中用到 first，next，in addition；such as 等词或词组；They are...; It includes...; It comprises of... 等句型进行列举。所列举的事例应当是并列或平行的关系。

范文：

There is a list of reasons to explain why the leisure industry is rapidly expanding in Japan.

It is a government-led leisure boom. Under pressure from the United States and other trading partners, who complain about the Japanese labor force working too much, the government is vigorously promoting the concept of "leisure". Japanese workers labor about 200 more hours per year than the average of their American counterparts, according to figures from Japan's Labor Ministry.

More leisure time is available. Some companies require employees to take longer vacations, and others are moving to eliminate the traditional Saturday workday so that people will get out and have more leisure opportunities.

Construction of more leisure centers. Hundreds of amusement parks, sports centers, and resorts are opening almost every day all over Japan. Leisure centers are trying to provide all kinds of leisure facilities and activities for the Japanese people to enjoy their leisure time.

Section B

I. 阅读技巧

Skim 略读，快读

在阅读时，如果为了获取某些具体的信息，回答某个问题时，常常需要快速阅读或者浏览（fast reading）相关的段或句。这种带有明确目标的快速阅读就叫略读法。略读要求读者专门关注那些帮助理解文章主旨的线索或者信息。读者快速移动视线的前提是迅速明确哪些信息是自己需要的。为了快速获取文章的核心大意，读者可以借助上下文线索例如斜体字或下划线部分，文章的小标题，间隔等，专门阅读相关句子，不需要逐字逐句阅读。

II. 词汇与短语详解

1. upbeat

[词义] *adj.* 乐观的，快乐的

[例句] The publisher says this character must not die and the book should end on an upbeat. 出版者说这个人物不能死，这本书应当以皆大欢喜为结局。

2. turn out 结果是，证明为

[例句] This is true for simple problems but, as I have said many times before, as soon as the problems become more complicated our mathematical knowledge turns out to be greatly deficient. 对于简单的问题确实如此，但是正如我以前多次说过，问题一变得更复杂，我们的数学知识最后会证明是很不够的。

3. interact with 互相交流，互相影响

[例句] Economic decline was the most serious problem, and it interacted with other aspects of social disadvantage.
经济衰退是最严重的问题，它与社会不利条件的其他方面互相影响。

4. hold out 坚持，支持，维持

[例句] Given their state, the soldiers had done well to hold out for so long.
考虑到他们的状况，战士们坚持了这么长时间已经是干得很不错了。

5. shy away from（由于厌恶、害怕、缺乏信心等）躲开，回避，退缩

[例句] All the others were talking and laughing happily while she shied away from being the centre of attention.
所有其他的人都在谈笑风生，而她却避免成为关注的中心。

6. show up 出现，露面

[例句] Real changes will show up only in the next ten or 20 years, and they would change people's lifestyles. 只有在10年或20年以后才会出现真正的变化，这些变化会改变人们的生活方式。

7. end up 结束，告终

[例句] No one is going to thank you if you end up making changes which cause real troubles in our work. 如果你最终做出的变化会给我们工作带来真正麻烦的话，没有人会感谢你的。

8. on sight/at sight 一见到就

[例句] He seemed to have hated her on sight, yet he knew nothing about her, except that she bore a physical resemblance to her father. 他好像是一见到她就已不喜欢她，然而他对她一无所知，除了她长得像她父亲。

9. in (the) face of 尽管，不顾;在……面前

[例句] In the face of difficulties, one should never give up, but struggle on and thus establish a strong will. 尽管有困难，我们决不应该放弃，而是要继续奋斗，这样建立起坚强的意志。

General Motors is promoting its latest models in face of falling demand in European markets.
面临欧洲市场需求的下降，通用汽车公司正在推销其最新的车型。

10. be about to do sth. 刚要做某事，行将做某事，打定主意要……

[例句] I could not believe that such a simple mistake was about to have such dire consequences. 我不能相信这样一个简单的错误将会造成这样可怕的后果。

11. thanks to 幸亏，由于

[例句] Today, thanks to overcrowding and overdevelopment, it is a bit of a nightmare for travelers to find any place of peace. 今天，由于过分拥挤、过分发展，让旅游者找到任何一个安宁的地方有点像是做一场恶梦。

12. at first glance 乍一看，乍看上去

[例句] At first glance, the pictures don't look good, but on closer examination you will find they're not bad at all. 乍一看，这些画画得不怎么好，但是再仔细看看，你就会发现它们画得相当不错。

13. have authority over 对……有控制能力，对……有管辖权

[例句] Senior managers are required to coordinate the work of subordinates by having authority over a wider area of work.
高级经理须管辖工作中更大的范围以对下级的工作进行协调。

14. substitute for 替代，用……来代替

[例句] No book or course of lectures can substitute for experience, but as you gain confidence in your practical ability, you can derive inspiration through reading the works of wise men. 虽然书和课程不能取代经验，但是当你增强了对自己实践能力的信心时，你能通过阅读智者的著作得到灵感。

15. break out 发生，爆发，突然开始

[例句] Fighting eventually broke out between the demonstrators and police in which at least 80 people were injured.
示威者与警察最终发生了搏斗，至少有80人受伤。

283

16. be blessed with 有幸得到，具有

[例句] Having been blessed with a cold mother, did I seek a cold wife?
我已经有了一个冷酷的母亲，难道要再去找一个冷酷的妻子?

17. count for 值，计

[例句] The lab's technical superiority counted for little as few people used its facilities.
由于几乎没人使用这实验室的设备，它的技术优势几乎无用。

Ⅲ. 难句解析

1. Some children grab for the treat the minute he's out the door. (Para. 2)

[分析] 本句中的the minute作时间状语，相当于as soon as 或 immediately ，意思是"一……就……"，引导时间状语从句。用于类似结构的短语还有the moment , the instant。

2. A survey of the children's parents and teachers found that those who as four-year-olds had enough self-control to hold out for the second piece of candy generally grew up to be better adjusted, more popular, adventurous, confident and dependable teenagers. (Para. 3)

[释义] A survey of the children's parents and teachers found those who could control themselves and continued to do what they were doing without giving in to the temptation of the candy at first when they were four years old usually are better adapted to different situations, more liked by others, more willing to take risks and try new things, feel sure about their own abilities and more reliable when they are in their teens.

[分析] 本句的主干为"A survey...found that..."。句中的that 引导的是宾语从句，作谓语动词found 的宾语。在宾语从句中，"who...had enough self-control...of candy"为限制性定语从句，修饰宾语从句的主语those。宾语从句核心结构"those...grew up to be...teenagers."。

3. When it comes to predicting people's success, brain capacity as measured by IQ many actually matter less than the qualities of mind once thought of as "character". (Para.6)

[分析] 本句中的 "When it comes to"为习惯表达法，to为介词，后面接名词或动名词，意思是"当谈到/说到/谈及……."。"as measured by IQ"为省略了"is"定语从句，修饰brain capacity; thought of as character 为过去分词短语作后置定语，修饰the qualities of mind。

4. At first glance, there would seem to be little that's new here. (Para.7)

[分析] 本句中的little 为不定代词，"that's new here"为限制性定语从句，修饰先行词little。注意，当先行词为不定代词时，定语从句的引导词必须用that。

5. When street gangs substitute for families and schoolyard insults end in knife attacks, when more than half of marriages end in divorce,...many of whom say they were trying to discipline the child for behavior like blocking the TV or crying too much, it suggests a demand for basic emotional education. (Para. 8)

[释义] When street gangs replace families and schoolyard insults become violent attacks in the end, when more than half of marriages break up,...many of whom say they were trying to punish the child for behavior like blocking the TV or crying too much, it suggests there is a need for basic emotional education.

[分析] 在这个长句中，出现了两个由when引导的排比 (paralleled) 时间状语从句。第一个由两个并列句构成，即 "When street gangs substitute for families" and "schoolyard insults end in knife attacks"；第二个为 "when more...in divorce"。"many of whom say...too much" 为非限制性定语从句，修饰parents。本句的主句为 "it suggests...education"。

6. **While many researchers in this relatively new field are glad to see emotional issues finally taken seriously, they fear that a notion as handy as EQ invites misuse. (Para. 9)**

[释义] While many researchers working in this relatively new field are glad to see that people consider emotional issues important and pay serious attention to them at last, they fear such a convenient term EQ is likely to be misused.

invite *vt.* 招致，导致，诱惑

e.g. His lazinesss invited his jobless. 懒惰使他失去了工作。

[分析] 本句中while 引导让步性状语从句，意思是 "尽管，虽然"。过去分词短语 "taken seriously" 作宾语 "issues" 的补足语。

Ⅳ. 重点语法讲解

"neither" 否定副词位于句首的倒装结构

否定副词neither 位于句首时，全句应该使用部分倒装的结构，即将be动词或助动词提到主语的前面，意思是 "也不"。类似用法的常见否定副词还有seldom（很少），hardly（几乎不），scarcely（几乎不，简直不能），barely (几乎不能)，no sooner（一旦……立即……）等。

Neither is it surprising that "people skills" are useful, which amounts to saying it's good to be nice. (Para. 7)

此说法也不令人惊奇，这就等于说与人为善是对的。

If he won't go, neither will she. 若他不去，她也不去

Just as you would not, so neither would they.

正如你们不愿意一样，他们也不会答应的

"Easily was a man made an infidel, but hardly might he be converted to another faith" (T.E. Lawrence)

"一个人可以轻易地变为不信宗教的人，但几乎不可能转而相信另外一种信仰。" (T.E.劳伦斯)

Ⅴ. 课文赏析

1. 文体特点

本文开篇讲了一个实验，激发读者兴趣，由这个实验得出结论，引出要谈论的主题。用事实来说话，以事实论据来说明问题。语言有力，运用排比，也是本文的一大特点。

2. 结构分析

Part Ⅰ (Para. 1-4) A candy experiment.

285

Part Ⅱ (Para.5-8) Implications and roles of emotional intelligence.

Part Ⅲ (Para.9) Conclusion.

Ⅵ. 课后练习答案及解析

Reading Skills

XV.

1. Those four-year-olds who had enough self-control to hold out for the second piece of candy generally grew up to be better adjusted, more popular, adventurous, confident and dependable teenagers.

2. The ability to delay reward.

3. When it comes to predicting people's success, brain capacity as measured by IQ may actually matter less than the qualities of mind once thought of as "character".

4. 20%.

Comprehension

XVI.

B A A C C   A B B

Vocabulary

XVII.

1. implications 译文：利用震动物体声音的变化来检查裂缝裂痕这一方法对工程师们很有意义。

2. dimmed 译文：一个孩童的世界充满了好奇和刺激，它是新鲜、美丽的，但对于我们大多数人来说，这种好奇感到我们还尚未成年时就已经淡化甚至完全消失了。

3. dependable 译文：研究人员发现那些能够抵制诱惑的小孩长大后能成为更加可靠的孩子。

4. notion 译文：我们所关心的是爱的概念，这是我们理解这本书的关键。

5. enhance 译文：我们高度赞同应该支持这一为了提高英国男网球队水平而订的新方案，这是合情合理的。

6. adjust 译文：我们强烈建议老年人应该根据健康食物指南来检查一下自己的饮食，根据需要进行调整。

7. virtually 译文：一旦零部件上了装配线，国外生产的汽车的质量，其实和他们在日本生产的差不多。

8. ingredients 译文：1950年首次出版的《艺术的故事》取得成功的必不可少的因素是敏锐的思维和严格的编辑。该书的作者是E·H·格姆布瑞克。

XVIII.

1. shy away from 译文：研究发现能保持乐观情绪的人不会逃避困难的工作和挑战。

2. counts for 译文：有些研究表明智商只占决定成功因素的4%，心理专家认为它并不能预测一个人的工作表现。

3. are blessed with 译文：他们两个能力超众，都能够为了某一目的而暂时放弃眼前的利益。

4. substitute the new ones for them 译文：提高个人的感情智能类似于改变一个人的习惯。负责指挥习惯的大脑要忘掉旧的习惯，然后用新的习惯去取代它们。

5. gave in to temptation 译文：孩子们知道如果他们能够等到实验者回来，他们就能够得到两块糖，但有些孩子还是抵挡不了诱惑，一把抓过糖就吃。

6. **When it comes to** 译文: 提到关于情感智能方面的著作, 丹尼尔·戈尔曼的《情感智能》被认为是一本独辟蹊径的书。

7. **on sight** 译文: 我大约在四年前买了这辆车, 事实上, 当我第一次看到它时, 就喜欢它了。

8. **held out for** 译文: 女工们继续罢工, 强烈要求和男性工人得到相同的薪水。

VII. 参考译文

个人要成功, "情商"起作用

人们发现, 通过观察一个四岁孩子怎样处理一块糖, 科学家可以预测其未来。研究人员将孩子们一个一个地请进一间普普通通的房间, 开始了小小的折磨。他对孩子说, 你们可以现在就吃这块糖, 但是如果你们等一会儿, 等我从外面回来, 你们就可以吃两块糖。说完他就走了。

一些孩子当研究人员一走就一把抓过糖来吃。另一些孩子等候了几分钟, 但还是忍不住吃了糖。还有一些孩子下决心等下去。他们或蒙上眼睛, 或低头不看, 或自己唱歌, 或玩游戏, 甚至还睡着了。研究人员回来之后, 把这些孩子经过努力赢得的糖果给了他们。然后等着他们长大, 再来看看科学的结论。

到这些孩子上高中时, 引人注目的事发生了。对这些孩子的家长和教师所作的调查发现, 那些四岁就能克制自己, 坚持等到第二块糖的孩子, 长大后通常有较强的适应力, 更合群, 富有进取心、自信心, 也更可靠。那些经不住诱惑的孩子更容易变得孤独, 容易受挫, 缺乏灵活性。他们受不了压力, 逃避挑战。

我们说到出众的才华, 就会想到爱因斯坦, 那个有生命的, 穿着不配对袜子的思考机器。在我们想像中, 取得卓越成就的人一出生就注定会不平凡。可是你也会问为什么随着时间的推移, 天才在一些人身上显露出来, 而在另一些人身上却暗淡下去。这就是糖块实验要说明的问题了。看来似乎能耐心等待收益的能力是最重要的技巧。这里, 逻辑性强的思考战胜了不负责任的思考。简言之, 这是情感智能的体现, 而这是在智力测试里表现不出来的。

在本世纪大部分时间, 科学家们一直重视大脑这个具体之物和理智这个无形之物, 而情感这一纷乱的力量却留给了诗人去谈论。但大脑研究理论就是无法解释我们最想弄清的问题: 为什么有些人似乎就是有过上好日子的才能; 为什么班里最聪明的孩子很可能最终并不是最富有的; 为什么我们对有些人几乎一眼就喜欢上了, 而对另一些人则信不过; 为什么有些人面对困难仍能保持乐观, 而另一些人则坚持不住, 沉沦下去。一句话, 心智或精神的何种素质决定了人的成功?

"情感智能"一词是研究人员五年前创造出来的, 用以描绘人的一些素质, 诸如对自身感觉的了解, 对他人感觉的同情, 以及"调节情感以更好地生活"的能力。由于丹尼尔·戈尔曼的新书《情感智能》, 这一概念很快会成为国内谈论的话题, 为方便起见简称为"情商"。戈尔曼将他花了10年的工夫, 研究头脑怎样处理感情的结果汇聚成书。在书的封面上, 他说他的目标就是要重新定义聪明到底是什么。这是他的理论: 要预测人的成功, 智商所衡量的大脑能力实际上远不如曾被看作"性格"的心智的素质重要。

乍一看来, 此说并无新意。它与感情掌管头脑的说法一样并无创见。人们常说"我气得无法思考"。"与人交往的技巧"非常有用，此说也不令人吃惊，这就等于说与人为善是对的。但如果事情就那么简单，这本书就不会引起那么大的关注，它的含义也不会引起那么大的争论了。

这决不是抽象的调查。戈尔曼在寻找方法恢复"大街上的彬彬有礼，社区生活中的互相关心"。他认为这处处都用得上，如公司该如何决定聘用什么人，夫妇该如何提高婚姻延续的可能性，父母该如何培养孩子，学校该如何教育孩子。当街头团伙取代了家庭环境，当校园辱骂导致了械斗，当半数以上的婚姻以离婚收场，当这个国家里死去的孩子大多死于父母之手，而这样的父母大都说他们是想规范孩子的行为，要他们不要挡着电视，不要大哭不休，当发生了这些现象，这就意味着需要进行基本的情感教育。

正是在这个问题上人们产生了争论。尽管在这一较新的领域里很多研究人员对情感问题终于得到认真对待感到高兴，但他们也担心像情商这样一个方便的概念会被误用。"人们的情感是多种多样的，"哈佛大学心理学教授杰罗姆·凯根说，"有些人能很好地处理愤怒，但却对付不了恐惧。有些人无法承受欢乐。因此每一种情感都应得到不同的看待。"情商不是智商的对立。一些人有幸两者都很高，一些人则两者都很低。研究人员想要弄清的是两者是如何共同起作用的；举例说，一个人应付压力的能力是如何影响他集中精力，运用智力的能力的。在成功的诸要素中，研究人员现在普遍认为智商约起20%的作用，其余部分则取决于从社会地位到运气等各种因素。

Section C
Ⅰ . 语言点讲解

1. **People with greater knowledge of their emotions are better pilots of their lives. (Para.3)**

   [释义] **pilot** *n.* 作为向导的人：飞行员，领航员，引水员

   e.g. The accident was caused by pilot error. 事故是由于领航员出错导致的。

   [分析] 介词短语结构"with greater knowledge of their emotions"为后置定语，修饰 people。

2. **When people who fear snakes are shown a picture of a snake, monitors attached to their skin will detect sweat, a sing of anxiety, even though the people say they do not feel fear. (Para. 3)**

   [分析] 这个长句为一个主从复合句。在when引导的时间状语中包括一个who引导的定语从句"who fear snakes"，修饰people。过去分词短语"attached to their skin"为后置定语，修饰monitors。

3. **Some preschoolers grabbed the treat immediately, but others were able to wait what, for them, must have seemed an endless 20 minutes. (Para.12)**

   [分析] "what, for them, must have seemed an endless 20 minutes"为名词性从句作wait 的宾语，在该从句中，"for them"为插入语。"must have seemed"为对过去发生事情语气较为肯定的推测判断。

4. **When you're faced with an immediate temptation, remind yourself of your long-term goals—whether they be losing weight or getting a medical degree. (Para.14)**

[分析] 本句的主干为 "remind yourself of your long-term goals..." 祈使句结构。破折号后面的 "whether they be losing weight or getting a medical degree" 为省略了should的虚拟句结构。

5. **The labs re staffed by engineers and scientists who are all people of great intelligence. But some still emerged as stars, while others wee never very successful (Para. 16)**

[分析] 本句中 "who are all people of great intelligence" 为限制性定语从句，修饰先行词 "engineers and scientists"。连词while，相当于转折连词but，表示对比或与前面相反的情况。

Ⅱ. 课文赏析

1. 文体特点

本文开门见山，提出写作目的，接下来条理清晰、脉络清楚地谈了构成情感智能的一些主要素质，以及如何来培养这些素质，并通过举例说明帮助读者更好理解文章。

2. 结构分析

Part Ⅰ (Para.1) The EQ is also one of the factors that determines success.

Part Ⅱ (Para.2-17) Five major qualities make up emotional intelligence.

Ⅲ. 课后练习答案及解析

Reading skills

XIX.

1. 20%.

2. 5.

3. Self-awareness, mood management, self-motivation, impulse control and people skills.

Comprehension of the Text

XX.

TFTFF TTT

Ⅳ. 参考译文

构成情感智能的主要因素

心理学专家一致认为决定成功的因素中智商只占了大约20%，而其他因素占了整整80%，包括我所说的情感智能。下面谈谈构成情感智能的一些主要素质，以及如何来培养这些素质。

1. 自我意识

能够在一种感觉产生的同时确认它，这一能力是情感智力的基础。能较大程度地认识自己的感情，这样的人能更好地把握自己的人生。自我意识的培养要求能注意到什么样的感情会使自己想做某事——确切地说，就是直觉。有时人们产生了直觉却没有意识到。例如，当怕蛇的人看到蛇的画面时，在他们体表上安放的监控器会测到排汗，这是焦虑的迹象，即使他们说自己并未感到害怕。

通过有意识的努力我们可以更好地意识到自己的直觉。举个例子，某一遭遇使人过后几小时都一直闷闷不乐。此人可能并未意识到自己的不快，如果有人提醒这一点，他还会感到吃惊。但如果他能确认一下自己的感觉，他就能改变这种状况。

2. 情绪控制

坏情绪和好情绪都给我们的生活增添了风味，也构成了我们的性格，关键是要平衡。

在所有人们想要避免的情绪中，怒气似乎最难处理。该怎样来缓解怒气呢？一种说法是把愤怒说出来会使人好受些。实际上，研究人员发现那样做是一个很糟糕的办法。怒气的爆发激起了大脑的兴奋系统，使人更加愤怒，而不是相反。较为有效的办法是"重新建构"，就是说有意识地以更积极的眼光来重新审度局面。

3. 自我激励

积极的动机，即积聚起高涨的热情、旺盛的精力和充分的信心，这对获得成就至关重要。对奥运选手、世界级的音乐家和国际象棋大师的研究表明，他们的共同特点就是具有促使自己坚持艰苦的日常训练的能力。

要激励自己获得成就需要有明确的目标，以及一种乐观的、"我能行"的态度。宾夕法尼亚大学的马丁·塞利格曼建议梅特莱夫保险公司雇用一批特别的求职者，他们经测试证实有很乐观的心态，虽然在一般能力测验上不及格。与另一些通过了能力测试但具有悲观心态的推销员相比，这些人第一年的销售就超出了21%，而第二年更超出了57%。

4. 克制冲动

自我调节情感的核心就是有能力做到为了某一目的而推迟近在眼前的利益。有一个实验说明了这一特性对成功的重要意义。实验是20世纪60年代由沃尔特·米歇尔在斯坦福大学校园内的一所幼儿园里做的。他们告诉孩子们可以马上吃到一样东西，比如一块糖。但是如果孩子们能等到实验人员出去办点事回来，他们就可以吃到两块糖。一些孩子抓过糖来一口吃了，但另一些孩子却能够等待对他们来说肯定是漫长的20分钟。

多年以后，这一实验的引人之处出现了。那些四岁时能够等到两块糖的孩子们，到了十几岁时仍能够为了他们的目标而推迟某种乐趣。他们的社会生活能力更强，也更有自信心，能更好地应付生活中的各种挫折。相反，那些当初迫不及待地吃了第一块糖的孩子到了十几岁时更有可能表现得缺乏灵活性，难以作决定，容易紧张。

抗拒诱惑的能力也可以通过练习来培养。面临着唾手可得的诱惑，提醒自己别忘了自己的长远目标——不管它是什么，减肥也好，拿医学学位也好。那样，你就不会轻易满足于只吃一块糖了。

5. 与人交往的能力

知道他人如何感受的能力在工作中、在爱情与友情中和在家庭生活中都是很重要的。卡内基-梅隆大学的罗伯特·凯利和珍妮特·卡普兰在贝尔实验室的一个研究说明了良好的交往能力的重要性。在实验室工作的工程师、科学家们都是才智很高的人，但是其中一些仍能够脱颖而出，而另一些则一直成就平平。

是什么造成了这种差距？表现出色者都有广泛的人际交往关系。凯利评论说，一个成就平平的人碰到技术问题时，"他向各位技术专家求助，然后就等待着。求助无果，他的时间就这么浪费了。而那些杰出人物很少碰到这样的局面，因为他们早已有了可靠的人际交往关系。因此当杰出人物与某人联络时，总会很快得到回答。"不论他们的智商有多高，还是情感智能使得杰出人物有别于表现平庸者。

五、知识链接

IQ is an abbreviation for "intelligence quotient", a measure of a person's intellectual ability. In 1916, Americans in general first learned about general intelligence thanks to a book by Lewis M • Terman, professor of psychology at Stanford University. The book was *The Measurement of Intelligence*. Terman explained: "The intelligence quotient (often designated as IQ)is the ratio of mental age to chronological age. , multiplied by 100, and is based on the scores achieved in an intelligence test." The two most important scales for measuring IQ are the Standford-Binet test and the Weschler test.

It is expressed as the ratio of mental age to actual age

Modern ability tests produce scores for different areas (e.g. language fluency, three-dimensional thinking, etc.). It is much more useful to know which are the strengths and weaknesses of a person than to know that he or she beats n percent of the populace in some "general intelligence" measure. Two persons with vastly different ability profiles may score the same IQ, but may exhibit different affinity to a given task, or may not be valued equally intelligent by other people.

IQ scores are sometimes taken as an objective measure of intelligence, and since intelligence is notoriously difficult to define, the definition "intelligence is what the IQ test measures" has been seriously proposed. However, IQ tests encode their creator's beliefs about what constitutes intelligence. Most people also think that creativity plays a significant role in intelligence; creativity is almost immeasurable by tests.

The modern field of intelligence testing began with the Stanford-Binet test. Alfred Binet, who created the IQ test in 1904, was aiming to identify students who could benefit from extra help in school: his assumption was that lower IQ indicated the need for more teaching, not an inability to learn.

The following numbers apply to IQ scales. Scores between 90 and 110 are considered average—so a person scoring 95 is simply average, not below-average. For children scoring below 80 special schooling is encouraged, children above 125 are "highly gifted". In previous years, scores below 90 were divided into ranges labeled moron, imbecile and idiot, while scores above 150 were labeled genius. Some say that such scores outside the range 55 to 145 are essentially meaningless because there are not enough people to make statistically sound statements.

智商IQ是 "intelligence quotient" 的缩写形式，用来衡量一个的智力水平。1916年，斯坦福大学心理学教授特曼出版了一本书《智力的衡量：白涅特–赛门智力标准的修订和延伸》，在这本书里，他首次提出给智力的量度一个名称和数植，那就是IQ。他解释说："IQ就是思维年龄和生理年龄的比值乘以100%。" 智商有两个重要的测量标准：斯坦福——比奈测试法和韦斯勒测试法。

能力测试的现代方法得出了测试大脑不同区域的分值（例如语言流畅性，三位思考等）。然而，了解一个人的强项和弱项要比知道此人在某些 "普通智力" 测试中排第几更重要。两个各方面能力相差较大的人有可能得到相同的IQ值，但完成同一个任务时会表现完全不同，或者不同人会认为这两人的智力水平是不同的。

有时，人们认为智商值是一种客观测量智商的方法。而且，由于很难对智商定义，"智商就是智力测试的分值"这种定义被人们很认真地推崇。但是，智力测验代表的是发明这种方法人的对智商由何构成的观点。甚至，大多数人还认为创造力在智商中非常重要；而创造力基本上是无法靠测验来测量的。

现代智力测试领域始于斯坦福-比奈测试法。该方法是阿尔弗雷德·比奈1904年发明的。他当时正计划确定哪些学生能够获得学校额外帮助。他当时的想法是：智商越低就意味着需要更多的教导，并非无学习能力。

下面的数字表示智商范畴。得分在90-110，智商水平一般。所以，假如某人的得分为95，那他就是个普通人，而非低于常人水平。那些得分低于80的孩子就应当鼓励接受专门的学校教育。而智商值高于125的孩子就是"非常有资质"。在以前，低于90的智商被分成不同的等级，即苯人，弱智和白痴；而智商值高于150的人则被称为天才。一些人认为不在55-145范围内的智商值是毫无意义的，因为目前尚未有足够多的人给出从统计角度上听起来比较满意的报告。

六、自测题

Directions: In the following passage there are altogether 10 mistakes, one in each numbered line. You may have to change word, add a word or delete a word. If you change a word, cross it out and write correct word in the corresponding blank. If you add a word, put an insertion mark (∧) in the right place and write the missing word in the blank. If you delete a word, cross it out and put a slash (/) in the blank.

The European Union had approved a number of genetically
modified crops until late 1998. But growing public concern
over its supposed environmental and health risks led several EU   1. _____
countries to demand a moratorium (暂时禁止) on imports of any
new GM produce. By late 1999 there were enough such country   2. _____
to block any new approvals of GM produce.

Last year, America filed a complaint at the WTO about the
moratorium, arguing that it was an illegal trade barrier because
there is no scientific base for it. As more studies have been   3. _____
completed on the effects of GM crops, the greens' case for them   4. _____
has weakened. Much evidence has emerged of health risks   5. _____
from eating them. And, overall, the studies have shown that
the environmental effects on modified crops are not always as   6. _____
serious as the greens claim. Nevertheless, environmentalists
continue to find fault of such studies and argue that they are   7. _____
inconclusive.

While Americans seem happy enough to consume food made from GM crops, opinion polls continue to show that European consumers dislike the idea. Europeans seem be taking the attitude which, since there remains the slightest possibility of adverse consequences and since it is clear how they, as consumers, benefit from GM crops, they would rather not run the risk.

8. _____

9. _____

10. _____

答案与解析

1. its改为their。本题考查了大家识别代词所指的能力，its 指代genetically modified crops (为复数)，所以应该改成their。

2. country改为countries。such country是指前面要求暂停进口转基因农产品的某些欧盟国家，所以应该改成复数。

3. base 改为basis。此处意为：因为没有科学根据支持暂停 (进口)，it 指the moratorium；base 基础，基地，根据地; basis (for) 基础, 基本, 根据; 科学根据只能说scientific basis, 有的同学把base 后面的for 改为 on，应该是受到了base on 这个短语的影响。

4. for 改为 against。the greens = the environmentalists 环保主义者。case 论点，论据，case for 后面的them指GM crops, case for sth. 支持某物的论点，case against sth. 反对某物的论点 (削弱了)。

5. much 改为little。逻辑错误，本句正常语序为Much evidence of health risks from eating them has emerged. 。根据andnd, overall, 或后的语意，此行应该把much 改为little, 说明没有什么迹象、根据表明吃GM crops对健康有什么危险。

6. on 改为of。本句的意思为：研究表明modified crops对环境造成的后果并没有环保主义者所声称的那样严重。Environmental effects of modified crops (modified crops对环境造成的后果)；很多同学看到effects 以为后面一定跟on 就错了。

7. of 改with, find fault with 批评，找茬，使固定搭配。

8. seem后面加to. seem to be taking固定结构，be 不能少。

9. which 改为that. taking the attitude that ...后为同位语从句，不能用which。

10. clear 改为unclear或者前面加not. 注意since 前面的and 表示前后语意一致。因为欧洲人觉得仍然存在使用GM food的不利后果，并且他们作为消费者从GM food中会如何获得好处也不清楚，所以他们不愿意冒风险。

答 案

Unit 1

Listening

Understanding Short Conversations

1. A   2. C   3. A   4. C   5. B   6. A   7. B   8. B   9. D   10. A
11. C   12. C   13. A   14. B   15. D   16. C   17. D   18. B   19. C   20. D

Understanding Long Conversations

1. C   2. A   3. B   4. A   5. D   6. C   7. A   8. A   9. B   10. D

Understanding Passages

1. B   2. C   3. A   4. A   5. D   6. A   7. B   8. C   9. C   10. D
11. B   12. D   13. A   14. D   15. B   16. D   17. A   18. C   19. B   20. B

Speaking

Practicing Conversational Skills

Speaking Task 2

Frequency: 1. Every two weeks

2. Every five minutes

3. How many times a week?

4. Take this medicine twice a day

5. never

6. Do I need to feed the fish three times a week?

Sequence: 1. after that   2. first   3. after   4. As soon as   5. What next?

Listening & Speaking

Listening, Taking Notes and Retelling

Integrated Task 1

1. They are revealed at the point where sadness and love meet.

2. It is friendship.

3. Friends of different ages and backgrounds.

Listening, Discussing and Role-playing

Integrated Task 2

1. Status is important for men.

2. Their failures rather than success.

3. To reach an agreement by discussion.

Unit 2

Listening

Understanding Short Conversations

1. C   2. A   3. B   4. C   5. A   6. D   7. D   8. D   9. B   10. A
11. A   12. B   13. C   14. C   15. B   16. D   17. A   18. A   19. A   20. B

Understanding Passages

1. B   2. D   3. C   4. C   5. A   6. A   7. B   8. B   9. D   10. B
11. C   12. A   13. B   14. A   15. A   16. A   17. C   18. D   19. C   20. B

21. D   22. C   23. B   24. C   25. C   26. B   27. D   28. A   29. B   30. C

Speaking
Practicing Conversational Skills
Speaking Task 2

Position: 1. opposite   2. on the third floor
            3. at the back of the classroom   4. To the left

Direction: 1. Go straight down this street to   2. Turn left and go one block until
            3. I'm a stranger here myself   4. Cross the street, walk on and take
            5. Go along the street, turn right at

Movement: 1. from   2. get to   3. leaving for   4. towards

Listening & Speaking
Listening, Taking Notes and Retelling
Integrated Task 1

1. The lovely figure of his little Tramp

2. The greatest actor in movie history

3. $ 10,000 a week

Listening, Discussing and Role–playing
Integrated Task 1

1. At the age of seven.

2. In Holland.

3. She was crazy about it.

Unit 3
Listening
Understanding Short Conversations

 1. A   2. B   3. B   4. C   5. B   6. B   7. C   8. D   9. A   10. A
11. B   12. B   13. B   14. A   15. A   16. B   17. D   18. C   19. A   20. A

Understanding Passages

 1. B   2. A   3. C   4. B   5. C   6. A   7. B   8. C   9. A   10. D
11. A   12. D   13. B   14. C   15. B   16. A   17. B   18. A   19. B   20. D
21. C   22. B   23. D   24. D   25. C   26. A   27. B   28. C   29. D   30. D

Speaking
Practicing Conversational Skills
Speaking Task 2
Conversation about Length and Width

1. 10 meters long and 5 meters wide   2. How long   3. the width   4. wide   5. long

Conversation about Height and Depth

1. How high   2. the depth   3. At what depth   4. in height   5. the highest

Listening & Speaking
Listening, Taking notes and Retelling
Integrated Task 1

1. Medicare and Medicaid   2. contribute more generously than others

3. Because the cost is very high

Listening, Discussing and Role–playing

Integrated Task 1

1. She found a lottery scratch-and-win card

2. Honesty

3. Some reward money and a free holiday to a destination of her choice.

Unit 4
Listening
Understanding Short Conversations

    1. A   2. B   3. A   4. D   5. A   6. A   7. A   8. B   9. D   10. B

    11. B   12. B   13. A   14. A   15. D   16. D   17. C   18. A   19. C   20. A

Understanding Long Conversations

    1. B   2. A   3. B   4. C   5. A   6. B   7. A   8. C   9. C   10. A

Understanding Passages

    1. B   2. A   3. A   4. B   5. D   6. D   7. A   8. B   9. A   10. B

    11. A   12. B   13. D   14. C   15. C   16. D   17. B   18. B   19. A   20. C

Speaking
Practicing Conversational Skills

Speaking Task 2

Definiteness and percentage

1. definite   2. definite   3. Definitely

4. percentage 5. percent of

Increase and Decrease

1. has been increased   2. increase   3. increase   4. Decrease   5. decrease

Listening & Speaking
Listening, Taking notes and Retelling

Integrated Task 1

1. Beating a drum

2. The Canadians

3. Television

Unit 5
Listening
Understanding Short Conversations

    1. D   2. C   3. A   4. C   5. C   6. B   7. C   8. C   9. D   10. B

    11. D   12. B   13. A   14. D   15. C   16. A   17. D   18. B   19. C   20. D

Understanding Long Conversations

    1. C   2. D   3. A   4. B   5. D

Understanding Passages

    1. D   2. A   3. B   4. C   5. C   6. C   7. B   8. D   9. A   10. B

11. C 12. A 13. C 14. C 15. D 16. C 17. D 18. C 19. C 20. A

21. C 22. B 23. D 24. D 25. B

Speaking

Practicing Conversational Skills

Speaking Task 2

Defining: 1. means 2. definition 3. definite

4. is 5. explained

Explaining: 1. do you mean 2. because 3. I mean

4. to say 5. other words

Interpreting: 1. get your meaning 2. that mean 3. it true

4. tell me 5. made myself

Listening & Speaking

Listening, Taking notes and Retelling

Integrated Task 1

1. He was an odd fellow who didn't plan by the rules.

2. He bought it with the money he had saved over the months.

3. They envied him.

Unit 6

Listening

Understanding Short Conversations

1. B 2. C 3. A 4. D 5. C 6. C 7. B 8. B 9. B 10. B

11. A 12. D 13. D 14. A 15. C 16. B 17. D 18. D 19. B 20. A

Understanding Long Conversations

1. C 2. D 3. C 4. B 5. D

Understanding Passages

1. B 2. A 3. D 4. C 5. C 6. C 7. A 8. C 9. D 10. B

11. D 12. C 13. B 14. D 15. D 16. C 17. C 18. B 19. A 20. D

21. D 22. D 23. C 24. B 25. C

Speaking

Practicing Conversational Skills

Speaking Task 2

Narrating: 1. doing 2. when 3. take place

4. forget 5. after

Describing: 1. look like 2. describe 3. What color

4. like 5. something about

Clarifying: 1. I mean 2. that's not 3. Frankly

4. saying 5. to make

Arguing: 1. to some extent 2. but 3. admit

4. don't you think 5. aren't there?

Listening & Speaking

Listening Taking Notes and Retelling

Integrated task 1

1. He was a director of National Schools.
2. Demanding substantial payments from the mothers of some students?
3. 12 years.

Unit 7
Listening
Understanding Short Conversations

1. C	2. D	3. B	4. D	5. C	6. A	7. D	8. D	9. A	10. D
11. B	12. C	13. D	14. C	15. A	16. D	17. A	18. B	19. A	20. C

Understanding Long Conversation

1. D   2. A   3. C   4. B   5. A

Understanding Passages

1. C	2. D	3. B	4. D	5. A	6. C	7. C	8. D	9. A	10. D
11. C	12. D	13. C	14. B	15. A	16. A	17. C	18. A	19. D	20. D
21. C	22. A	23. B	24. D	25. D					

Speaking
Practicing Conversational Skills

Speaking Task 2

Generating: 1. In general   2. As a rule   3. On the whole
           4. goes without saying   5. By and large

Conclusion: 1. reached the conclusion   2. In conclusion
           3. reach an agreement; put it aside
           4. conclude my words   5. divided

Listening & Speaking
Listening, Taking Notes and Retelling

Integrated Task 1

1.prove innocence   2. identify fatherhood   3. identify soldiers

Integrated Task 2

1. In the early 1980s.

2. By showing that their DNA does not match the sample found at the crime scene.

3. By showing that their DNA does not match the evidence such as the blood on clothing.

4. To use DNA typing.

5. Compare the DNA from the body to those in the stored samples.

Listening, Discussing and Role–playing

Integrated Task 1

1. 6 billions.

2. People have different looks, personality and behavior.

3. People share ways of looking, thinking and being.

4. By studying our genes.

5. Our size, build, coloring, sex, ways of thinking and behaving.

6. 80,000.

Unit 8
Listening
Understanding Short Conversations

1. A 2. C 3. B 4. B 5. B 6. B 7. B 8. C 9. C 10. D
11. C 12. B 13. A 14. D 15. B 16. D 17. D 18. D 19. A 20. B

Understanding Passages

1. C 2. B 3. B 4. A 5. D 6. D 7. A 8. C 9. D 10. D
11. D 12. B 13. D 14. A 15. C 16. C 17. A 18. B 19. A 20. D
21. D 22. A 23. A 24. B 25. C 26. A 27. A 28. D 29. D 30. C

Speaking
Practicing Conversational Skills

Speaking Task 2

Causing and Effect: 1. Because 2. as 3. reason
4. because 5. for

Aims and Purpose: 1. so that 2. so as to 3. In order to
4. in case 5. for; to

Listening & Speaking
Listening, Taking Notes and Retelling

Integrated Task 1

1. Hispanic; 58; 35.3
2. first; belonging to more than one race
3. 7; multiracial
4. shrinking ; 69 ; 76
5. new immigrants; Asia; Latin America

Integrated Task 2

1. The U.S. is a more ethnically and racially diverse country.
2. Hispanics.
3. In places where people of different races have long intermarried.
4. Non-Hispanic whites.

Listening, Discussing and Role–playing

Integrated Task 1

1. Slavery.
2. To bring history to the American masses.
3. The rebellion aboard a 19th century slave ship and the trial of those involved in the rebellion.
4. George Washington and Thomas Jefferson.
5. They did so of their won free will.
6. They did no come to the U.S. out of choice.
7. they have no roots.

Unit 9

Listening

Understanding Short Conversations

1. B   2. B   3. D   4. A   5. C   6. A   7. D   8. C   9. C   10. D
11. B   12. D   13. B   14. D   15. C   16. A   17. B   18. C   19. A   20. D

Understanding Long Conversations

1. C   2. A   3. D   4. C   5. B   6. B   7. B   8. C   9. D   10. A

Understanding Passages

1. B   2. C   3. C   4. B   5. A   6. C   7. B   8. D   9. C   10. A
11. C   12. B   13. A   14. C   15. A   16. A   17. C   18. A   19. D   20. D

Speaking

Practicing Conversational Skills

Speaking Task 2

Concession: 1. Although there were only 200 foreign students

2. Even if the sun isn't burning

3. Difficult as it is

4. whether it rains or not

5. in spite of the fact that she is world famous

Real Condition: 1. If the survey indicates there is a need

2. as long s you promise to be back

3. press the second button; press the third button

4. in case it rains

5. I have to face these challenges

Unreal Condition: 1. If I were you

2. If he hadn't spent so much time on his part-time job

3. but for the pronunciation

4. Without your help and advice

5. under more favorable conditions

Supposition: 1. Suppose the air on the earth could not be breathed

2. is supposed to be

3. Supposing that it rains

4. it was supposedly

5. I'm proceeding on the supposition

Hypothesis: 1. Assuming that were true

2. working on the assumption that

3. assuming that computers have artificial intelligence

4. I'm working on the hypothesis

Listening & Speaking

Listening, Taking Notes and Retelling

Integrated Task 1

1. for different reasons

2. had to work very hard to survive

3. would be melted down into 100% American.

4. valuable and close to their hearts

5. not a melting pot, but a mosaic

Integrated Task 2

1. The first wave of immigrants: The early settlers came mainly in the 17th and 18th centuries, mostly from Britain. The second wave of immigrants: In the middle decades of the 19th century, a much larger wave of immigrants arrived, chiefly from Ireland and Germany. The third wave of immigrants: A really huge wave reached the U.S. between 1880 and 1920. These later arrivals were mainly from eastern and southern Europe and various parts parts Asia.

2. All these immigrants had to adapt themselves to the new conditions and all had to work very hard to survive. They helped one another in the new environment. Besides, the common conditions tended to draw people from diverse backgrounds together. That is why for a long time the U.S. was regarded as a melting pot.

3. The speaker argues that the U.S. culture instead of a melting pot is a mosaic culture, which consists of many patterns and colors represented by the various racial and ethnic groups. The American culture contains many elements that come from other cultures. And each of these has contributed to making the whole nation ever much richer, stronger and more interesting.

Listening, Taking Notes and Retelling
Integrated Task 1

1. The melting pot means that people with different cultural and ethnical backgrounds immigrate to the States, live together, get mixed and build up this wonderful culture that we call American culture today.

2. Even though the American school did have a devise student body with about 40% international students. However, they were not integrated with native Americans. They could be in the same class, but rarely could they become great friends. This is because of the cultural difference.

3. No. The immigrants feel like outsiders to America culture and find it difficult to really become part of American culture. That is the reason why America cannot be counted as a melting pot. That is because the immigrants know a lot of American culture whild Americans don't know much of their cultures. Through the author's personal experience the author finds that the immigrants and Americans don't share many things in common. The lack of mutual understanding, the imbalance and almost one-way traffic in understanding is surely the unpleasant side of the melting pot.

Unit 10
Listening
Understanding Short Conversations

1. D   2. A   3. D   4. B   5. C   6. A   7. A   8. C   9. D   10. D

参考答案

11. C   12. C   13. B   14. A   15. B   16. D   17. D   18. D   19. C   20. A

Understanding long Conversations

1. D   2. C   3. B   4. A   5. A   6. D   7. B   8. C   9. C   10. A

Understanding Passages

1. C   2. A   3. C   4. C   5. D   6. B   7. D   8. B   9. A   10. B

11. A   12. D   13. B   14. B   15. C   16. D   17. B   18. A   19. B   20. C

Speaking

Practicing Conversational Skills

Speaking Task 2

Exception: 1. besides their rich nutritious elements

2. with the exception of

3. Besides this dictionary

4. except for a few spelling mistakes

5. except that

Restriction: 1. that will restrict

2. are severely restricted by

3. should be declared off limits

4. without limit

5. limit your essay to

Part and Whole: 1. two parts of flour to one part

2. the whole of April

3. is twenty-fourth part

4. two parts orange juice and one part

5. Two halves makes a whole

Connection Between Parts: 1. in 10 parts

2. it should be good in parts

3. the best part of my holiday

4. for the most part

5. It was partly my fault.

Listening & Speaking

Listening, Taking Notes and Retelling

Integrated Task 1

1. to worry about their technological competitiveness

2. have automatic technological superiority

3. scientists or engineers; when to bet on new technologies

4. facing their companies today

Integrated Task 2

1. It is because American firms no longer have automatic technological superiority. If managers from the rest of the world understand the forces of technical change better than their American competitors do, they can overtake their American competitors.

2. If the managers today want to be winners they have to understand what is going on in

technology. They have to be managers who understand when to bet and when not to bet on new technologies.

3. Schools of Management are expected to produce a generation of managers who will be solving today's and tomorrow's problems. If they are successful in doing so they will become tomorrow's captains of business.

Listening, Discussing and Role-playing

Integrated Task 1

1. He keeps in touch with others through e-mail, telephones, fax machines, etc.

2. The most important lesson Oskin learned is that everyone in the organization is important and vital. It is people who make the difference. It is with people's commitment and involvement that Oskin succeeded.

3. A young person, if he wants to become somebody some day, he should commit to whatever he does. He should always be curious about anything new to him and try to be more creative in his work. At the same time, he should keep himself approachable and show care for others, willing to offer help.

4. Oskin wants to make a difference every day. He wants to continue to expand his global knowledge base and to surround himself with the best possible talent he can find.

常用后缀

–'s 1. 所有格 (a.) today's 今日的

–'s 2. 店铺 (n.) greengrocer's 菜场

–a 构成复数名词 (n.) stadia 视距 单数um结尾

–ability 可…性 (n.) dependability 可靠性

–able 可…的 (a.) inflammable 易燃的

–ably 可…地 (ad.) suitably 合适地

–aceous 有…性质的 (a.) carbonaceous 含碳的

–acious 具有…的，多…的 (a.) sagacious 聪明的

–acity 性质等（抽象）(n.) veracity 诚实，真实

–acle 构成名词 (n.) manacle 手铐

–acy 性质等（抽象）(n.) fallacy 谬误

–ade 1. 行为等 (n.) blockade 封锁

–ade 2. 物（…制成）(n.) lemonade 柠檬水

–ade 3. 人和集体 (n.) cavalcade 骑兵队

–age 1. 集合名词 (n.) foliage 叶子

–age 2. 场所、地点 (n.) orphanage 孤儿院

–age 3. 费用 (n.) postage 邮资

–age 4. 行为 (n. pilgrimage 朝圣

–age 5. 状态，身分 (n.) reportage 报告文学

–age 6. 物 (n.) carriage 马车，客车厢

–ain 人 (n.) chieftain 酋长，头子

–aire 1. 人 (n.) millionaire 百万富翁

–aire 2. 物 (n.) questionaire 调查问卷

–al 1. 有…性质的 (a.) continental 大陆的

–al 2. 行为（抽象）(n.) withdrawal 撤退

–al 3. 人 (n.) rival 竞争者

–al 4. 物 (n.) manual 手册

–ality... 性，（抽象）(n.) technicality 技术性

–ally 方式，程度等 (ad.) conditionally 有条件地

–an 1. 属于…的 (a.) metropolitan 大都市的

–an 2. 人 (n.) pubican 旅店主人

–ance 情况等（抽象）(n.) buoyance 浮力

–ancy 情况等（抽象）(n.) elegancy 优美，高雅

–aneity 性质等（抽象）(n.) contemporaneity 同时代

–aneous 有…性质的 (a.) subterraneous 地下的

–ant 1. 属于…的 (a.) luxuriant 奢华的

–ant 2. 人 (n.) participant 参与者

–ant 3. 物 (n.) excitant 兴奋剂

–ar 1. 有…性质的 (a.) consular 领事的

–ar 2. 人 (n.) liar 说谎的人

–ar 3. 物 (n.) altar 祭坛

–ard 人（贬义）(n.)

–arian 1. 人 (n.) parliamentarian 国会议员

–arian 2. 兼形容词 (n,a) vegetarian 吃素者（的）

–arily 有性质地 (ad.) extraordinarily 不寻常地

–arium 场所，…馆 (n.) planetarium 天文馆

–ary 1. 有…性质的 (a.) customary 习惯的

–ary 2. 场所，地点 (n.) apiary 养蜂场

–ary 3. 人 (n.) secretary 书记，秘书

–ary 4. 物 (n.) glossary 词汇表

–asm 性质（抽象）(n.) sarcasm 讥讽

–ast 人 (n.) enthusiast 热心者

–aster 人（卑称）(n.) medicaster 江湖医生

–ate 1. 做，造成 (v.) activate 激活

–ate 2. 有…性质的 (a.) private 私人的

–ate 3. 人 (n.) graduate 毕业生

–ate 4. 职位，职权 (n.) professoriate 教授职位

–ate 5. 构成化学名词 (n.) acetate 醋酸盐

–atic 有…性质的 (a.) diagrammatic 图解的

–ation 1. 行为，情况 (n.) invitation 邀请

–ation 2. 行为的过程 (n.) reformation 改革

–ative 与…有关的 (a.) affirmative 肯定的

–ator 做…工作的人，物 (n.) calculator 计算机

–atory 1. 具有…的 (a.) exclamatory 感叹的

–atory 2. 场所，地点 (n.) observatory 天文台

–cian …学家 (n.) clinician 临床医学专家

–cracy 统治 (n.) bureaucracy 官僚主义

–crat 参加者，支持者 (n.) democrat 民主主义者

–cy 性质，状态 (n.) infancy 幼年期

–dom 1. 情况，身分 (n.) freedom 自由

–dom 2. 领域，…界 (n.) sportsdom 体育界

–e 构成复数名词 (n.) larvae 幼虫 单数以a结尾

–ed 1. 构成过去式 (v.) showed 展示 规则动词

–ed 2. 构成过去分词 (v.) published 出版 规则动词

–ed 3. 已完成的 (a.) destroyed 毁灭的

–ee 受动者 (n.) employee 雇员

–eer 关系者，管理者 (n.) volunteer 志愿者

–en 1. 含…的，…制的 (a.) golden 含金的

–en 2. 使成为 (v.) widen 加宽

–ence 性质，状态，行为 (n.) existence 存在

–ent 有…性质的 (a.) deterrent 妨碍的

–er 1. 人 (n.) fighter 战士

–er 2. …的住民 (n.) villager 村民

–er 3. 制作者 (n.) hatter 帽商

–er 4. 物 (n.) harvester 收割机

–er 5. 更… (a.& ad.) better 更好的 比较级

–ern 在…方的 (a.) northern 北方的

–es 1. 构成复数名词 (n.) bushes 灌木 单数或原型结尾 ch,is,o,s,sh,x,z

–es 2. 第三人称单数 (v.) does 做

–ese …民族的 (a.) Japanese 日本的

–ess 阴性 (n.) airhostess 空姐

–est 最… (a.& ad.) nicest 最佳的 最高级

–et 小 (n.) floweret 小花

–fold …倍的，…重的 (a.) multifold 多倍的

–ful 1. 有…性质的 (a.) beautiful 美丽的

–ful 2. …的量 (n.) teaspoonful 一茶匙

–fully 有…性质地 (ad.) carefully 小心地

–fy 使…化 (v.) electrify 通电

–graph 信号 (n.) electrograph 电传真

–hood 性质，状态 (n.) childhood 童年

–i 构成复数名词 (n.) fungi 真菌 单数以us结尾

–ial 1. …的 (a.) industrial 工业的

–ial 2. 行为（抽象）(n.) trial 审判

–ial 3. 人 (n.) official 官员

–ial 4. 物 (n.) material 材料

–ian 1. …的 (a.) antemeridian 午前的

–ian 2. …民族的 (a.) Canadian 加拿大的

–ian 3. …的人，…学家 (n.) custodian 保管人

–ibility 可…性 (n.) responsibility 责任

–ible 可…的 (a.) possible 可能的

–ibly 可…地 (ad.) terribly 可怕地

–ic 1. …的 (a.) basic 基本的

–ic 2. …的人 (n.) critic 批评家

–ic 3. 学科 (n.) logic 逻辑学

–ical …的 (a.) identical 全等的

–ice 行为，动作，状态 (n.) service 服务

–icious 具有…的，多…的 (a.) suspicious 可疑的

–icity 性质 (n.) authenticity 真实性，可靠性

–ics 学科 (n.) physics 物理学

–ies 1. 构成复数名词 (n.) counties 县 单数以y结尾

–ies 2. 第三人称单数 (v.) cries 哭 原型以y结尾——ing 1. 构成现在分词 (v.) hoping 希望

–ing 2. 正在进行的 (a.) developing 发展中的

–ing 3. 构成名词 (n.) feeling 感觉

–ious 具有…特性的 (a.) glorious 光荣的

–ise 使…化 (v.) surprise 使惊愕 BrE

–ish 1. …民族的 (a.) Turkish 土耳其的

–ish 2. 有点…的 (a.) tallish 稍高的

–ish 3. 有…性质的 (a.) foolish 笨的

–ish 4. 造成，致使 (v.) finish 结束

–ism 主义，学说，状态 (n.) socialism 社会主义

–ist …主义者，…家 (n.) novelist 小说家

–it …的动作 (n.) pursuit 追求

305

–ity 性质，状态 (n.) solidarity 团结

–ium （化学）元素名 (n.) calcium 钙

–ive 有…性质的 (a.) attractive 迷人的

–ize 使…化 (v.) initialize 初始化 AmE

–kin 小 (n.) princekin 小王子

–less 无，没有，不 (a.) hopeless 绝望的

–let 小 (n.) booklet 小册子

–like 似…的 (n.) catlike 猫样的

–ling 小（轻蔑）(n.) starling 小星星

–logy 学科 (n.) astrology 占星术

–ly 1. 像…的 (a.) friendly 友好的

–ly 2. 方式，程度等 (ad.) chiefly 首要地

–ly 3. 每隔…发生的 (a.) monthly 每月一次的

–ment 行为，结果，手段 (n.) implement 工具

–most 最… (a.) utmost 极端的 不是最高级

–ness 性质，状态，程度 (n.) illness 疾病

–or 1. 人 (n.) emperor 皇帝

–or 2. 物 (n.) tractor 拖拉机

–or 3. 状态，性质 (n.) color 颜色

–ory 1. 有…效果的 (a.) satisfactory 令人满意的

–ory 2. …的处所 (n.) category 目录

–our 状态，性质 (n.) favour 好感

–ous 具有…特性的 (a.) dangerous 危险的

–que 概念 (n.) techique 技巧

–ress 阴性 (n.) actress 女演员

–ry 1. 性质，行为 (n.) rivalry 敌对

–ry 2. 境遇，身份 (n.) slavery 奴役

–ry 3. 种类 (n.) jewelry 宝石

–ry 4. 行业 (n.) forestry 林业

–s 1. 构成复数名词 (n.) rockets 火箭

–s 2. 第三人称单数 (v.) plays 玩

–s 3. 构成副词 (ad.) indoors 在家

–ship 1. 动作 (n.) courtship 求爱

–ship 2. 身份 (n.) citizenship 公民身份

–ship 3. 关系 (n.) friendship 友谊

–sion 动作，状态 (n.) revision 复习

–sis 性质，状态，动作 (n.) crisis 危机

–some 引起的 (a.) troublesome 烦人的

–teen 十… (num) fifteen 十五 13~19

–th 1. 行为，结果 (n.) death 死亡

–th 2. 第… (num) sixth 第六 基数个位   4

–tic 有…性质的 (a.) romantic 浪漫的

–tion 行为，状态，情况 (n.) contribution 贡献

–tious 有…性质的 (a.) cautious 谨慎的

–ty 1. 性质，情况 (n.) safety 安全

–ty 2. …十 (num) ninety 九十 20, 30, ..., 90

–ure 结果，动作，过程 (n.) procedure 程序

–ves 构成复数名词 (n.) calves 幼仔 单数以 f,fe结尾

–ward 向，向…的 (prep.& a.) backward 向后

–wards 向 (ad.) skywards 朝上地

–y 1. 充满，有…性质 (a.) handy 手巧的

–y 2. 亲昵 (n.) kitty 猫咪

–yst 1. 人 (n.) analyst 分析者

–yst 2. 物 (n.) catalyst 催化剂